BELLADONNA

MICHAEL STEWART

BELLADONNA

HarperCollins*Publishers*

HarperCollins books may be purchased for educational, business, or sales promotional use. For information, please call or write: Special Markets Department, HarperCollins Publishers, Inc., 10 East 53rd Street, New York, NY 10022. Telephone: (212) 207-7528; Fax: (212) 207-7222.

FIRST EDITION
Designed by George J. McKeon

Library of Congress Cataloging-in-Publication Data
Stewart, Michael, 1946–
   Belladonna / Michael Stewart.—1st ed.
     p. cm.
   ISBN 0-06-017982-1
   I. Title.
   PR6069. T464B4 1992
   823'.914—dc20   91-58361

92 93 94 95 96 ❖/RRD 10 9 8 7 6 5 4 3 2 1

This book is for Martine and
for our daughters, Amelia and Cressida

Here is Belladonna, the Lady of the Rocks,
The lady of situations.

—T. S. Eliot, *The Waste Land*

"MANDRAKE": a root of rude human appearance with aphrodisiac and
narcotic properties. It is said to shriek when uprooted and to be lethal to
whoever pulls it out.
*   It is supposed to be a creature having life, engendered under the earth*
of the seed of some dead person put to death for murder.

—Levinus Lemnius, *Herball for the Bible*,
(tr. Thomas Newton, 1587)

The known is finite, the unknown infinite; intellectually, we stand on an
islet in the midst of an illimitable ocean of inexplicability. Our business in
every generation is to reclaim a little more land.

—T. H. Huxley (1825–1895)

When any particular organized system ceases to exist, as when…an ani-
mal dies, its organizing field disappears from that place…and can reap-
pear again physically in other times and places, wherever the physical con-
ditions are appropriate.

—Rupert Sheldrake, *The Presence of the Past*

ACKNOWLEDGMENTS

Especial thanks are due to the following for their kind and generous help in the research for this book: Dr. Susan Blackmore, University of Bristol; Professor John Casey, University of Virginia; the Librarian of the Royal Society, London; Oliver Sacks, M.D.; Dr. Rupert Sheldrake; the Society for Psychical Research, London; Professor Ian Stevenson, M.D., University of Virginia; and finally, the many students of Mr. Jefferson's "Academical Village" to whom I owe such authenticity of place and atmosphere as I may have achieved.

I would like further to express my sincere gratitude to my publisher in the United States, Ed Breslin, and to all my friends and helpers there. Above all, once again, my most profound thanks are due to my publisher and friend, Eddie Bell, for his consistent guidance, inspiration and conviction throughout the writing of this book.

I owe a most especial debt to Helen Peacocke, whose own personal story provided me with the seed idea for the book and who has shared her experiences with me with a true and unstinting generosity of spirit.

And finally, my most heartfelt gratitude goes out to the person who is at once my muse and my severest critic, whose scholarly work, *The Literature of the London Underworld (1660–1720)*, I have shamelessly plundered, and who is ultimately the reason I go barefoot up this Everest every time—my wife, Martine.

PART I

ONE

The night was alive with dark excitements, and in the sultry air hung the smell of reckless midsummer dangers. Despite the stifling heat, Matthew shivered. He prowled about his rooms high under the eaves, too uneasy to settle, too restless to concentrate on his work. He yearned for distraction, but he could not allow himself any respite. Yet danger sought him out. It came to him unbidden, and it was to alter forever the course of his life.

The hour was late. Across the city a ragged chorus of clocks was chiming eleven. Matthew had his windows flung full open into the night. The heat outside hung like a lead curtain, with scarcely a breath of wind to stir the sluggish air. Beneath slabs of clouds brooded the spires and battlements of the college skyline, cast now and then into startling relief by a flash of sheet lightning. From the darkness below his rooms came sporadic bursts of drunken laughter, while from the Great Quad some way beyond, muffled by the canvas of a vast marquee, thumped the heavy beat of a rock band. This was the end of the academic year, and the whole university was alight with parties and grand dances.

Matthew refilled his glass and forced himself back to his desk. He struggled to close his ears to the seductive call of the night. Part of his mind, as always, slipped easily back to the seventeenth century, to the company of his fond familiars, Isaac Newton and Robert Boyle and, above all, to Nathaniel Shawcrosse, that tantalizing, enigmatic maverick of his time whom he'd made his own special subject. But another part cried out in protest: this was the 1970s, not the 1670s! Here he was, in England, on a Rhodes scholarship to Oxford, at the end of a path that had taken him from the leafy suburb of Portland, Maine, where he'd grown up and through the red brick lecture halls of Harvard where he'd taken his masters. He was twenty-two, healthy and fit and *alive*. Surely there was more to life than a doctorate and a career in the tenured towers of academe?

A burst of flirtatious laughter rose from the quad below. With a tormented groan, he pushed back his chair and went to the bathroom. There he held his head under the tap until the cold water hurt. If he didn't submit his thesis on time, he'd *have* no career. Mortify the flesh now to gratify it later: That was the deal.

With the noise of the water, he barely heard the knock at the door.

When it came again, he decided to ignore it. He couldn't afford the interruption. It was probably some inebriate from the ball looking for a bathroom. The tapping continued, light but insistent. Rubbing his head dry with a towel, he stalked over to the door and pulled it open.

He caught his breath.

A girl stood before him. The most astonishingly beautiful girl he'd ever seen. Dazed, stupefied, he slowly drank in the vision.

Her hair, the color of fine gilt, was piled high and fell in ringlets about her oval face. Her complexion was as pale as alabaster, its pallor heightened by the scarlet of her lips. Her eyes, a deep electric violet, wore an expression at once serious and whimsical. High on her upper lip, accentuating her mysterious half-smile, lay a small, dark beauty mark. Her whole skin seemed to glow with an inner luminosity, like a marble figurine lit from within.

Then his eye fell upon her dress. He gave a start. Was he hallucinating? She wore an exquisite period ball gown of cream silk, cut high and square so as to force up her breasts, with a tight corsetted waist, ruched sleeves and a long flounced skirt trimmed with lace and blue silk. She had walked straight out of the seventeenth century. He could be standing face to face with Robert Boyle's daughter or Isaac Newton's sister or any great beauty of the period.

He let out a small crazed laugh, but in the next instant it died upon his lips. He realized, of course, this girl was dressed for the college ball! She was evidently looking for someone and come to the wrong room. He felt a stab of disappointment.

When finally he could summon his voice, he hardly recognized it as his own.

"Can I help you?"

For an answer, she fixed him with her deep violet eyes and slowly broadened her smile. It broke over him like a wave in slow motion, surging through him, sweeping him off his feet in its swell. He felt powerless to resist.

"You're looking for someone?" he began again, reaching out a hand. The hand felt clumsy, made of rubber.

She nodded, and her smile grew arch.

"I was."

Her voice was strangely low and soft. It had a trace of an accent, perhaps a regional strain of English. Even slightly archaic.

"You were?" he echoed dumbly.

Her smile faltered. Her expression grew questioning. Suddenly he was struck with the bizarre sense that she had actually *recognized* him and she was puzzled that he didn't recognize *her*. But he'd never met her in his life. How could he ever have forgotten those deep, far-off eyes, that mysterious smile, the powerful presence flowing around her like a magnetic flux?

Her eyes grew softer, the shape of almonds. She took a step forward.

"Nathaniel," she said.

It was a statement, a greeting, not a question.

He gave a violent jolt at the name. He must have misheard. He'd been living like a hermit these past weeks, night and day, with only Nathaniel Shawcrosse and his alchemist friends of three centuries ago for company. Surely she had seen his name painted over the door in the traditional college style: MR. MATTHEW CAVEWOOD.

Then it came to him. Lyall had sent her round! The old rogue had thought he was working too hard: He'd got a girl to dress up in costume and address him as Nathaniel Shawcrosse, to jolt him out of his reclusion and get him to come and join the party.

He would play the game. Yet when he tried to move, his legs seemed locked rigid. With effort, he took a step back and held the door open. He sought the right thing to say. Why was his brain numb like a love-struck adolescent's?

"I'm sorry. Do come in, please."

She gave a small mock curtsey and flashed him a cheeky, complicit smile, as though this were already a familiar game between them, then stepped into the room. As she passed he caught a trace of her perfume. The scent filled his head with a light, elusive fragrance. It was spicy like sandalwood, smoky as saltpeter, yet with a strange, cool undertone of electricity that matched her violet eyes.

Game or no game, his mind was in a whirl. He had to keep his hands busy, keep talking, cover up the confusion he felt. He went to the sideboard and bent to open the cupboard. He cleared his throat.

"Can I offer you a drink? Gin? Sherry? And white wine in the fridge. As for ice ..."

He shrugged apologetically. He was about to remark that this university was, after all, seven hundred years old and what could you expect?— but he checked himself. It seemed not just trivial but somehow unnecessary, like everything else he could find to say.

She made no reply. As he straightened, he glimpsed her reflection in the sideboard mirror. Her long, pale neck was thrown back and she was unbuttoning the fine lace ruff at the throat. He watched, rooted to the spot, as her fingers descended to her dress and she began unlacing the tight, curving bodice. Her eyes met his in the mirror, and briefly she stopped.

His throat was dry and swollen. He reached into the small built-in fridge for the wine. With a shaking hand he poured two glasses, then turned to give her hers. She had shed the ball gown and she now stood before him, barefoot, in a tightly whaleboned shift, from the top of which two pearly white breasts struggled to escape. Underneath, he could see she wore yet more slips and stays. Extraordinary, he thought distantly; that's *exactly* how they dressed in those days.

She was no game of Lyall's and she was no trick of his mind. She was absolutely authentic. And curiously, potently, familiar.

He offered her the glass in silence, but she wouldn't take it. Instead, she tilted her head back and pursed her lips. Obediently, filled with a trance-like sense of unreality, he took a step closer toward her. As he drew up to her, he had the sudden feeling of stepping through an invisible membrane into a different kind of space, a space somehow strangely energized and, in the midst of the stifling heat, uncannily cooler.

He held the glass against her lips. She parted them slightly. Her tongue sought the rim, explored its shape, its rigidity. He tilted the glass. The pale liquid trickled into her mouth, but she did not swallow it at once; instead, she let it lie pooled in her lips for a moment, lapping her tongue, glistening her teeth. He let his gaze wander over her face. He felt like a climber cresting a hill onto a sudden, breathtaking landscape. Her whole complexion bore a soft, opalescent glow. Slowly her mouth lifted into a smile, that same knowing half-smile he'd first seen. It eddied around the corners, making the small mole on her upper lip dance. Her eyes held him spellbound. He was suffocating. His stomach was melting. An eternity of time was theirs. Everything seemed so slow, swollen with such sweetness and inevitability. An exquisite sense of perfection and harmony rose within him. There were no questions. No puzzlement, no awkwardness, no doubt. Only a sense of complete knowingness. They had been here before.

Without surprise, as though he'd seen it coming from a long way off, he felt her reach for his hand and, putting the glass aside, slowly draw it down onto her chest. Her shift was undone at the top. Gently she guided his hand inside and closed it tight around a breast. She gave a small sigh of pleasure. The touch of her skin, the roundness of that young breast cupped in his hand, the nipple swelling between his fingers ... gradually a wild roar rose in his blood and exploded through his body. Tightening his grasp until she cried out in pain, he tore at the garments with his free hand. The sound of rending silk filled the air, but nothing would stop him until she stood before him, trembling and breathless and completely naked.

Matthew drew his gaze away from the window and looked back down at the diary. Damp fingerprints showed where he'd clasped it tightly, just as he'd clasped her breast. He was trembling inside. Downstairs, he could hear Hazel sorting out packing cases, her footsteps echoing hollow in the bare house. He glanced back at the diary. He couldn't abandon the reverie just yet.

"Sanctus Spiritus College, 22 June 1976," began the next day's entry. It was short, despairing. "Catastrophe. She's gone. Vanished. I can't work, can't think, can't breathe. Am cracking up."

As he stood there in the large, dusty room that he'd earmarked for his study, surrounded by crates of books and papers accumulated over the intervening fifteen years, he felt again the vicious stab of panic on waking the following morning to find that the girl, his magical spirit of the night, was gone. He remembered searching his rooms for a note. Staring out of the window for her. Waiting for a call. It was crazy, but he'd actually begun to believe she was real, not just an incredible dream. There were no obvious signs, true—no upturned furniture or shattered glasses or torn sheets or marks upon his body of a night of passion—and yet he just couldn't believe he'd imagined something so absolutely vivid and tangible. And unique: in all his life he'd never experienced anything remotely like this. He'd literally taken leave of this earth. This girl, this total stranger, had swept him into another world, a world beyond all imagining, a realm of soaring, timeless delirium. She *couldn't* have been a figment of a dream!

For days he couldn't work, eat or sleep. He blanked out in the middle of giving a seminar on "Alchemy and the Scientific Method." He cut his supervisor dead in the High. His friend Lyall—who was quite innocent of any trick—came round one night with a bottle of college port and enough methaqualone to put the U.S. army to sleep. Lyall diagnosed "reticular formation overload," his way of saying overwork. It wasn't that. It was far more serious. He was in love. In love with a girl in a dream.

He told Lyall. He even joked about being lovesick. They talked about formulating a pill for it: "HEART-EEZE, The *E*-motion Sickness Tablet." They'd go into business and make a million.

But nothing could ease his heart. He'd caressed that scented skin, he'd kissed those soft lips, he'd slaked his craving upon that lithe and slender body. How could he have just invented her? Although he told himself it was crazy, he would catch himself looking around for her. He loitered at the foot of his staircase, lurked around the quad, spun out small talk with the porter on the main gate. Twenty times a day he checked his pigeonhole, and at night he left his door ajar. Lying in bed, he would imagine her footfall in every creak of the old building, and with each silence he'd die a little inside. He went around the city on invented pretexts but actually in search of her. He looked in the libraries, the pubs, even the river where the gilded youth, fresh out of Finals, were out on the punts, braying raucously and hosing one another with champagne. He checked the tea rooms, the Union lounge, even a theatrical costumers, for surely she'd hired that dress? She had to be *somewhere!*

He felt, at times, close to suicide. The prospect of never seeing her again was intolerable. This girl, this phantom of the night, had changed his life; she'd taken him to another level of being, shown him a glimpse of the ultimate. "Can there ever be another woman for me after this?" cried one despairing diary entry. (Of course there were other women, not a few of them, and now there was Hazel, certainly the best and definitely the last.) He'd been meant to hand in his thesis the following week before flying back to the States, but he hardly cared any more. This girl was all he could think of. Yet he didn't even know her name! Or why she had come to him like that, in the heat of the night, a complete stranger, right out of nowhere. Hadn't she been with a partner, or planning to meet one? He knew nothing at all. All he had was a strange, nagging suspicion that somehow this was more than a chance encounter. She'd known exactly where she was and what she was doing. She *had* been looking for someone, just as she'd said. And found him.

In his dream, of course. Not in real life. She had been nothing more than a shade of the night.

"Matthew? Where are you?"

Hazel's voice from the hallway downstairs echoed hollowly in the empty house. Matthew snapped the diary shut and slipped it back into the packing case beneath a pile of leather-bound books, part of his collection of early scientific treatises.

"Here," he called back.

"Where's here?"

"In my study."

"Your what?"

Footsteps mounted the stairs, the heels clattering on the uncarpeted boards. Half way up, they stumbled. There came a muffled oath.

He thrust a handful of packing foam on top of the books and busied himself checking off the cases on a list. He was still shaking. He felt guilty, but for what? For keeping the diary? True, a historian should know better than to hoard compromising personal papers. Or was it for the event itself? But it had only been a dream, goddammit! A dream, all of fifteen years ago, about a girl he'd never set eyes on since. Yet he felt guilty about the power the memory still had to disturb him. And for keeping it from Hazel. He loved Hazel, he was going to marry her, and he wasn't going to muddy the future with the past. But if it *was* the past, why did it still affect him so?

Hazel's voice from the landing cut into his thoughts.

"Someone had better get those stairs fixed," she was saying, "or someone else is going to break their neck."

She stopped just inside the room and cast provocatively about her. A single shaft of the yolk-rich autumn sunlight slanting in through the bay window caught her eyes and fired them a pale jade green. She ran a hand through her dark copper hair in mock exasperation.

"Your study?" she protested. "Excuse me, Matthew. This is my private sitting room."

"Downstairs is for sitting, Hazel. Upstairs is for—"

"Entertaining my gentlemen visitors."

"Just the one, if you don't mind." He drew her toward him. She made a modest pretense of resisting. "And he's sure no visitor."

"No gentleman, either," she mumbled through the kiss. "You're a pig, Matthew. I knew you'd grab the best room in the house for yourself."

"I always go for the best."

The soft touch of her lips stirred his senses. She was everything, all he ever wanted. Holding her was like coming home. His hand was working beneath her blouse, rising up the naked skin. She let out a small, convulsive shiver, then pulled away.

"Not now, Matthew. I've got the sheets to sort out and the food to unpack. Don't make me late getting back. Ben's got homework still to do."

He turned back to his lists with an ironic smile.

"Amazing how the human race perpetuates itself. When do busy people get the time?"

"You need the place as well as the time."

"What's wrong with right here?"

"You know what I mean, Matthew."

Of course he knew. A "place" meant a proper family home. Not the apartment in a high rise in central Washington in which she and Ben lived, already too small for his bike and skateboard and model airplanes and the rest of the surfeit of toys that invariably belonged to the only child of a single parent. A "place" meant a big house like this, a house with room for a proper photographic studio and darkroom for herself and a proper bedroom and playroom for Ben and for other children they might have of their own, with a yard big enough for a pool and a tennis court and maybe even a paddock, a house in a leafy residential area of a quiet and elegant town like this Charlottesville, where the air was clean and life was gentle and you could walk the streets without fear.

He went to the window and peered through the dusty panes. The glass was old and flawed, and for a moment he watched the fair-haired eight-year-old boy kicking tracks through the leaves, his figure now elongated, now foreshortened, now split in two. He felt a swell of affection for this bright, tough, young kid. He'd have wished him to be his real son.

"Ben looks happy," he said.

Hazel's hand reached for his.

"Like he's at home," she sighed.

"He *is* at home."

She turned and rested her head briefly on his shoulder. He closed his eyes and breathed in the familiar soft fragrance. It smelled rich with the promise of love and contentment. Then, reaching up, she gave him a kiss and drew away. At the door, she paused and cast a final glance around the room, then left, muttering as she went, "The best view in the house, and he grabs it for himself." Matthew smiled; she herself had told the removals men to deposit his books and papers up here.

He'd returned to checking the lists when a gleeful cry from outside caught his attention. He glanced back out the window. Ben had found a rickety climbing frame buried in the shrubbery and was dragging it out into the open to play on. Slowly and with contentment, Matthew scanned the large, neglected grounds that were now theirs. The sun, a disk of molten amber, was slipping down behind the coppice of silver birches that vaguely defined the western boundary of the property. To the right, just visible through gaps in the trees, stood their nearest neighbors' house, a mansion of red brick and white columns set behind a high security fence and approached by a wide, manicured driveway through razored lawns. Full ahead, at the end of a clearing in the scrub rose a majestic plane tree, ankle-deep in fallen leaves.

His gaze lingered on this tree. Its branches stood out bare and startlingly white against a bank of darkening thunder clouds. It looked as though white paint had rained down upon it, or acid had been flung at it, peeling back the flesh to the bone. An image flashed across his mind. It was of an early engraving that depicted an experiment given before the Royal Society: Stretched out on a wooden board lay the naked corpse of an aged man stricken down by the plague ... the flesh meticulously flayed by the scalpel, the skin pinned back onto the board, baring the sinews and exposing the bones from the thickest femur to the tiniest digit, all gleaming this same searing white ... and pressing close around the slab, a group of bewhiskered men in top hats and frock coats, in the center of which, apprised in the act of drawing some stringy substance out through a nostril with a pair of pincers, stood the fresh-faced, clean-shaven and unhatted figure of Nathaniel Shawcrosse.

Abruptly, Matthew turned back to his lists. Twilight was falling rapidly and within minutes it was too dark to read. The room was bare and as yet unlit. He stood in the center and looked about him. He felt the despair rising as he saw the work that had to be done to the place. The ceiling plaster was hanging off in slabs, exposing the naked laths. The floorboards sank spongily with every step. The fireplace had been taken out and the surrounding mantel, perhaps dating back to the house's colonial origins, was badly distressed and its carving clogged with generations of paint. This was just one of twenty such rooms in this vast, rambling wooden ruin. Had they any notion of what they were taking on? Or rather, what *he* was taking on? The plan was that he would live here and do it up, while Hazel remained with Ben in the apartment in D.C., two hours' drive away, coming down just for weekends. When the place was finished, they'd get married and she and Ben would move in properly.

As a plan it seemed fair enough. But what about his work? Could he really write a major biography and totally renovate a house at the same time? This was the critical year in his academic career. Yet he also had a lot going for him. He had a generous research fellowship from the University of Virginia, the oldest and one of the finest universities in the nation, and an almost nonexistent teaching load. He had the dean's implicit promise of an associate professorship at the end of the year if his work went well. He had a woman he loved, who was supportive and ambitious for him and who had a son whom he loved as his own. And finally he had the perfect house for a family home: this peeling, reeling, aged clapboard homestead, situated on a winding street off Rugby Avenue, a short drive from the university, and surrounded by an assortment of interesting neighbors—academics cheek by jowl with architects and attorneys, town alongside gown, new money rubbing shoulders with old money and no money. No doubt about it, this was going to be the year of his life.

From downstairs he heard Ben's high-pitched voice.

"Matt? Mom says we've got to go. You coming down?"

"Be right with you," he called back.

He glanced at his watch. He hated this moment each weekend, but unless Hazel and Ben left now they'd hit the worst of the Sunday evening traffic returning to the capital. He tossed aside his clipboard and hurried downstairs. Hazel was already outside, packing up her red Pontiac compact, impatient to get on the road. He met Ben struggling down the porch steps, with the binoculars Matthew had bought him that weekend slung around his neck and his arms laden with his "finds": a die-cast toy fire engine, a half-rotted baseball bat, a patch of what looked like the fur of an opossum, a large branch off a yew tree. A squirrel fled across their path and scurried around the blind side of a silver birch.

"You're taking that tree with you?" he asked the boy.

"It's to make a bow."

Hazel looked up from loading the car.

"Leave it behind, darling," she said. "Matthew will look after it."

"I'll guard it with my life," promised Matthew, helping the boy into his seat belt. "Well," he smiled, "what do you think of the new ranch? Think we can knock it into shape?"

"It's just great."

He bent forward and kissed him on the forehead.

"Work hard, Ben, and take care of your Mom," he said.

"And you take care of my bow, okay?"

Hazel climbed into the car. She started up the engine and blew him a kiss through the window.

"There's cannelloni in the fridge and chili in the freezer," she called. "I'll call you from home. From the apartment, I mean. 'Bye, darling. Love you."

Matthew stepped back onto the porch and waved them off. A few yards down the drive, the car skidded to a halt and Hazel jumped out again. Leaving the door open and the engine running, she hurried back, drew him into the doorway out of sight and pressed a long, passionate kiss hard onto his lips, then skipped lightly back to the car and headed away into the road. Within moments the last notes of the engine had faded away into the dusk, and all that was left was the imprint of her kiss upon his lips.

He stood on the porch for a while, familiarizing himself with the new sounds: rustlings in the undergrowth, the crash of a heavy pigeon breaking cover through the laurel, the faint purr of traffic from Route 29 half a mile to the west, which Hazel would shortly be joining. High overhead, a plane scored a slender trail in the sky. From the neighbors' house came the yelp of their guard dog, muffled by the evergreen shrubbery, the sound punctuated by a gentle *chink* just behind him of wind chimes stirred by the evening breeze. Matthew let out a deep breath and closed his eyes. Hazel's face filled his mind, her green eyes smiling, her sensual mouth parting in a kiss. Gradually a resolution began to form in his mind. It was a small act but a significant one, and much overdue.

Turning, he strode indoors and up the stairs to his study. There he retrieved the diary from the packing case and took it back down into the large, bare living room. Kneeling down by the fire, he tore it up, sheet by sheet, then went in search of matches.

The flames devoured the thin dry paper greedily. One sheet curled free and dropped onto the hearth. On it he could just make out a fragment of the writing: *Can there ever be another woman for me after this?* He picked up the burning paper and held it until the flames reached his fingers, then tossed it back into the dying fire and, finding a broom handle lying nearby, proceeded to pulverize the embers until nothing was left of the memory but dead ashes.

TWO

Rain began to fall as Hazel skirted Manassas, and by the turn-off to Dulles airport a violent cloudburst had reduced the traffic to a crawl. The pavement was awash and the storm gulleys ran red. Fierce gusts buffeted the car and hammered on the roof, all but drowning out the radio. Through the rain-bleared windshield she could see only a smear of taillights. She turned the radio up. An overturned truck had closed the 14th Street bridge and traffic was backed up to Columbia Pike. She couldn't wait to quit the city.

She thought of the long weekend just past, of the night they'd spent in a country inn and of their trips to Waynesboro and Staunton, to Culpeper and Orange, in search of antiques and knick-knacks for their new home. She thought of their foray up Skyline Drive, that high and winding trail along the spine of the Blue Mountains, and she smiled to recall how they'd had to stop at every overlook and let Ben out to scour the forest through his new binoculars for grizzlies and golden eagles.

She thought, too, of the small apartment in D.C. to which they were now returning, with its kitchen that doubled as a dining room and its doors that slid on rails to save space, and she compared it with the large ruin of a house she'd just left, with its spacious hall, its vast utility areas, its endless attics and cupboards and rooms to make into studies and libraries, bathrooms and dressing rooms, snugs and salons, television dens and music rooms, its rooms for dining and rooms for withdrawing and its generous family kitchen living-room, and for herself, at long last, a proper darkroom and studio. She was exaggerating, true, but couldn't a girl born and raised in a family of six in a four room apartment over a diner in a poor suburb of Philadelphia be forgiven for that?

She sighed. No transition was quite that easy, of course. There was her work, for one thing. She'd invested a good deal in building a career as a commercial photographer, and it took a lot to change direction successfully. At her own initiative she'd persuaded Otis McDowell, Virginia's staunchly Republican senator, to agree to an exclusive photographic profile, and she was pitching this hard at *People* magazine. If she got them to bite, it could be the break she needed and lead to more work of the same kind—portrait photography, work she could run from home, down in Charlottesville. And the money? Shooting advertising stills for dog food and detergents might not be aesthetically fulfilling, but it was very nicely paid. For that, however, she had to be on the spot, in Washington. Still, there was no going back now. She'd made up her mind. And however the new venture fared, she wasn't going to be dependent on Matthew's income. She'd darn well *force* the magazine to buy.

Ben's silvery voice interrupted her thoughts.

"Mom, does this mean Matt won't see the exhibit?"

"I'm sorry?"

"The projects exhibit. You know. It's on just for this week." He turned his serious brown eyes on her. "Mom?"

"Well, I'll make it, darling, of course I will."

"But Matt?"

She reached out and squeezed his hand. Along with the rest of his grade, Ben had been given a nature project for the vacation. He'd chosen to record a day in the life of an ocean rock pool—a "marine eco-subsystem," in Matthew's typical phrase—near the house on Virginia Beach they'd rented for the summer. Matthew had spent hours with the boy, helping him photograph and record his findings and collate them into a proper scientific report. And now Ben naturally wanted Matthew to see it on public display. It was her fault—she'd forgotten to remind him. There was just too much going on to remember everything.

"He may be too busy to come up," she warned. "You saw the state of that place. And there's his book, don't forget."

Ben sighed and looked out of the window.

"It's okay, Mom," he said.

An ambulance was pressing hard on their tail, its lights flashing and siren wailing. She pulled over to let it pass. Ahead, the road was flashing with police lights. A car had overshot an exit and skidded down the embankment onto the freeway, landing on its roof. A group of figures, bent against the rain, stood over a man stretched out on the ground, while two cops in reflective jackets were vigorously waving the traffic on. Funneled into a single line, the cars began to move faster now, and within a minute the road was clear. Hazel shivered. That is somebody's father or brother or husband, she thought, and here we drive past, cocooned in our steel boxes, quite untouched, unable to help. We can only remember that it could have been our father or brother or husband. Not her own father, of course, God rest him. But Matthew? One day it could be Matthew. Her ear picked out a snatch of a song on the radio: "I'm a one-man woman … and I want a one-woman man." I'm yours, Matthew, she whispered silently to the drumming rain, and you're mine, and we will be together forever, promise me. Don't ever leave me, Matthew, don't ever die on me.

"What's wrong, Mom?"

She jerked back to reality. "Nothing. Just thinking."

"You're making funny faces."

"Well, daydreaming."

She drove on more slowly. You could love someone too much. She only had to see an accident or read of a murder or a death to know she loved Matthew too much. It made her feel vulnerable. You should always hold back just a little bit of yourself, in case.

"Mom," broke in Ben, "I want a soda."

"That's not how you ask."

"May I have an ice-cream soda *pleeeease,* dearest darling Momma?"

"Can't you wait? We're nearly home."

"I'll pay. Matt gave me five dollars."

"No television till you've done your homework, then?"

"I'll pay for you, too."

"Yes or no?"

"All right, Mom, it's a deal."

She laughed and, pulling off the freeway toward a shopping mall, headed for the sign of a Hardees and a welcome break from her thoughts.

It was late at night and the storm was still blowing when Matthew returned home from Lyall's house. Lyall, his English friend from his postgraduate Oxford days, held the chair in Theoretical Physics at the university, and it was largely at his instigation that Matthew had come to Charlottesville. A biography of a seventeenth-century physicist spanned the disciplines of both history and science, and Lyall had persuaded his own faculty board to put up half the research funding, arguing that here was a positive chance to help bridge the communication gap between the arts and the sciences. He'd put a lot into fixing it, and much of his own personal prestige rode on the outcome. The result was that Matthew had two masters, was the Dean of Arts and the Dean of Sciences, but also had two sources of money. Substantial money, too. The surplus was going to go a long way toward paying for the refurbishment of the house.

Lyall and his Bostonian wife, Myra, lived a few miles west of town, not far from the exclusive Farmington Country Club, of which, incomprehensibly to Lyall who thought the place gossipy and snobbish, she was an enthusiastic member. Knowing Matthew was alone in a new house, they'd invited him over for supper. He'd stayed rather longer and drunk rather more than he'd meant to. Driving back, he'd missed the exit and made an illegal turn on the main highway, and at the intersection down the road he'd jumped a red light.

As he swung his aging gray Mercedes into the driveway, he glanced at the large gaunt house ahead, silhouetted against the turbulent sky. He frowned sharply.

A light was on in an upstairs window. But how? He hadn't been able to fix the circuits for the upstairs floor.

Slowing, he peered through the rain-lashed windshield. The light came from the room on the corner, the room they had set aside to be their married bedroom—what Hazel called their "nuptial chamber." It was a strange kind of light, now he came to think; more a luminous greenish glow. The car was rolling forward by itself, and before he was aware what was happening, it lurched to one side and a wheel sank into a pothole. He struggled to haul it back on track, but when he looked up again the light had gone. Of course: it was just the hall light reflecting up the stairs.

He parked around the side and hurried up the steps onto the porch. He was standing with one foot propping open the outer screen door, fumbling for the key, when a thought made him stop. It was a bay window up there, divided into three sections. Why had the light shone in only one?

He hesitated. Rain scoured the porch. His shoes were already over the welts in mud. He wasn't dressed for this. Yet he knew he wouldn't feel easy otherwise. He had a phobia of loose ends; he couldn't rest in his mind if something didn't fit. He called it being scientific; Hazel called it being obsessional. Turning up his collar, he retraced his way on foot back to the entrance of the driveway. Then, following the path he'd driven, he walked slowly back, keeping his eyes fixed on the upper window. No light of any kind showed from any angle of view. There was no streetlight to cast a reflection, no moonlight to glint off the glass. Nothing. And, now that he remembered, the hall light couldn't possibly shine up there anyway: to block out drafts, he'd closed all the upstairs doors.

He went indoors and checked the downstairs windows. Burglars? Nothing had been disturbed as far as he could judge. He searched for the flashlight, but it was evidently still packed, so he lit a kerosene storm lamp and, switching off the lights, made his way up the staircase to bed. Upstairs, all the doors were closed, exactly as he'd left them. He went into the nuptial bedroom. Empty and undisturbed. His eye briefly lit upon the large French brass bedstead, standing dismantled against the wall, which he'd bought the day Hazel agreed to marry him, and he smiled to recall how she had asked for time to think his proposal over, when he knew she'd already made up her mind—he'd come upon some real estate particulars of properties in Charlottesville in a drawer in her apartment. This room was hallowed ground. They had vowed to keep it untouched and the bed unslept in until the night that they were married.

Puzzled, he closed the door and headed off to the bathroom. No doubt it would all seem clear in the daylight. Hazel had made them up a bed in the guest room across the landing, and there he finally retired. He took with him a copy of his old doctoral thesis; the bibliography would make a starting point for his new research. As he climbed into bed, he found a love note from Hazel tucked in between the sheets, signed with the imprint of her lips in bright carmine lipstick. As he read it, he could hear her voice and feel the soft touch of her lips. With a shiver of pleasure, he slipped the note onto the bedside table beside the storm lamp, then turned to the thick volume and looked up the references on his subject, Nathaniel Shawcrosse.

Question marks. Lacunae. Loose ends. And, as always, the big puzzle: Why the sudden, deafening curtain of silence at the end?

He scanned the biographical sketch for the few known details of the life of this brilliant, shadowy figure. Born somewhere around 1645. Mentioned first as a member of the secretive Oxford-based "Invisible College," a year before its transformation into the Royal Society. Performed experiments as recorded in early proceedings of the Society. Corresponded with eminent names of the period, such as Newton and Hooke. Worked for a while alongside Boyle. Made a fellow of Sanctus Spiritus College, Oxford, in 1671, and, four years later, appointed to the Lucretian Chair of Natural Philosophy. Involved in bitter conflicts with the all-powerful university clerical body. Gave public lectures in which he proposed highly advanced, rational explanations of comets, the Flood, the Resurrection. Published a major anti-Trinitarian polemic in 1678. Accused of heresy. Attempts made to expel him from his chair without success. And then finally, in early 1681, the last surviving reference: a lengthy, rambling *Apologia,* in which he promised shortly to publish the result of his life's work, to be entitled, *Revelations.* After that, nothing more. Not a word, not a mention. A total blank. A wall of silence. *Damnatio memoriae.* Erasure from the record.

Why?

Matthew turned to an excerpt of the *Apologia* he had included as a footnote.

As to the Dangers & Persecutions I shall expose myself to by my forthcoming Revelations, I know my Duty as a Christian and do resolve to hazzard all in the World rather than be unfaithful to the Hidden Truth of Christ, or suffer the People to be any longer so grossly blinded and mis-led by the Tyranny of the Church, which is become but the Mask & Mouthpiece of the Antichrist.

Such a profane denial of the Church was, of course, an unspeakable heresy. One could hardly imagine in our own century the bitterness and hatred this must have provoked at the time. But what was the core of it? What was this "Hidden Truth of Christ"?

Now Shawcrosse had been in contact with Newton in Cambridge; they exchanged results of their alchemical experiments in a coded correspondence. Alchemy was more than just the attempt to transmute base metals into gold and silver; it was the search for the ultimate nature of matter—for the spirit itself. In a letter, Newton described the spirit as "an exceedingly subtile and unimaginably small portion of matter diffused throughout the mass of which if it were separated there would remain but a dead and inactive earth." The search for the ultimate nature of matter was thus the search for the essence of life, the *anima.* To bring the spirit under the control of human art was to obtain the key to the survival of death. The "Hidden Truth of Christ" was the secret of the Resurrection, a secret open to everyone through science.

Matthew laid the volume down and closed his eyes. The answer to the riddle had to lie here.

At the time, the Church was fighting for its life against the growing tide of reason and enlightenment. To provide a material account of the immortal spirit was to offer an alternative path to the life after death, and that was ideologically intolerable. Such a heresy struck at the mainspring of the Church's authority as sole mediator between this life and the next. How would the clerics be expected to react? Surely, by demanding either that the heretic recant or that he be removed. Shawcrosse wouldn't recant; he'd inveighed hard enough against Galileo for *his* recantation before the Inquisition. Nor could he be removed from his chair; they'd tried that, and failed. No, he had to be silenced. Once and for all. Could this be the reason for his sudden complete disappearance from the record after 1681?

A violent squall of rain against the windowpanes broke Matthew's train of thought. A sheet of lightning fleetingly lit up the room. The storm lamp flickered. Suddenly he heard a sharp *crack* from downstairs. He jolted upright. The bedroom door was open. Through it, he could see the wall of the staircase, lit mauve-white with a second flash of lightning. He swung himself out of bed and reached for his bathrobe. As he did so, a gust caught the flame of the storm lamp. It leaped, flared briefly, faltered, then abruptly sputtered out.

Smothering an oath, he groped his way onto the landing. At the top of the stairs, he hesitated. A chill frisson prickled his skin; he felt like a swimmer at sea entering a colder patch of water. Something strange was going on here. He felt cold outside, yet hot, even feverish, inside. A confusion of feeling surged through him—excitement, anticipation, terror. Nervous, erotic feelings, too, like those he'd known as an adolescent going to meet his first date. His heart was racing, his throat tight and dry.

Suddenly he froze.

Her scent! He could smell that same elusive, haunting perfume! Spicy like sandalwood, smoky as saltpeter, and beneath always that strange undertone, something like the smell of static electricity, of air ionized around a neon tube ...

She ... she was here!

He gripped the bannister post. With his other hand he clasped his forehead. Hold on, he told himself half-aloud. You're imagining. It's the strain of the past weeks, the unfamiliar surroundings, anxiety about your workload. Smell is the most evocative of the senses, of course, the oldest, most primordial sense, the first the human infant develops. The lightning ionized the air; memory evoked the rest.

Cautiously he made his way down the stairs in the darkness and struck out across the hallway until he met the far wall, then he felt his way along to the kitchen. He tried the lights there. They were out—the fuse probably blown. In the cupboard he found a candle and book of matches, and then went to examine the breaker switches. The override buttons had sprung out; somehow he must have overloaded the system. (Overloaded the system? But he'd turned things off, not on ...) In the morning he'd get a repairman to come by. Meanwhile, he'd put the whole thing out of his mind and get some sleep.

Holding the candle ahead to light his way, he retraced his steps back up the stairs. He had just reached the top stair when a sudden violent jolt, almost like a physical blow, struck him between the shoulder blades. He reeled forward, only just managing to keep the candle alight. Again that familiar sickly mix of dread and anticipation swept through him, and he found his limbs trembling uncontrollably. Gradually, as he stood clasping the railing, he became aware of that curious scent again, but somehow sweeter and rounder, warmer even, as though someone were actually there, standing very close by. He stood absolutely still and peered into the dark shadows, filled with nameless terrors.

Nothing, and no one.

Slowly he mastered his nerve and returned to his bedroom. There he closed the door firmly and stood for a moment composing his thoughts. Lights at windows, scents on stairways—this was the mind at work, inventing the nonexistent. These ghost sensations existed only in the brain's neuronal system, not out there.

He heaved a deep breath, shocked at his childish need for such reassurances. Disturbed and ill at ease, he laid the thesis aside and climbed into bed. As he leaned to blow out the candle, his eye fell upon the small love note Hazel had left him. He felt the tension in his body relax, his taut features soften into a smile. Thank God for some sweet certainties.

He looked closer. His smile hardened.

There, quite unmistakably, full across the lipstick kiss, spread a dark, discolored streak. A scorch mark. He reached out to touch the storm lamp; the glass was quite cold.

* * *

Matthew lived by lists. Each morning he'd start the day with his tasks freshly written out on yellow legal pad, and last thing at night he'd transfer the uncompleted balance onto the next day's sheet. He had two separate sections: one for Action—phone calls, correspondence, purchases—and another, usually longer, for Thought—references to check, ideas to explore, points to follow up. The scope of his chosen world of study was seemingly without limit, and these lists served in some way as marker-buoys to guide him in a universe of ideas awesome in its open-endedness.

To the Action section he now added another list: Ashlawn. Ashlawn was the name of the house, although there was not an ash tree throughout the property nor anything much resembling a lawn. Hazel had a theory that a previous owner had facetiously named it after James Monroe's rather modest residence up in the hills overlooking the town, to poke fun at their neighbor's mansion, a perfect scaled-down replica of Monticello, Jefferson's nearby and far more palatial seat. She refused to consider changing the name for fear it would bring bad luck. Though reluctant to yield to superstition, Matthew didn't want an argument. By a happy chance, the name board was old and rotten, and he could rely on the simple devices of time to erase the name for him.

By the end of the morning, the Ashlawn list ran to three pages. The roof needed major attention: The tiles, felt and battens, the chimneys, gutters and downspouts, all needed complete renovation. Under successive seasons of sun and rain, the exterior woodwork had cracked and warped, so that on all sides the clapboard panelling was split and large sections of the fretwork tracery around the porch and balcony were missing. As for the inside, the plumbing and wiring needed complete renewal and several floors would have to be entirely replaced. The house had been uninhabited for six years while a probate suit was being contested, and even the surveyor, for all the fee he'd charged, had refused to guarantee that no dry rot, death watch beetle or other infestation lay beneath the boards and behind the plaster. Still, Matthew was not going to let details deter him. Everything that really mattered was right about the place—the size, the location and the money. Most of all, as Hazel affirmed, it *felt* right.

The storm had blown itself out in the night, leaving two silver birches by the neighbors' security fence fallen and the surrounding trees robbed of their remaining foliage. The day was bright and unnaturally serene, with something of the stillness of a truce, and a new chill had entered the air that confirmed the change of season and foretold colder, harsher times ahead. Even the sunlight lapping in through the study window seemed already on the ebb.

Matthew felt a coil of excitement quicken within him. This was the time of year he loved best—the equinox, when day turned on the cusp of night. As he gazed out of his study window, his eye fixed on the giant plane tree dominating the acre of scrub and grass below and standing so crisp and clear that he felt he could count each twig on the furthermost branches. As he stared, the tree seemed to transform itself into a cast he'd once seen of the veins inside the human brain, a white multibranching web of exquisite intricacy proliferating from the arterial root to the finest capillaries. He rubbed his eyes. He was tired. Fatigue heightened the imagination. Trees might look like brains, but only by poetic distortion did trees *become* brains. Equally, only in the poet's world did kisses actually smolder.

He glanced down at Hazel's note, lying on his desk. He'd deliberately kept his mind off it all morning, busying himself with his lists, but he couldn't keep himself from confronting the puzzle any longer.

Taking an identical piece of paper, he went into his bedroom and lit the storm lamp on the bedside table, then propped the paper up against the lamp in the same position as before. Could a draft have blown it onto the hot glass? He experimented. No, that was impossible. The chimney was protected by an open-wire mesh sleeve, itself quite incapable of producing a long, diffused scorch mark. Finally admitting defeat, he slipped the note away and consigned the problem for later thought.

He spent the next two hours on the telephone to builders and carpenters, plumbers and electricians, arranging for quotations. In the early afternoon, already running late for a meeting he'd asked for with Lyall, he stuffed a bundle of papers into his briefcase, threw on a jacket and headed for the door. He was closing the outer screen when he noticed a small parcel on the porch steps. From the label he recognized it as the antique carriage clock he'd bought from an estate sale the previous week. He really must get the doorbell fixed. He hurried indoors with the parcel and took it upstairs to the master bedroom to add to their "nuptial treasure." But just as he was turning to leave the room, something caught his eye. A distinct, discolored patch on the floorboards just beneath the center sash.

He went over to examine the mark. Gradually his frown tightened. What had done this? Not wood varnish or floor polish or anything like that. It was more like the mark left by a hot iron, only larger and circular. He bent down. A smoky, charred odor rose from the boards.

This was a burn mark. A fresh burn mark.

Now, wait a minute. This was getting out of hand. What the hell was going on here?

He left the house in deep disquiet and, heedless of the time, he drove slowly to the university. It was a short journey, and one he usually enjoyed. Down Rugby Road he passed small groups of first-year undergraduates rushing sororities, but he hardly noticed them. By the gaunt stone chapel he had to jam on his brakes to let a trio of tracksuited jocks cross the road. Here and there on the sloping lawns of the grounds, between the magnolias and the tall fir trees, he glimpsed solitary figures sitting immersed in books or lying stretched out in the sunshine. At one remove, he took in the familiar route. He followed the campus bus at an obedient crawl along McCormick Road and past the main libraries and social halls, all a uniform stately blend of red brick and white stone that seemed to embody noble ideals of pride and honor and, perhaps for that reason, always reminded him of a military academy. Crossing Emmet Street, he wound his way through the science and psychology areas and finally reached the plain, square red-brick block that housed the physics department. There he drew up in a visitor's parking lot and tried to piece together a workable hypothesis.

Back at high school in Portland, Maine, he remembered building a Wimshurst machine, an old-fashioned creation for generating electricity, using two of his father's old 78-rpm records and some silver tinsel for brushes. He could recall with total immediacy the peculiar smell of the electricity as it discharged in fat sparks between the two copper knobs. Thunder storms involved immense electrical discharges; obviously this had been the cause of the strange smell the previous night, and his imagination, fired by nostalgia at reading the diary, had construed it as the perfume of the girl in his dream. But what about the weird scorch marks? It might be possible to account for those on the floor. Suppose a bolt of lightning had passed through the window and struck the floor—possibly even at the very moment he'd been coming down the drive? That would account for both the scorching and the strange luminous glow at the window.

But then there was the notepaper. No one could seriously imagine a bolt of lightning rolling down the corridor, skipping in through the bedroom door, hopping nimbly onto the bedside table and leaving a delicate trace upon a piece of paper, without burning it up, let alone doing serious damage on the way. And not only delicate but somehow deliberate. Why there of all particular places, gashed right across the kiss, a sign so grotesque he couldn't help seeing a deeper meaning in it?

Irritably, he climbed out and hurried up the front steps of the department building. He'd given this absurd business too much thought already. Hazel was right: he was obsessive, and he was taking it all too far. He had far more pressing concerns right now. Foremost was how to twist Lyall's arm into letting him have the use of a lab where he could work on replicating some experiments of Nathaniel Shawcrosse's. Lyall ran one of the nation's leading particle physics laboratories, and rehashing antiquated alchemical nonsense wasn't going to win any Nobel prizes. Perhaps when he'd made his pitch to get him here, Lyall hadn't reckoned that historical biography could actually involve historical bench work. If so, he hadn't reckoned with Matthew.

"I've been doing my homework," said Lyall from his chair, riffling through a leather-bound volume that Matthew recognized as some of the early proceedings of the Royal Society in seventeenth-century England. "Of course, you aren't serious."

"Wait a minute ..." began Matthew.

Lyall held the book at arm's length and squinted.

"What's this? 'Experiments of including living Animals ...'" His face registered mock pain. "'Of including.'" What kind of grammar is that? I tell my students, if you can't express yourselves properly, clear out and take up road sweeping."

"'Including' means enclosing ..."

"Very well. 'Enclosing living Animals and kindled Coals and Candles in a large Glass to observe which of them will be first Extinguished.'" He scrutinized Matthew with an owlish stare. "My God, Matthew, you *are* serious."

"Come off it," smiled Matthew, trying to make out how far Lyall was joking. He had never grasped the English sense of irony.

"And what about this?" continued Lyall, quoting from the book. "'Experiments as of cutting the Spleen of a Dog: of the effects of Vipers biting Dogs: of injecting various Liquors and other Substances into the veins of several Creatures.... Experiments with a poisoned Indian dagger:

of making Flesh grow on after it has been cut off: of the reviving of Strangled Animals by blowing into their lungs: of transmuting the Blood of
one Animal with another ...'" He paused, relishing the effect. "My dear
fellow, are you quite sure you've come to the right place? You have biology
across the road. And, next to it, experimental physiology."

By now Matthew was chuckling: This was the old Lyall, pulling his
leg. True, Nathaniel Shawcrosse had done his share of nonsensical work
and no doubt participated in some ghoulish experiments on live animals.
At the time, for instance, it had seemed perfectly reasonable to drain the
blood out of a dog and then feed it back in again, on the assumption that
if blood carried the essence of life, then life should return with the blood.
Certain work in the twentieth century was little more advanced. Shawcrosse's essential work was concerned with the search for the "vital substance," the spark of life that lay imbedded in all living matter. The absolute separation of mind from body, of spirit from flesh, was a later idea, an
idea that found its clearest exponent in Descartes and one that had infected
every area of thought since. Today, advanced physicists in departments like
Lyall's were at last dissolving this dualistic illusion. Yet back in the 1670s,
way ahead of his time, Shawcrosse had explicitly proposed a quantum
world in which mind and matter merged. Such was the thrust of
Matthew's thesis. But the surviving historical records were scanty, and
much had been suppressed after Shawcrosse's demise. The only way to fill
the gaps and reach the truth, Matthew believed, was to step into his shoes
and painstakingly reconstruct his path of inquiry. Lyall probably thought
it quite crazy.

Lyall had laid down the book and was initialing some memos in a For
Signature folder. Matthew cleared his throat.

"Lyall," he began, "I have a favor to ask."

"Let me just kill these and then we'll go."

Matthew sat down on the edge of the chair opposite and waited. This
was all going wrong. He studied his friend for a clue to his mood. Lyall
was a short, stocky man with a flattened face and bushy eyebrows and with
the fixed upper lip and permanent lipless smile of a ventriloquist's
dummy. He was ten years older than Matthew, and his thinning hair and
pouchy eyes showed he wasn't wearing them well. His office, a large airy
room dominated by a vast executive desk and high-backed leather swivel
chair, reflected his chiefly administrative role. Perhaps the strain lay there.

Finally, he put the folder in an out box, slipped a beeper into the pocket of his white lab coat and rose to his feet. Standing, he seemed actually to grow shorter.

"Ready, willing and able?"

He led the way out of the room. Matthew followed, mystified. Every few yards, Lyall stopped to exchange a few words with passing colleagues, approving a schedule change here and agreeing an agenda there. As they rode the elevator to the top floor, he listened while an attractive young research technician briefed him on the latest work being done by Abdus Salam in Trieste. Even the students in the corridors made way for him with a deference Matthew had rarely seen in other universities. Perhaps they did indeed operate a different code of behavior at UVA; or perhaps Lyall simply radiated a presence that commanded respect.

Finally they reached a heavy-duty door with a small wire-glass window and a lock that operated by a magnetic card. Lyall slipped a card into the slot to open the door, then handed the card to Matthew.

"Yours," he said. He threw open the door. "Well, I hope it'll do."

Matthew stepped into the lab and looked around. A large bench ran the length of one wall, laden with instruments, while a screened-off area at the end offered a desk with phones and a computer terminal. On a central table, in whimsical contrast to the sophisticated modern equipment all around, sat a large antique crucible and an apothecary's pestle and mortar.

He caught the expectant look on his friend's face.

"You old devil, Lyall," he smiled.

"Whatever you want, you only have to ask." Lyall went over to the desk and handed him an internal phone list. "I've told the people in Requisitions to see that you have any materials you need and charge them to me. The facilities department is on standby for equipment; just fill in a yellow form here. I'll fix you up with your own computer ID, too, so you can access the mainframe. Oh, and when you want to book time on the accelerator or the spectroscopy unit, go through my office. I'll introduce you to Sandra. She'll handle any typing and secretarial work for you, too."

"You're a real pal," said Matthew, genuinely moved.

The other man's expression softened into a wry, almost weary smile.

"I miss the real thing, working at the sharp end. I'm not a bench man any more, Matthew. I'm a butt man. I drive paper around a desk."

"Take a sabbatical," urged Matthew. "Work with one of your own project teams."

"Gamekeeper turn poacher?" Lyall shook his head, and his expression took on a sudden fervor. "No, I'm thinking of your work. I feel ... I feel it's important not to lose sight of the big questions. Science and religion: Can they be reconciled? Ninety-eight percent of the world believes in a soul that survives death: Can they all be wrong? What *is* the soul? Is it a force field, a resonance? Can we detect it? Big questions. But it's time we asked them seriously. And I think we can begin to expect some answers. These are thrilling times, Matthew. We're already half way toward a biology of consciousness. Let's go for a physics of consciousness, too." He broke off, as if surprised by his own forthrightness.

"I never saw you as a religious man, Lyall."

The professor smiled self-deprecatingly.

"I'm a thinker who would rather be a believer."

Matthew gestured around the room. "So that's the reason for all this?"

"That, and other things. Things that have happened." He eyed him sharply, intently. Then, as if he were satisfied with something, his manner eased. "We go back a long way, old chap," he said. He touched him briefly on the arm in a rare gesture of affection, but withdrew his hand as though he'd overstepped the boundary of propriety, then went on more briskly, "Well now, there are people in the building you'll need to meet. Shall we make a start?"

Matthew wasn't listening. Lyall's cryptic reply echoed in his ears: *That, and other things. Things that have happened.* He thought of the things that had happened to him just the previous night, and he shivered. And he thought of Lyall's earlier remark, *Ninety-eight percent of the world ... can they all be wrong?*

"Matthew?"

Lyall's voice broke across his thoughts. He mustered a smile and cleared his throat.

"Sure, let's go."

THREE

Far ahead of her, at the end of a long, straight gravel drive lined by lime trees, stood Hanover Park, an imposing red-brick colonial mansion. On either side, beyond white post-and-rail fencing, stretched rolling meadows of tall, yellowing grass on which cattle grazed, knee-deep in the late fall mist. Closer to the house spread a large paddock in which a well-groomed horse was being exercised, its breath steaming in the sharp morning air. Hazel slowed; perhaps the rider was the Senator's daughter, Josie. Then she glanced at the dashboard clock and accelerated. She mustn't be a moment late for this assignment.

She parked to one side of the entrance and, lifting her cases of camera equipment out of the back of the car, hurried across the frost-crisped gravel to the tall white portico. A lady of advancing years, clearly once a great beauty, met her on the steps and ushered her indoors, across a hallway with a checkered marble floor and through a pair of mahogany doors into a small anteroom, and tapped at an inner door.

From within, a gravelly, cigar-rich voice called, "Come."

Otis McDowell rose from behind his desk as Hazel entered. He was a lean, silver-haired man who projected an instantly commanding presence. His manner was youthful and vigorous, and only a closer inspection of his complexion, with its thin, parchmentlike translucency, and his eyes, where a faint milky film had begun to veil the pupils, betrayed his true age. He greeted Hazel with an outstretched hand—his left hand. He'd lost half his right arm in an accident with a punt gun, he explained. Josie, his daughter, had saved his life.

The phone on his desk buzzed, and while he excused himself to take the call, Hazel glanced around her. It was a fine room, with treble-sash windows and book-lined walls. Framed photographs stood on every shelf, mantel and table. One, on the desktop beside her and faded by sunlight, showed a leggy young girl of about eight standing beside a woman who, to judge from the extraordinary likeness, was her mother. Hazel had read in the cuttings files about the family tragedy. Otis had never remarried. There was a son, a few years older than Josie, who appeared in a couple of photos, but all the rest that she could see were of father and daughter alone—on vacation in Mexico, deep-sea fishing perhaps off the Florida keys, or sharing a barbecue with the President, possibly at Camp David.... If Josie was home right now, could she persuade the Senator to let her photograph them both together?

Otis was relaxed and good-humored during the photo session, and at the end, feeling relieved and confident that she'd got some great shots, she broached the question. Otis looked at his watch, then picked up the phone. He called the stables; apparently, Josie was out riding. Briefly he hesitated, then cast Hazel a mischievous smile and rose to his feet. He strode across the room, took a Stetson from the hat rack and swung the door open for her.

"Come on, young lady," he said, sweeping her out of the room. "I have an idea where we'll find her. And you can see a bit of the old homestead on the way, too."

"There's been a McDowell living on this land for three hundred years," Otis was shouting above the roar of the Jeep. He drove one-handed, from time to time using the elbow of his other arm to help steer. "Not in the same house, of course. Things got knocked down and rebuilt with the changes in fashion. And fortune."

"And the next three hundred?" smiled Hazel.

He shrugged, then gestured out of the window. "Some things don't ever change."

They were bumping over a rough track that led through rolling grassland toward a distant line of fir trees. Thin skeins of mist still lingered in the dips, swamping the vehicle one moment and whipping past the windows like ragged white scarves the next. Hazel stretched her gaze to the middle distance. Over to her right lay a small group of plywood cabins, where she could imagine farmhands had lived since the days of slavery. Briefly she glimpsed a woman reaching up to hang out washing, her dark skin a striking contrast against the white sheets. Beyond stretched apple orchards, where she could see the pickers hard at work—hurrying, Otis told her, to bring in the crop before the frosts came.

She felt a strange sense of timelessness washing over her. Nothing here really had changed in three hundred years. True, the plantations had long since been taken out of tobacco and given over to fruit farming—but then, tobacco had never done well north of Richmond—and the pickers were no longer the local blacks but Mexicans shipped in for the season in fleets of bright yellow buses. But as the Jeep forged through meadows once worked by horse and hoe and long since left to lie fallow, with the broad Pamunkey river snaking its silvery path in from their left to meet the lake glinting through the fringe of trees ahead and all around stretching the ageless, sorrowful beauty of the tidewater marshes, she felt that here was a pocket where time had truly never moved on. Perhaps this was just the very feeling that Matthew had during those hours he spent lost in his seventeenth-century world. It was like looking through a misted windowpane, but at a real world nonetheless.

"There she is!" came Otis's shout.

Ahead stood a great bay hunter, tethered to a tree. Beyond, Hazel could make out movement in the tall grasses. Abruptly a figure emerged, a girl of about twenty, in hacking jacket and jeans. She came forward, smiling, her blond mare's tail swinging as she walked. She clearly grasped the situation in a flash.

"Hi, I'm Josie," she said, holding out a hand as Hazel climbed out. She sized her quickly up and down. "I admire your guts. Dad's a maniac driver."

"I drove like a mouse," protested her father. "Ask Miss—"

"It's Hazel," interposed Hazel. "I came to take some photos of the Senator, and—"

"Dad, I'm sorry," said Josie, "but I told you. I won't do it." She turned to Hazel with a sigh of fond exasperation. "I keep telling him he should give it up. He doesn't need the hassle. He's getting on, and he's got no one to look after him when I'm away at college—don't look at me like that, Dad, you know why it's Northeastern—and politics is so stressful. He's dead set on going for another term. And now here you are, and it's all beginning again."

"Hazel isn't part of that," he objected.

"It's all publicity."

"Josie, be honest. You want to put me out to pasture?"

Josie shook her head and, putting an arm round his shoulder, gave him an affectionate squeeze. "All right," she smiled to Hazel, "what do you want me to do?"

"Just hold it there," said Hazel and reached into her case for the Hasselblad. "That's just great."

Hazel wiped the back of her rubber-gloved hand over her forehead and let out a sigh. Even wearing just a long loose T-shirt and skimpy panties, she was sweltering in the small, cramped darkroom. She glanced at the timer-clock. Matthew would be wanting to get on the road. He'd driven up to D.C. for the evening to see Ben's exhibit; it was well past ten now, and he was still reading the boy bedtime stories. He was spoiling him, or turning him into an insomniac like himself.

She checked the temperature of the developer and, reaching for a pair of tongs, slipped the paper from the enlarger into the dish. Slowly, filled with excitement, she watched the next image come up. What an amazing scoop! She'd come away with far more than she'd dreamed of, and already the results looked sensational.

Here it came now, a fond family portrait of father and daughter, taken in that wonderful pearly morning light, with the lake stretching in the background and the far treeline fading out of focus. In the foreground, on the top step of the jetty, sat Otis, a wry, relaxed smile spread over his face, while behind him and leaning forward with her arms round his neck, stood his daughter Josie, blond, classically beautiful, with a strong, forthright face and eyes that smiled. The magazine just had to love it.

There was a tap at the door.

"Hang on," she called. She gave the photo a final stir and slipped it into the hypo bath. "Okay now."

Matthew came in and closed the door quickly behind him. He paused for a moment while his eyes adjusted to the low red light, then stepped forward and peered into the dish.

"And you say the camera can't lie," he grunted.

"Forget the man's politics. Do you like the photo?"

He picked up the print with the tongs and examined it more closely.

"You have a real talent for people, Hazel," he said quietly. "You capture what makes them tick. Their essence."

"Bull! You just want to ogle the girl." With a laugh she took the photo and reached above her to clip it onto a line to dry. As she stretched up her arms, she felt him step behind her and his hands reach to her breasts. She shivered.

"Matthew ..."

"Don't say a thing."

Slowly he ran his hands beneath her T-shirt over her naked skin. In the darkness she half pretended he was a stranger. The stranger was bending her forward over the workbench. Her hair clung clammily to her face. Her breath was coming faster. The stranger was now inside her, moving with long, slow strokes. Her breasts swung heavily back and forth. Fuck me, she rasped as the first convulsive waves shuddered through her. The room was swirling in and out of focus. She gripped the sides of the bench to steady herself. Wave after wave swept through her. She was spiraling upward, out of control. She had no sense of how or when it came to an end, she was only aware of floating gently down to the ground like a falling leaf, to find herself folded in his arms. Taking his hand, she placed it high on the inside of her thigh. The muscles there were trembling uncontrollably.

"See what you do to me?" she whispered.

"I love you, Hazel," he murmured.

"More than anyone ever before?"

"More than anyone ever."

"There'll never be anyone else?"

"Never."

"I'd kill them. And then I'd kill you."

"You wouldn't collect on the life insurance."

"I mean it, Matthew."

In the gleam of the safety light, his neck and arms glistened with perspiration and his eyes were lost in deep pools of shadow. The small darkroom was stiflingly hot, yet she felt she never wanted to leave it. This was a womb of love. She had never felt so close to anyone before. She held her breath, wishing that time would hold its own too.

He shifted his arm. She could tell he was angling his wristwatch so as to see the time. She shook him angrily.

"Bastard!" she cried. "For that, you're staying the night."

"Hazel, I've got builders coming at seven."

"Then get up at five."

"Let's be sensible."

"Be sensible? God forbid!" Abruptly she regained her strength of mind. "Go, then," she said, pulling away. "See you next weekend."

"Here." He drew her back to him.

"You've had your share. Now, beat it. I've got work to do."

He hesitated. "Hazel?"

She caught the look on his face, part manly and defiant, part forlorn as a little boy, and she broke into a smile. Suddenly they burst out laughing together. She flung her arms around him and kissed him hard.

"Drive safely," she said. "Promise me."

"You bet your life."

"Now get lost," she laughed and pushed him away.

He seized her again in a brief, violent embrace, then he broke free, turned and left the room. She heard him whistling softly to himself as he put on his old leather flying jacket and searched around for his car keys. The front door opened, shut, and there was silence.

She closed her eyes and yielded to the flood of senses surging through her body. Every fiber of her felt charged with a love and a lust she'd never felt before. A swell of pure joy rose within her, and she stood there in the center of the small darkened room, swaying backward and forward and smiling idiotically as the tears streamed uncontrollably down her cheeks.

The night was clear and starry, and a razor-sharp crescent moon lit the buildings and countryside on each side of the highway with a cold, stark brilliance. Matthew drove unhurriedly, with the carefree ease of a satiated lover. His pulse quickened as he pictured Hazel in that red-lit darkroom, bent over the workbench, her naked buttocks thrust out toward him. He brushed his fingers past his nose and inhaled the delicate traces of her body's most intimate scent. His senses reeled. A blast of a truck's horn jolted him back to the present, forcing him to swerve sharply.

Did other men know such feelings? Had Lyall ever drawn such ecstasy from the body of that waspish wife of his? Were any such heights of passion being scaled at that very moment behind the drawn curtains in that motel over there or in those dimly lit rooms of that apartment building? His mind turned on its well-oiled grooves to Nathaniel Shawcrosse, his ever-present familiar. Had he lusted after the flesh? Had he concocted potions of cantharides in his laboratory and slipped them into his wife's nightcap for a night of unbridled passion?

Nathaniel Shawcrosse. In his mind's eye, Matthew could see the figure in the engraving as clearly as if the man himself stood before him. A youthful, fresh face, boyishly round, with sensual lips and wild unkempt hair, a face full of zest and vigor and sexual energy. What had the private life of this brilliant, mysterious figure really been like? So little was known. He'd married a bishop's daughter, Mary, who'd borne him six children, only one of whom, a boy named Barnabas, survived beyond the age of twelve. He'd lived in a narrow, stone-built house in Merton Street, Oxford, a short walk from Sanctus Spiritus college, where he'd kept rooms and maintained a laboratory in an annex at the back of the Great Hall. His public lectures and private tutorials had raised passionate feelings and vehement debate. But what about his sex life?

Matthew amused himself for the rest of the drive, fantasizing scenarios. He imagined orgiastic feasts behind bolted doors, he invented trysts with students, pretty boys with long ringlets and pale, studious faces, such as his assistant Lapidus, to whom he'd addressed love poems. He constructed passionate dalliances with dons' daughters and tavern girls and buxom serving wenches, too. In the all-male world of academia, a passing fancy for one sex didn't preclude a lusty interest in the other. Nathaniel could have had a regular mistress. He very probably did. Infidelity by itself carried no great social stigma in his day. This man, thought Matthew, was unquestionably one for the ladies. I'd give him a bubbling bosomy young mistress any day.

He reached home with hardly any recollection of how he'd got there and pulled up in the front driveway. Still smiling to himself, he stepped lightly up the porch steps and groped for the right keys. The neighbor's guard dog was barking loudly, a stupid, relentless noise that began to eat away at his good humor. Once indoors, he poured himself a drink and took his messages off the answering machine, trying to ignore the dog's incessant barking. He noted down the messages on a pad and, putting on a record of a Sibelius symphony, settled down to plan the rest of his week. Then he realized he'd left some papers in the car. Fetching the keys, he went back out into the chill, clear night.

As he headed toward the car, he stopped. The dog was barking in unabated frenzy. He could hear the tormented creature half strangling itself as it strained against its collar. He stepped around the back of the house to see what was going on. Across a stretch of rough grass, between a large camellia bush and a clump of trees, he could see the German shepherd straining at the limit of its chain, bristling, slavering, struggling after something it had evidently seen on his side of the fence. Something, or some*body?* But surely no one would just stand there all this time, drawing attention to himself?

Gingerly, he stepped forward. He had reached the edge of the grass when he gave a violent jolt.

A figure, all in white. More exactly, a kind of whitish luminescence. A shape somehow without edges or outline. And yet identifiably human.

He knew that human figure.

How, why, he couldn't tell. There was no reason or recollection in it. He simply knew he knew her.

Her?

She turned, though he couldn't say how or from where she turned, for she seemed to have a body that neither began nor ended anywhere that could be defined. She looked at him. He couldn't actually see her eyes, yet she held him transfixed. Very steady, very still.

Remotely, he heard a shout from the neighbors' yard. Floodlights burst on, swamping the woodland and blinding him. His neighbor Herb was lumbering heavily forward, ordering the dog to heel. He called out to Matthew. Matthew came forward but tripped over a root and fell to the ground. Clambering to his feet and shielding his eyes, he scanned the patch of woodland where the figure had been standing. But she'd gone, turned transparent, like flame in sunlight. Herb was at the fence now, asking if he was all right, whether he'd seen an interloper. Beside him the dog stood growling suspiciously. But Matthew hardly registered any of this. All that existed for him was the smell in the air—that dangerously familiar smell—and the unmistakable coolness in the air and, above all, the afterimage of that strange figure seared indelibly onto his brain.

FOUR

Matthew leaned back in the swivel chair and pressed his thumb and forefinger hard into the inner corners of his eyes against the throbbing migraine. Splinters of gray afternoon light filtered into the laboratory through chinks in the blinds where the slats were bent. He'd been having headaches on and off for the past ten days. In fact, ever since.... Maybe he should get his eyes tested. Deciphering old texts put a great strain on the eye muscles, not to mention sitting in front of a flickering CRT screen for hours on end, struggling to put a database onto the computer. Eyesight ought not to start going until after forty, and he was a good five years off that. But his sight *had* been playing tricks. How else could he explain what he'd seen?

More likely it was just the strain of taking on too much. Hazel was right: He ought to get in a single building contractor to do the renovation work rather than try and save money by hiring in the skills separately and managing the project himself. Yet the savings represented the price of a ten-by-five-meter heated swimming pool. He rubbed his eyes harder. Damn it, he'd never been ill in his life! He was impatient of illness in others and he refused to accept it in himself. He was sound in body. And in mind.

The phone interrupted his thoughts. It was Lyall calling from his office, asking if he could spare a minute. Matthew said he'd be down right away. He'd better get moving if he was to get to the library on the way home, too. Hazel and Ben were arriving early for the weekend and Herb and Norma had invited them to meet-the-neighbors cocktails at their mini-Monticello next door. He swallowed a couple of Tylenol with a beaker of stale tap water and, stuffing his briefcase with papers, made his way unsteadily to the door.

As he was leaving, he noticed a letter lying in the wire basket on the door. It was a circular from a conference-management company and bore a computer-printed label addressed to a Dr. Clark Tauber. He slipped it in his pocket, locked the door and headed for the elevator. He'd get Sandra, Lyall's attractive young secretary, to forward it.

Sandra looked up as he entered. She sized him up and down with a rapid, practiced eye, then smiled, holding his eye just a fraction longer than was entirely professional. In a slow, silky voice, she invited him to go on through. As he went past, he handed her the letter.

"This came to the lab by mistake," he said. "Could you redirect it?"

"Sure." She glanced at the addressee. Instantly her expression tightened. She shot him a quick, troubled glance, then hastily put the letter to one side, face down. "That shouldn't have happened," she said. "Yes, I'll see to it."

He hesitated. "Who is Dr. Tauber?"

"He was, uh, one of the faculty. He had your lab before …"

"Before what?"

"Before … you." She rose to her feet. Her cheeks were slightly flushed. "Let me show you in."

"No, no, I can see myself in. Thanks."

Lyall was busy updating a plastic wallchart with colored magic markers as Matthew entered. It was a departmental schedule, listing the professors and lecturers down one side and the course modules across the top. Matthew was intrigued to find him doing this by hand; any of a dozen linear programs could do the job at a keystroke.

Lyall turned and greeted him with a dangerously friendly smile.

"I know this is a hell of an imposition," he began.

"What's the deal?"

"I have rather an embarrassing gap here," said Lyall, pointing to the chart. "Roland Burnside from Harvard was scheduled. He's going in for major surgery that day. It's an open lecture. Thursday at five p.m., in Cabell Hall. Two hundred students. Subject of your choice." He paused and held his eye unflinchingly. "Sorry about the short notice."

"Is this your call?"

"This is my call."

"Then I'd be honored," Matthew replied sweetly. "I can offer you 'A Molecular Approach to Masonry Repairs,' or 'Applications of Fluid-state Physics to Domestic Plumbing'..."

"My dear chap, I don't mean to tax you that far. I was thinking of your 'Alchemy and the Scientific Method' paper. Half the civilized world may have heard it, but I don't believe you've ever delivered it in this university." He paused, maintaining a deadpan face. Matthew suppressed a grin. "Alternatively," he went on, "you could offer us a foretaste of your offering for the Faraday conference in Oxford. When is that, now?"

"The first week in December."

Lyall smiled benevolently.

"You'll need a travel grant. For two, of course. I'm sure we can stretch a point."

"Hazel will be too busy. Besides, there's Ben."

"Nonsense. It'll do you both good. Relax amidst the dreaming spires. Relive the old memories." He smiled, then his manner grew more businesslike. "What title shall I put down for you? 'Science and Magic?'"

Matthew sharpened. How did Lyall know that? He'd told him the subject of the talk he planned to give at the Oxford conference, but not the title. He'd only thought it up the previous evening while sketching the outline on the computer in the lab.

"You know me too well, Lyall," he responded.

"Well enough, I think."

The two men exchanged a careful smile, and with a slight sense of unease Matthew made for the door. Sandra had recovered her composure, and as he passed she bade him good-bye with her usual blend of efficiency and intimacy.

He hurried out of the building and into the dull, overcast afternoon. Turning up his collar against the wind, he wound his way through the maze of pathways that crisscrossed the grounds. Taking a short cut across Emmet Street and around the back of the social halls, he finally reached the imposing building that housed the Alderman Library.

It was there, and only by chance, that he made the curious connection.

He duly collected and signed for the book he had ordered, a copy of the *Prolegomena* of Robert Boyle, which he'd obtained by interlibrary transfer from the John M. Olin Library at Cornell. It was an exceptionally rare and valuable copy, containing important marginal notations in Boyle's own hand. The transfer was processed so smoothly that Matthew found himself with a few minutes to spare, and he decided to call up a copy of some of the early Proceedings of the Royal Society and check the agenda of a meeting at which both Boyle and Shawcrosse had been present. As the book was in the stacks, he filled in an application form and took it to the desk; he'd pass by the following day and collect it. The librarian keyed the application into his computer terminal, then shook his head. The volume was already out on loan. Then Matthew remembered this was the particular one Lyall had had in his office. He was turning to go when he noticed the librarian was staring at the screen with a puzzled frown .

Matthew bent forward to look. A shiver rippled over his skin.

The borrower's name on the file was not Professor Lyall Markson. It was Dr. Clark Tauber.

"How do I look?"

Hazel swept through the front door and did a pirouette on the porch. Her red wrap-around dress hugged her figure to the waist and flared into a full, gypsy-cut skirt, and she wore her cream Lagerfeld coat over her shoulders like a cape. Her coppery hair whirled in waves as she spun. Apart from a trace of lipstick, she wore barely any makeup, and in the outdoor light this somehow rendered her eyes the palest translucent green.

"Like a million bucks," responded Matthew. He drew her toward him and slipped a hand between the folds of her top. She was naked underneath. Her nipple hardened to a small point.

She pushed his hand aside.

"I asked how I look, not how I feel." She stood back and scrutinized his clothes critically. "Herb is in construction, not deconstruction. Wouldn't you feel more comfortable in something less slovenly?"

"Hazel, I know Norma and Herb. They *want* academics to be badly dressed. They want us to wear bow ties and brogues and elbow patches. That's why they live here. They'd be on Palm Beach otherwise. It's culture by osmosis. It creeps across the boundary with the weeds."

"What garbage you talk, Matthew," she smiled. "Where's Ben?"

"Around the back, getting himself nice and messed up. Academics' kids are supposed to be dirty and disheveled, too. The day there's real money in learning, where would they be with their bourgeois materialism? Hazel, we *have* to look scruffy. It's unneighborly not to. You're looking far too glamorous."

"I'm not an academic, in case you've forgotten."

"You'll soon be married to one."

"Don't expect me to answer to 'Mrs Matthew Cavewood, Academic's Wife,'" she warned, rising to the bait by reflex.

"Socially and legally, my sweet betrothed," he smiled, "that's precisely what you will be."

"I can't take you in this facetious mood," she said tartly. "We're late already. Where *is* that child?"

She called, and eventually Ben emerged, his fair hair neatly brushed, his shoes gleaming and his clothes perfectly tidy. She glared at Matthew, then gradually her expression softened into a grudging smile.

"Just don't be too smart with them, Matthew, okay?"

"Relax. There'll be only one topic of conversation—the old girl who owned the house before us. Can't get too smart there, can we? Are you all ready?"

Matthew knew he was drinking too much. Hazel kept shooting him glances like poisoned arrows. For a while he tried to join in the flow of the talk, but he could hear himself sounding exaggeratedly fascinated. Norma, a tall, sardonic woman with a voice sharpened by gin and a complexion carapaced in makeup, was talking about a big postmodern Japanese exhibition in New York she'd been to see. New York was her home town, and she made it clear that anywhere else was deeply provincial. Charlottesville was positively the boondocks. Her husband Herb was laughing a lot in a nervous high-pitched giggle that sounded curious from a man of his size and substance. The Japs were too darn big in everything, he was saying; Pittsburgh, his home town, had been virtually wiped out by Japanese steel imports. Look at the automobile industry, look at electronics....

"Look at our yard," offered Matthew with the best intentions. "Overrun by bamboo."

"Bamboo comes from China," muttered Hazel *sotto voce*.

"You can't do a goddamn thing about bamboo," agreed Herb. "Don't get Norma onto the subject of gardening."

"Are you gardening folk?" enquired Norma with steel-edged sweetness, dead on cue. "Your yard used to be a real showpiece when Blanche Morrell had it."

"Blanche ran the local women's garden club," explained Herb.

"*She* never had a problem with kudzu."

"Another lousy Jap import," chuckled Herb.

Matthew winced beneath Norma's eye. That terrible ivylike plant was sweeping like wildfire through their property; it had already overrun a large clump of trees in the wilderness with its vast, hand-size leaves and was creeping toward the boundary fence. Nothing short of napalm would arrest it.

"Blanche was out in her yard day and night, cutting and pruning," Norma continued pointedly. "I can see her now, pottering around, all dressed in white."

"Always in white," echoed Herb. "Ever since her husband passed away, that's all she wore. White apron in the garden, white duster in the house. Said she felt closer to him like that."

Matthew felt a sudden chill prickle his skin. With a sense of detachment, he heard himself ask the question.

"Blanche Morrell died at home?"

"In her sleep," replied Herb. "Peaceful as an angel."

"Tell me, which was her bedroom?"

Hazel chipped in. "Matthew," she cautioned, "I don't think anyone wants to pursue this."

But Herb was eager to oblige.

"On the right, upstairs. The one with the large bay window," he responded.

"And she always dressed in white?" persisted Matthew.

Norma gave a harsh chuckle. "Everything white. Even her ashes. You know your large camellia bush, the one by the silver birch trees, next to the fence. That was her favorite spot. She had her ashes sprinkled there."

"Bone meal," grinned Herb, until quenched by a reproving glance from his wife.

Matthew's hand tightened around his cocktail glass. His gaze locked onto the olive bobbing through the oily meniscus of the gin. His thoughts were racing. He felt a madman's compulsion to go on. He lifted his stare to Herb and edged his back to Hazel so as to avoid her looks.

"You had your German shepherd then, too?"

"We've had Carlo since he was a puppy," replied Herb readily. "I trained him myself. Take the leg off an intruder soon as look at him. Mind you," he added in a consciously fair-minded tone, "he was soft as a kitten with Blanche. But then, she used to spoil him. She'd feed him cookies and tidbits through the fence. He put on a helluva lot of weight." Herb patted his generous stomach. "Like his old man."

"Difference is, honey," said Norma sweetly, "Carlo took it off."

"The dog knew her, then?" Matthew continued obstinately. "It wouldn't ... bark at her?"

Herb chuckled in an effort to ease the tightening atmosphere.

"I get you. Sorry about the other evening. Carlo will soon get used to you."

But Norma wasn't satisfied.

"Something on your mind, Matthew?" she asked.

Hazel intervened quickly. "Don't take any notice. Questions, always questions. That's life with an academic."

"That's life with Norma, too," said Herb jovially. "Keeps a boy on the straight and narrow. Huh, Matt?"

At this point, Hazel stepped in to take over and elegantly switched the conversation, even managing to draw Ben into it. But Matthew had stopped listening. He stood immobile as a rock while the cocktail party chatter swirled about him. Deep within him spread icy tentacles of dread. Dimly he grew aware that the room had grown quiet. He felt a hand on his arm and started violently. Norma was staring intently at him, her thin ribbon lips twisted in a smile of false concern.

"Are you quite all right, Matthew?" she asked. "You look as if you've seen a ghost."

His throat was too tight and too dry to reply.

Hazel reached for his hand and dug her fingernails into the palm. With a sweet smile round the room, she said she thought they'd better be going; it was well past Ben's bedtime, and if he didn't get his sleep ... Herb put his arm round the boy's shoulder and sympathized, saying he himself was good for nothing the next morning if he didn't get his full eight hours. Norma took the cue to launch into a discourse on a new Japanese technique known as "super sleep" whereby the normal night's sleep was condensed into four hours, and the whole conversation would have started full circle again if Hazel hadn't led the way to the door and politely but firmly made their excuses again, offered their thanks and left.

Before he quite realized, Matthew found himself being hurried down the gravel drive. Behind them, their hosts were standing on the steps of the columned portico, courteously seeing them off. Ahead, at a command from the house, the large, heavily spiked front gates swung slowly open.

"What the hell was all *that* about?" hissed Hazel when they were out of earshot. "You behaved disgracefully."

Matthew bit his lip. He glanced to his right where, through the security fence, he could just glimpse the clump of silver birches and, beyond, the large camellia bush reduced to a dark, dead silhouette in the falling twilight. He said nothing. There was nothing he could say.

By the time he had finished reading Ben his bedtime stories, Matthew felt more sober, but his migraine had come back worse than ever, and as he sat down to the Cajun chicken Hazel had prepared, he found he could literally see only half the plate before him. A scotoma: had that been it? A shape somehow without edges or outline ... a body that neither began nor ended anywhere that could be defined. Perhaps it had simply been a blind spot on the retina, like now. Or a hallucination, quite common in migraines. Yet he'd been feeling fine at the time—never better, in fact. Besides, there had been a witness: That dog had seen something, too.

Hazel sat down opposite at the temporary kitchen table and uncorked the wine. As she reached to fill his glass, she paused.

"Something is the matter, Matthew, isn't it?" she probed gently. "Is it to do with the book? Or the house?"

"Nothing. Just a slight headache."

She shook her head and gave a light laugh.

"That won't do tonight, Napoleon. I've missed you too badly."

He rubbed his eyes. A good third of his vision was blotted out. It was not a hole so much as a void. A nothingness. Not like then. Then he'd at least seen *something*.

"Hazel, I know this may sound crazy, but I wonder if we should rethink where we have our bedroom."

Her manner stiffened.

"What ever for?" she demanded, then she understood. "You aren't serious!"

"If it really is where the old girl died ..."

"Don't be ridiculous! Every house with any age has its history. Birth, copulation and death, what's new? Why should it affect us? She's *dead*, Matthew. She died peacefully, if that makes you feel easier." She reached out a hand and her tone softened. "Do I need to start worrying about you?"

He strove to pull himself together.

"You're right. It's ridiculous."

"Try and eat. You drink too much and eat too little. You haven't touched the cannelloni I left you, or the chili. I want my man with some meat on him. He'll need it for the ride."

Matthew mustered a smile and tackled the chicken. He felt sickness rising in his gorge. Finally, with an apologetic grimace, he pushed the plate aside and poured himself a glass of water. He felt a deep inner chill wrap round his soul. Hazel had got up and was standing behind him, stroking his forehead.

"What you need," she said, "is a good, hot tub and a nice, slow massage all over. What do you say?"

He tilted his head back and nestled into her soft, reassuring body. Slowly she bent forward and, her hair falling like a curtain around them, pressed her lips against his. In that warm and sensual touch all his anxieties gradually began to ebb away, and as he turned to draw her closer he felt that his fears were just fantasies and the only reality that meant anything was here, in the arms of the woman he loved.

The lecture hall, a steeply tiered amphitheater, was packed. Some students were sitting on the stairs and others lined the back wall. Matthew could not recall speaking before such a large and attentive audience since his visiting fellowship year at Chicago University. As usual, he focused on one or two individuals in the audience—here, a pretty blond chewing a pen in the right quadrant and a thick-set youth with a studded leather jacket and designer stubble in the upper left—but throughout the lecture he was uncomfortably aware of a thin, bespectacled student in the center of the front row who held him in an intense, unblinking stare. Lyall sat on the end of a row to one side, nodding his agreement to each point.

Matthew sat perched on the edge of the desk, talking without notes. He spoke for fifty minutes, deliberately raising and lowering the tension as he built his proposition up to its climax. He felt he held his listeners in the palm of his hand. It was a heady, seductive sensation.

The root of modern science, he suggested, was magic. Today's scientist owed his entire method and approach to the ancient magician.

Magic meant far more than mere illusionist's tricks. It was, to quote della Porta in 1658, "nothing else but the knowledge of the whole course of Nature." The whole emphasis of natural magic was on empirical discovery, on what things worked together to produce what, with little concern about *why* they worked. Causes, being indiscernible by experiment, were considered inscrutable, occult. But the particular could infer the general, and by the exercise of inductive thinking Nature could be forced to yield her secrets—a method, enunciated by Francis Bacon and developed by Isaac Newton, that became the foundation stone of modern science.

Both men were profoundly affected by the magical tradition, in particular by the belief in a universal occult principle of life. All matter was, in a real and potent sense, alive. This was, of course, a fundamental tenet of alchemy. Newton himself was a clandestine alchemist. His library was discovered to contain all the Hermetic texts, Zoroaster, Orpheus, the Cabbala and the writings of Eirenaeus Philalethes and the other magi. The work, however, went on strictly behind closed doors: it was dangerous. Alone and in secret, Newton labored at his furnaces in his laboratory in Cambridge, playing with gold and mercury and lead and creating complex alloys unfamiliar even to modern chemists. Even his alchemical communications with his close friend Nathaniel Shawcrosse were always written in code....

At the mention of Shawcrosse's name, the thin student started violently. His hand flew to his mouth to choke back a cry. Matthew was thrown momentarily off balance, and though he recovered quickly, throughout the rest of the lecture he was uncomfortably aware of the student's penetrating, stricken gaze upon him. At last he brought the lecture to its conclusion, rounding it off with a final rhetorical flourish.

"The science that put a man on the moon," he declared, "the science that has split the atom, eradicated innumerable diseases and doubled man's life expectancy, the science we think of as objective, detached, rational, 'scientific,' this science owes its methodology not to Aristotle and the Schoolmen but to the ancient traditions of natural magic and alchemy. I'd go as far as suggesting that modern science today is closer to these roots than ever before. The world of high-energy physics, with its quarks and gluons and charmed lambdas, is in a profound sense the world of the magician, and its preoccupations with understanding the fundamental nature of matter and what animates it—spirit, mind, force field or whatever you chose to call it—these are the very preoccupations of the seventeenth-century alchemist." He paused to give weight to his final proposition. "Isaac Newton the magician and Nathaniel Shawcrosse the alchemist are alive and well and living among us today."

Silence greeted his ending, and for a moment he thought he'd misread the mood of the audience. But gradually the applause broke out, sporadically at first, then rising to a sustained swell. Lyall was beaming. He came forward and shook Matthew by both hands, in the manner of a conductor congratulating a soloist. The students began to pack up and disperse, now laughing and chattering at the top of their voices.

The thin, bespectacled youth from the front row, however, detached himself from the others and came forward. His face was pale and his manner agitated. Matthew felt Lyall's hand at his elbow drawing him aside. But the student pressed closer.

"Sir?" he asked in an urgent tone.

Lyall intervened. "Dr. Cavewood has a meeting with the Dean of History right now, Thomas." It was true, but Lyall couldn't have known it.

"I'm sure I have a moment," said Matthew, pausing.

"You spoke of the work being dangerous ..." began the boy.

"Yes," explained Matthew. "You mustn't forget what it was like in those days, with the Church having a monopoly on divine authority. Alchemy offered a way of mastering the occult principles of life and growth, a way to share in the power of God, to make man divine. If you could get access to God through the laboratory, what was the need of churches and priests?"

"No, no," objected the student, "I mean the *real* danger. The danger that lives on."

Lyall interposed himself between them.

"Thank you, Thomas," he said smoothly. "I don't think Dr. Cavewood—"

"I have seen it!" cried the student. "*I was with Dr. Tauber!*"

"That will do, Thomas," said Lyall crisply. "Now, if you'll excuse us." He steered Matthew away toward the exit. In the corridor outside, he turned to him with a small, forced laugh. "Sorry about that. The kid's brilliant but a fruitcake. You always get one or two. It's statistical."

Matthew didn't respond. He followed Lyall out into the open. At the top of the steps, he paused and stretched his gaze up the long rectangular lawn ahead, enclosed on either side by mellow brick pavilions and classical white colonnades, to the majestic Rotunda at the far end, cast in misty twilight shadows, with just the tip of its pediment still gilded by the dying sun. Abruptly he turned to Lyall.

"Who *is* this man Tauber?"

Even in that light, Lyall visibly blanched.

"Tauber was an associate professor in the department. Brilliant but unstable. Always in and out of mental institutions. Tragic case." He shot Matthew a careful glance. "Often the case with geniuses. You know how it is. Nature tends toward the norm. Compensates for a gift with a flaw."

For a brief while the two men walked together. Lyall talked effusively about how well the lecture had gone and was already proposing setting up a regular series. After a short distance their paths diverged. They shook hands, and with yet more thanks, Lyall turned to go.

Matthew laid a restraining hand on his arm.

"Tell me," he said. "What was he working on, this guy Clark Tauber?"

Lyall's manner sharpened and his eyes flicked quickly between Matthew's. He seemed momentarily caught at a loss for words. Matthew realized he had supplied the man's first name, Clark, himself.

"He was a particle physicist," he responded shortly.

"Not a science historian?"

"My dear chap, your field doesn't have a monopoly of the brains." He looked at his watch. "You'll have to excuse me. A thousand thanks once again. It was a triumph. Give my love to Hazel."

Matthew watched the short figure take off with a springy step and disappear down the winding pathway toward Jefferson Park Avenue. His final works echoed in Matthew's ears. Had that been a denial? Or was he merely being British and embarassed to talk about mental illness?

Briskly he turned and headed down the gentle incline toward Randall Hall, a small, square building half submerged in the ground that housed the history department. He didn't have time for all this idle speculation. The dean of the history faculty was expecting a progress report. And he wouldn't want to hear about roofs and wiring and central-heating systems.

FIVE

As autumn turned to winter and Hazel watched the house coming together, a faint unease crept into her gladness. At first she put it down to what Matthew would call "proximate causes": anxieties over her career switch and worries over a change of school for Ben. In early November she received a letter from *People* magazine accepting her photo profile of Senator McDowell, and a week later she found a school in Charlottesville for children of UVA faculty where Ben felt instantly at home, and yet her sense of foreboding still persisted.

She watched the roof of the new house being relaid and the clapboard cladding stripped off and repaired. She watched the dumpsters fill with old plumbing and pipework and the whole yard, back and front, being laid to waste by the tires of heavy trucks, so that for several weeks they had to park at the end of the driveway and walk on duck boards through the thick, deep mud. When, on the weekend before Thanksgiving, she arrived to find the upstairs windowframes taken out and the gaping holes covered over with polyethylene sheeting barred by thick, crisscrossed battens, she understood at last the cause of her unease. She was building a prison for herself. The nest was turning into a trap.

She recognized it all stemmed from a conflict within herself, a conflict whose causes were not hard to trace in the events in her past.

Her father, a second-generation immigrant of mixed German-Polish blood, had ultimately, and literally, worked himself to death struggling to provide a meager livelihood for his family out of a small diner in a suburb of Philadelphia. As the eldest of six, with a mother who had weak lungs and was frequently too sickly to work, Hazel had had to grow up fast and learn to rely on herself. For the sake of her mother's health, they moved to Atlanta, Georgia, replicating their situation at another, though larger, diner. At nineteen, Hazel made the break. She set off across the country until she arrived in California, where she worked her way through college. She had always dreamed of being a photographer, and her father had encouraged her in this. Over the years he'd saved money, a dime here and a quarter there, mostly from tips, and with this he now bought her a single-lens reflex Hasselblad, a professional's camera. None of her siblings had managed to escape the gravitational pull of the family: her two younger sisters ran the diner, now expanded, and her three brothers still lived within a half hour's drive, and every Sunday they all met for a family lunch.

In her final year at college, Hazel met Clay. He seemed so sincere, so convincing. They lived together for a year in a small rented apartment in San Francisco. She worked nights in a restaurant and devoted the days to photography, and in between she ran the home, just as she had in her own family. He dealt privately in high-performance cars, matching buyer with seller and taking the margin. One day, on impulse, they got married. Determined to own a home of their own, she threw herself into her work harder than ever. Often when she returned home late at night he'd still be out; sometimes he wouldn't return until dawn. She never suspected anything. He always had a perfectly good explanation for where he'd been, and the money flowed in to prove it.

Then she discovered she was pregnant. It wasn't planned, but she welcomed it. For her, a family was the point and purpose of a marriage. Still, she chose her moment to tell Clay. One evening, knowing he'd be at the apartment, she left work early. She'd never forget unlocking the door and being gripped by a terrible conviction that something was wrong. In the living room, she found the first signs—a half-empty bottle of vodka and two glasses—and down the corridor, leading not to the bedroom but to her small photographic studio, the tell-tale squalid trail of underclothes. Through the door she could hear heavy panting and grunting. A vicious, cramping pain jabbed her in the stomach. She was going to be sick, to vomit up this fruit of his faithlessness. Then rage, *out*rage, seized her. She kicked the door open. There, naked on the couch, beneath her own spotlights and before the eye of her own camera, sprawled Clay, groaning with the ecstasy of being pleasured by a blondhaired girl in exotic underwear crouching on her knees before him.

She didn't know how she survived that night of screaming and recrimination. It was a miracle the life within her survived, too. In the early hours, she flung his belongings out of the window into the street, and when he ran out semi-naked to retrieve them, she slammed the door behind him and chained it shut. She never saw him again. She hadn't even told him she was expecting his child, for it was his child no longer; he had forfeited any claim. Gradually the truth about his life came out. The lies. The other women. The systematic deceptions. The alibis so incredible in the light of reason that she couldn't imagine how she'd been so gulled. She veered between hysteria and depression, she had terrible pains and serious bleeds, and more than once she was convinced she would lose the baby. To cauterize her heart against any lingering feeling, she developed the film and forced herself to look at the grotesque obscenities. Beside this, the demands and summonses that came daily through the mailbox seemed as nothing: He had conned his way through the city, defrauding banks, stores, garages and innocent folk, old and young alike. But Clay himself had vanished. He never appeared to contest the divorce, and her lawyers' letters were sent back marked RETURN TO SENDER.

There followed a period when her life was at its lowest ebb. She was sick, tired, impoverished and alone. Her father died, struck down by a series of coronaries. She went home to help out for a while, but she resisted the lure to stay, just as she rejected the simple solution of terminating the pregnancy. She was determined to have the child. It was going to be *hers*. She'd rear it by herself, with every ounce of her love, they'd be complete unto themselves, and never again would she commit her trust to a man or lay her heart so open to abuse.

The child was born, and she named him Ben, after her father. She got free-lance work taking photos for mail-order catalogues, then took a job as an in-house photographer for an advertising agency and moved to Washington. Times were never easy. For eight years now she had struggled to raise Ben by herself while at the same time carving out a career that would support them both.

Then, as if by a trick of fate, the moment she felt she had finally secured her ambition, she met Matthew. They met in the self-service restaurant at the Smithsonian. She'd gone to the Institute to take photographs for a poster for a forthcoming exhibition. He was there doing research in the library. She had taken her solitary tray to a table for lunch when a lean, angular stranger, carrying a solitary tray of his own, politely asked if he could join her. She'd never felt anything so powerful, or so sudden. Matthew was the polar opposite of Clay. And she, too, was a different person. She hadn't meant to fall so completely in love, and the power of her feelings still frightened her. She felt at the top of a slippery slope, down which she might slide at any moment and lose all that she had so laboriously gained in those years of struggle. Behind it all lay the inescapable legacy of Clay. For all that she loved Matthew beyond any love she had ever known, for all that she knew he would give Ben the father he needed, for all that she yearned for a proper family home, a happy, noisy, warm, querulous hearth such as she'd been raised at, nevertheless, at the very core of her soul, there always remained this indelible hesitation. She had been burned once. Could she ever fully commit her trust to anyone again?

In the way of things, all came to a head when least expected.

On the day before the Thanksgiving vacation, she collected Ben from school shortly after lunch and headed out of city into a pale, wintry sun. She reached Charlottesville early and, knowing that Matthew wouldn't be home, decided to take a drive around the town.

The place always gave her a friendly, welcoming feeling. Matthew had once suggested it was because the earth was rich in irons and people were literally attracted there. She smiled to herself; sometimes she couldn't tell if he was serious or joking. The town felt comfortable and safe, if perhaps a little smug. Low unemployment. Just enough crime to keep things colorful. And, unlike D.C., no real racial tensions. According to Herb, the last time there had been trouble was back in the early seventies when a black kid was caught stealing from a supermarket and his friends set the building on fire. The town had its blue-collar area, Belmont, where the "grits" lived, and its black community around 10th Street, but even here the inexorable process of gentrification was in evidence. She took Ben for a Coke at the Virginian, a student hang-out on Main Street across from the University grounds, and sat for a while contemplating her prospective new home town. Yes, it felt altogether right.

She arrived at the house to find Matthew had long been back and was putting the finishing touches to a grand transformation for the weekend.

She went from room to room, filled with amazement. He'd got the main kitchen units in place and working, albeit with temporary wiring and plumbing. In the living-room area, he'd had the carpenters cover the bare joists with hardboard to form a makeshift floor, on which he'd laid rugs bought at a house clearance auction. He'd had the chimneys swept, dislodging a jackdaw skeleton which Ben immediately claimed for a wall trophy, and he'd made a fire grate from bricks and a metal foot scraper in which a log fire was blazing. Every available vase and jar was crammed with flowers—lilies, gardenias, winter jasmine—whose scent filled the whole house, smothering even the ubiquitous smell of paint and putty.

That night they all had supper in style, before a roaring fire, with a silver service and crystal glasses and an old claret to complement the turkey. The atmosphere was enchanted. In the flickering candlelight, the room with its ragged, unplastered walls and patched ceiling became an old Florentine palazzo, and even the polyethylene sheeting over the windows took on the milky quality of early glass. Ben started the evening in high spirits, but gradually his day's wild careering around the yard took its toll, and finally over the pumpkin pie he fell asleep. Matthew carried him upstairs and put him to bed, then returned to the fireside and a second bottle of claret.

They sat on the hearth rug, staring into the fire, silent and content. Occasionally she glanced across at his strong, lean features, his dark eyes sunk deep in shadow, his high forehead knotted in a passing thought. Finally he let out a sigh.

"I wish—" he began, then checked himself.

"Go on. Tonight anything can come true."

"It doesn't matter." He drew a breath. He was incapable of holding things in. "I do sometimes wish we had more time alone together," he began. "Go off on a trip. Just us."

"You're not still talking about Oxford, Matthew," she said quietly. "I've said I can't come."

"I didn't mean that specifically, but since you raise it, yes. I do wish you were coming. We could use the break."

"It's not a break, it's work."

"Not all the time. You know what these conferences are like."

"I don't, thank goodness. Anyway, I meant it's *your* work."

"You could bring your camera."

"Don't patronize me, Matthew," she said, feeling her smile tightening.

"I'm saying it's a vacation. I've got to show up at a reception, dine at the college a couple of nights and deliver a paper, that's all. The rest is free time. Time we don't ever get. Time to *ourselves*."

She could feel the enchantment of the evening melting fast.

"I'm sorry if you feel Ben gets in the way," she responded.

"It's nothing to do with Ben! I love Ben, you know I do. I love having him here. I feel he's like my own son. The point is simply, we never get time alone, you and me."

"I'm sorry," she said, momentarily chastened. She reached for his hand. "But why Europe? Why not just a weekend on Virginia Beach? I love the ocean in winter. Ben could stay with Suzannah for a couple of nights."

"Why *not* Europe? We're only talking about a week. Suzannah can handle that. You pay her good money; she's not working for charity. And Ben is quite old enough to be left on his own for one week. Besides, you haven't got any appointments you can't reschedule. I know—you left your calendar open."

"Matthew, let's not spoil a lovely evening."

"I'm serious," he persisted. She recognized that obstinate tone of voice, the terrier with a rat, worrying the issue to death. "I'm going to book you on the flight first thing. You don't need a visa for England these days. I'll upgrade the hotel room to a suite—"

"Drop it, Matthew. Please." She withdrew her hand.

"But *why* won't you? The money's no problem. You know Lyall's even come up with a travel grant. If it's not the cost, or the time, or Ben, then what is it?" He leaned forward, his eyes burning in the dark. "I'll tell you, Hazel. It's the same old story. You won't really ever commit yourself. You're afraid to get too involved in *my* life because you think that means giving up *yours*. Hazel, you must find your independence *within* our setup, *within* the family! It's no good running away whenever the water gets deep."

"I'm not running away!" she retorted, shocked by the suddenness of the downward spiral of the evening and yet unable to reverse it. "I'm simply preserving myself as a separate person. Can't you see how intrusive you are? You're always trying to run my life, trying to absorb me into *your* plans, making me fit into *your* scheme of things. I can't stand it! I'm used to being me, thinking for myself, chosing my own way. It's the same old story with you, Matthew. Your trouble is you have to be at the center of everything. You're a typical only child. The world revolves around you and your wants. People exist only for you and your needs. That's why you're so obsessive about everything."

"Hazel," he said in a pained tone, "all I ask is that you choose. The moment you commit wholeheartedly to our life together, that's the moment I'll stop pressuring you. I won't need to then."

He touched her lightly on the shoulder, but she shook him off. She was surprised, and alarmed, by the force of her own reactions. Why had this hit such a tender nerve? Of course she wanted to be part of his life, to stand behind him, to champion him; she admired his work and wanted to share his trials and triumphs in it. But he was like a whirlpool: The closer she grew to him, the stronger the forces sucking her in. Perhaps she had overreacted just now; the issue of going or not going to this damned conference was insignificant in itself. But it was symptomatic of a larger and more fundamental conflict she had to resolve within herself. And one, in truth, for which no blame could be laid at his door.

She put her arms round his neck.

"I'm sorry, Matthew," she whispered. "I don't want to fight."

As she drew him closer and kissed him on the temple, she caught the movement of a shadow in the doorway behind. A floorboard creaked in the hallway just outside, followed by a muffled cough. A pang of shame shot through her. Gently she disentangled herself from Matthew's arms and tiptoed over to the door. There, just beyond the threshold, hovered the wan figure of Ben, his face white and fallen.

She knelt down and hugged him tight to her.

"Couldn't you sleep, darling?" she murmured, stroking his hair comfortingly. "Come by the fire and get warm."

Matthew had risen to his feet, too, and was advancing with arms outstretched. Together, each holding a hand, they led the small boy to the fire and sat down in its warm glow, and as a special treat Matthew began to recount him his favorite made-up story of the time-traveling cowboy. Gradually a tentative, conditional harmony was restored. But never, she vowed, would she let this happen again. Matthew was right. She knew her heart, but she had to make up her mind.

For the next two weeks, Matthew was frantically busy.

The final works to the exterior of the house had to be finished before December brought the bad weather, and there were constant unforeseen problems to face and decisions to make. A gale struck before the roofing had been fully laid, which ripped off tiles and sent them crashing to the ground fifty yards away. One struck his Mercedes and gouged a jagged hole in the hood, causing a time-wasting controversy between the builders and the household insurance company as to who was responsible. Then a ready-mix concrete truck got stuck in a ditch and had to be winched out by a breakdown crane, in the process of which the main water pipe was severed and the entire site was flooded. Even the simple repairs to the outside woodwork received a setback when dry rot was discovered in the balustrade and much of the fretwork of the porch. Matthew was growing frustrated and worried. The contingencies of time and money he'd built into both the schedule and the budget were fast being eaten up.

His work was a source of anxiety, too. To save duplication, he'd planned to give as his conference paper the text of the first chapter of his biography of Nathaniel Shawcrosse. He'd expected to have it finished by now, but as the date of the trip approached he began to realize this was a near-impossible task. Talking in general terms around the subject to second-year students in Cabell Hall was one thing, but at an international academic conference he would be facing his peers, a highly erudite and ruthlessly critical audience. After innumerable false attempts, he saw that any scholarly overview of a man's life and work required a complete understanding of the man himself, and here he kept coming up against the same brick wall. He still hadn't unlocked the secret to the central mystery to Nathaniel Shawcrosse: Why the abrupt silence, the cessation of historical references, the sudden and total erasure of his name from the record? What had actually become of him? Had he been deliberately silenced, and if so, by whom? As the deadline grew near, Matthew sank into despair. His study at home filled to the ceiling with books, his lab bench groaned under the weight of printouts. It was hopeless: He was trying to find the answer in one single bound to the puzzle that he'd set himself a year to solve.

In one respect, perhaps, he was fortunate to be so busy because it meant he had no time to dwell on Hazel. In fact, when she called the weekend before he was due to leave and suggested it might be better if she and Ben stayed in D.C. and left him alone to work, he was frankly relieved. He only wished he'd made the suggestion himself. He knew he'd been putting too much pressure on her recently, and he sensed the danger he was courting. You didn't catch a runaway horse by chasing after it; you stood still and let it come back of its own accord. He knew this was troubling her, too. Sex was inevitably the barometer of the emotional weather, and ever since Thanksgiving this conflict had shown up in that quarter. One moment she'd surrender herself with uninhibited abandon, the next she'd hold herself back, giving her part and taking her due with almost mechanical detachment. One night he woke to find her weeping silently, her pillow drenched with tears, but she wouldn't say what the trouble was. Were they subject to the same commonplace laws that ruled the balance of power between immature first lovers, slaves to the depressing truism that a person pursued will flee, but one rejected will redouble their affections? As far as he was capable of it, he forced himself to back off. He gave up his habitual goodnight call, and when she called him he strove to sound slightly distant. He even managed to persuade himself it was best that he was going on the trip alone. The time apart would take the heat out of the issue. She was the most precious thing in his life, and he wasn't going to risk losing her by a simple error of tactics that even a sticky-palmed adolescent in love wouldn't commit.

Finally, the day of his departure arrived. He'd booked on the overnight direct flight from Washington, D.C., to London, and he spent the day at the word-processor in the lab cobbling together a final version of his paper. He was incorporating a good deal of the material he'd meant to keep for the book, which meant taking a chance on his work being plagiarized, but it made up for the gap in the Shawcrosse account. It was the best he could do and it would simply have to suffice.

Darkness was already falling when he finally hurried home. He threw some clothes into a suitcase and left a list of instructions for the workmen. He called Hazel, but was only answered by her machine. It caused him a stab of disappointment, even jealousy, and he tried not to think what it might mean. They'd already said their good-byes over the phone late the previous night, and that should be enough for mature adults. Casting it out of his mind, he climbed into the rented car—his Mercedes was still having its hood fixed—and set off in a light, cold drizzle in the direction of Dulles airport.

He parked in the long-stay area and caught the shuttle coach to the departures terminal. There he joined a line of passengers being asked routine security questions, then headed unhurriedly for the check-in desk. Already he was settling into his familiar long-distance travel mode in which he gradually allowed his world to shrink into the lozenge of his own body space and his thoughts to turn inward upon themselves. He was only dimly aware of the flight announcements over the public address system and of the other passengers, mostly businessmen, standing ahead in the line for the Club check-in. He certainly failed to notice the woman in the long, cream coat standing slightly to one side and observing him with a gentle, wry smile. Even when he presented his ticket at the desk and was told that a seat had already been allocated to him, the fact registered no particular surprise.

It was only when he had picked up his ticket and boarding card and was turning away that he paused momentarily, and then it was just the faintest scent of a familiar perfume that arrested him.

He looked up. Into Hazel's pale green eyes.

"My God!" he exclaimed, flooding with delight. "What a lovely surprise." He glanced at a clock. "I don't have long, but there's time for a cup of coffee."

Then he noticed she was holding a ticket and boarding card, too. She smiled.

"We have all the time in the world," she said simply. "I'm coming with you."

"All the way?"

She held his eye levelly.

"All the way, Matthew."

Oxford wore its finest face for their arrival. The days were piercingly cold and clear, and until well after midday the frost lingered on the north-facing stonework, bearding the gargoyles with rime and distorting the patterns of the mellow stone tracery. From the window of their suite in the Randolph Hotel, they gazed out over stone-tiled roofs and slender Gothic spires as though at a canvas traced in fine silverpoint, and if they stretched their eye further they could see the distant blue-hazed hills that formed the rim of the gentle bowl within which the city alternately stirred and slumbered.

They spent the first two days strolling through the colleges and parks, absorbing the atmosphere. On the afternoon of the second day the conference opened with a reception and a dinner. The following morning, Matthew was due to give his paper, and that evening they were to dine on High Table at Sanctus Spiritus college as guests of his old supervisor, Ralph Corcoran. After that, they were free; they could go wherever the mood took them—London, Stratford, Bath, bed. In the meantime, fired with excitement and enthusiasm, Matthew determined to show Hazel everything—the colleges, the libraries, the pubs, his old haunts, even, if he could get into them, his actual rooms in college. Equipped with an old guide book and his memories, he took her on a grand tour of the city. He saw her smiling to herself, but she allowed herself to be swept along. She'd put herself entirely in his hands. Was this the new shape of things?

The first afternoon, he walked her around Trinity and Balliol, Magdalen and Christ Church. They dipped into the smaller colleges—Pembroke and Exeter, Lincoln and St. Edmund's Hall. On the second morning, refreshed and free of jet lag, they set out for his own college, Sanctus Spiritus. The moment he stepped through the main gate, the memories came flooding back. He recounted anecdotes as they came into his head. He told her of the time Lyall bought an old Aston Martin and, to the horror of the chaplain, had it christened with full ceremony by a Greek Orthodox priest in the Fellows' Garden. He recalled the time a bunch of rowdy oarsmen, celebrating victory on the river with a Bump Supper, smashed all the downstairs windows in the Great Quad. And the time he woke up after a particularly wild night with a dining club to find himself in bed with a woman—a marble bust of a woman, in truth, which, with the abnormal strength of the inebriated, he had lifted off its plinth in the restaurant and smuggled half across the city to his rooms. He returned it, of course, with profuse apologies and a check for amends, but even with the help of two friends he'd barely been able to lift it. There were incidents that shamed him to recall, incidents that reduced Hazel to tears of laughter, and others that belonged to his bachelor past and which he thought it wiser to censor out.

His steps took him automatically to the small quad where, on the upper floor in one corner, he'd had his rooms. There had been superficial changes over those fifteen years: the ancient stonework had been washed and restored and now gleamed with a brash newness, while the giant mulberry tree in the center of the lawn showed the passage of time in the reverse way, with its low-sweeping boughs propped up by supports like an octopus on crutches. But the atmosphere of the place had hardly changed. To his surprise, as he entered his old staircase, he walked straight into his old scout, Jock, the college servant who had looked after his rooms. The old fellow had grown thinner and more bent and his skin had taken on the parchment translucency of age, but Jock recognized him at once, exclaiming, "Dr. Cavewood, sir! Now let me see ... seventy-five to seventy-six, wasn't it, sir?"

Matthew introduced Hazel, and for a while they reminisced about old times. In traditional fashion, Jock bemoaned the passing of the good old days. The young gentlemen weren't what they used to be. And, of all horrors, the college now admitted *women!* They even had female scouts. Matthew exchanged a discreet smile with Hazel, then asked if by any chance he could show her his old rooms. With a conspiratorial wink, the scout beckoned them to follow.

The smell of the staircase with its dusty bare boards, of linseed oil and disinfectant ... fifteen years evaporated in the instant. It was a young and relatively green American postgraduate student that climbed the stairs behind the wheezing scout. His knew each tread, the ones that were high and twisted, the ones that sank in and creaked. As they arrived at his rooms, he felt faintly surprised to see a different name painted above the door. The scout tapped peremptorily, as though not expecting an answer, and entered. Matthew followed. Hazel lingered momentarily in the corridor, looking at the view from the window.

Quite suddenly, it hit him. That scent. Spicy like sandalwood. Smoky as saltpeter. And underneath, that ionized, electric smell. Very faint, but *there.* In his nostrils.

He felt his senses lurch, and he grasped the back of a chair for support. At that moment, the door opened. *She* came in. The girl in the cream ballgown.

The images flooded upon him all in a rush.

It was her! Her beauty robbed him of breath. She was unbuttoning the tight curving bodice. Her skin was opalescent, it glowed from within. She put aside her glass. She reached for his hand and closed it around her small, full breast. The touch of her skin, the roundness of the breast cupped in his hand, its nipple swelling between his fingers ... a roar exploded within him. He tightened his grasp until she cried out in pain. He tore at her clothes with his free hand. The sound of rending silk filled the room. But nothing would stop him until she stood before him trembling and breathless and completely naked.

"Matthew?" Hazel's voice catapulted him back to the present. "Matthew, are you all right?"

She grasped him by the arm. Her eyes were wide with alarm, her face chalky white. He shook his head to clear it and drew a deep breath. He was trembling in every nerve.

"Just a bit dizzy," he said gruffly, "The climb up the stairs."

She hugged him to her.

"Jesus," she breathed, "I thought for a moment you were going to pass out."

He groped for a lighter excuse.

"Just overcome with nostalgia, I guess," he said.

"Nostalgia? With memories, you mean," she hissed into his ear. "Just don't tell me what you've been up to in this room!"

He felt the oppressive weight gradually lift off him. He managed a small chuckle. She could drag him out of any mood; she had an in-built knack. He never could work the same on her. Perhaps he lacked the trick, or maybe her moods ran deeper and she was genuinely inconsolable. And when he did try he always somehow ended up sounding carping and cajoling. At the scowl of mock jealousy painted over her face, he broke out laughing. He took her by the hand and led her to the door.

"Come on, let's get some lunch. Jock, how do they rate the Elizabeth these days?"

"I'm sorry, sir?"

"He means, is it as good as it used to be when he was swanning about up here?" interpreted Hazel.

The old retainer shook his head.

"I don't hear it spoke of much, sir. Different class of gentleman today."

"Let's try it anyway," said Matthew, heading out of the room. "No memories there, I promise."

"None you were sober enough to remember, you mean."

He led the way down the staircase. At the foot, he bade Jock goodbye, assuring him he'd look in again before he left. The scout was visibly moved by this figure returned from the past. Matthew hurried Hazel across the quad at such a pace that she called for him to slow down. He, too, had been moved by the figure returned from his past, and he wanted to leave it behind as far and as fast as possible.

Drinks were served before dinner in the Senior Common Room, a long, low room steeped in the echoes of centuries of academic banter and intrigue and soused in the aroma of tobacco, port and old leather.

Ralph Corcoran led them in, a tall, stooping man with hyperthyroid eyes and a cadaverous grin. From the moment they entered, they found themselves the center of attention and eagerly questioned about life in American academia. At first Matthew thought the attraction must be

Hazel, for though she had deliberately dressed in a demure gray suit and low-heeled shoes, even in sack-cloth she'd have looked glamorous. It was when the unhallowed topic of money came up that he finally understood. He was witnessing the British brain drain at its wellspring.

"We live in parlous times," Ralph Corcoran explained as he led the way up the narrow back stairs to the dining hall. "Four university chairs empty and won't be filled. In this college we've cut our fellowships by a third. The undergraduates are having to borrow to pay their fees; last year, we had two bankruptcies and a suicide. We called in a professional fund-raiser, but he's cost us more than he's raised so far. We had to sell off half the college silver to refurbish the library. Still, we get the odd bequest." He paused. "Which reminds me. There's a portrait that came into our hands recently you'll be interested in. I'll show it to you afterward."

He took Hazel's hand and courteously ushered her through the small paneled door that opened onto the rear of the Great Hall. Ahead spread the High Table, laden with silver salvers and cut glass decanters and dishes stamped with the college crest, while each place was set with half a dozen knives and forks and as many fine crystal glasses. To the side stood a line of college servants, the senior butler at their head. Beyond and below, in the body of the hall, lit by small parchment-shaded lamps on the long dark-waxed refectory tables stretching the length of the room, past the gilt-framed portraits to the ornately carved reredos that formed the main doors, stood some two hundred gowned students in hushed expectancy. Amid shuffling of feet and a low buzz of chatter, a grace was rapidly spoken from a lectern. Matthew smiled at the familiar words. *Nos miseri homines et egeni,* it began. We wretched, needy mortals. At the final *Amen,* a pent-up burst of conversation exploded across the hall and rose in consort with the din of scraping benches to echo high among the tall, smoke-blackened rafters.

Ralph Corcoran examined the printed menu like a critical text. The first course, of eight, was a lobster soup. He nodded to a scout offering him a chilled manzanilla and leaned toward Hazel at his side.

"We may be parlous," he smiled, "but we have our priorities. Feed the body, nourish the mind. Tell me, I believe you're a professional photographer ..."

Somewhere between the *canard en croute* and the sorbet, the undergraduates in the body of the hall finished their less lavish supper and filtered out, leaving the place quieter and emptier. But the talk on High Table, fueled by the wines, had risen in volume to compensate, and their departure passed almost unnoticed. Matthew sat listening to the conversations around him, though not to the argument so much as the cadence. It had a carping, bleating quality that was unfamiliar to him. Academics were a bitchy, incestuous group on either side of the pond, but here he detected a new defensiveness in their tone, a scrambling for life jackets on a sinking ship, a grabbing of seats in an inexorable game of musical chairs.

They withdrew to yet another room for dessert and port, but there the conversation lightened up as gossip and anecdotes were swapped around the table. Hazel sat between a fleshy philosophy don and a lean young geneticist; occasionally he caught her eye across the candles and she pursed her lips in an invisible kiss. The evening seemed to fly by. Matthew was aware he was drinking too much, but he felt high. His paper had gone down well that morning, he'd spent a magical afternoon in bed with Hazel, and here he was now, in the company of some of the finest minds in their fields, drinking port of a timeless vintage and eating fruit off plates of solid gold that had somehow survived the depredations of both the Civil Wars and the current economic straits.

Gradually, as he sat there, he felt himself slipping into a time warp. This was the seventeenth century. Nathaniel Shawcrosse himself was sitting across the table, eating the same fruit from the same plates and engaged in some barbed theological debate with the Dean, a figure in rich clerical robes and a black skullcap....

He felt Ralph's hand on his shoulder. The table was rising. The geneticist was solicitously holding Hazel's chair as she got up, talking intensely all the while. The Dean was bidding the room goodnight. He pressed Matthew's hands in a strangely fervent clasp, almost a masonic benediction, then moved toward the door. Hazel shot Matthew an appeal for help, but before he could come to her aid, Ralph had taken him by the elbow.

"I haven't shown you our new portrait."

He steered him to the far end of the room. The walls on each side were lined with gilt-framed portraits, each lit with a dim glow by a small shaded light above. Matthew hadn't paid much notice to them: with the candles and the general subdued lighting, they'd merged into the general background. Now, as he approached the far wall, the intended portrait came beneath his gaze.

A sudden bolt of electricity shot through him. He stopped abruptly in his tracks.

He rubbed his eyes. It was the drink. Port on top of red wine on top of white. What did the French say? *Rouge sur blanc: tous foutent le camp.* Fatal.

He glanced at Ralph's face, then down at the rich carpet, then across at the devastated table. No, he wasn't drunk. Cautiously, hardly daring to confront what he had seen, he raised his eyes again to the oil painting.

It was a quarter-length portrait of a young woman. A woman he knew well. Very well.

Words came whispering into his mind. Familiar words. Words he had written himself: *Her hair, the color of fine gilt, was piled high and fell in ringlets about her oval face. Her complexion was as pale as alabaster, its pallor heightened by the scarlet of her lips. Her eyes, a deep electric violet, wore an expression at once serious and whimsical. High on her upper lip, accentuating her mysterious half-smile, lay a small, dark beauty spot. Her whole skin seemed to glow with an inner luminosity, like a marble figurine lit from within.... She wore an exquisite period ball gown of cream silk, cut high and square so as to force up her breasts, with a tight corsetted waist and ruched sleeves trimmed with lace and blue silk ...*

He felt sick. Suffocated. Stunned.

It was *her!* It was her, *exactly!* Down to the smallest detail. Her face, her smile, her skin, her hair, the beauty spot on her lip, her dress ...

He reeled. This was some terrible trick of the mind. He was possessed. He was projecting.

But no, it was her. The girl who had come to him in the night. As real in this picture as in the living flesh. The very same person.

"Her name was Isabel," Ralph Corcoran was saying. "Isabel Hardiment. Her father was dean of the college in the seventies and eighties."

Matthew could barely bring out the words.

"The *sixteen*-seventies and -eighties, of course," he croaked.

"Why, yes," replied the other man, a trifle surprised. "The portrait's a Kneller. One of his best, wouldn't you say?" He cast Matthew a studied glance. "I thought you might find it interesting."

"Should I?" asked Matthew sharply.

"Well, it's only secondary evidence of course, and there's nothing in the college records to substantiate it, but there was a suggestion that this Isabel Hardiment and Nathaniel Shawcrosse were ... romantically attached."

"She was his mistress?"

His supervisor nodded.

"I don't pretend this is my field, Matthew, but that fact—if it *is* a fact—can hardly have helped endear him to the dean and the clerics. There's some hint she came to a sticky end, too, but whether that's connected or not ..."

"When did she die?" he rasped.

"In 1681, I believe."

"My God."

1681: precisely the date at which all the surviving records on Nathaniel Shawcrosse abruptly broke off. Matthew's thoughts were whirling. All kinds of wild solutions to the mystery flew into his mind. But then the real shock spun back like a boomerang and hit him a dizzying blow. He gripped the edge of the table to steady himself. He became aware of Hazel standing beside him, her eyes wide with concern. Ralph had stopped in midspeech and was asking if anything was the matter.

He couldn't speak. His mind was scattered like grapeshot. He could only stare numbly at the portrait on the wall ahead.

He had known this girl, he had spoken to her, he had touched her, he had made love to her. And she had died three hundred years ago.

PART II

SIX

A man's brain, Matthew remarked to Hazel on a walk through the snowy countryside that Christmas, is physically different from a woman's. Its aptitudes are more centered, its structure is more compartmentalized. By contrast, in a woman's brain the two hemispheres are far more densely connected. As anyone knows who has witnessed it, a mother can feed one child, mind another, help a third with his homework and answer the telephone, all at once. She "multiplexes" in a way a man simply cannot. Men tend to separate the areas of their mind's concern and focus single-mindedly on one operation at a time. They will break a problem down into its component parts, separating the emotional from the rational, the moral from the ideological, while women will tend to see the same problem, whether confused or coherent, as a whole. For this reason—or so Matthew hoped to persuade himself by raising the subject in the first place—a man should be better able to cope when faced with an apparent total and utter physical impossibility.

But he wasn't. He could find no way of coming to terms with what had happened that night in Oxford. Common sense and sanity told him there was no conceivable way the girl who had visited him in a dream one long-ago midsummer night could actually be Isabel Hardiment. His guts, however, told him exactly the opposite. He'd never seen that portrait before, but he knew it was one and the same girl. In his dream (was it a dream?) he had touched that small beauty spot, he'd kissed that mouth, stroked those cheeks, breathed in the perfume of that neck ...

No amount of effort of mind could wish the problem into a convenient compartment. It affected everything in his life, including things with Hazel.

Hazel clearly sensed that something was wrong, though he felt sure she didn't connect it with the incident at the dinner. At the time, he'd covered up his reactions as best he could, feigning a scholarly interest in the portrait. Back at the hotel, she'd pulled him onto the bed and made passionate love to him, and for a few moments he'd lost himself in sensual oblivion. But afterward, he'd lain awake half the night, wrestling with the impossible conundrum, and he spent the days that followed wandering about in a disorientated daze. He would lose the thread in the middle of conversation, and often he simply wouldn't register what people were saying. He'd snatch an hour here or there when Hazel was otherwise occupied, or he'd invent a lecture he had to attend, and he'd hurry off to the Bodleian to unearth whatever he could on Isabel Hardiment.

While Hazel was at the hairdresser's one afternoon, for instance, he slipped into the college library and examined the Deanery archives. By the time he'd finally traced Ralph Corcoran's source, a letter that hinted at a liaison between a certain "N. S." and the Dean's daughter Isabel, he had lost all sense of time and he arrived at their rendezvous at the Ashmolean just as the museum was closing. He felt as though he'd wandered out into the center of a frozen lake and the ice was beginning to crack. He groped for an explanation, testing one possibility after another in a continuous internal inquisition, but he couldn't even convince himself there *was* an explanation.

When Hazel asked what the matter was, he brushed it off as nothing at all or else he fabricated some weak excuse. She must have felt herself to be somehow at the root of it, for she redoubled her efforts to be happy and lively and to make the trip enjoyable for him. The pathos of the situation pained him deeply, but he felt powerless to change either her belief or his own behavior. Finally, however, when over one dinner she began to question whether she should have come along at all, he pulled himself together sharply. With a supreme effort of will, he threw himself into filling their remaining time with all the enjoyments he could think of, and he vowed that on their return to the States he would keep his work to regular office hours and devote the evenings and weekends uninterrupted to his family. Once or twice he geared himself up to tell her, but in the event he always flunked it. The whole notion was too crazy. Besides, he remembered what he'd told himself at the time when he'd come upon his old diary. The past was past; Hazel was the future. Why risk muddying one with the other?

Except that the past had become the present.

Christmas arrived that year amid a furious blizzard. Temperatures fell to ten below, transforming the yard overnight into an arctic wilderness. Matthew, Hazel and Ben awoke to find the snow had drifted high up the porch, jamming the outer door tight shut, while around the side the cars lay buried up to their windows. Work on the exterior of the house had at last been finished, and their home was warm and weatherproof. More snow was on its way, and Ben was hoping they'd be snowed in; he had made an inventory of their rations and declared they could survive for several weeks—maybe, with luck, the full school semester.

That year, Christmas and New Year's Day fell on a Saturday, and the week between stretched naturally into a single vacation. Hazel took charge of the arrangements. Determined to make it a proper family event, she set about organizing the decorations and the presents, the food and the games, and even insisted they go to the midnight service at the university chapel on Christmas Eve. Matthew's heart swelled. It seemed she really had made her commitment.

In the months to come, that brief period of tranquility would stand out in his mind as the calm before the storm. He had put the whole gnawing puzzle on hold, like a plane in a stacking formation; it was always there, going ceaselessly around and around, and yet somehow it was contained. As the new year approached, however, he knew that he couldn't keep this up much longer, and as the vacation came to its end and Hazel and Ben returned to Washington and the normal routine of life reasserted itself, he turned his energies back to his research. And now he tightened his focus upon Isabel Hardiment.

So far, the link between Nathaniel Shawcrosse and this girl was based merely upon a single reference in a letter of Isabel's father, identifying the lover by the initials "N. S." Certainly, Shawcrosse had been in the right place at the right time—he'd been at Sanctus Spiritus college between 1670 and 1681—and the hostility toward him felt by the dean, a leading churchman, was well documented. In a letter to the astronomer Edmund Halley dated May 1679, for instance, Shawcrosse warned that Halley's achievement in establishing the orbit of comets would once and for all overthrow the clerical doctrine that comets were supernatural events and "cause Sore Vexation to those who base their opinions upon Belief, not Proof, among whom I count the Dean and Chapter of my Oxford College foremost, having upon this very point engaged in much grievous and inimical Dispute."

The evidence, though strong, was still only circumstantial. "N. S." could perfectly well refer to some otherwise unrecorded student who had earned the Dean's disfavor by dallying with his daughter. Something more positive was needed.

Matthew went back to Shawcrosse's private papers. By interlibrary transfer from the Smith Collection at the University of Pennsylvania in Philadelphia, he obtained a small group of love poems. He had read transcripts of these before, of course, but now he examined the originals more closely. In most cases the poems were not addressed to anyone specific, but where there was a name, however, it was invariably that of his young lab assistant, Lapidus. This assistant was referred to elsewhere; he was recorded, for instance, in the Proceedings of the Royal Society as attending upon Shawcrosse during an experiment to form a regulus of antimony and lead. "Lapidus" was a pseudonym, of course: it derived from the root of *lapis,* the Latin for "stone," and in its age would have been a perfectly common and well-understood reference to the Philosopher's Stone, that mysterious powder ascribed with the power to transmute base metals into gold and forever one of the central quests of the alchemists.

In fact, the whole tone of these poems rang with alchemical references. One, not perhaps the finest, held Matthew's attention; he had a curious sense that a vital clue lay buried in these lines. The poem, a sestet in iambic hexameters, ran as follows:

> *If thou should'st ever doubt the power of my love,*
> *Sweet Lapidus, or seek that I its strength should'st prove*
> *And fiery trial of its potency prepare,*
> *By Egypt's ancient art I hereby to thee swear:*
> *Eternity's elixir swift shall I achieve*
> *Lest e'er my love the loss of life's sweet breath should'st grieve.*

Nothing especially difficult or unusual here. The references were perfectly commonplace for their time. "Fiery trial," "potency," "elixir" were familiar enough concepts in alchemy. Indeed, "Egypt's ancient art" directly referred to alchemy itself: It was an Arabic word, formed from the definite article, *al,* and *kimia* or *khemia,* "black land," or Egypt, from the Egyptian name. The poem gained further meaning, of course, in the context of Shawcrosse's search to find the material basis for the spirit, through which he could unlock the elixir of eternity, the secret of everlasting life.

Matthew paused. He felt convinced that something more was being signaled.

And then it hit him. The simplest of all coded messages. If ... Sweet ... And ... By ... Eternity ... Lest ... The initial letters of each line, taken together, spelled a name: I-S-A-B-E-L.

Under careful scrutiny, the other poems now began to yield up their secret. Phrases such as "most sweet and fragrant basile" and "basile that inflames the senses" did not, after all, refer to the aromatic herb basil ("basile" in its Old French form), nor, as one scholar had suggested, to the basilisk, the fabulous iguanalike creature noted by Pliny for its fiery, death-dealing eyes. "Basile" was quite simply an anagram of "Isabel."

With this new insight, everything began falling into place. All except one piece of the jigsaw that obstinately refused to fit. Matthew turned back to the love poem. "If thou should'st ever doubt the power of my love, / Sweet Lapidus ..." Why would Shawcrosse address a poem ostensibly to his assistant Lapidus while covertly intending the message for his mistress Isabel? It was like writing a love letter to one person and addressing the envelope to someone else. It didn't make sense.

Still, he'd established to his own satisfaction that there was a link. He could say with confidence that Nathaniel Shawcrosse had felt passionately for the dean's young and beautiful daughter, Isabel Hardiment, and that Isabel had died at just about the time Nathaniel's own story came to its abrupt end.

The next step was to work from Isabel's end.

Matthew was later to wish that he had heeded the warning signs. The creeping paranoia. The fatal muddying of a personal quest with a professional inquiry. The odd, disturbing events that began increasingly to dog his steps. And, perhaps most dangerous of all, the insidious blurring of reality with imagination.

He began to develop a suspicion of the people around him. He became increasingly mistrustful of Lyall in particular. And, so he believed, with good reason. A few days earlier, he'd called up his record file on the computer terminal to check how much CPU time he'd used to date, when one entry caught his eye. In one particular week, the first in December, he had only accessed his data base on one single occasion, whereas on other weeks he'd made at least twenty entries over the same period. Then he remembered he had been in England at that time. How come there were *any* entries, then? Someone else had gained access to his files. Someone who knew his user ID. It could be only one person, the man who had allocated him the ID in the first place: Lyall.

What did Lyall want? To keep abreast of his progress? Why hadn't he simply asked him? Or at least, told him afterward what he'd done? No, the reality was more sinister: Lyall was snooping. In fact, the more Matthew thought about it, the more he began to wonder about his old friend's motives from the start. Lyall had gone to quite unusual lengths to lure him to Virginia. He himself had been looking for a university with a specialist library—UCLA perhaps, where the William Andrews Clark Library contained a unique collection of scientific first editions, or Toronto, where the Thomas Fisher Rare Book Library offered a rich collection of works of Boyle, Hooke, Newton, Lavoisier and other leading scientists of the period.

But Lyall had made it virtually impossible for him to refuse. He'd twisted arms within the Center for Advanced Studies to procure him an irresistibly generous funding package. Then he'd set him up in a laboratory, supporting the overhead from his own budget (a laboratory in the same building, moreover, where he could keep him under his eye). He'd offered him the use of his own secretary (a neat way of keeping track on his work). He was even following his research personally—witness that volume of the Proceedings he'd taken out of the library. Correction: that Dr. Tauber had taken out, and Lyall had *kept* out. And who was this Clark Tauber? Lyall had brushed the question aside: *an associate professor ... brilliant but unstable ... in and out of mental institutions ... tragic case.* Had he been working on something similar? And why did everyone refer to him in the past tense? Had the "tragic case" been a fatal one?

Matthew held back from confronting Lyall. Something was going on, but he didn't want to show his hand until he had proof. He began to avoid the professor. When he saw his energetic, tubby figure coming down the corridor, he'd duck quickly into a doorway or else pretend he was lost in his thoughts and simply hadn't seen him. His window had a view over the parking lot, and he took to waiting until Lyall's car had gone before leaving the building himself. Inevitably, however, their paths crossed. One Saturday when he was out of the house, taking Ben to a Toys "Я" Us in a nearby mall, Lyall phoned and spoke to Hazel. He returned to find she had invited him and Myra round for supper the following weekend. There was no escape, and he spent the week steeling himself for an evening of evasion and false bonhomie.

On top of this came the incident of the strange boy in black—or rather, the incidents, for he saw this curious figure on at least three occasions.

He wasn't even certain what attracted his attention about this young man. Not his face, for he never saw him at close enough quarters. Not really the way he dressed, either, although his broad-brimmed hat and long dark coat gave him a disheveled, almost Hasidic look, but then many of the students wore fairly eccentric clothes. Perhaps it was simply the striking visual contrast his dark clothes made against the white snow. Perhaps, too, it was that wherever he was, this boy always seemed to be watching him.

He first glimpsed the figure from his car as he was driving home one evening. Twilight was falling. He'd pulled up at the intersection where McCormick Road filtered into University Avenue and was checking over his shoulder that nothing was coming up behind when he caught sight of this young man standing beneath a lamppost across the road. Though he couldn't make out his face beneath the brim of his hat, he sensed that he was looking at him intently. Distantly he wondered what he was doing there. He couldn't be waiting for a bus; the campus shuttle stopped further along the road. Maybe he was waiting for a ride, yet he stood on the right side of the road, leading into the grounds, not away. A gap appeared in the traffic, and Matthew slipped out into the flow. As he did so, he glanced up in his rearview mirror. The boy had vanished.

He would have forgotten entirely about this insignificant incident had he not glimpsed the figure once again, a week later, this time standing at the back of a lecture hall. Matthew himself was sitting at the front on the end of a row. The lights were down, and an epidiascope behind was projecting diagrams onto a large screen ahead. At one point, turning to look at the lecturer, Matthew caught a movement among the shadows at the back of the hall. It was the boy. He was wearing the same black hat and coat—but indoors, in a centrally heated room? In the dim light reflected from the screen, Matthew had the feeling once again that he was being stared at. A minute later, the lecturer called for the lights to go up. Matthew scoured the rows of faces behind, but the boy's was not among them.

It was on the Friday, however, the day before Lyall and his wife were due for dinner that Matthew had a real jolt. He was packing up at the laboratory at the end of the day, in a hurry to arrive home before Hazel and Ben. He stepped over to the window to check the parking lot below. Peering out into the dusk, he could see Lyall's maroon Oldsmobile still in its space, parked beneath the cold fluorescent lights. He swore softly; he'd have to risk an encounter. As he was turning away, he stopped abruptly. A sick jolt shuddered through him. There, down below, in the center of a broad triangle of smooth, crisp snow, stood the young man, his face upturned toward the high window. Matthew felt mesmerized. Even across that distance, he felt the power of the stare. Finally he broke away and, grabbing his overcoat, hurried down the elevator and out of the exit at the rear that led directly into the car lot. His pulse was pounding, though he told himself not to be ridiculous. What was so unusual about a kid hanging around outside a building?

His footsteps crunched on the icy crust, grooved deep by car tracks. From ground level, the sky appeared a dense, inky black. In the buildings looming darkly all around, the last lights were going out, while ahead a slow-moving line of vehicles snaked its way down Gilmer Road toward the main streets and out of town, their exhausts billowing in the frosty air. Matthew unlocked the Mercedes and tossed his briefcase inside. As he was climbing in, he shot a glance across the half-empty car park to the stretch of lawn where the young man had been standing. To his relief, he saw he had gone.

Then he halted. In the fringe of light from a streetlamp he could see quite clearly that the snow in the triangle was entirely unmarked. Puzzled, he went over to take a look. A mass of footsteps had scuffed up the snow on the pathways that edged the patch of lawn, but the snow on the lawn itself was untrodden. He drew a line of sight up to his lab window. The boy *must* have been standing out in the center; anywhere else, and he'd simply have been out of sight. Matthew took a step into the snow. His foot sank in up to the ankle. Beyond, the surface of the snow was intact, unbroken. No one had walked here since the last snow had fallen, two days before.

* * *

Hazel glanced critically at her reflection in the dressing-table mirror. Her lipstick didn't quite match her red silk blouse, but it didn't matter; Lyall and Myra weren't expecting the *Vogue* treatment. She leaned forward and put a final touch to the makeup. Small smile lines eddied round the corners of her mouth. There was a fullness, even a smugness, in her look that she hadn't noticed for so long. She couldn't remember when she'd last felt so profoundly contented. From the moment she'd decided to go with Matthew on the trip, a whole new mood of ease and confidence had settled over her. She felt she could relax at last. She was no longer alone, yet she still owned herself. There was more freedom to be found within a trusting relationship than alone in the vastness of the great outside world.

Her new mood showed in her work, too. The photo profile of Otis McDowell in *People* magazine had brought a small flood of assignments, and for the first time in her career she was in a position to turn down work. The house was coming along on schedule, if not on budget, and she and Matthew had set a date in mid-April for their marriage, by which time the whole renovation should finally be complete. Ben was looking forward to moving down to Charlottesville. He had already designed his room, complete with a bed in the shape of a Ferrari that Matthew had promised him and with the ceiling made into a planetarium with stars and planets in luminous paint. For Christmas, Matthew had bought him a canvas-and-straw archery target and a quiver of bamboo arrows, and he would spend hours in the freezing cold in the yard at the back playing with his bow that Matthew had helped him make from the yew branch he had found. It was wonderful watching them together.

From downstairs floated snatches of a symphony, Saint-Saëns perhaps, or some tortured late Romantic composer, the kind of thing Matthew played when he felt intense. She frowned briefly. Just recently he had been acting rather strangely. Quick-tempered, nervy. He only seemed really himself when he was playing with Ben. He was under terrific stress, of course. She tried to ask how the book was going, but he wouldn't talk about it. Once, when he was out with Ben, she'd looked in on his study and couldn't help reading the papers on top of his desk. Who was this woman, Isabel Hardiment? Was he veering off on a tangent? She thought it best not to interfere, though. For the time being, until the book was finished, she could help him best by making his weekends as relaxing and free from troubles as possible. Maybe she shouldn't have invited Lyall and his wife over without asking him first; he'd reacted most oddly when she'd told him. She glanced at her watch. They would be arriving any minute now. She put a dab of perfume on her wrists and behind her ears, then rose to her feet. It was up to her to see the men didn't talk shop. Even if it meant spending the evening talking horses and hunting with Myra.

Myra Markson was a wolfish woman with a barking laugh and too many teeth. She wore a cable-stitch cardigan and a Black Watch plaid skirt and held her graying hair back with a velvet Alice band.

"What are you?" was the question she fired at Hazel as she handed her a second gin sling.

Hazel replied that she was a photographer. Surely she remembered?

"I mean what *sign*," barked Myra.

"Taurus," responded Hazel with surprise.

"I had a Taurean once. A wild brute. I had to ace him every time I took him out. In the end I had to put him down. The wretch kept foundering."

Hazel took a moment to realize she was talking of a horse, not a husband. What, she inquired conversationally, did "ace" mean? Why, doping the horse with tranquilizer, replied Myra, astonished at such ignorance. "Foundering" was when the animal ate too much rich pasture, its legs swelled up and splayed apart and it ended up grounded on its belly. And Myra went on to describe at length the gruesome details of putting a foundered horse down.

Hazel glanced at Matthew. He was drinking his whisky in long, deliberate gulps, like a medicine. Hazel slid up to him and put a restraining hand on his.

"Go gently," she whispered. "I don't want you too aced."

"To waste?" He hadn't been following. He took a more careful sip of his drink. "I wouldn't waste a drop."

Out of the corner of her eye she noticed Lyall observing him closely. His bushy eyebrows were knitted in a frown and his thin upper lip was set in a tight line. He raised and lowered his glass but didn't appear to be drinking.

Myra's voice cut through her thoughts. She had launched into a story about a friend of hers, a true blue First Family of Virginia, who'd had someone suspended from the hunt for inviting a black horse master along to a meet.... Hazel wasn't listening. She excused herself and went to the kitchen to see to the supper. From the hall she could hear Ben in his room upstairs, playing a video game on his computer. Thank God for the young generation, she thought.

She was basting the roast when she heard a step on the boards outside. Lyall came in.

"Ah, Hazel, it's you," he said, feigning surprise.

He took up a position by the stove and stood nursing his glass, his legs crossed at the ankles. He opened his mouth to say something, then closed it again. To put him at his ease, she gestured around the bare plaster walls and naked piping and at the paint cans and tools and builder's materials pushed away into the corner.

"You see why we haven't invited you over before," she said, pulling an apologetic face. "You may end up getting putty for paté."

He smiled edgily and shot a glance at the door.

"Hazel," he began, "can I ask you something? In private?"

"Is this private enough?"

"I'm serious. It's about Matthew." He hesitated. "He is okay, isn't he? You haven't noticed anything ... odd about him recently?"

"Why?" she asked quickly.

"It's just ... I wouldn't like to see him go overboard. You know what I mean?"

She closed the oven door and turned to face him.

"I'm not sure I do," she replied carefully. "Matthew's under a lot of pressure right now. It's quite a lot to take on, the house *and* the book."

"Hazel, I've seen what can happen."

"Matthew's tough. He can handle it."

Lyall seemed not to hear her reply. He was fumbling in his jacket pocket. He took out a card and handed it to her.

"My direct line at the labs. You have my number at home. Call if ever you need to, Hazel. Night or day. Do you get me?"

"I hear you, Lyall, but I don't really think—"

"Just keep it by you."

She took the card, puzzled by the urgency of his manner. It was a plain card with just a phone number, written by hand. Evidently he had come intending to give it to her. Now his mission was completed, his manner abruptly eased. He took a slug of his whisky and showed a sudden interest in the food she was preparing. He was surprisingly knowledgeable about culinary affairs, and soon they were comparing recipes for pasta sauces and salad dressings. He helped her serve the courses and take in the plates, and throughout the evening he was in an ebullient and jocular mood—in stark contrast to Matthew, who seemed distant and self-absorbed and, in spite of his patent efforts, never quite part of the company.

As she looked across the table at Matthew's quick, nervy mannerisms and listened to his short, broken laughter, she fingered the card in her pocket. Was he uttering a cry for help that she wasn't hearing? She would do well to keep a careful eye on him for a while.

Night closed in suddenly, and by five o'clock the sky was dark as pitch and the windows, lashed by wintry squalls, glistened like black mirrors, reflecting the laboratory in a dozen splintered angles. Matthew focused harder on the computer screen before him. Time was racing past. Fridays always came round too quickly, an irritating, artificial end to work just as he was getting into the flow. He typed at a furious pace, heedless of syntax or spelling, just desperate to get as much down as he could before he had to break off. He'd unearthed a good deal more about Isabel Hardiment, and at last he felt he was really getting a fix on his target. Her own papers revealed a covert correspondence with Shawcrosse. Again, they were addressed in code, mostly simple plays on words or devices based on the palindrome N-a-t-a-n which seemed designed more to tease her lover than to protect his identity.

The more he read, the more he felt a strange closeness to her. A strong, even familiar, personality seemed to emerge from her pen. At times, he could almost hear her voice behind the words, speaking directly to him.

A *ping* from the computer brought his thoughts sharply back into line. He glanced at the digital time display. Five-fourteen. He was cutting it fine. He always made a point of being at home when Hazel and Ben arrived, weary and eager, from Washington.

He was tired, too. He felt dizzy and alternately hot and shivery, as though he were coming down with flu. His brain felt loose in its moorings, and when he turned his head too sharply his vision went into a nauseous swirl. Even rubbing his burning eyes seemed to knock some inner gyrostat out of true and make him momentarily lose his sense of orientation. With a groan, he held his head in his hands and pressed his fingers hard against his temples. God, he felt lousy.

The computer whirred softly. The rain scrambled across the windows like a horde of sharp-clawed rats. Distantly, a door banged shut, and somewhere outside a car started up. He yearned to drift off to sleep. Gradually, like a man on a cliff edge no longer able to hang on, he began to feel himself slipping. Just two minutes, he told himself; a catnap to refresh the system. The room was warm, the noises grew more distant, his own breathing seemed to come from further off ...

Suddenly, a cough.

Soft, muffled, but distinct enough. A human cough.

Christ, someone's in the room!

He jerked his head up. His brain whirled sickeningly. A black wave washed over his vision, leaving stabs of brilliant color in its wake. As his senses cleared, he became aware of a figure standing by the door. A figure dressed in a black coat, white scarf and broad-brimmed hat.

It was the mysterious boy who'd been dogging his steps.

In the murky no-man's-land between sleep and waking, between reality and unreality, between what is and what might be, a single word, a name, slowly wormed its way to the surface of his consciousness. He opened his mouth, but all that came out was a throttled croak. "Lapidus?"

The young man smiled. He took a step into the room.

First, the smell. It hit him like a blow in the face. That sickeningly familiar electric smell.

Before he could recover from the shock, two further blows struck in the same instant. As the face came into focus, he saw the beauty spot. And in that very moment the young man swept off his hat with a flourish. A cascade of blonde ringlets fell out, and the sound of young girlish laughter pealed around the room.

Matthew drew back in his chair, choking.

Isabel!

As he struggled to stand, one foot became twisted in the leg of the swivel chair, and he tripped. He caught himself before he fell to the floor and quickly straightened, but when he looked up again, she was gone. Vanished entirely, leaving no evidence behind but the faint scent of her perfume lingering in the air and the door of the laboratory gently swinging.

Hazel phoned the labs, but the switchboard was closed and, to her infuriation, she'd left the number of Matthew's direct line back at the apartment in D.C. She had Lyall's, though, and on the off chance they were caught up in a late meeting together, she called his number, but there was no reply. She kept Ben up as long as she could, but by nine o'clock she decided to put him to bed. By then the supper was overcooked and growing cold in the oven. She checked the phone for incoming calls in case there was a fault on their own line. As the time passed, she grew seriously worried. It was so unlike Matthew not to call. Had he had an accident? She worked herself into such a state of anxiety that she actually called the University of Virginia Hospital, but no Matthew Cavewood had been admitted. She switched on the television and flipped through the channels, but found nothing to take her mind off her worry. She would simply have to sit it out as patiently as she could.

Finally, an eternity later, she heard his car drive up. She rushed to the door. She barely recognized the figure that staggered into the porch light. His clothes were askew, his face was wild and blotched, and a gash of blood streaked across his cheek. He'd crashed the car. Or got involved in a fight.

With a cry, she rushed forward.

But the instant she took him in her arms, she knew the truth. The evidence hit her full in the face. The smell of a woman's perfume, a light, elusive fragrance. The gash across his cheek, scratched by fingernails. Above all, the look in his eyes. Shame, horror, and incomprehension.

SEVEN

In that moment something died within Hazel. It burst like a puff ball and scattered its seeds of hope to the winds. With a howl of anguish, she thrust Matthew away and stumbled back indoors. This isn't possible! she cried to herself as she pounded her head with her fists. Christ in heaven, say this isn't happening!

She fumbled her way across the hall and into the kitchen, slamming the door firmly behind her. Nine years of her life suddenly collapsed to nothing, and for a moment she was back in her small apartment in San Francisco, arriving home to find the half-empty vodka bottle and the trail of underclothes and the obscene grunts and groans coming from the studio, then kicking the door open and finding her lover sprawled naked on the couch.... A different man this time, but the same crime. And the same suffocating pain.

The room lurched and swayed. She was going to be sick. As she steadied herself against the sink, wild notions flew through her mind. She'd kill the cheating bastard. A carving knife glinted at her from the draining board. She'd stab him. She'd catch him in the hall, on the stairs, in the bathroom, and she'd stick him in the guts. No, she wouldn't. She'd just pack her things and get out. She'd haul Ben out of bed, bundle him into the car and drive back home to D.C. Right now? Well, maybe she'd leave it to the morning, not to upset the poor kid more than she had to. Then she'd pack their cases, load the car, and go. No fuss, no fight, just a controlled and dignified exit. She'd take Ben for one of his favorite nature rambles in the forest, then stop off for brunch on the way back and explain it all to him. She'd teach him the ugliness of deceit. She'd make him learn what an unforgivable sin it was to elicit someone's trust and then exploit it, to take someone's heart and betray it ...

The doorhandle was turning. She spun round, backing against the sink. Through her tears she saw Matthew standing in the doorway. His dark eyes were staring. He struggled to focus on her.

"Uh, I guess I'm a bit late."

"Don't say anything!" she cried. "I can see for myself."

He cast a glance at himself in the mirror, and frowned. His hand rose to his cheek. He felt the gash carefully.

"Ah." He swallowed. "Don't get it wrong, Hazel. It's not how you think."

She whipped her head to one side. She didn't want him to see her tears.

"I don't want to hear, Matthew. You'll only make it worse."

"I saw this ... person," he began. "She just appeared, out of nowhere, just for flash ... then she was gone." His words came out broken and disjointed. He was looking at her, but his eyes weren't seeing her. The expression in them was glazed, deranged. "I ran after her. I followed her out of the labs and across the grounds. I lost her somewhere beyond Jefferson Park Avenue. In the undergrowth. It got too thick and thorny. She just ... kind of ... melted into the bushes."

She looked at him in horror and disbelief, consciously keeping her distance.

"Who is this 'she'?" she rasped.

"I don't know."

"You *don't know?*"

"I mean, she wasn't real. Not *really* real." He smote his forehead. "Oh God, I can't explain. I don't understand, myself."

"Stop playacting, Matthew," she snapped, mustering all her inner strength. "It's childish and demeaning. I'm not getting involved in your absurd semantic quibbles. The facts are real enough."

"She was there one moment," he cried in a tormented voice, "then gone the next. Like an apparition."

"Look at the shape you're in!" she said coldly. "How can you pretend? Don't insult me."

He stepped forward and caught her by the sleeve.

"Please, angel, just *listen*—"

"Don't touch me!" she cried, tearing away.

She wormed past him to the door and stumbled across the hall to the living room. Matthew followed on her heels, pleading with her to listen.

"Sssh!" she hissed. "You'll wake Ben." She retreated to the far corner of the room. "Just leave me alone. God, is there nowhere in this house, in this *universe,* where I can be free of you?"

He held back and his gaze fell to the carpet. When he spoke, his voice was quavering.

"Hazel, I need your help."

"You need help all right!" she agreed bitterly. She turned away. "I don't know what you did to make me fall for you, but I loved you, Matthew, I loved you like I never imagined I could ever love anyone. You were wonderful, incredible. Everything was going to be different." She broke off.

Matthew had slumped into a chair, his face pressed in his hands. He spoke in a muffled, disjointed, often incoherent tone, heavy with despair and bewilderment. He sounded like a man cut adrift from reason, lost beyond hope, struggling to make sense of some incomprehensible act of fate. She couldn't make out how far he was acting, or how far even he was taking himself in.

"See," he fumbled, "I thought it was a guy. A kid I'd seen around the campus. Weird clothes. Staring eyes ..." He trailed off briefly. "I was in the labs. Guess I must have dozed off. I looked up, and, Christ! there he was. Only it was *her.* Isabel. Then I got it!" He looked up, his expression suddenly fervent, urgent. "You see, she was his assistant all along! *She disguised herself as a boy.* That way, she could join his classes, work with him in his lab. Women couldn't do that in those days. She had to be a boy to be close to him!"

Hazel looked at him with growing horror. Here was the man she was going to marry, reeking of fornication, inventing some garbage about the girl he'd just been screwing disguising herself as a boy. Did he think that made it any better? She put her hands over her ears.

"I don't know what you're talking about. I don't *want* to know. It's all lies, lies." Her voice was faltering. "It's no use, Matthew."

But he wasn't hearing her.

"The perfect cover!" he continued insistently. "She can come and go as she pleases. Stay late in the labs, when everyone's gone home and the place is empty. No one could possibly suspect. Neat game plan for an affair, heh? Until one day—"

"Spare me the sordid details!"

"—her father finds out. He's the *dean,* Hazel, and there's no love lost between them at the best of times. So when he finds out who his beloved daughter is mixed up with ..."

She blocked her ears to the gobbledegook, but some phrases still slipped through. He spoke of the dean's daughter, but the dean didn't have a daughter—he wasn't even married.

"Matthew," she began carefully when at last she could meet his eye. "We've had Dean Colbert to dinner. Don't you remember? He doesn't have children."

"Not Colbert," retorted Matthew impatiently. "Hardiment. Dean Hardiment."

"I thought Hardiment was the dean of your old Oxford college."

"He was."

"Back in sixteen-eighty something."

"Exactly! That's just what I've been trying to tell you."

"Wait a minute." She had to get this right, to know the measure of his madness. Had he grown so obsessed with his work that in his mind the past had become merged with the present? The whole idea was so absurd that she couldn't keep the irony out of her tone. "Are you telling me this has something to do with this fantasy girl you've been getting it on with?"

"That was Isabel! And we weren't 'getting it on,' for God's sake."

"Isabel?"

"You're not listening, Hazel. Isabel Hardiment. The girl in that portrait Ralph Corcoran showed us, remember? You'll say it's crazy, it's impossible, but I know it was her. Not just someone like her. It actually was her."

Hazel assumed the cautious, placatory half-smile appropriate for idiots with dangerously volatile tempers.

"But of course, Matthew," she said levelly, "you know that *is* quite impossible."

"Impossible *and* possible. A *and* not A. Aristotle's fourth principle of logic. The wild card. Describes perfectly the quantum effect."

A taut silence stretched between them. The mantel clock struck the quarter hour; ten, or eleven? She couldn't see from where she sat. The radiators rumbled gently, in need of bleeding. Overhead a floorboard creaked:

had they disturbed Ben, or was it merely the old house settling its timbers for the night?

Her mind flitted from one commonplace thought to another, avoiding the moment when it would have to confront this mountain of confusion and contradiction. She stared hard at Matthew. Watching the way he twisted his limbs as he sat wrestling with his thoughts in inner torment, she began to wonder if insanity might not be still more painful to confront than infidelity. His words reverberated through her mind: *I need your help, Hazel.* God help them all.

She took a deep breath and prepared herself.

"All right," she said, "you'd better tell me about it. Everything. From the beginning."

Hazel canceled her Monday appointments and spent the hours while Ben was at school wandering through the city. She passed the morning strolling around Georgetown in the frosty sunshine and the afternoon sauntering through the galleries of the Smithsonian. She stopped for coffee in the restaurant where she and Matthew had first met, but all that seemed so far away now, a meeting between two different people, and she left without touching the drink. She felt she must look to any casual observer a typical, carefree visitor, a tourist maybe, but it was the very burden of her cares that drove her to prowl public places, moving restlessly from one to another, looking at objects and exhibits but not really seeing. She'd never felt so completely at a loss before. She was frozen into paralysis by confusion, like a mouse mesmerized by a snake.

The questions and issues all bled one into another in one great and insoluble tangle. She didn't even know what she herself really felt. Shocked, perplexed, disappointed, angry, incredulous, scared: all of these, and yet none clearly enough, or maybe none singly enough, for her to be able to say, "That's how I really feel, so this is what I shall do." She had left Charlottesville early on the Sunday morning, forcing Ben reluctantly back home on the pretext of a work deadline she had to meet. All through the Saturday she had tried to act as normally as possible, for his sake. In fact, it hadn't been hard, partly because Matthew himself seemed so incredibly normal, having offloaded his mental burden, but partly, too, because she didn't feel anything clearly. Forces were tugging her in all directions equally powerfully, so that her heart remained in the center of the spinning disk, still and motionless.

When she could escape the numbing effect of Matthew's own conviction and strip away his absurd fantasies, however, it became perfectly clear what had happened. It was simple. This girl was one of his students who'd taken a shine to him. She had chosen a moment late on a Friday afternoon when the labs were empty and she could be reasonably sure he'd be alone. Maybe she knew his car and could tell he was still there. Under the pretext of a problem with her work, she'd gone up to seek his help. Just another case of a pupil with a crush on her tutor. Whether they'd done anything almost didn't matter. That was the minor problem.

The major problem lay with Matthew and his reaction. Why had he needed to invent that ludicrous business about a seventeenth-century girl come back to life? He might feel guilty for whatever he did do, but why go to these absurd lengths to fabricate such an improbable fiction? Why not just say, "So-and-so came to see me. She had a problem with her thesis and I sorted her out. It took a bit longer than I expected. I'd no idea how late it was. Sorry, honey. What's for supper?" And while they'd eaten tepid duck and overcooked vegetables, he would have launched into one of his domestic lectures on quantum physics and all would have been smoothed over.

Instead, he'd tried to suggest she wasn't really real. Was his sin so terrible or his guilt so harrowing that he found it more comfortable to deny her reality altogether? Could conscience so outweigh common sense?

Oh my God, she thought suddenly. Maybe, for him, this girl actually was real. Maybe he'd invented her. And she was a direct product of his mind, a figment of his own creation—born, of course, out of his obsessive fixation with the historical character of Isabel Hardiment. He was always going on about the mind's phenomenal powers of autosuggestion. If saints could weep blood and make stigmata bleed, if prophets and priests could see visions of holy beings and heavenly cities or hear divine voices commanding them, if the asylums of the world were filled with tormented souls believing themselves under attack from spiders or spacemen, if people could heal themselves of cancer by laughter and cure illness by adjusting their thinking, then why couldn't one man with an especially powerful intellect, perhaps more sensitive than most and certainly more obsessive, be able to conjure up a being which he believed to be absolutely and utterly real? She'd have thought there must be something to give the lie to the image, some obvious giveaway. But not necessarily, to the sick mind. Think of the martyrs that went to the stake prepared to burn for their convictions, or the wretched patients in those asylums who would sooner die than deny that God himself was speaking to them. Interpreting the evidence to fit the idea—that was the very mark of the sick mind.

Abruptly she broke off her train of thought, shocked by the implications. At the bottom line, she was saying that Matthew was profoundly mentally disturbed. He wasn't deluding her—he was deluding himself. Weren't these the classic symptoms of schizophrenia?

Unless he was actually right.

She shivered. Was she now saying that Isabel Hardiment might really have come back from the grave? Was she now going mad?

Yet this was Matthew's absolute conviction. He had advanced all kinds of theories about collapsing wave forms and quantum effects to support it, all muddled up with a mass of stuff about Shawcrosse and concepts of matter and spirit in seventeenth-century alchemy. Deep into the night he'd struggled to account for the experience, but never once had he doubted it.

She needed desperately someone else's opinion. Someone who was at home with quantum physics and had some understanding of psychiatric disorders. Above all, someone who knew Matthew well enough to care while also being discreet enough to respect her confidence.

Lyall?

She was standing at the foot of the staircase of the National Gallery of Art when the idea came to her. She fumbled in her purse for the card he had given her and cast about for the nearest phone. Then she hesitated. Lyall was a friend, but he was also Matthew's departmental head. He wore two hats. His loyalty couldn't be entirely relied upon.

But as she turned toward the exit, it occurred to her that Matthew was groping for a scientific theory because that was the language in which he naturally interpreted the world. Instead of a physicist or a psychiatrist, perhaps what she really needed was an expert on the psychic.

The previous summer, when they'd rented a house at Virginia Beach, she remembered driving past a complex of buildings on Atlantic Avenue, overlooking the ocean. In front of the main block, a large structure in buff concrete, curiously reminiscent of the plug-on memory store on Matthew's computer, stood a signboard which read THE ASSOCIATION FOR RESEARCH AND ENLIGHTENMENT. Matthew had explained that this was an internationally renowned center of research into the paranormal. A revolution was currently going on in modern science, he'd said: By the time Ben was their age, the paranormal would be proven to be quite normal, the supernatural perfectly natural. They'd fallen to talking about ghosts—"entities" was the term he'd insisted on using—and she'd been mildly surprised to find a man of his scientific rigor admitting freely he believed in their existence. At the time, she'd thought he was merely playing devil's advocate, as he so often did, just to be argumentative. Now she began to wonder how serious he'd been.

She called up the organization. It was after hours and the director himself answered. He began questioning her about the "entity experience," and she found herself saying she was researching a piece for the Charlottesville *Daily Progress*. Why couldn't she confess she was directly involved in the case? Was she ashamed?

If the director saw through the pretense, he was too professional to say so. He began by describing typical cases of apparitions of the dead. Substantive proof, however, he said, was very elusive; the cases always fell far short of what he called "policeman's proof"—witnesses and proper hard evidence. Ghosts were most often observed by a single person only, even when others were present, a fact which by itself ruled out any notion of a physical reality as we knew it. For an entity to be really real, it must be perceptible to anyone using their normal five senses, not just to one individual possessing a sixth. Had the girl in question been seen by more than one person? Hazel doubted it; she thought Matthew had been alone in the labs.

If witnesses weren't available, she asked, what about hard evidence? Here the shortcomings were more telling. Poltergeists might leave behind a trail of broken crockery. Ghosts might even be tangible: people said their touch was like fine muslin. But in all the countless recorded cases, she pressed him, did they ever leave anything behind of themselves? A dropped handkerchief? A shed slipper? Fingerprints on a glass, footprints in the snow? Touch a ghost and did the perfume rub off? Could a ghost scratch you and draw blood?

No, the director had to admit.

When Hazel finally put the phone down, the inescapable conclusion was already crystallizing in her mind. She'd disposed of the crazy outside shot. Now she was back in the real world, with choices she could come to grips with. Either Matthew was lying or he was sick. Each raised its own implications. In either case, she had Ben to think of: Did she want to bring him up in an atmosphere of mental illness and instability? And of

Matthew himself: What should she do there? She shook her head in despair. Goddamn it! Why did it have to happen now, when everything at last seemed set so fair?

Her first thought was to confront Matthew and force him to see a psychiatrist. But she could foresee his reaction. He simply would not accept that he had a problem.

She decided to bide her time. During the week, when he called to discuss a choice of bathroom fittings or alternative wallpaper for the hallway or to wish her goodnight at the close of day, she studiously avoided any mention of what had happened at the weekend. She listened to the timbre of his voice, so reasonable, so balanced, so relaxed, so much the essential Matthew, that she even began to wonder if it hadn't all been a figment of *her* mind. Yet though the problem might not be in evidence all the time, it had not disappeared. It lurked in the background, stalking her waking thoughts, ready to snare her in unguarded moments. Finally, as the weekend approached, she steeled herself to break the uneasy truce and bring the issue out into the open.

She chose that Saturday afternoon to have it out. Around three o'clock, she drove Ben to their friends', Harry and Elaine. Harry taught earth sciences at the university, and they had two boys of Ben's age at his school-to-be.

The day was bright and piercingly cold. Fresh snow had fallen during the night, and the snowplows had not yet cleared the smaller lanes that wound through the wooded slopes around Rugby Avenue. On the way back from dropping Ben, she took a shortcut and, needing time to prepare her thoughts, she pulled up off the road.

She walked up the hillside to a point from which the land fell away steeply, commanding a fine view of the town. Standing beneath a sturdy beech tree on which last year's leaves still hung, curled and withered, she stretched her gaze over the checkered tapestry spread out below. The university campus was contained within a rough square, divided from the town by the railroad to the east and crisscrossed within by a lattice of roads and pathways that stood out starkly against the white patchwork of roofs and lawns. If she screwed up her eyes she could just pick out the Lawn itself, the heart of the university, spread out like the shirt of a recumbent white giant with the majestic Rotunda for its head and the Pavilions for its flanks. She picked out the other buildings, too, the libraries and halls, the chapel and the school of medicine. A formidable fund of knowledge and ability lay cupped within that gentle bowl. Surely someone in some study or laboratory could provide the help they needed? With the right will, they could find the right person. The first task was to coax Matthew into agreeing to seek help. Could she somehow tease the idea out of him in such a way that he'd think it was his own?

Confirmed in her resolution, she retraced her steps to the car and started up. The back wheels spun vainly in the snow, refusing to grip. The more she revved, the deeper the car sank. She thrust the gears into reverse, then forward, then reverse again, hoping to rock it out of the rut, but the tires only dug in still deeper. Finally, she climbed out. The car was grounded up to its axle in compacted snow. With a smothered curse, she slammed the door and headed back home on foot. She'd have to get Matthew to tow her out with the Mercedes.

She trudged up the lane, fuming. At the turn where it steepened, she passed another abandoned car that had evidently missed a driveway and skidded into the gatepost. Her shoes were soon sodden, and more than once she slipped and fell sprawling onto the crusty snow. The sun had disappeared behind the upper line of trees, and a chill wind had risen that knifed through her overcoat. What an idiot she'd been to risk pulling off the hard surface! Matthew would say something, meaning to tease her, she'd take it as patronizing, and the real discussion she'd meant to have would get off on the wrong foot.

Finally, the house came into sight, looming tall and gaunt in the encroaching twilight. She dragged her steps wearily into the drive. Briefly, she wondered if they shouldn't have painted the whole thing a warmer color, a rusty barn red or maybe a Tuscan ochre ...

A movement in an upper window caught her eye. In the bay window on the far corner, their nuptial bedroom. It was Matthew. The light was off, but as he wore a pale jersey she could make out his movements quite clearly. He held a small object in his hand which he was slowly raising and lowering as though sweeping something.

She hesitated momentarily in her tracks, puzzled. What on earth was he doing? Wiping the windows? He was standing too far back for that. Measuring up for curtains? They'd already bought the curtains. After a moment he bent double and appeared to become engrossed in something on the floor. Perhaps he was trying to get out that scorch mark she'd noticed on the boards. But why bother? They were having the room carpeted wall to wall.

She hurried on down the driveway and let herself in the side door. Shivering, she kicked off her shoes and hugged the kitchen radiator for a moment to restore her circulation. The door was open onto the hall. Hearing voices, she stepped forward into the doorway. Matthew's voice, upstairs, broken and hesitant. Did he have company?

A sudden sick jolt shot through her. That girl! He'd brought that wretched girl into the home! Not real, he said!

She crossed the hall to the foot of the stairs. It sounded more as if he was dictating something. Perhaps it was a pocket tape recorder she'd seen in his hand.

Then her blood froze, and a giddy swirl of nausea rushed to her throat. His voice came filtering down the stair well. A soft whisper. Coaxing. Caressing.

"Isabel?"

The name struck her like a knife in her heart. A pang of jealous rage streaked through her like acid. That name! And the tone. She knew that seductive sweetness, that tender tone of intimacy. This was how he would speak to her in bed, lying beside her, arousing her for love.

"Come on, Isabel," he was murmuring. "Show yourself. I'm here. I'm waiting. Don't be afraid. Do you remember this? 'If thou should'st ever doubt the power of my love ...'"

Poetry! Jesus Christ, he was reciting *poetry*!

She couldn't listen to any more. Tears welled up in her eyes. She started up the stairs, then checked herself. All her resolution had ebbed away. Slowly she sank to her knees and crumpled up on the bottom stair. A long choking sob broke from the depths of her soul.

The man she loved was in love with another woman. A woman dead for three hundred years.

EIGHT

Matthew straightened. He switched off the small hand-held detector. No apparent change in the electromagnetic field in this room either. He'd now tested every location where he had sighted her, but he'd got no hint of any abnormal reading. He sighed with exasperation. Any entity must leave *some* trace.

And a real entity she was. Not a dream image, certainly; he'd felt drowsy, true, but he hadn't actually fallen asleep. For one thing, if he had been asleep he'd have had to wake up, and the continuity of his experience was perfectly seamless. He hadn't been hallucinating, either, as he followed her fleeing figure down corridors and stairs and across lawns and roads until she had disappeared into the thorny shrubbery. A trance would have snapped long before then.

If he half-closed his eyes he could see her strange, chilling smile as clearly as if she stood before him now. It was an intense, magnetic smile that hardened for a fleeting moment with a flash of pure, cold malevolence. And in his ears still echoed the sound of her laughter, a light, trilling laugh, at once flirtatious and mocking, spiteful even.

He rubbed his aching forehead. The malevolence, the mockery and the spite, these were surely projections of his own paranoia, his own guilt. God, he thought, how was it ever possible to untangle reality from illusion?

But then he remembered the one piece of hard evidence: his watch. After losing her in the stretch of woodland that ran along the far side of

Jefferson Park Avenue, he'd returned to the labs to record all he could remember. As he was feeding the information into the computer under a new, secure ID code, he'd noticed his watch had stopped. Exactly at the time she must have come into the room. It was a cheap watch, an imitation Rolex he'd bought for fifty dollars in the back streets of Singapore years ago, and it was certainly not antimagnetic. That had given him the idea. Suppose she had created a force field around herself sufficient to stop a watch, couldn't he then detect some residual traces? He'd searched the labs and found a small hand-held magnetometer, but the field seemed to have dissipated. He hadn't really held out any hope of getting a reading in this room at home either.

Maybe this was all too crude. He was seeking to detect gross physical changes when the mysterious processes that governed her actuality must operate at the subtlest quantum level. Instead of measuring electromagnetic fields and temperature differentials, maybe he should be thinking in terms of some superposition of macroscopic states. He groaned. Frankly, what the hell did that mean?

A soft sound caught his ear, like muffled sobbing. He shot a glance through the window. Hazel's car was not in the drive. A wild hope flashed across his mind. He raced to the top of the stairs.

"Isabel?"

The name died on his lips. There, at the bottom of the stairs, staring up at him with red eyes and a face swollen with tears, crouched the figure of Hazel. In an instant he understood.

He hurried down and knelt beside her, flushed with regret.

"God," he choked, "I had no idea you were back."

"I heard you!" she hissed, drawing away.

He swallowed. "I was just running a check. For resonances. Residual traces."

"Here? This woman has been to this house?"

"Well, not as such."

"Not as such?" she repeated, her eyes blazing like copper in a flame. "You haven't slept with her in our house *as such,* is that what you're saying, Matthew? You haven't lured the little slut back and screwed her in our bed *as such?* Get away from me! You disgust me!"

"Hazel!" He grabbed her by the shoulders, but she wormed free. "I've told you, it's not like that!"

"If you can't be faithful, at least be honest. Where's your self-respect?"

"I am being honest. I can't pretend it away. That would be a lie."

"Admit you're completely infatuated with her."

"She is ... intriguing ... fascinating ... elusive. I can't come to grips with it."

"She's just some young thing who's turned your head. Admit the truth, Matthew, and be done with this ridiculous nonsense."

"I know what you think and I know it sounds crazy, but—"

"Don't push me, Matthew ..."

"—it *is* Isabel!"

"Matthew, I'm warning you! I can't take much more of this."

"But listen—"

"Cut it out!" she screamed, thrusting her fists over her ears. "Are you trying to drive me crazy? You're sick, Matthew. Sick, do you hear?"

She was growing hysterical. He reached out to calm her, but thought better of it and withdrew his hand.

"Hazel," he faltered, "let's be adult. I don't pretend I can explain. I only know what I saw. You've got to believe me! You're the most precious thing in my life, Hazel. I'd never do anything to hurt or upset you. Don't you think I've asked myself a hundred times if I'm going out of my mind? I know it seems crazy and contradicts all reason, but you've got to try, Hazel, believe me, for my sake, for our sake. I can't just wish her away as though she didn't exist."

"But she doesn't!"

"She does, Hazel." He gritted his teeth. He hadn't wanted to say this. "This wasn't the first time. I have seen her before. I have actually touched her."

"Up there in the bedroom just now?"

"No, no. I was just checking."

"Oh yes, checking for resonances."

"Look," he began again, his anger rising with his frustration, "I don't exactly know what I'm looking for. But there *is* something strange in that room. Have you ever noticed there's a weird patch over by the window where it always seems quite cold?"

"I don't believe this! If it's cold, it's because the double glazing doesn't fit, or the radiators aren't working. I suppose you were measuring the draft. And all that sweet talk? Some ode to the north wind?"

"You're being ridiculous now."

A sudden flash of understanding lit her expression, and she shrank back in disgust.

"I get it! I know what you were doing up there. It's that blond Barbie doll across the way, the one that's always giving you the eye. You can see their house from the window. What was she doing, huh? Treating you to a striptease? I've seen her, the cheap slut with her whore's makeup and false eyelashes. You could fall for that, Matthew? Well, you can have her. Go over there now, go on, have her while she's hot, don't let me stop you—"

Her hysteria was out of control. He raised his hand. "Hazel, stop this!" he shouted, appalled.

"Go on," she taunted. "Go check her resonances. Make traces together. Only don't expect to find me here when you come back."

He beat his fist against the stairpost, spending its pent-up rage. "You're impossible! I can't talk to you in this mood."

"Don't try!" She backed across the hall. "I won't be ... humiliated like this."

Filled with despair and frustration, he followed her to the kitchen. She was standing by the window with her back to him, her whole body shaking. He hesitated, not knowing how to approach her.

He heaved a breath to calm himself. "Let's talk it through sensibly," he began in a reasonable tone. "There's no use in getting hysterical."

"Why shouldn't I get hysterical," she cried, "when I find the man I'm supposed to be marrying having an affair—"

"An affair of the *mind*, Hazel ..."

"—with a cheap broad round the corner?"

"There is no cheap broad anywhere! I'm talking about Isabel. Isabel Hardiment. How many times must I say it?"

"So what is it, then? Necrophilia?"

He paused, trying to control his welling anger.

"She died," he replied carefully, "but I guess she's not dead."

"Died, but not dead," echoed Hazel sarcastically. She scrutinized his face, and her voice fell to a whisper. "You really do mean it! God help us all." Gradually a new look entered her eye, wary and fearful, like that of a doctor faced with an unknown disease. "Matthew, do you realize what you're saying?"

"Sure, it's difficult—"

"It's not difficult, it's deranged. This girl lives only in your mind." She sat down at the table, her head in her hands. "I just don't believe this is happening."

"Angel—"

"You want to talk it through sensibly? All right, I'll tell you how it really is." She met his eye defiantly. "You see an ancient portrait of a young woman in some smoky dim-lit dining room. It's late at night and you've had a good couple of drinks. Months go by, and you're back home on the other side of the globe when you catch a fleeting glimpse of another girl, and although the first girl happens to have died three centuries ago, you swear that they're actually one and the same." She sighed. "Come *on,* Matthew."

The silence lengthened between them. She could never share his absolute certainty.

"She even had the mole on her upper lip," he said quietly.

"The mole on her upper lip!" She feigned incredulity.

"A beauty spot. But it was her whole person, her face, her smile, her perfume ..."

"She smelled of port and cigar smoke, I suppose? She didn't by any chance speak?"

"She did the first time, yes."

"And she spoke like the portrait? Now that's strange. I was there in the room, if you remember, and I can't recall hearing the portrait talk." She raised a quizzical eyebrow. "I presume she spoke pure Jacobean English, and not with the teeniest trace of a Virginian accent?"

He bit his lip. His case couldn't be argued; it rested on blind faith. No point in trying to convert the disbelieving. Isabel would have to appear to Hazel in the flesh for that. If only he could find a way of recalling her.... My God, just think what that would mean! If he could get her to talk, imagine what she could tell! She was, literally, a voice from the past. She'd actually worked alongside Shawcrosse. It was every biographer's wildest dream.

He glanced up to see Hazel looking at him, her fury and hurt given way to anxiety. He could almost hear her thinking, *"He's cracked, he's gone completely around the bend, he's got some terrible brain disease, I'd better get him to a specialist."* When she finally spoke, her question took him by surprise.

"Do you like her?"

"She ... she was considered quite a beauty in her day."

"That isn't what I asked."

He reached forward. "It doesn't change what I feel for you, Hazel."

"Oh no?"

"Of course not!" He put his arms round her. She didn't respond, merely sat as stony as a statue. "There's no one else in the world, angel, you know that. You surely can't be jealous!"

"Jealous of a three-hundred-year-old woman?" She laughed a bitter, cracked laugh. "How absurd."

"Well, then."

He moved forward to kiss her, but she turned her head away and continued to stare out of the window at nothing in particular, her face set hard and her eyes, unblinking, gradually filling with tears. He frowned. He'd said too much, as always. He should have bluffed his way out instead of spouting the whole thing out. It was too late to backtrack now. To the extent she believed the girl was real, she would be jealous; to the extent she didn't, she'd reckon him demented. A no-win situation. What the hell could he do? Cling to the one known fact in this sea of madness and unreason.

"I love you, Hazel," he mumbled.

He hugged her more tightly, even roughly, as if to squeeze the mood out of her, but she remained inflexible. He felt a stab of panic. He knew her so well in this mode. The right thing was always to withdraw and leave her completely alone to come to terms with the situation by herself, but he was temperamentally incapable of doing that. His nature was to persist, to argue, to press his suit to the point of destruction. But he also sensed that their whole future was on the line and that at any moment he might push her over the limit and she'd walk out of his life, forever. Mustering all his self-control, he let go of her and, brushing her hair with a gentle hand, he crossed to the door and let himself quietly out of the room.

Hazel lay in bed staring up at the ceiling and tracing a wedge of bright moonlight along the cornice and across the fresh plasterwork. Beside her, Matthew's breathing was growing slower, deeper. She eased herself onto an elbow and studied his long face with its strong features, pronounced brow and generous, sensual mouth, now softened and relaxed in sleep. He didn't *look* mental. It wasn't the face of a liar and a cheat, either. Was the whole thing some expression of genuine frustration she couldn't fathom, that cry from the heart to which she'd been deaf? Was

this Isabel a kind of imaginary friend, such as children sometimes invented? Was all this talk of quantum effects, of force fields and resonances, just
so much noise to shout down the voice of common sense? She had no way
of knowing—she was no expert. She'd already ruled out a paranormal
explanation; she had yet to check out whether there might be a genuine
physical one. It meant taking the risk and consulting Lyall. She'd let
Lyall's judgment settle the question.

Her own feelings were gradually crystallizing out of the turmoil.
She'd overcome her first, automatic impulse to quit before she got in too
deep, and now her dominant reaction was one of outrage. Suppose it
wasn't one of his students or even that cheap broad across the way after all;
suppose it really was some creature he'd imagined walking out of the
pages of his book? Was she going to give in and leave the field to a merely
illusory rival? She had made her commitment and she would see it
through. Who the hell was this figure risen from the grave to poison their
life? She wouldn't stand for it!

She'd set a time limit. She'd give it, say, a month.

But she'd be clever. She'd learn about her imaginary adversary. She'd
investigate her history. Instead of contradicting Matthew, she would agree
with him, play along with his whims. If he wanted to say he had talked
face to face with a woman who had died three centuries earlier, then she'd
accept it as a matter of course. She would be positive. Perhaps she'd even
offer to help him in tracking this girl down, or recalling her, or however
he put it. Perhaps she'd even suggest they met. Why not offer to invite her
to supper? They could strike up a friendship. What conversation! All
those questions about how life was lived in the seventeenth century, the
manners and mores of the time and those small vivid human and domestic
details. She'd get her to sit for her portrait, too. *People* magazine would go
wild. "Introducing Miss Isabel Hardiment, aged twenty-one, born in
1660." Or *Vogue.* "How to keep your complexion at three hundred." Ha!

She squeezed her eyes tight to rein in the galloping mania. At all
costs, she must avoid mocking him. Whatever he believed, she would
believe, too. That way she might just possibly enter his mind sufficiently
to turn it from within and, by some piece of mental jujitsu, use its own
power to destroy its own creation.

She leaned closer and brushed a kiss across his neck. Then, stirred by
the sweet familiar smell of his body, she ran her fingernails lightly across
his chest, tracing her way slowly down to his stomach. Gradually, through

his slumber, she felt him growing aroused. Gently she eased her body on top of his, her breasts softly caressing his cheek. Barely wakening, he began to respond. His breathing came stronger and his thrust quickened, but she held him back. She would play with him, tease him, drive him to the limit before giving him release. She'd show him what real love was, the love of a woman of flesh and blood.

That Monday afternoon, Hazel drove out to Washington National airport to meet Lyall, who was flying to Detroit for an interuniversity meeting of heads of physics faculties. After much agonizing, she'd finally called him at the labs early that morning. She'd given his secretary a false name, as a precaution against it getting back to Matthew. Lyall had sounded unsurprised to receive her call, and he didn't ask any questions. She'd suggested lunch later in the week, somewhere well off campus, but he'd insisted on meeting that very afternoon. For such a busy man, his own plans seemed remarkably flexible, and they agreed to meet at the airport at two o'clock, allowing her time to get back and pick Ben up from school.

She found him waiting for her in the center of the main concourse. He was without briefcase or baggage; he must have already checked it. He took her arm and steered her to a small lounge for members of a frequent travelers' club, where he sat her down in a deep plush chair and ordered coffee for her and a brandy for himself. Then taking off his glasses to polish them, he fixed her with a long and careful regard. Naked, his eyes looked pinkish and watery, and their gaze was strangely open, even vulnerable. This was a man she could perhaps, after all, trust.

Steeling her nerve, she plunged straight in.

"You're going to think this is crazy," she began, "and I'm relying on you to keep this strictly between ourselves. The fact is, I *am* worried about Matthew. He's been having some strange … experiences recently. He has his technical explanations, and I don't pretend to understand. I need you to tell me if there's anything in what he says. From a purely scientific point of view."

Lyall replaced his glasses and, with them, a professional mask.

"You're going to tell me he's been imagining things," he said.

"Why, yes." She was taken aback. "Has he told you?"

"No, no. Matthew has said nothing to me. In fact, he's been avoiding me." He smiled innocently. "Call it inspired guesswork. Tell me what's on your mind, Hazel."

She summarized the situation as succinctly as she could. At the end, Lyall spread his hands as if to express the infinite inexplicability of the human mind.

"Just because you can't see an obvious explanation, it doesn't mean there isn't one," he said. "Think of the magician sawing the lady in half. You see something happen which you know is impossible. Which do you believe, your eyes or your reason? You believe what you see." He smiled. "We shoehorn our reason into some kind of fit, and if it won't go, we call it magic. We don't go back and deny we ever saw it."

"But it's got to obey natural laws. The lady is not actually chopped in two and then joined up again. That *would* be impossible."

"Maybe." He signaled to the waiter for another brandy, then sat back and composed himself. "I think you should tell me the whole story, Hazel," he said. "From the beginning."

Time passed. Lyall sat listening intently. He seemed quite unconcerned about his flight. She told him all that had happened, as objectively and unemotionally as she could. The question was simply whether, according to the latest thinking in physics, there was just a shred of a possibility that Matthew might, after all, be right. She didn't need to know how or why. She'd long given up trying to understand the conundrums. She was sick of hearing about particles being in two places at the same time, about an infinity of alternative universes, about Schrodinger's imaginary cat in the box which was both alive and dead at the same time and only the act of opening the box to look actually determined which. Absurd though it seemed to a mind used to a world of three dimensions and time which ran conveniently in one direction only, all she wanted to know was whether a woman who had died three centuries ago might, however briefly and tenuously and under whatever unique circumstances, *theoretically* become actual and visible again.

When she'd come to an end, he let the silence lengthen. He frowned, rubbed his eyes, shook his head, began to speak then broke off. Finally he let out a long breath.

"Do you want the short answer or the long one?"

"Just the right one. I have to know."

"Of course you do." His frown deepened. "You're really asking two questions."

"Am I?"

"One about this woman Isabel as a physical object, the atoms and molecules that make up her skin and bones, her clothes, and so on. We now know that matter is made up of little packets of pulsating energy. It follows that you can create matter out of energy, and that includes mental energy. Imagine the mental energy of a man like Matthew in his manic obsessive mode. I'm talking pure theory, mind you."

"And the second question?"

"That concerns Isabel *qua* Isabel, the actual person that she is. What some people might call her soul, or her spirit. If what Matthew saw was actually her, it must incorporate the thing that makes her *her*. Otherwise it could be Joan of Arc or Boadicea or my great aunt Jemima. Do you agree?"

"Sure, but the soul is not a physical entity."

"At the quantum frontier, it could be physical in the way that energy is. It's a function of the brain—the brain's model of itself, if you like—but it's certainly not physical in the sense of a load of brain cells. You can't cut out a piece of brain tissue and say, 'Here's consciousness, here's the soul.'"

She leaned forward.

"But if the brain dies, the soul dies, too, doesn't it?"

"Not necessarily. Two plus two will equal four whether or not there's anyone there to think it. The software, if you like, can exist independently of the hardware. There's increasing evidence that the brain harnesses quantum effects at normal body temperatures. If that's so, the death of the brain needn't mean the death of the mind."

"So, the soul could survive bodily death?"

"In modern physical theory, yes."

It was all so bizarre, so far from everyday reality, and yet Lyall was repeating just the kind of stuff Matthew had been on and on about. She held his eye levelly.

"And here, in this case, with this woman Isabel?"

"What do *you* think?" he replied, raising his eyebrows.

"I think Matthew's got himself so immersed in the book that he's reading something into it all. Shutting his eyes to the simple and obvious explanations. What's your view, Lyall?"

"You must make up your own mind."

"I came here to ask you."

He watched her carefully as he replied.

"I'm a scientist," he said with a ghost of a shrug. "I'm comfortable with hypotheticals."

He wouldn't offer anything more substantial than that. The conversation drifted on for a minute or so, then the Denver flight was called. With a glance at his watch, he rose to his feet. He walked her back to the concourse and, cupping her hand in both of his, told her just to let things settle down and not to worry. Then, with a final word of reassurance, he headed off toward the departure gates.

On her way back to the parking lot, Hazel thought over their meeting with annoyance and frustration. What had she really got out of it? She was back where she'd started. In this mysterious world of atomic physics, anything seemed possible; the maddest notions were theoretically plausible. But people weren't particles! They operated by perfectly well known laws. If there really was something in what Matthew was claiming, then why in all the thousands of years of recorded history hadn't it ever happened before? And why to Matthew Cavewood and not any one of a billion others?

All that mattered in the end, she told herself as she left the terminal building, was that this crazy nonsense was real enough to him. She was fighting not a person but a belief; this girl existed only in his mind. Yet there could hardly be a more potent adversary than that. She would have to take the battle right into his mind itself if she was to have any hope of ridding him of the delusion.

As she reached the car, she stopped in her tracks. Something else had been niggling away at the back of her mind the entire time. Lyall had shown no surprise at what she'd told him. He'd known. How? "Inspired guesswork"? Come off it, Lyall.

And then another small but puzzling thought struck her. He'd gone for the Denver flight. Hadn't he said his meeting was in Detroit?

NINE

Isabel this, Isabel that.

The name drove Hazel frantic, yet she gritted her teeth and suppressed her feelings. Behind every smile lay a pang of pain. She dug her nails into her flesh rather than protest, and once or twice she even had to go and stand outside the room, drawing deep breaths, until her frustration and fury were back under control. Who was this figment, this interloper, this literal nobody? Matthew spoke of her with such familiarity, such casual ease, that she could have been just an old colleague of his who'd happened to be passing through town and chosen to look in on him at the labs.

She just couldn't understand what was going on in his head. Could he be so obtuse as to believe she really shared his absurd delusion? Or so blind to her feelings that he lacked the simplest appreciation of the pain it was causing her? Alone, when driving to an assignment or working in the darkroom or lying awake in the small hours of the night, she would feel a sudden stab of heartache, and a terrible, suffocating panic would rise to choke her, and she'd have to pull into the side of the road or rush out of the room or throw off the bedclothes, all feverish and breathless and frantic for light and air like a prisoner immured alive in a tomb watching the final bricks being cemented into place.

But the hurt was inescapable if she was to stick to her plan, and that she was determined to do.

She deliberately encouraged Matthew to speak about Isabel. She asked him questions about Isabel's life and her significance for his book. She got him to show her the transcripts of Isabel's love letters to Nathaniel Shawcrosse and to decode their recondite references. He had obtained a color slide of the portrait from his old college in Oxford, and she spent one evening in her darkroom printing an enlargement for him. She kept a smaller copy for herself, however, and this she studied carefully and in secret from time to time, scrutinizing the pale, oval face with its high forehead and intelligent eyes and the strangely tantalizing beauty spot on the upper lip, trying to read the mind that lay behind the mask in the hope of finding some insight into her elusive adversary. One day, in a fit of temper, she tore up the photo. She was falling under the spell of the same idolatrous fascination. But that evening, she made herself another print. For she had grown to realize that her rival was not this woman, the actual historical Isabel, but rather the image that she represented in Matthew's mind. It was not a person but a perception that she had to destroy.

This realization, however, brought fresh pangs of hurt. Why did Matthew need another woman, real or imaginary? What did she herself lack, or what was she failing to give him, that drove him to this bitter mental infidelity? All her secret doubts about herself, all the never-to-be-confessed anxieties of any woman about her relationships with men, all those feelings of insecurity she'd fought to overcome during the past years, these came flooding back in an overwhelming tide, and she had constantly to take herself in hand and remind herself who she was and how far she'd come, how successfully she'd coped so far on her own and how independent she was of the need of a man in her life. And anyway, this was all part of a conscious plan she had set in motion, which she could at any moment easily close down.

Some days, she felt full of strength and determination; on others, however, she could see only the hopelessness of it all. But by rehearsing this litany over and over, she began to regain her confidence and reaffirm her commitment to see the business through to its end.

To add to the pressure, there were certain immediate, practical decisions to be faced. The date for the wedding grew steadily closer, and as February slid into March, she awoke to the realization that the appointed day was just six weeks away and that they'd fixed only the most basic arrangements. In this as in everything else, Matthew seemed to have not the slightest notion of anything amiss. He exhibited an unwavering certitude that all was right and fine. After supper one evening they sat down with pen and paper and shared out the remaining tasks—confirming the pastor, sending out the invitations, booking caterers for the reception and, not least, finalizing their honeymoon vacation, a taste of paradise on Jost Van Dyke, a small island off the coast of Florida with no phones or cars and only accessible by boat.

The blithe manner in which Matthew took their whole future for granted was, she supposed, testimony to the success of her strategy. Her open acceptance of Isabel had eliminated this as a divisive issue. He clearly felt perfectly comfortable and content. He was his usual animated and talkative self once again, full of wild ideas and enthusiasms. He was loving and attentive toward her, too, and to all outward appearances it seemed that the appearance of this girl really had made no difference to his feelings.

As the days passed, with some unease Hazel found herself slipping into her own new way of thinking. She began to talk about Isabel with genuine curiosity; once she even caught herself referring to her in the present tense. It was an intriguing story, she had to admit: a mysterious seventeenth-century beauty and her helpless infatuation with a married man fifteen years her senior, against a background of clandestine alchemy and religious persecution. She began to do research of her own. When she learned that the young Isabel had been a noted herbalist, for instance, she visited Heartwood's, the bookshop close to the university, and bought several books on herbal recipes and remedies, including a fine facsimile copy of Thomas Newton's *Herball for the Bible,* which she took back to Washington and studied intently in spare moments during the following week.

By degrees, Isabel Hardiment was becoming one of the family. She was ever-present in the background of all they said and did, the invisible stranger at their hearth, the absent guest at their table. Hazel knew this was of her own doing; she had enabled it. She had collaborated in the deception and lent endorsement to the illusion. It was only when she was back in the capital, working in her busy professional world and plagued by all the pressures of modern city life, that she could see the situation for what it was, for what she had made it. At such moments the pain and the puzzlement bit deepest. What the heck was she doing encouraging this lunacy? Why was she even tolerating it?

She was playing with fire, and it was dangerous. How could she remain sane while playing a madman's game? The moment you engaged, the moment you allowed yourself to enter his world, you were sucked into the whirlpool.

She wished there was someone she could really talk to, but she knew what all her friends would all say. Sally, perhaps her closest friend, a political journalist on the *Washington Post* and a hard-headed realist, wasn't likely to let her get beyond the first sentence. There was always Pauline, the manager of a large modeling agency in town, a breezy, extravert soul with a big heart and broad shoulders on which all her girls had wept at some time or other. Pauline would tell her right off to fly the cuckoo's nest.

She'd simply have to cling to her own inner voice of reason. But that was so difficult. Matthew's disturbed world was so coherent, so internally consistent, so much all of a piece. He saw no demarcation between real and unreal, normal and abnormal. For fifty-nine minutes in any hour, he would talk and behave like any normal person. Then, without the slightest change in tone of voice, he'd drop in a mention of Isabel, and a minute later, with an equally seamless transition, he'd be back in the world of the normal and the sane. She felt she was watching some kind of conjuring show. The doublethink left her dumb.

She passed from outrage to compliance, from anxiety to rejection, until finally she reached the only workable way of living with the problem. Rather than cure it, she would only try and contain it. She'd think of Matthew's mind-fix more as an aberration than a disability, something like a lisp or a stutter or an odd tic. Given patience and, above all, the will to see it through, she could live with it. Gradually, at last, she began to relax. And that in turn made the atmosphere at home more relaxed. At the weekends the house rang with laughter once more, and a sense of conviction returned to their preparations for the wedding.

And then, with the day approaching fast, a series of incidents occurred that brought her up sharp and made her realize just what a dangerous fool's paradise she'd been living in.

The Saturday was cruelly cold, with an ice-pale sun and brittle clear air. Around every corner swept a biting wind that stung the cheeks and snatched the very breath from the mouth. It seemed nothing would ever unlock the land from winter's grip.

Matthew had taken them all to a football game in Lambeth Field. Afterward, huddled in overcoats and scarves, they drove back to Main Street and took refuge in the warmth of Armand's café. Ben's face was aglow with excitement of the game, and as they followed the waitress to their table he chattered irrepressibly. Hazel exchanged a smile with

Matthew. At moments like this she felt that nothing could come in the way of their happiness. She ordered a hot apple cider, Ben chose a Slush Puppy and Matthew went for a Rolling Rock beer. While the drinks came, the males fell to a heated debate about the game and the tactics. She tuned out. Her father had been crazy about football; he'd lived with the television on in the diner, and it became all he'd ever talk about. The great heroes of the game became like members of his own family. She shivered; that idea was all too familiar.

Idly, her gaze wandered to a wall of posters advertising university activities. The Commonwealth Ball, dance workshops, an appeal for platelet donors. A wildlife poster of an otter with the slogan beneath, "Now Disappearing at a Location Near You." Cards advertising a typing service, the Wellness Center, an AIDS help line. A bill advertising a production of *Romeo and Juliet*.

The waitress arrived with their order, creating a natural break in the conversation. Hazel pointed to the playbill.

"Ben might like that," she said. "I think he's old enough. If we're going to live in a university town, we might as well get the benefits."

Matthew assumed a declamatory voice.

"'And shrieks like mandrakes' torn out of the earth,

That living mortals, hearing them, run mad ...'"

He smiled. "Isabel talks a lot about mandrake. Or mandragora, as she calls it, in the Latin."

Hazel felt the sting a full second late. By then Ben was speaking.

"Mandrake?" the boy piped. "Like the magician?"

Matthew chuckled.

"No, it's a plant. An herb with weird and wonderful properties. The root looks a bit like ginseng—half human. There's an old folk tale that it will shriek if you pull it out of the ground when the moon is full. You've got to look the other way or you go mad."

"What if you do it when the moon *isn't* full?"

"Ben, I guess they just didn't think of that." He glanced at Hazel and went on in a musing tone, "Shakespeare doesn't say so exactly, but mandrake was probably the drug Juliet took to feign her death. It's certainly a powerful narcotic. It's a sensory suppressant, lowering the body function levels. In small doses it acts as a somnifer."

"Matthew," Hazel reminded him mildly, "we're not at a lecture."

"What's a somnifer?" asked Ben.

"Something that puts you to sleep."

"You mean, like math?"

"C'mon, darling," smiled Hazel, "you love math. You got an A last semester."

"Ben's so smart he can do his sums in his sleep." Matthew reached out and tousled the boy's hair. "I'll tell you something else interesting. Like a lot of drugs, it's poisonous in larger doses. Deadly nightshade is just the same. A drop in the eye widens the pupils—very fashionable for society beauties—but much more is fatal. People still die of belladonna."

"They poison themselves to look pretty?" asked Ben with incredulity.

"Not any more. But women did. They did all kinds of things. Rubbed white lead into their faces to look pale. Bled themselves to make themselves faint. They carried little razor contraptions to cut themselves on the back of the legs and let the blood."

"Ugh," shuddered Ben.

Hazel intervened, "I don't think we want a survey of early cosmetic practices, thank you, Matthew."

"We were talking about mandrake. You know, it might have killed off Romeo, too. Remember what the apothecary tells him?"

> *Put this in any liquid thing you will*
> *And drink it off; and, if you had the strength*
> *Of twenty men, it would despatch you straight.*

"Describes an overdose of mandrake perfectly."

"Don't listen to him," Hazel warned Ben. "He's complicating things as usual. *Romeo and Juliet* is a sweet love story that ends tragically, all the result of a misunderstanding. We'll read it together, and you'll see. You'll enjoy it. It has a very simple plot. And the language isn't too difficult."

She found herself talking on and on. Matthew's expression had taken on a familiar distant look and she could guess where his mind had gone. Eventually, she knew, he would have to share it with her. He turned to her when she finally came to a pause.

"Just had an idea," he began. "Remember that letter where Isabel talks of feeding Nathaniel a 'potion of mandragora'? I'd assumed she was offering him a Valium, as it were, to help him sleep. But what if she were actually threatening to poison him?"

"Why should she want to do that?" Hazel responded automatically.

Here she went again. They could be talking about Sally or Pauline or Lyall's secretary, Sandra, or any of a dozen young women of their acquaintance and the affairs they were involved in.

"Maybe Isabel is giving him the classic ultimatum: 'It's your wife or me, but choose her and I'll kill you.' It figures."

Ben was sucking noisily at his straw.

"Who's Isabel?" he chipped in.

Hazel flashed Matthew a glance. This was his one to field.

"Someone who's very involved in my book," he said.

"Who *was* involved," muttered Hazel.

"Has she been to see us?" inquired Ben.

"Of course not," replied Hazel firmly. "She's dead. She lived three hundred years ago."

"But Matt said—"

"I know, darling. He likes to imagine his characters are alive and running around the place. It makes them seem more real." She signaled to the waitress for the tab. "It's time we got home. What would you like for supper, Ben? And don't say burgers: you've had burgers every day this week."

"Burgers," said Ben.

Matthew was still far away. "I wonder ..." he mused to himself.

"Just wonder to yourself," she responded crisply. The tab arrived on a plate, and she covered it with a bill from her purse. "This is mine."

He pulled himself abruptly out of his reverie. He replaced her bill with one from his own wallet.

"Ours," he corrected, then rose to his feet. "C'mon, let's brave the arctic. Got everything?"

He led the way to the door, laughing and kidding with Ben for all the world as though he hadn't heard what she'd said about Isabel. As she followed into the biting wind outside, she realized that he had heard but it hadn't touched him. For him, Isabel was both dead and living, and he simply didn't see anything odd in that.

As the week back in Washington began again, Hazel's doubts about what she was doing returned once more. Then, on the Wednesday, something happened to confirm the danger with which she had been flirting.

She had an assignment out of town all that day. She returned late to pick Ben up from their friends', where he'd been taken after school, and it wasn't until she'd finally bathed him and got him off to sleep that she had time to take the day's messages off her answering machine. The realty company had called saying they'd received an offer on her apartment; she would deal with that in the morning. Next, a message from Sally inviting her to some glitzy party where the whole of Washington society would be showing up; she wasn't in the mood for parties. There followed a few *clicks* where someone had called without leaving a message.

And then Lyall's voice. There was an edge to his tone that instantly arrested her.

"Hazel," he began hesitantly, "it's Lyall. It's ... uh ... probably not important, but I thought you should know. It's about Matthew. He's been requisitioning certain chemicals from lab supplies. He's taken the stuff off the premises ..." A pause. "Some of those early herbal drugs can be pretty dangerous in their synthetic form. I'm sure he knows what he's doing, but after our conversation the other day, Hazel.... Anyway, I just wanted to let you know. Call me if you need me. You have my numbers."

An icy shiver ran through her. She thought back to the conversation in the café and Matthew's intent musing as they were about to leave. Requisitioning chemicals ... herbal drugs ... with a flash of insight she guessed what was on his mind. She snatched up the phone and dialed the house in Charlottesville. The line was engaged. She tried it again, and then again. After five minutes she checked with the operator. The phone had been taken off the hook.

She moved fast. Within twenty minutes she had got the girl from the family in the apartment opposite to babysit, checked Ben was soundly asleep, thrown on her overcoat, taken the elevator down to the basement parking lot, collected her car and was speeding out of town into a bright, starlit night.

Matthew sat in his swivel chair with his hands resting on the edge of the desk as he stared up at the enlargement of Isabel's portrait, pinned to the study wall and spotlit with a thin pencil beam. On the desk and directly in his line of sight stood the portable television, tuned off station to give only a hissing, flickering snowstorm. White noise, a flickering image, all other obtrusive sensory inputs suppressed. Maybe under these conditions he could go on the trip he wanted.

As he stared into the deep, hypnotic eyes, he began to hear the strange voice again, beckoning him. He'd been hearing this voice off and on all day, whispering in his inner ear, like a tiny implant in the very core of his mind, speaking somehow without words, in the language of the mind.

Come, beckoned the thought. *Come to me.*

He was coming. He would meet her in the half-world, the shadowy limbo between sleeping and waking, between the here and the hereafter. He would fly to her upon the wings of mandrake. He would follow in Nathaniel's path, he'd go where Nathaniel had gone, to the frontier between life and death, the no-man's-land where mind and matter met, the secret garden of the soul where death could be reversed and the body resurrected.

He glanced at the glass beaker at his elbow, unsure if he'd taken enough. But then it came, the cold and drowsy humor, seizing each vital spirit. Already his eyes were growing heavy, his pulse dwindling. With a massive effort he dragged his sluggish gaze toward the television screen. The world about him was receding. He was growing lighter, insubstantial, emptying of matter, filling with nothingness.

The mind-voice grew louder, closer, sweeter. *Come to me, Nathaniel ...*

Nathaniel?

Yes. I am coming.

Slowly, gradually, an ineffable joy suffused his whole being. It was like a glow of warmth and light that grew from within until it consumed him entirely in a blaze of wonder. A stupendous surge of hilarity flared through him. He was air. He was light. He was laughter. He was a particle dancing upon the very cusp of being, now matter, now mind, flicking back and forth between one state and the other like a ripple of sunlight coruscating upon the surface of the ocean. He was everywhere, in everything, and also nowhere, in nothing. He was spinning, whirling and swirling dizzily through the great tumultuous rush, and in the small silent spaces in between he could hear the very ticking of the universe.

Isabel!

She was there. Far away. Connected to him by a silver thread snaking across the chasm of eternity. She stood naked, reduced to essence. Her arms were outstretched, inviting. She was smiling, a warm, beneficent smile. Her eyes promised the ecstasy of perfect union. Her gaze was magnetic, impelling him irresistibly toward her. She was his other self. She would complete him. He understood. He knew how it would be. At the moment of contact, just for an instant, they would become one again, a single whole, two specks of one being, sundered billions of years ago in the birth pangs of the universe and now, for an infinitesimal breath, reunited, yet in the next instant to be annihilated by the very force of the impact and sent spinning away into the infinite nothingness that existed before time and space were ever born.

He was coming closer, obeying the pull, spinning faster and faster, closing on her, steadying for the collision....

"Matthew!"

Hazel shook him violently. His body was rigid and transfixed, his eyes were rolled back into his head and his breathing was shallow and faltering. She grabbed his wrist; she could barely detect a pulse. She shook him again. Christ, what the hell had he done? Her arm caught the glass beaker. It spilled, sending a yellowish fluid fizzing across the papers and filling the air with volatile fumes. What in God's name was he thinking of?

"Matthew! Can you hear me? Matthew, speak to me!"

He waved his arm clumsily to fend her off. His voice was thick and slurred.

"Go away," he growled. "Leave me alone."

"What have you taken?" she demanded, shaking him angrily now.

"I'm losing her!" he fumbled, pushing her off. "She's going! Wait, wait!"

Hazel's temper snapped. She swung back her arm and slapped him hard across the face.

"Stop that!" she cried. She slapped him again, and again. "Stop it! Snap out of it!"

"Don't," he warned, clumsily warding off the blows. "You don't understand."

"I understand all too well," she snapped.

She switched on the lights and turned off the television, then crossed to the mantelpiece and, seizing a vase, tossed out the flowers and flung the water straight in his face.

"Pull yourself together, you stupid fool," she commanded. "What's this shit you've been taking? What's it done to you? Do I need to get you to the hospital?"

"It's okay," he pleaded groggily. "It'll wear off." He pressed his fists into his eyes. "Why did you do that, Hazel?" he choked. "You stopped it, just as it was coming. She was there. I'd just gotten to her ..."

She grabbed him by the hair and wrenched his head back. She pressed her face close to his.

"Listen, you dumb jerk," she hissed, "just cut this crap! I won't have you blow your brains on some junkie trip to fairyland. Don't screw yourself up, Matthew, not while I'm around, not while you've got me to deal with. So just shape up and stop being such a stupid half-assed cretin."

He tried to protest, but he could hardly manage to get the words out. His whole body began to sway, his eyes closed, his mouth fell agape, and he crumpled up, falling unconscious on the desk top, his arms dangling limp to the floor. She felt for his pulse again; it seemed stronger. His breathing was steadier, too, and it rose and fell in the gentle rhythm of sleep.

She reached for the telephone and called a doctor. Hardly had the phone begun to ring when she put her finger on the cradle and dialed Lyall's number instead.

Lyall stayed just long enough to help Matthew into bed and to be sure he was not in any danger. He examined two small vials he found on the desk and pronounced himself satisfied that the apparent dose was unlikely to cause any ill effects beyond a monumental headache in the morning. He said very little, restricting his comments to short, curt remarks. She had the sense that he was more worried than he was showing. As he left, he clasped her hands and thanked her with a surprising warmth of feeling. She was puzzled. *She* should be grateful to *him*.

She waited an hour or more until she decided she could do no more by staying. Matthew hadn't stirred. He was lying exactly as they had left him, snoring deeply. She hesitated for a moment on the landing outside the room. There an idea occurred to her, an idea so absurd that she felt ashamed at the very thought, yet she knew she had to obey the impulse.

Quietly, she tiptoed along the landing to the nuptial bedroom. Inside, she closed the door and went over to the window. Before her spread the front yard with its slender silver birches gleaming silver-cold in the moonlight. She craned her head to see if it was possible to see into the house across the way. No, the house was too far away and anyway the view blocked by a crop of trees.

As she stood there, she became aware of a strange, penetrating chill creeping over her skin. It seemed to envelop her until she felt cold to the bone. Matthew had told her the men had finished this room. She felt the windows for drafts, but the frames were sealed tight. She took a step backward; there, to her astonishment, it seemed perfectly warm. In that one spot, the air seemed distinctly colder. With a sudden shiver of unease, she realized that this was the exact spot where she had found Matthew "looking for resonances."

Abruptly she turned and headed downstairs and, after scribbling him a brief note, left the house.

Had she chanced to look up behind her as she took off down the driveway, had she glanced in her rearview mirror or cast a final look over her shoulder at the house that was soon to become her home, she might have seen the cold, greenish, oval-shaped luminance hovering in the window of that upstairs room.

As it was, on the drive back to Washington, when she found her thoughts turning back to the strange chill in that room she put her foot down harder on the accelerator. This was a perfect example of the treacherous power of the imagination. She was damned if she'd let herself be taken in by the illusion.

TEN

Quite suddenly, over the space of a few days, spring arrived. The great plane tree at the back broke into bud, and within a week the chestnuts in the driveway had unfurled fledgling leaves. An invisible hand passed over the countryside, dusting the hedgerows green and drawing forth the tender shoots from the fields, while in the warmer, sweeter air the song of nesting birds mingled with the scent of hawthorn and flowering currant.

For his part, Matthew felt himself awaking from a hibernation of his senses. Its culmination had been that foolhardy experiment with mandrake. Yet, though he knew it was a stupid, dangerous thing to have done, he was also frustrated at failing to reach his goal. He'd been within an ace of touching the infinite, and he'd been dragged back to the mundane. A pioneer had to take risks. For the rest of that week he felt too ill to work, but in between bouts of vomiting and migraine he began to realize the greatest danger of all—the danger of losing Hazel.

In his obsessive fascination with Nathaniel Shawcrosse he had simply ignored the effect it was having on her. How cruelly this constant harping on Isabel must have hurt! Why couldn't he see what he was doing to her?

When on the Friday morning she called to say she had too much to do in Washington that weekend and she and Ben would only come down for the day on Sunday, the coolness in her voice filled him with alarm. What could she be doing that couldn't just as well be done from Charlottesville? She was the best thing that had ever happened in his life, and he was throwing it down the tube.

He rose from his sickbed, showered and dressed, then groped his way outside. The bright sunlight dazzled him, and his head swam as he filled his lungs with the giddy green scents of spring. Gradually he felt life and hope returning. In the fresh new world unfolding about him, anything and everything seemed possible. He was free, he was happy, he was young, and he was about to marry the woman he loved. Isabel was no part of this world. She belonged among the archives of the dead. He would do his biographer's duty by her, but no more. He'd consign her to the pages of his book, and when that was finished, forget her. Never again in Hazel's hearing would he let that name pass his lips.

The drive to Washington passed swiftly. He drove recklessly, with the radio on full blast to Bruce Springsteen, UB40, Bonnie Raitt, Tom Petty—pop music, as suited the day and his mood. He arrived feeling exhilarated. He stopped at a flower shop round the corner from Hazel's apartment and bought up half the stock. He stayed just long enough to watch the first bouquets arrive with the doorman, then he climbed into his car and headed back to Charlottesville.

Once home, he changed into his jogging clothes and went for a run. He was going to take himself properly in hand, physically as well as mentally. His limbs shrieked and his lungs burned, but he relished the pain. It made him feel alive. He ran past the large, comfortable houses of his neighbors, sitting securely within their grounds, fearless in their own confidence and certitude. He looked at them with the lost eyes of a stranger. Where had his own confidence and certitude gone? He'd been living like a mental exile.

But an exile no more. He was rejoining his world. Burying the past. Isabel was a footnote. He'd clean up his act and stop messing about with drugs, too. And he'd kick the paranoia and make it up with Lyall. He'd come home to find a message from his old friend from Chicago whom he'd asked to be his best man saying he was in hospital from a skiing accident and he wouldn't be back on his feet in time for the wedding. This was the perfect opportunity to mend fences. He'd ask Lyall to stand in and do the honors.

A great weight seemed to lift off his shoulders. His steps felt lighter, fleeter. He bounded along the woodland paths, he leaped over logs and boulders, he punched the air and whooped aloud, until a root tripped him up and he fell flat on his face in the mud, laughing.

* * *

Hazel arrived home that evening to be greeted by a profusion of flowers. She understood. Deep within her a cautious smile unfurled. So typically Matthew—impulsive, extravagant, excessive. She read the subtext, too. This was more than an appeal for forgiveness for the hurt he'd caused her, he was trying to say that he'd come to his senses. Yet she didn't quite trust the turnabout. How often did a cheating lover promise with all his heart and soul that he had given up the other woman only to be caught out later, still carrying on, only more covertly?

We shall see, Matthew, she said to herself. We shall see.

At first she was reassured by what she saw. Sunday was a perfect spring day. She packed a picnic and left Washington in time to arrive with Matthew mid-morning. They drove out to Skyline Drive and found a sheltered spot in the sun where they built a camp fire and roasted sausages skewered on sticks. Afterward, Matthew showed Ben an old Navaho Indian trick for snaring rabbits, and while the boy went off to try his new art with a piece of fishing line and a couple of ash twigs, she and Matthew lay down together on the rug in the sunshine. Warm and relaxed, she began to feel the desire uncoiling irresistibly inside her. Ben was well out of earshot, but this was still a public place. The danger of being seen sent a thrill shuddering through her body. She pulled the rug over them. "Quick!" she whispered, her fingers racing with their clothes.

Then a distant whoop broke through the whirl of her senses.

"Matt! Mom! I've caught one!"

"And I've just lost one," growled Matthew in her ear.

She wriggled free as feet came pelting through the woodland. Matthew leapt up and intercepted the boy as he arrived. Flushed and disheveled, she clambered to her feet, but her knees gave way beneath her. Unsteadily, she followed the two into the woods. She arrived to find Ben pointing to a spot on the ground.

"It was a great big one," he was saying. "But I let it go."

Matthew suppressed a smile at the transparent fib. "That's a shame. We could have had rabbit pie."

"Ugh!" shuddered the boy. "I'm glad I'm not an Indian. Still, your trick sure works."

"I made it all up," confessed Matthew. "Like you did just now."

"I wasn't making it up," protested Ben, blushing.

Hazel took Ben by the hand. She recognized the underlying cause. It couldn't be easy for him, sharing her with Matthew; all credit to him for the way he'd handled it so far.

"I think you did just the right thing, letting it go," she said gently. "Come on, let's pack up and go back home."

Ben picked up the remains of his trap and led the way back to the car. They strolled in silence. The air was growing cooler and the sun was already inching below the treeline. Somehow, out here in the open, set in the greater context of things, her worries seemed to shrink into insignificance.

Matthew cleared his throat.

"Hazel," he began, "why don't you stay over and get up early?"

She faltered. "Ben's got homework to do."

The boy overheard. "I did it yesterday, Mom," he objected. "Come on, let's stay. It's much more fun here."

A small warning note sounded in her head. She looked from one to the other, their faces bright and expectant.

"It'll mean getting up at dawn, darling," she warned her son.

"You can help me cook supper, Ben," proposed Matthew. "What'll it be?"

"Burgers," said Ben at once.

"You'll eat beef but not rabbit?"

"A hamburger doesn't look like what it comes from."

"Ah, Ben, you must see beyond the outward form of things to the inner reality."

"You won't find a cow inside a burger."

"He's got you there, Matthew," Hazel laughed. "Admit it."

"Sweetheart, this boy's a budding genius. Come on, Ben. Race you to the car. Let's see how smart you are on your feet."

As they pulled up in the driveway, Ben sprang out of the car and ran ahead to unlock the door. On the porch he bent to pick up a package. From a distance it looked to Hazel like a Federal Express pouch.

"It's from the University of Illinois," called the boy.

Matthew's expression tightened. He climbed quickly out of the car.

"I'll take it," he said firmly.

Hazel lingered outside, reluctant to go indoors just yet. She strolled around the yard, thinking about how it could be laid out. There was so much to be done. Blanche Morrell had gone crazy on flowerbeds, and a lot of thought needed to go into redesigning the back area, particularly where to site the pool. She looked about her at the signs of burgeoning spring. In just a single week, shoots had sprouted all over the grounds, beneath the trees and among the scrub: crocuses, wood anemones, daffodils, narcissi. She recalled Norma and Herb speaking of the old lady, out in the yard day and night, and she felt she could almost visualize her aged figure, dressed all in white, bending over her flowerbeds, cutting and pruning.

The daylight was now failing, and a low, doleful wind had risen. She looked up at the window of their bedroom-to-be, and she shivered, recalling the strange sensation she'd had there. Blanche Morrell had died in that room. Could she still be there somehow? But ghosts were supposed to be troubled spirits, the souls of those who'd died violently or unnaturally, unresolved beings who had not made their peace with the world, and Blanche Morrell had died peacefully, hadn't she? Hazel frowned. What nonsense was this? The only form in which the old girl survived was here, in her garden. Her spirit was expressed in the rebirth of the bulbs and flowers she had planted. People lived on through their work and thought, not as disembodied entities floating around, interfering with the lives of the living. She mustn't let herself get spooked.

Resolutely, she turned her steps indoors. She found Matthew standing at the foot of the stairs, absorbed in reading a sheaf of closely printed papers. His face was drawn in a troubled frown. He started when he heard her.

"Bad news?" she asked.

"What? No, it's nothing. Nothing at all."

He shuffled upstairs, still reading. She called after him to ask if he'd like a drink, but he merely grunted, and a moment later she heard his study door close with a slow, thoughtful *click*.

He came down a good while later, well after she'd fed Ben and put him to bed. He made a transparent effort to snap out of his self-absorption and began preparing steak and salad for themselves with a levity that didn't deceive her. In moments of silence, a deep frown would close over his face, and when she spoke he'd look up quickly, nervously, as if caught thinking forbidden thoughts. After supper, remembering the early start the next morning, they went to bed. They made love, but she could sense his mind was only partly with her. Then he turned over and within a few minutes he was fast asleep.

She lay wide awake, staring out through the half-open curtains at the starry night sky. She thought of taking a Valium, but decided it would make her feel worse in the morning. The thought of drugs brought back images of Matthew in his swivel chair, his eyes rolled back into his head, his breathing shallow and faltering, and that dangerous yellowish liquid fizzing across the desk....

Eventually, she rose and went to the bathroom for a glass of water. The water from the tap tasted stale, so she slipped downstairs to the kitchen for a Perrier. Then slowly, reluctant to return to her sleepless bed, she retraced her steps upstairs.

On the landing she hesitated. Ahead lay Matthew's study, the door ajar. She honed her ears. A heating pipe gurgled, a stair board eased itself, the wind curled softly around the roof. Otherwise all was silent. Quickly, decisively, she let herself into the study, closed the door and switched on the desk lamp.

Before her, stacked neatly in the center of the desk, lay the sheaf of papers that had arrived by courier that afternoon. On top was a cover letter, written on paper headed, FROM THE DESK OF THE SENIOR LIBRARIAN, THE UNIVERSITY OF ILLINOIS, CHAMPAIGN-URBANA. She skimmed it quickly.

Dear Dr. Cavewood,

My sincere apologies for the delay in replying to your letter, but I'm afraid that the majority of the broadsheets and pamphlets we carry from the period in question are not as yet fully indexed and cross-referenced.

However, I believe I have tracked down a collection of papers bearing directly on your research. I enclose photocopies of the most relevant. Please feel free to consult the originals here at the library, or else I can arrange for microfilm to be sent to Charlottesville.

The most revealing documents, in my view, are the Ordinary of Newgate's *Accounts of the Behavior, Confessions and Last Dying Speeches of the Prisoners Executed at Tyburn.* The specifically relevant account is that dated 3rd May 1681 and refers to the hanging of one Isabel Hardiment, aged 21, condemned to death for murder...

Murder?

Slowly, filled with foreboding, Hazel drew up the chair and settled down to read.

A gruesome picture of crime and punishment in seventeenth-century England revealed itself through these papers.

The whole process of justice, from crime to final punishment, exerted a macabre fascination over the imagination of the day. The public, she learned, streamed through Newgate prison to peer at the chained prisoners in the condemned hold. Crowds joined the hanging procession as the cart of felons wended its way to Tyburn. There, throngs of spectators scrambled for a place at the "triple tree" to watch a show as elaborately staged as any entertainment that might be witnessed at Drury Lane or Bartholemew Fair. The gallows, sited conspicuously at a main crossroads in the center of London, inspired a calculated blend of horror, fear and dread.

With a mixture of horror and fascination, Hazel read of the meticulous ritual and ceremony surrounding these public hangings. On an execution day, the crowds would arrive early. They'd jostle for a view; the fortunate found a seat in the wooden stands erected around the scaffold, others paid to stand in the carts of tradesmen with the wit to exploit the opportunity. As the tumbril arrived, one figure, all in black, stood out among the wretched prisoners. This was the chaplain of Newgate Gaol, known as the Ordinary, offering final prayers, extracting last-minute confessions and reconciling the condemned souls to their fate. The hangings were frequently held up while the Ordinary talked some particularly obstinate victim into making a last-minute confession—often to the impatience of the rabble who wanted to see the execution despatched. The prisoner might make a final speech, and this sometimes would even move the crowd to tears.

Finally, however, the Executioner stepped forward and roped up the condemned and, after any final pleadings, the Ordinary consigned their souls to the Almighty. Then, with a crack of the whip, the horses drew away the cart, leaving a row of kicking, squirming bodies dangling by their necks. Some might have relatives who had bribed the captain of the guard to cut down the body as soon as the signs of life had expired and let them take it away for a decent burial. Some even had a physician on hand, and it was not unknown for a corpse to be revived and live on, disgraced but free. Those without relatives or means could well be left for hours before being brought unceremoniously to a pauper's grave.

All along, the Ordinary would be keeping a record, and within a couple of days he would bring out his official account of the malefactors' crimes, confessions and conduct in their final hours, which rolled off the presses in their thousands to be snapped up by an avid, sensation-thirsty public.

Hazel came to the final document. It was a thin, stapled photocopy, printed in a jumble of different typefaces and the lettering of the period. She felt her pulse quickening as she read the majestic rubric.

It was nothing less than the account documenting the crime and fate of Isabel Hardiment.

A True
ACCOUNT
Of The
Behaviour, Confession
And
EXECUTION
Of
ISABEL HARDIMENT
For Murder
Who Received Sentence of Death on the 25th April last at
JUSTICE HALL in the OLD-BAYLY, and was Executed at
TYBURN
On <u>Friday</u> the <u>3rd</u> of this May 1681.

The preamble thundered:

"Still it appears, notwithstanding the many precendent Examples Justice has made of Offenders, that divers are so besotted or deluded by wiles and Temptations that regardless of their Safety, Lives or Reputations they will rashly run themselves to Ruin and Disgrace, neither fear of Shame nor Severity being of force sufficient to keep them within the Bounds of Honesty and God-fearing Behaviour ..."

Then, with barely a break, the text launched into details of the crime:

"This Isabel Hardiment, a young woman of good Birth and most Righteous Parentage, had upon this 15th April last been Apprehended, Indicted, Tryed, and found Guilty, for the Murder in London city of Mary Shawcrosse, wife of Nathaniel, Fellow of Sanctus Spiritus College in the city of Oxford ..."

Mary, his *wife?*

Hazel felt an icy shiver run down her spine. With mounting dread, she read on.

The story gradually unfolded.

Nathaniel Shawcrosse made frequent trips to London to attend meetings at the Royal Society. This, however, was a special occasion—a celebration to mark the thirtieth anniversary of the founding of the Society—and his wife Mary accompanied him on the fifty-mile journey by coach and horse to the capital. Largely through the favor of the king, Charles II, the Society had risen from the original "Invisible College," a semiclandestine, peripatetic Oxford group, to a national institute with the full status of a royal charter. The founding Fellows had now been summoned to court to receive various honors and other tokens of the king's favor.

The presentation ceremony took place in the late afternoon of April 10. A furious storm had raged over London all day, and by the time the palace footmen were ushering forward the carriages to collect the departing Fellows and their ladies, the sky was as dark as night, and in the furious squall the torches of pitch illuminating the palace courtyard could barely be kept alight. Nathaniel and Mary Shawcrosse were waiting their turn in the vestibule. A grand dinner had been arranged at a private town mansion afterward, and the mood among his colleagues was high and boisterous. One carriage after another rolled under the shelter of the cloister and collected its charges. Finally, summoned by the majordomo, Nathaniel Shawcrosse led his wife by the arm into the open. A footman opened the carriage door. Another folded down the steps. A third helped her up the steps and into the dark, plush interior.

Suddenly the dark came alive. Nathaniel caught the fleeting movement. He saw the lithe figure spring suddenly out of the shadows. He caught the swift flash of the blade. Then he heard the scream. Mary turned, clutching her stomach, her eyes wide with horror, the scream strangling in her throat, then slowly her legs folded beneath her and she crumpled to the carriage floor.

But already the assailant—a young boyish figure in a black coat, his face concealed beneath a broad-brimmed hat—was up and away. He wrenched the far door open and sprang to the ground. The knife fell clattering on the cobbles. Before the guards could challenge him or give chase, he had darted through the cloisters and, weaving in and out of the carriages lumbering down the drive, fled through the palace gates, to disappear into the storm-swept streets of the city.

A hue and cry was raised. The culprit was discovered, demented and hysterical, taking refuge in an inn. As the constables laid hands on him, his hat flew off, revealing long blond hair. This was no man at all but a young woman! Isabel Hardiment, the daughter of the dean of

Nathaniel Shawcrosse's college, Sanctus Spiritus, in the city of Oxford.

Raving, deranged, the girl confessed to her crime, even boasted of it. Under interrogation, a tragic tale of passion and jealousy emerged and, with it, the motive for the murder.

Isabel Hardiment had been consumed with lustful desire for her tutor and mentor, Nathaniel Shawcrosse. She loved him with a "celestial passion." They were two souls destined for one another, partners in a bond forged in another world. In natural law, she, not Mary, was his rightful wife. She had worked with him on his discoveries, too. They were a joint achievement. Having shared the work, did she not have the right to share the recognition? It was intolerable that his wife, who'd had no part in it, should now stand at his side and receive the king's favor. This was the last straw, and it drove Isabel to her final act of desperation.

She was tried, convicted and condemned to hang.

She spent the week before her execution in Newgate jail. There, as the account testified, "she Utterly Refused to receive Instructions from Mr Ordinary how she might be Fitted for her Death," and she remained "Obstinate and Unrepentant to the end." She refused to attend chapel or follow the Ordinary in his prayers for her, conduct which by itself put her beyond hope of a royal pardon. She seemed unmoved by the heinousness of her offense and the consequent ignominy and humiliation of a public death upon herself and her family, and this provoked the Ordinary in his account to a long and angry diatribe upon the "Wickedness of Women and the Dangers of Lustful Passions."

On the day of her execution, she was taken to Tyburn in the cart along with two other malefactors due to hang, one for coin clipping, the other for robbery. At the appointed hour, the cart began on its slow procession. It wound its way past St. Sepulchre's church, whose great bell tolled the prisoners' doom, through St. Giles where the condemned received a customary free bowl of ale, along Holborn Hill and finally to the tree at Tyburn, gruesomely dubbed the "deadly evergreen" for it bore its ugly fruit all year round.

At her final moment, Isabel addressed the crowd with great calm and composure, saying she admitted to the murder but in no way repented of it, believing she had committed no sin in the eyes of God. She had made her peace with the Almighty, her heart was "weaned from this World of Illusion and placed upon the True Heaven" and her eyes were fixed upon "the World Beyond, where I may hope, trusting in the Infinite Necessity of Being, that I shall be reunited with the One of whom I am the other Part, as the face on a Coin is to its Reverse, with him who has gone before to await me ... to which realm I therefore go without Sorrow or Remorse but with a heart filled with great Gladness." The Ordinary, hearing dangerous heresy in this obdurate young woman's words, abandoned the attempt to extract a repentance and, consigning her soul to God's mercy, turned to the Executioner and commanded him to make haste his work.

Hazel spent the night in a torment of unease. There was a murderess in the house. A wife poisoner. A girl with blond hair who went about her deadly business disguised as a boy dressed all in black. (My God, wasn't that just how Matthew had described the visitation at the labs?) Her own thoughts echoed around inside her head: "*Ghosts are troubled spirits, the souls of those who have died violently or unnaturally....*" And in counterpoint to it all ran the constant, insidious whisper of the name: "*Isabel Hardiment, Isabel Hardiment, Executed for Murder.*"

Dawn was already breaking when she fell into a fitful sleep, and she woke tired in mind and body. Over a snatched breakfast, she tried to prize out of Matthew a clue to his own reaction. She couldn't admit she'd been snooping, and she didn't want to raise the issue anyway, least of all now, but somehow she needed reassurance. In all he'd said about Isabel, he'd never given the least hint she might be evil.

"What are you up to today?" she asked as she stacked the cereal bowls in the dishwasher. "Working on that stuff that came yesterday? Was it useful?"

"So-so," he shrugged.

"I thought it must be really hot news. You seemed pretty preoccupied all evening."

He looked at her sharply.

"Why do you ask?"

"Darling, why do I ask anything? Because I know it's all you think about."

"Well, I guess it fills in a few gaps."

He wasn't to be drawn, and she left it there. From his manner she could tell the revelations had affected him more than he dared show. And that in itself disturbed her more than she dared admit.

On the drive back to Washington, they hit the traffic and she was late delivering Ben to school. She arrived at the apartment with her nerves frazzled. She took the phone off the hook and sat down with a cup of coffee to try and work out just where things were going wrong.

She was falling into the trap of believing in Isabel. They did not have a murderess in the house. The wife poisoner was dead and buried centuries ago. And yet this creature from the long-dead past was somehow influencing their lives as actively as if she was living and breathing now.

There was only one solution. She had to kill Isabel off. And kill her off in the place where she had been born—in Matthew's mind.

First, she needed to understand his condition properly, and for the next few days, she combed the libraries for everything she could find on mental disorders. The closest diagnosis seemed to be schizophrenia, yet that was really a catch-all category for a host of ill-defined conditions, and no one appeared to understand its cause any more than offer a cure. The neurologists she read said it was to do with enlarged ventricles in the brain, the psychoanalysts to do with infantile psychological trauma, and there was an entire spectrum of views in between.

The one clear conclusion, though, was that Matthew was suffering from a serious delusional disorder. He didn't need scans to test for anomalies in brain structure or sessions with a shrink to relive his birthing trauma. It was simpler than that. He'd created the delusion himself. Isabel was his invention. He had thought her up. In principle, therefore, all he needed to do was to *un*think her.

How in hell's name could she get him to do that?

The wedding was now just ten days away. As a gesture of respect to an ideal of virginal innocence, they'd agreed they would not see each other from now until the day itself, when she would arrive at the house for the ceremony. The very thought of marriage filled her with increasing unease. She couldn't go through with it until she had found a way of removing the shadow of Isabel from their lives. She had to rid Matthew's mind of the fiction. The stakes all around, she sensed, had risen, too. It was more than a question of his sanity now; it could even be a matter of her and Ben's physical safety.

It was a call from Pauline suggesting lunch that gave her the idea. As she drove to the small restaurant in Georgetown where they'd arranged to meet, a plan crystallized in her mind. Pauline was the perfect person to help. She knew every model in town, and many had passed through drama college and were now professional actresses. It was a long shot, and catastrophic if it backfired, but it was all she could think of. And possibly, just possibly, it might work.

ELEVEN

Matthew dressed slowly and with care: starched shirt, wing collar, cravat with pearl pin, gold cuff links. And his grandfather's old black morning coat and pin-striped trousers, altered by a tailor to fit his taller frame. The others would be in suits, some probably in casual dress, but this was the first—and the last—time he was going to do this and he felt it merited formality.

He glanced at his watch. The guests would start arriving any minute. He closed the bedroom door with finality. Crossing the landing, he glanced into the room in which they would be spending that night and the rest of those to come. Sunlight streamed in through the large three-section window, glinting off the intricate brasswork of the bedstead and making a dazzling snowfield of the white lace bedspread. White lilies filled the room with a cool fragrance, in chaste contrast to the bowl of deep red roses beside the bed. Tucked into the coverlet was a card on which he'd written out a short sixteenth-century love poem. He knew no fitter words to profess his love.

Downstairs, everything was bustle. The caterers had taken over the kitchen and hall, and the florists were making last-minute adjustments to the flower arrangements. He sauntered through the hubbub and let himself out by the French doors into the large open-sided marquee in the backyard. Helpers were setting out chairs in rows on the sprung floor they'd laid—Hazel had organized a surprise "entertainment" for afterward, which was to include dancing—while at the far end the young pastor was busy transforming a trestle table into a small altar with its richly embroidered cloth and ornate silver cross. Lyall broke away from a group of students he'd co-opted into overseeing the parking and came forward, perspiring heavily, his pouchy, flattened face wreathed in smiles. He grasped Matthew's hand and pumped it vigorously.

"Well, this is it," said Lyall cheerfully. "Time to tie the knot."

"Or the noose," smiled Matthew. "Any news from the hotel?" Hazel had taken a room at the Silver Thatch, a nearby country hotel, to change and get ready.

"She'll show up, don't fret. You could do with a drink." He beckoned a waiter, but Matthew declined. "Relax, old chap. It's everybody's first time once. Gets easier with practice. Myra's my second. Number three will be a piece of cake."

"I'm going into this for keeps, Lyall. Try and remember that when it's time to give your speech."

"It'll be nothing but the raw, untarnished truth. The inside story on your young and headstrong Oxford days."

"I didn't realize you'd been taking notes, Lyall."

"I've always kept an eye on you, Matthew."

Matthew checked himself. He hadn't had it out with Lyall yet about the snooping and the hacking, but this wasn't the moment to broach it. Anyway, the time for paranoia was over.

Lyall was looking quizzically at him

"Something bothering you?" he asked.

"This speech of yours," Matthew bluffed. "Don't I get editorial approval?"

Lyall shook his head and chuckled. "Don't I get a fee?"

At that moment the doorbell rang and, exchanging a careful smile with his best man, Matthew returned indoors.

He found a throng of people all arriving at once. First came Norma and Herb from next door, laden with an extravagantly wrapped present. Then Pauline, wearing a figure-hugging pink dress, together with other friends of Hazel's from Washington. Beyond, just turning into the drive, he glimpsed a black limousine with tinted windows. It pulled up to one side. No one got out. Matthew hesitated, feeling a flicker of unease, then checked himself. What was he expecting, on this of all days—Isabel?

Before he could see who it was, Hazel's mother came forward onto the porch. She clasped him in a bony embrace and in a trembling voice said how happy Hazel's father would have been if he'd lived to see this day. Behind her followed Hazel's eldest sister, with Ben in tow. Ben shook hands with him and said his penguin suit was really cool.

He was swept deeper into the house as yet more guests swelled the hallway. There were colleagues and pupils from UVA, old friends from Chicago, neighbors and friends from the local area. The clamor grew deafening, the table steadily piled with presents. Matthew glanced at his watch. Five minutes to go. More people arrived, and still more. He could hardly imagine they'd invited so many. At last his own parents arrived. He'd fixed them up on a flight to arrive mid-morning and sent a car to meet them at the airport, but the plane had been delayed. As he hurried forward, he noted with alarm that his father was walking more stiffly, and when he greeted them he realized his mother wasn't catching all he said. He felt a flush of self-anger. Here again, his obsession with the book had led him to neglect those he loved and felt responsible for. Well, all that was going to change. When he got back from honeymoon, he'd fly to see them in Maine, with Hazel and Ben. It was time Mom and Dad got to know their new family properly.

Just then a shout from the house made him turn. Hazel was arriving! He hastened through to the marquee and, weaving his way through the crush of guests shuffling into their seats, took up his position next to Lyall at the front. Gradually the chatter dwindled until a hush fell over the gathering. A small organ broke into a processional anthem and the gathering rose as one. He threw a glance over his shoulder.

There she came, a solitary figure walking slowly, unfalteringly, her eyes fixed steadily upon his. She wore a long, pale silk dress, high to the neck, with a headband of white flowers. She looked so beautiful he was left breathless.

She took her place across the aisle. The young pastor stepped forward. He looked at each, and smiled.

"Dearly beloved ..." he began.

After the ceremony came the speeches.

Being used to addressing audiences just as large and a good deal less attentive, Lyall delivered his speech without notes or microphone. He was succinct, witty and polished, flattering the bride and teasing the groom. In reminiscing about their Oxford times and alluding to Matthew's present work, he never gave the slightest hint of the bizarre skew his life had recently taken on.

Matthew began at last to relax. The deed had been done, the knot tied and blessed, and it had all gone off without incident. During the past nights, his sleep had been plagued by horrific anxiety dreams. Once he'd dreamt that the marquee caught fire, scattering the screaming crowd, and a ball of flame latched itself onto Hazel. Another time, he'd imagined a violent tornado struck the tent aloft and tore through the gathering at the very moment they uttered their vows, plucking people off their feet and sucking them high into the air. He would wake up drenched in terror, certain that some dire presence was stalking his steps and was awaiting its moment to strike. But now the danger was over and his fears had proved unfounded.

Prolonged laughter and applause signaled the end of Lyall's speech. It was now his own turn. Casting all other thoughts out of his mind, Matthew stepped forward and began his list of thanks.

Then followed the reception party. Hazel glided through the crush, smiling, laughing, radiating happiness. Matthew would join her for a moment, then veer off to speak to other guests, glancing back every few moments to catch glimpses of her. His hand ached with the congratulations pressed upon him. Yes, he was darn lucky. At one point he glimpsed Hazel speaking intently to Pauline with an anxious expression on her face, but by the time he'd made his way over, she'd moved on and he found Pauline exchanging racy badinage with Lyall.

He spotted Hazel by the dais at the back of the marquee, signaling to someone in the wings. Casting him a mischievous smile, she stepped onto the dais and clapped her hands. Voices hissed "sssh," and within seconds complete silence had fallen.

"We've arranged a small entertainment for you today," she announced in a bright, clear voice. "Friends, ladies and gentlemen, please welcome two stars from the University of Virginia Shakespeare Players. They're going to give us three short scenes which I hope you'll find appropriate to the occasion."

An actor in doublet and hose sprang onto the dais and bowed with a flourish, followed by a girl with cascading blond hair and wearing a high-waisted period dress, who gave a demure curtsey. A burst of applause broke out. Music, added Hazel, was being provided by the UVA Minstrels, on original instruments. At this, a group of three youths in medieval outfits with viols and sackbuts appeared briefly on the dais, then withdrew to the side and struck up a lovelorn melody.

Hazel returned to Matthew's side just as Romeo's great love speech from the balcony scene began: "But, soft! what light through yonder window breaks?"

Matthew glanced around at their guests, standing silent and entranced beneath the spell. He squeezed Hazel's hand. "You brilliant devil," he whispered.

There was a ripple of applause as the piece came to an end and the young lovers parted. The actors assumed a different stance: Romeo was now Petruchio in *The Taming of the Shrew,* having a flaming domestic fight with Katharina. The scene brought a chorus of approbation from the women in the gathering. Finally the actress stepped forward and announced that, as a sop to the chauvinists in the audience—

"Specially for you," whispered Hazel to Matthew.

—she would like to give them Katharina's final speech when she is subdued beneath her lord and master's thumb. Groans from the ladies in the audience and cheers from their menfolk.

> *Fie, fie! unknit that threatening unkind brow,*
> *And dart not scornful glances from those eyes*
> *To wound thy lord, thy king, thy governor ...*

The speech rose to its climax, and an outburst of applause marked the end of the performance. With a quick bow the actors left the stage to mingle among the audience, while the minstrels suddenly acquired violins and struck up a wild hillbilly tune. Waiters appeared from all corners to replenish glasses and hand around canapes, and the chatter and laughter rose to a deafening pitch. Hazel introduced the actors to Matthew, who thanked and congratulated them warmly. They chatted for a moment, then took their leave, and Matthew found himself alone in a small clearing. He cast around to check everyone was enjoying themselves and to see whether anyone was stranded or ...

Isabel!

... needed to be rescued ...

He whipped back. Jesus holy Christ!

It was Isabel! In person!

Impossible! He cast around him wildly. People had their backs turned.

No one was paying any special attention. They didn't seem to notice. Maybe they took her for one of the players ...

But there she was, standing right before him, across the clearing, no more than six feet away, looking exactly as she had when she'd first appeared in the doorway of his rooms that long-ago night in Oxford. She had walked straight out of her portrait, true in every detail. Pale silver-gold hair, piled high and falling in ringlets around her oval face, scarlet red lips, the telltale beauty spot on her upper lip, her dress that same exquisite ball gown: cream silk, cut high and square, tightly corsetted at the waist, the sleeves ruched, the skirt flounced and trimmed with lace ...

Hazel had seen her, too. She turned slowly and looked directly at him. For a moment the three of them made a triangle, with empty floor space between. Time froze. His mind was paralyzed.

"Isabel?" he choked in a whisper. He turned to Hazel.

But Hazel stood like a statue, watching him intently, saying nothing.

Then the girl, the phantasm, this creature of flesh or figment of fantasy, *moved!* She took one step forward. Slowly, with a kind of austere dignity, she held out a hand. He found his own reaching out to hers. Their hands remained just apart, untouching.

"Nathaniel," she said slowly in that strange archaic accent he recalled so well. "Nathaniel, I have come to say good-bye."

Matthew was robbed of words. Hazel hadn't moved a muscle. She was observing it all with a close, penetrating scrutiny. What was she thinking?

Isabel smiled. A small, sad smile, that flickered at the corners of her mouth.

"I have come to wish you well," she said gravely. "To wish you both happiness in your life together as husband and wife." She turned to Hazel. "I give up all claim over this man. Take him. Love him. Cherish him. He is yours." She reached further toward Matthew until their fingers were an inch apart. "I am going now. You will never see me again. I am leaving your life for ever. Farewell, Nathaniel. Farewell and adieu."

Briefly, for an instant, their fingers touched. A violent jolt shot through him and he lurched backward. Hazel ran forward to catch him. He staggered, clutched at her for support, slipped and fell. His last conscious image was the slender figure of Isabel disappearing through the parting throng, before the people, the faces, the marquee, everything began to swim before his eyes until all was blotted out in a fine white mist and gradually dissolved into nothingness.

* * *

Matthew drove the old Mercedes slowly through the dark, winding country roads. Thick prowling clouds masked the moon, and large drops of rain had begun to fall, smearing the windshield. He glanced across at Hazel stretched back in the seat beside him. She wore a drowsy, contented smile. They'd had a wonderful meal at a large country club up in the hills. They'd talked about everything, they'd laughed and gossiped about the guests, reminisced about the entertainment and amused each other with little anecdotes. He had only once mentioned the scene with Isabel, and then Hazel had just made some teasing remark about his passing out from drink. He'd barely had a glass.

He'd come round from the faint to find a crowd of guests pressing around him. Hazel was kneeling beside him, helping him to a glass of water, while Lyall stood urging people back to give him air. He'd struggled to his feet and called to the minstrels to strike up again and let the party continue. He'd passed the incident off as lightly as he could, but the shock left him feeling dazed and disorientated. It was only when Hazel slipped away to change into a dress for dinner that he suddenly came properly alive again. He still felt dizzy, but this time with a giddy sense of liberation. He felt like a prisoner casting off his fetters and standing up at last a free man. For the rest of the evening he deliberately tried not to think about what had happened but merely enjoy the heady sense of release.

Yet how could he let something so extraordinary pass quite so unresolved? He glanced again across at Hazel, wondering whether he should risk spoiling the evening by raising the old familiar specter. But she had been there, at the scene. She'd seen and heard everything. She was smart. How did *she* figure it?

"Angel," he began cautiously, "I don't want to dwell on it, but ... well, about what happened .... Did you ...?"

She half-opened an eye.

"I don't know any more than you do, Matthew."

"But you were right there. You saw it. I mean, you saw *her.*"

"Matthew, give it up."

"You believe me now, don't you? You see I wasn't inventing her." He frowned. "God, I wish I *understood.*"

She reached for his hand.

"Don't think about it any more, darling," she said quietly. "I don't know. I don't need to know. She's gone; that's all that matters. Gone for good. Understand what she said. We're free of her, Matthew."

He breathed a long, deep sigh. He could feel the great slab that had been oppressing him all these months lifting off him. He bent across to take her hand and kiss it.

"Thank God for you, Hazel," he murmured.

"Just concentrate on getting us home," she smiled.

She reclined her seat and closed her eyes. In the headlights of the oncoming cars, she looked so beautiful, so desirable. He drove faster, impatient to get home. By now the caterers would have cleared everything away and they'd be alone at last to enjoy their first night together in their new and sacred bedroom. He bit his lip. That room: that would be the test. He eased his foot off the pedal. Maybe he didn't want to arrive quite so soon.

Yet the very moment he opened the front door, he sensed something was different. Something about the atmosphere had changed. In a way it never quite had been, it seemed somehow benign. He led Hazel upstairs to the bedroom, and by the warm yellow light of the candelabra on the dressing table, slowly and silently he began undressing her. She slipped on a silk robe and slid away into the bathroom, leaving him briefly alone. He looked over toward the window. This was the moment for the test.

He stepped across to the spot just beneath the window sash. His shirt was open to the waist and loose at the cuffs, but he felt no chill on his bare skin, no hint of a draft, not even the slightest frisson.

He looked up to see Hazel standing in the doorway of the bathroom. Their eyes met. An infinity of understanding seemed to flow between them in that gaze. Slowly she crossed the room toward him and entered that same small space. She smiled into his eyes and, folding her arms about him, she gradually steered their steps toward the bed.

Morning. Peace. Spring sunshine flooded into the bedroom. Birds chattered outside. A distant church bell pealed. The occasional car purred past, going down to the mall for the Sunday papers, maybe, or off for a day's fishing. Hazel asleep in the crook in his arm. Serene. So wonderful, so beautiful. And the trace of a satisfied smile on her lips.

Matthew closed his eyes. He was home. Home from a long and dangerous voyage, weary but triumphant. This was all he had wanted and all he would ever want.

Toward the end of the morning, he went round closing up the house. He watered the plants, threw out the perishables from the fridge and left a note for the domestic help and a check for the contractors due in later to take down the marquee. The utility room sink was still awash with bottles of champagne in half-melted ice.

He took a bottle and two glasses on a tray upstairs to Hazel, still lazing in bed after a long night of love. As he reached the top of the stairs, he heard her speaking on the phone. Pausing outside the room to arrange the tray, he caught a snatch of the conversation. She was talking in a half whisper.

"Utterly, utterly brilliant," she was saying. "Worked like a dream. And the dress, my God!" She whistled softly. "A real knock-out, huh?"

She looked up sharply as he entered. Blushing fleetingly, with her voice raised to normal pitch, she brought the conversation abruptly to an end and put the phone down.

"Who was that?" he queried mildly as he undid the foil on the bottle.

She lay back among the lace pillows and stretched luxuriantly.

"Pauline," she yawned. "We were talking about the costumes. Didn't you think they were stunning?"

"I didn't know Pauline had a hand in that."

"She didn't. I was just saying."

"Saying?" He repeated, confused.

"Saying how great it all was. For God's sake, Matthew, tell your brain to go back to sleep." She arched an eyebrow at him. "If we're going to survive the vacation, may I suggest you leave your head behind?"

"And just bring the essential equipment?" he smiled.

As he handed her a glass, she reached up and planted a kiss lightly on his lips.

"Essential—you said it," she shivered.

"C'mon, or we'll be late for lunch," he said, pulling away. "Aren't you hungry?"

"Ravenous," she replied huskily and, hooking her hand around his neck, drew him firmly and irrevocably down onto the bed and into her warm, wanting embrace.

Josie turned up the tape cassette and opened the car window an inch. A fierce draft swept her face, misting her skin with fine rain. She lowered the window further and drew in deep breaths of the cold night air to clear her head. Outside, it was pitch dark, and the wipers beat a counterpoint to the rhythm of the music. The Beach Boys—a tape she'd brought for Dad, to help him unwind.

It had been a hell of a day. She'd got up at dawn to finish writing up a chemistry experiment, but she'd been too late leaving campus and missed her flight to Washington. The political convention was holding its reception dinner at a country club near Lynchburg, on the far side of the state beyond Charlottesville. She'd planned to drive to Hanover Park and ride out with her father, but as it was she'd had to drive direct and meet him at the venue. The reception had dragged on, with the usual interminable speeches, introductions and handshaking, then came the dinner with more drinks, more speeches.... She'd left her father behind, facing a night of meetings with aides and managers. It really was time he retired from it all. She'd only come for his sake, to be at his side, and there was a limit to her own tolerance, too.

She reached forward to the glove compartment on the passenger side. The music was wrong; she needed something hotter, something heavier.

The lock on the compartment lid was sticking, and she leaned further over to fiddle with the catch, steering the car with her left hand. She began wrestling with it, and for a moment she took her eyes off the road. Finally the lid flipped opened, and she glanced back up.

Suddenly, a figure ahead!

There, in the middle of the road, caught in her headlights and looming up at terrifying speed, stood a figure in white, the figure of a young woman of about her own age with blonde hair piled high and falling in ringlets about a pale, oval face, and wearing some kind of old-fashioned ball dress, it seemed, cut high and square at the chest.... She stood directly in the road, yet she just stared at her, stared through her, without faltering or flinching....

Josie gripped the wheel and, bracing herself, swerved to the left. But too late—she was suddenly upon her. Yet the girl made no attempt to step back, she merely stood there, frozen, watching, almost waiting. Then came the moment of collision. A flash of white glancing off the hood, whipping past the windshield, sucked in the instant into the dark behind. But no sound of impact, no thud or jerk or shattering of glass. The car seemed to pass through her, as though she were somehow insubstantial, like a skein of low-lying mist.

Josie whipped the wheel straight to correct her swerve, but she oversteered. The car turned nose-in to the side and the back swung around violently, skidding on the wet road. Briefly she managed to regain control and prevent the car flipping into a spin.

Except the bend was tightening.

Suddenly, ahead, right on the bend and in the middle of her lane, stood a vast truck, stationary, its hazard lights flashing. She hit the brakes and swerved hard. She missed the truck, but the car now went out of control. It shot across the road, its tires howling, and ricocheted off the central crash barrier. Propelled by its own momentum, it skated broadsides across the span of the road, then spun a half-turn and left the road tail-first down a shallow incline, flipping hood over trunk and landing upside down on its roof with its windshield shattered and the front end crumpled into a tree. She heard her own scream die away into the distance as a thick wave of blackness engulfed her.

She came around moments later to find herself lying upside-down, jammed against the wheel. Frantically she wriggled free and wrenched at the door. It wouldn't move. Seized with panic, she kicked and hammered at the lock. Suddenly the door broke open. She scrambled out and fell headlong onto the wet grass.

Dizzy, crazed, she fought her way up the bank in the pounding rain. She reached the road. A car flashed past in a squall of spray, its horn blaring away into the distance. Ahead she could see the flashing hazard lights of the stranded truck. She blundered forward, gasping, sobbing. Another car whipped past, narrowly missing her. She tripped and fell, grazing her hands and face on the gritty road surface, but she struggled to her feet and stumbled forward again.

She could see the truck driver sitting in his cab, his light on. Finally, she reached the truck, but the cab was high above her and the door on the near side lay out of her reach. She called out, but the man didn't hear her. She stepped around in front of the truck. Suddenly dazzled by the headlights, she threw up her hand to shield her eyes. The driver saw her now. She glimpsed him opening his door, she heard him yell out.

Just as she stumbled round into the road, blinded and disorientated, a car sped round the bend. She was way out in the open. She saw the headlights. She watched what followed take place with an appallingly slow inevitability. She saw the lights now bearing down upon her. She heard the horn screeching in her ears, the tires howling and shrieking. And then came the impact. Black turning to violet turning to blue turning to yellow turning to orange turning to red turning to white. Total whiteout.

White light, dissolving slowly. Something was coming through. Form, shapes, people, noise, bustle, the clang of emergency bells.

She saw it from above. She watched it unfold. She observed every step with detachment. She saw her own body lying stretched out on a trolley. The gurney was being rushed down a corridor. Paramedics and nurses ran alongside, some steering, others holding aloft drip bags. She saw a needle sink into her arm, but she didn't feel the prick. The gurney was being wheeled through plastic flap-doors into an operating room. The body was manhandled onto the operating table. It was as limp as a dead fish. From above, she saw the surgeons hastily robing up, snapping on gloves, calling out instructions. One looked up to reangle the overhead light, and she caught sight of his masked face, his eyes full of alarm and anxiety.

Why alarm, why anxiety? It's all okay. Nothing hurts. I'm not there. It's not my body any longer. I don't want it back. I want to stay out here, up above it all. I'm a balloon, a light, airy balloon, made of light. A thin silken thread attaches me to that body. Break the thread. Set me free.

Below, one surgeon was clamping two metal discs to the girl's chest. He shouted an order. Beside him, a nurse hit a button. The body jerked in a violent convulsion, then sank back.

Let me go! I don't want to come back.

The nurse adjusted a dial and hit the button again. The body almost shot off the table. Another nurse jabbed a needle into the flesh of the thigh. Instruments were being wheeled forward and attached to the mouth, nose, arms. And as the first nurse began daubing the girl's chest with an antiseptic swab, the surgeon flexed his fingers and reached for the bone shears.

From the sidelines, the presence watched. It watched, poised for the moment so long awaited.

The silken thread was retracting, towing the girl's soul back into her body. Any second now soul and body would be reunited.

Now! Quick!

The presence swooped. In through the open window of the body it flew, diving down, down into the dark red pumping cavern of its new fleshly cloak.

A thrill of triumph ran through every nerve of the new body. Peals of wild ecstatic laughter rocked every fiber of the new being.

She was there! She was there first!

Now, at long last, she could fulfill her destiny—her destiny of revenge.

TWELVE

Otis stood at the foot of the broad, columned porch. Shielding his eyes against the glare, he peered down the long gravel drive to the distant gateway through which the limousine would appear at any moment, bringing his daughter, Josie, home from hospital. At his side, nuzzling his hand, stood her aging gray lurcher. On his shoulders he could feel the warmth of the ripening summer sun, and his head swam faintly with the fragrance of the wisteria blossom that festooned the front of the old colonial mansion.

He felt strangely nervous. He wasn't sure how she would react—he wasn't even quite sure how he should behave himself. Ever since the accident there had been something profoundly odd about her. The strange things she'd been saying, the funny looks she gave, the familiar names that escaped her, the memories she seemed to have forgotten ...

Give it time, he told himself. Ten weeks is far too soon to tell.

In fact, it was a miracle she was alive at all. The surgeon at Martha Jefferson, the hospital where she'd been taken, said later that at first they'd genuinely feared they'd lost her. As she was being wheeled into the operating room she had undergone a massive coronary infarction and, for two critical minutes, she had—clinically speaking—died. Otis clenched his jaw against the pain of the memory. He'd been in the middle of a debriefing meeting when he'd received the call from the Nelson County police, and he'd rushed over to the hospital at once. All that night he'd stayed at her bedside. He would never forget the sight of the bloodless, bruised figure stretched out on the bed, her head swathed in bandages and tubes and wires feeding out of every part of her young body.

Her recovery had been remarkable. The sheer force of her willpower had astonished the doctors. She had been lucky, too. She could have suffered serious spinal injury, but all she'd broken was a collar bone and several ribs. Scans had showed minor skull fractures, but these were fast mending, and there was no evidence of damage to the brain itself. She'd undergone intensive physiotherapy—and here again, her drive to get well amazed the specialists—and she could now walk and move around unaided. Physically, she would be back to normal within a matter of months. Psychologically, however.... He fought down a gnawing anxiety. At least she was home now. Once in her familiar surroundings again, everything would fall back into place.

A flash of sunlight in the distance cut short his train of thought. The limousine was turning into the driveway. Instinctively he took a step forward. The dog beside him gave a yelp and keened its ears. The car grew rapidly closer until it reached the wide sweep of drive in front of the house and, with its tires scrunching in the deep gravel, finally pulled up. The driver climbed out, but Otis had already reached the rear door. He flung it open.

"Josie, Josie," he beamed, helping her out. "It's damn good to have you home."

She stood falteringly, holding his arm for support. Her face was desperately pale, the skin almost translucent. Screwing up her eyes against the bright sunlight, she looked slowly about her. Her gaze came to rest on the house, and her face took on a strange expression, partly puzzled and partly knowing.

"Home," she echoed in a murmur.

The lurcher was circling her, sniffing at her clothes. Its ears were flattened and a low growl rumbled ominously in its throat.

"Hey, cut that out!" Otis chided the dog. "That's no way to welcome your mistress home." He smiled at Josie. "He's gone senile, missing you."

But the dog's growl turned into a snarl. It took up a position between Josie and the front door, barring the way, its teeth bared and its spine bristling. Defiance and suspicion glowered in its yellow eyes. Josie stood frozen to the spot, her face white. Suddenly, snapping and snarling, the creature sprang forward and shuddered to a halt just inches away from her.

She shrank back with a cry of terror. Otis lunged forward. He grabbed the dog by the scruff of the neck and dealt it a furious blow across the muzzle, then flung it bodily across the drive, where it scrambled to its feet and, still eyeing Josie with savage hostility, slunk reluctantly away into the shrubbery.

"Let him try that again," he said between clenched teeth, "and I'll shoot the critter. You okay, Josie?"

"Sure. Fine."

He put his arm around the girl and steered her toward the house. She was shaking badly. Jesus, what a start to a homecoming. He forced a lighter tone into his voice.

"Now, let's see what you'd like to do. I guess you'll be needing a rest. Amy's got your room ready. She's put some of your books and other stuff from college in the spare room. I've fixed it up as a study. It's going to be great, having you here."

He squeezed her arm as he led her indoors. He'd seen her every day over these past weeks—far more than he ever did during semester time—but he'd missed having her home. Amy was an attractive, intelligent woman, a housekeeper who could double competently as a hostess, and there was always a cocktail or a dinner party or some other social event going on in the house, but when Josie was not there the evenings always felt somehow empty. Without her, the place felt more of a hotel than a home. She'd soon be well enough to resume her studies, and he'd had serious thoughts about having her transfer to a university closer by. But he wasn't going to raise the issue right now.

They reached the oval hallway, where she paused and looked about her. She ran her eye over the curved mahogany double doors that led off in each direction, over the checkered black-and-white marble floor beneath her feet and the elaborate Venetian chandelier above her head, over the gilt-framed family portraits that stretched along the walls and up the sweeping staircase to the upper floor. As she gazed about her, he studied her expression out of the corner of his eye. He chuckled to himself. Anyone would take her for a visitor seeing it all for the first time. Nothing here had changed in the past ten weeks. In fact, not a lot had changed in the past ten decades. That was the beauty of it. Here she could feel safe and secure among all the familiar memories of her childhood.

"Good to be back?" he asked.

A slow smile spread across her face and flickered in her gray-blue eyes.

As she turned, she briefly caught her own reflection in a pier glass, and paused. She touched her cheek with the tips of her fingers, feeling the substance of its flesh with a novel, intent curiosity. Something in her expression seemed to shift. The smile took on a sly twist, and behind the flicker in her eyes he fancied he could detect a glint of something almost like ... triumph.

She met his gaze levelly. The smile was frozen on her lips. And when she spoke, her voice sounded strangely unlike her own.

"Very," she replied slowly. "Very good to be back."

The issue came up a few days later, and it was Josie who raised it.

It was Friday, the day he reserved for working from home. He'd had a tough morning, first holding a conference call with colleagues on the Foreign Relations committee, then working on a difficult speech he was due to give to a group of lobbyists the following week. He'd finished the plate of sandwiches Amy had brought in to him on a tray and he longed dearly to break his resolve and light a cigar. The triple-sash window was open, and through it filtered the distant buzz of a motor, while on the soft breeze floated the green scent of freshly mowed grass.

His thought turned, as they did whenever he had pause to think, to Josie. The day was seductively fine; it cried out to be enjoyed. He'd give himself a break and take a stroll to look for her. Normally, he'd have taken the dog along for company, but since the ugly moment the other day he'd sent it off to the estate manager's house to be looked after. Josie had been badly shaken, and he wasn't going to risk upsetting her again. All the same, it was rather puzzling that such a faithful, devoted animal should react like that. Shaking off the thought, he rose from his desk and headed for the door. He knew where he'd find her.

He found her as he'd expected, sitting in the sun in the old stable courtyard, perched on a stone step with her back against a flaking stable wooden door. Beside her lay a small pile of notebooks she was reading. She was so engrossed that she only looked up when his shadow fell across her page. She gave a start and quickly closed her book, placing it face down on the pile. He caught sight of the front cover as she did so. It was her diary, from five years ago. Why was she reading her old diaries?

"Sorry if I startled you," he said. "May I sit with you?"

He lowered himself onto the step beside her and sat for a while sharing the silence. The sun cast a warm, drowsy spell over the courtyard. He looked idly about him. Across the cobbles stood another row of stables with a clapboard clock tower surmounted by an ornate weather vane, all now fallen into disuse. These buildings were, in fact, the oldest part of the house; their origins went back to the seventeenth century. Alice, his wife, used to come here sometimes when she wanted to be alone. Right up to her death she'd had the nurse wheel her out here. She said it had a very peaceful atmosphere—but then, she felt psychic about everything. Josie had never shown any interest in the place before, but ever since she'd come back from hospital she seemed to be drawn there. Maybe her mother had been right and the old stones did somehow give out "healing vibes." Who could tell?

To his surprise, Josie opened the conversation. She'd been so taciturn up till now, rarely initiating the dialogue and responding mostly in mono-syllables. But that morning she'd sought him out and told him, quite vol-untarily, that she wanted to quit Northeastern and transfer to the University of Virginia at Charlottesville. It was music to his ears, but of course it wasn't quite so easy. For one thing, she was insistent on starting right away. That very week, if possible.

"Dad?"

"What is it, sweetheart?"

She fixed him with a wide, open gaze. He gave an involuntary shiver. There was still something about the look in those eyes, something he'd noticed ever since the accident. He couldn't pinpoint it, but her look was somehow ... different. But then, you couldn't go through all she'd been through and expect to come out exactly the same. A person physically dies on the operating table and is brought back to life, and nothing changes? Impossible.

"Dad, I'm serious. I need you to set it up."

"You know what the doctors say," he replied gently. "You can't go back to college before the fall, at the earliest. Getting well takes time."

"But I *am* well!"

He swallowed. He didn't mean physically well. He'd been contemplat-ing calling in a psychiatrist, but he didn't want to have to explain to her why. Maybe the problem would go away with time—if it was a problem.

"It's too late to register now, anyway," he responded. "The summer semester has already begun."

"I have to get to UVA!"

"I know you want to, sweetheart. And I'd like to see you there, you know that. I'm all for having you closer to home." He took her by the hand. "Look, I'll call the dean of graduate studies and see if he can bend the rules and take you in with the fall admissions."

The university owed him one: Over the years he had made a number of substantial benefactions. He looked at her carefully. What could she do to keep herself occupied in the intervening months? Being incarcerated in Hanover Park couldn't be good for her, however interesting he tried to make things there for her. She had quite lost her appetite for social life, though. She had no interest in seeing her friends: When young Charlie Eastman came over she fled the house and took refuge in the woods. Maybe, when the doctors said she was up to it, she should consider taking a part-time job for the interim. Like the job in that crazy old shop in Fredericksburg she'd taken last summer and really loved. Yes, that was just the kind of thing she needed.

Carefully he dropped the suggestion. It was received with a puzzled frown.

"Which shop?" she queried. She reached involuntarily toward the pile of diaries as if in search of a prompt.

"The old apothecary's shop. In Fredericksburg. You remember."

"Ah." She stared sightlessly out across the courtyard through half-closed eyes. Slowly the frown lifted and her voice fell to a far-off whisper. "Yes. That's it. Of course."

Otis found himself chattering on, gladdened and relieved. She could start as soon as the doctors gave the okay. The chauffeur could drive her back and forth each day if she didn't feel up to driving herself. It would provide her with an interest, take her out of the house, give her the chance to meet people and make new friends. It was only after a few minutes that he realized she wasn't listening. He fell silent, and after a moment rose stiffly and, kissing her lightly on the head, left her.

As he reached the parterre that led through a tall yew hedge back into the front drive, he dug into his top jacket pocket for a good, fat cigar. Damn the Surgeon General and his warning. He knew chain-smokers who'd lived to one hundred and abstainers who'd died in their prime. What did doctors know about how the human body really worked, let alone the human mind? He bit off the end savagely and spat it out, then felt in his trouser pocket for the lighter. He stopped in his tracks. It must have fallen out when he was sitting down with Josie.

He retraced his steps. He found her once again absorbed in reading the diaries, only this time he noticed that it was the diary for the previous year, and from her place he guessed she was reading about her job that summer. Was she just reminding herself what had happened, or was she somehow—the crazy thought struck him—learning about it all afresh?

The figure moved silently through the darkness, her white nightgown luminous in the muted moonlight. She glided swiftly across the open lawn and, plunging into the thick shadows beneath a giant sweeping cedar, followed the border of the main lawn to the far limit where the formal flower beds ended and the shrubbery and undergrowth began. From time to time she paused and stooped to examine a plant, only to move away and resume her search further on.

Once at the shrubbery, she delved around her with quick birdlike movements, bending to pick a leaf here or a flower there. Eventually, growing alongside a rotten tree stump, among the fungi and the brambles, she found what she was looking for. Holding out her nightdress to form a lap, she snipped off the tiny, delicate heads until she had collected a small pile, then returned to the house.

She slipped indoors through the back entrance and felt her way along the unlit passage until she came to the kitchen. There she emptied her gleanings onto the large table in the center and reached into a cupboard for a pestle and mortar. Slowly and carefully she sprinkled the small blooms into the mortar, a handful at a time, and ground them to a soft pulp. Finally she drained off a quantity of pale greenish yellow liquid into a glass and put it on one side while she searched the cupboard for a packet of dog biscuits.

A minute later, she was carrying the bowl out to the shed by the back door where the dog used to eat and sleep, and laid it down on the straw. Then, satisfied, she returned upstairs to bed. Should the animal make its way back home, it would find a welcome of its own.

Amy, the housekeeper, putting on the coffee in the morning, stepped on one of the small blooms that had accidentally fallen onto the floor, and crushed it. Later, the maid sweeping the kitchen floor brushed up the remains along with the rest of the droppings. Neither chanced to see the delicate little flower intact or note its purple starlike petals and spikey yellow tongues, and even if they had they might well not have recognized it as *Atropa belladonna,* the deadly nightshade.

* * *

Otis stared out of the car window at the changing townscape. They had left behind the grand boulevards of the state capital and the towering glass and steel high rises of the downtown business district and were heading east out of town. As the street numbers rose, the buildings grew lower and the neighborhoods poorer. Town houses gave way to tenements, where lines of washing hung between iron fire escapes and groups of youths idling on the sidewalks eyed the limousine with unfeigned hostility. Before long all the shops were fortified with metal grilles and the walls sprayed with graffiti, while on empty demolition lots kids waged war among the car wrecks and the rubble.

Otis frowned with dismay. He'd seen enough of this kind of living in the shantytowns of the third world, but here in modern America? He checked the door lock. He'd be glad when the meeting was over and he could hit the Beltway and head back down to Richmond. This was like a descent into chaos, a brush with madness. He felt he didn't understand what was happening out there, that he didn't understand anything any more. Josie had set him all at sea with himself.

The meeting, a morale-boosting session with an influential local community leader and longtime supporter, dragged on interminably, and Otis found it hard to muster more than token enthusiasm. His mind was preoccupied with thoughts of Josie. She had been home for three weeks now, and while every day saw her grow physically stronger and healthier, her behavior was as strange as ever. Something he couldn't fathom was going on inside her head. He would find her sitting on the floor in her room, surrounded by the archives of her life—old family photographs, school reports, college yearbooks, newspaper cuttings, chemistry notebooks—checking and cross-checking as if to piece together a continuum that had somehow become broken. Other small incidents left him puzzled, too. She often used odd, inappropriate words, for instance. Once she referred to his cigar as made of "sot weed," the old word for tobacco. Another time, while mildly delirious with a fever, he heard her ask the doctor for "sassafras"; later he asked the doctor what this was and learned that it was a tree of the laurel family whose root was used in early colonial times as a drug to thin the blood. Was this core knowledge in graduate chemistry study? And then there were the things she seemed to have to relearn: using her personal computer, for instance, and even simple activities like dialing phone numbers.

But above all it was the look in her eyes. In some indefinable way she simply looked different. She would sit for long periods with a blank cloud masking her expression, and when she'd glance up and see him, he'd feel a strange, unnerving jolt. Those were Josie's gray-blue eyes, but was it really Josie behind them?

He reached Hanover Park shortly after lunch. Josie was not in the house, but the day was brilliantly fine and he guessed she'd be in her usual place in the old stable courtyard. He took the long way around, to give himself time to relax after the wearying drive. He strolled along the broad gravel path that ran along the rear of the mansion, then decided to make a brief detour to the greenhouses to see how the orchids were coming along.

As he entered the first greenhouse, he drew up sharp. Involuntarily his hand flew to his mouth. The heavy, humid air was fetid with the smell of putrefying flesh. Flies buzzed in thick clusters around a bundle of sacks that lay on the floor at the far end. Half choking, he stepped forward. As he approached, the flies lifted off in a swarm around him, blundering into the glass panes with a sound like the patter of heavy rain and revealing the object on which they had been feasting. He felt a rush of nausea.

Lying on the sacks, its belly distended and its limbs rigid, lay the gray lurcher. Its muzzle was peeled back to the gums and frozen in a contorted snarl while small white grubs wormed around the hollow sockets of its eyes.

He backed away into the open and, clutching a post for support, he doubled up and retched emptily into the undergrowth.

Eventually, with his stomach quieted, though still unable to rid his nostrils of the sweet-sour stench of rotting flesh, he went in search of the gardener and set him to work digging a trench in which to bury the dog's corpse. Slowly he turned his steps at last to the old stables. He wasn't sure if he should break the news or not.

He found Josie, as expected, sitting in the sun with her books. For a while he sat with her, telling her about his morning and suggesting plans for the weekend, until finally he knew he couldn't keep the sad news from her any longer. Very gently, he told her that the dog she'd loved, the dog she'd raised from a puppy, was dead. He watched her closely as he spoke, ready to cope with any sign of distress. But to his surprise she made no reaction at all. Only when he'd finished did the slightest expression cross her face. It was the hint of a small, knowing smile.

No! NO!
That laughter. That hideous, howling laughter.

Those leering faces, ugly and vulgar, with blackened rotting teeth and sweaty unwashed skin, jeering at me, taunting me, pressing so close that the coachman has to use his whip to clear a path for the cart. That laughter drowns out even the imprecations of the chaplain standing in front of me, dressed all in black, one hand clutching the cart rail and the other his fatuous book of prayer. I can shut my eyes but I cannot shut my ears. The jeers, the taunts, the cruel jests, the cheap ribaldries, and always that terrible laughter swelling as the throng thickens.

We must be nearly arrived. The moment is upon me. I fear I shall swoon. I am suffocating with dread. The cart jolts violently, throwing me forward against the chaplain. I smell his malicious sanctity, his greedy breath, the prurient excitement beneath that starched and powdered cloak of godliness.

Ahead, the captain is forcing a path through the mob. Fingers pluck at me, searching for a brooch, a ring, a fragment of my clothing, or seeking merely to touch me, to touch the flesh of the condemned. My hands are tied behind my back and I can do nothing to resist. Far ahead I glimpse the gibbet. Three ropes with nooses dangle from three sturdy beams. On either side as we approach I see rows of stands thronged with spectators. The soldiers close tighter around the cart. Out of the press a face leaps at me. My father! Beside him stands Dr. Fell with his bag of physicks. Oh Nathaniel, where are *you* now? My sight is beginning to blot out. The drug is already claiming me. I shan't be able to stand, my legs will not support me, I shall disgrace myself at the final moment....

Rough hands force me to my feet. The rope dances before my eyes. The executioner is testing the knot. The chaplain is hissing in my ears, "Repent, recant, confess, save thy soul!" I can barely hear him above the jeering and the catcalls and that hideous laughter, crackling like greedy flames all about me. Oh Nathaniel, where are you? Don't leave me! Don't let this be!

I feel the rope brush against the side of my neck. The executioner is playing to the crowd. The roar drowns out my thoughts. The chaplain is railing. Why is the potion taking so long? Dear God in your mercy, make it work fast. My head is thrust through the noose. The rope tightens around my throat. The laughter is growing distant, I am going. The veil is falling. An icy hand is working up through my body, numbing my limbs and dimming my senses. At last! It is beginning! I will cheat death yet. All is fading, fading.

An order shouted. A whip-crack. A violent jolt. Suddenly I'm falling.
A savage, wrenching jerk ...

Josie woke with a sickening jolt. Panic tightened its tentacles around
her throat. She jerked upright and looked about her frantically, feeling
fragmented and disorientated. Her eyes fell on the framed photograph on
the bedside table. For a moment her mind slipped: Who was that girl
kneeling beside the large gray dog, smiling at her out of the picture? Then
suddenly it all flipped back into focus. Of course she knew.

She wiped a hand over her forehead. It was dripping with perspiration.
Shakily she climbed out of bed and, clutching her throat, groped her way
to the bathroom. There she bathed her face and neck in a basin of ice-cold
water until gradually she felt calmer. Still trembling, she raised her head
and stared at her reflection in the mirror.

She frowned and looked a little closer. Something, a speck of dirt
maybe, seemed caught on her upper lip. She raised a finger to wipe it
away, but it wouldn't move. She touched the skin more carefully. A cold
shiver of excitement rippled through her body, and a broken smile gradually unfurled across her features.

This was no speck of dirt, no spot or blemish. It was the first faint
hint of a mole.

PART III

THIRTEEN

L eft, right, left right ...

Matthew forced his pace ruthlessly, keeping the same strict tempo up the steep woodland paths as down the gently sloping streets that threaded along the contours of the hillside. Today it hurt—badly. His feet were leaden and his head felt thick. Last night they'd had Lyall and a Nobel laureate in cryogenics from UCLA he was wooing for the university over to dinner, and they'd all drunk too much. Why didn't he take his exercise like Hazel—a forty minute aerobic workout at the health club in the afternoon in return for forty minutes more of sleep in the morning? Because he couldn't spare the time. He'd slipped behind on the book, pursuing that dangerous obsession with Isabel until it had almost destroyed him, and only by dint of furious exertion had he managed to make up the ground lost. Perhaps the reason was simpler: Exercise was like medicine—only if it hurt could it be doing good.

Gradually his muscles grew looser and his body lighter, and he felt his senses opening to the delight of that early midsummer morning. Pale shafts of sunlight filtered low through the leafy woodland, dappling the undergrowth and illumining the dells where pockets of mist hung as yet unstirred. The air smelled sweet yet somehow undeveloped, like a wine brought up from a cool cellar, waiting for the warmth of the day to swell it to its full fragrance. His path swung left beneath a large oak tree, from which he glimpsed the university campus spread out far below, lying asleep in the dawn haze, then abruptly rejoined the road. This was his turning point on the run, and from here on the gradient fell in a gentle zigzag around the streets back to the house.

He lengthened his stride. At the intersection with Oak Drive he passed the postman and exchanged a greeting. Further on, he overtook the skeletal figure of the aged professor of patristics, shuffling doggedly round his daily circuit in a forlorn attempt to outrun the grim reaper. As he turned into his own street, he came upon the girl from number 22 across the way, jogging in the high-stepping run of a Viennese horse and wearing stereo headphones turned up so loud he could hear the tinny beat as he passed. Keeping his eyes firmly away from her generous, articulated breasts, he greeted her with a neighborly smile. She smiled back from a thousand miles away, locked in her self-contained capsule. This was Hazel's "blond Barbie doll." His smile lingered on well down the road. How long ago that all seemed now! He could hardly imagine they'd ever been through those terrible times. The magical, mysterious, extraordinary day of their marriage had changed everything. It had been like switching on a light in a darkened room. In a stroke the terrors and torments seemed banished for ever and their lives infused with a happiness and a harmony such as he'd never imagined possible. The nightmare was over, the demon buried.

The neighborhood was stirring to life. Across the street, Joshua Grabinski, Jr., realtor, was flopping heavily into his stretch. Here, the Bateson kids were piling into their beige wagon, on their way to a Quaker school over in Staunton. A scaffolding truck was arriving at Ed Carey's mansion-style home; Ed was a successful plastic surgeon, permanently obsessed with changing the face of his home. Next door, in Herb and Norma's house, the drapes were drawn and the window grilles were down, the only sign of life being the van from the security firm who were house-sitting while they were away on vacation. Matthew thought back to the bad period and how he would jog past these houses and look at them with the lost eyes of a stranger. He remembered thinking how he lived among these people and yet felt an exile. Now everything was different. He felt a glow of neighborliness as he scanned the row of large, comfortable houses, each sitting secure and confident within its own boundaries. He shared their security and confidence. This was a community, a family, and he was a part of it. He could see things with his proper eyes again. He had Hazel to thank for this, as for so much else; she had rescued him.

As he turned in to their own driveway, he eased to a walking pace. He cast his eye over the house with a sense of satisfaction. The honeysuckle and roses Hazel had planted were already climbing up the trellis on the front porch, and from each corner the Virginia creeper was spreading its way over the white clapboard facade. The porch itself was filled with comfortable clutter: a wicker rocking chair and table, a shuttlecock net and poles, Ben's ex-army camouflage tent, a windsurf sail that had somehow got separated from its board. Hazel had been on at him to tidy it up, and one day indeed he would, but really he liked it that way. Untidiness made a house into a home.

He walked on around the side, past their two cars, each with its roof and hood badly sticky with the sap from an overhanging lime tree—something else he'd get around to doing something about—and made his way into the kitchen by the back door.

Here the comfortable clutter had become creative chaos. On the sideboard, the dinner-party dishes that hadn't fit in the dishwasher fought for space with cookbooks and flower vases and plant pots and those old-fashioned utensils Hazel was forever picking up at garage sales—knife grinders, butter molds, stone grain jars, copper pans, enamel coffeepots, pine dishracks. More of the same hung from the shelves above, interspersed with bunches of flowers hanging upside down for drying. The refectory table in the center served as a marshaling yard for Ben's train set, a battlefield for his galactic warriors and a study area for his homework, as well as a workbench for Matthew himself and the nerve center from which Hazel ran her photography business. On the walls hung several of her portraits of Ben and himself—perceptive, tender yet unsentimental work—alongside samples of Ben's own artwork from school, revealing a surprising talent, and a profusion of other pictures, ranging from a large canvas of a nude in neo-impressionist style to a postcard of a plain lemon with the rubric, "When life deals you lemons make lemonade." Matthew smiled to himself as he put on a pan of water to boil. If creativity was the process of making order out of chaos, didn't you have to start first with the chaos?

While the morning tea brewed—a taste he'd acquired in England those many years ago and never given up—he showered quickly in the pool changing-room and, feeling refreshed and invigorated, slipped into a toweling robe and returned to the kitchen. There he poured two cups and carried them on a tray upstairs. From Ben's room came the familiar sputter of electronic buzzes and crashes from a computer video game. He continued on down the corridor to their own bedroom and gently pushed open the door.

Hazel lay asleep on the large bed. She stirred lightly at his footfall, stretched out a long bare arm, then fell back to sleep again. He set down the tray and stood over her for a moment. How lovely she looked. Her strong, fine features were softened in repose, her lips half-parted as if robbed of a kiss, her copper-beech hair strewn in abandon across the pillow. He reached out a hand and lightly stroked her cheek. The skin was soft and warm. Her fragrance aroused his senses. Filling with desire, he slipped quietly in beside her and folded her into his arms.

It took Hazel a reunion with Pauline to show her how much her own life had changed and how deep her new contentment ran. Her old friend from Washington had called to say she was passing through Charlottesville and could they meet for lunch? Although the rendezvous was right on Main Street, Hazel arrived late. She'd spent the morning photographing a professor of English who had just won a grand literary prize, and the session had taken far longer than normal. The professor combined the pedantry of an academic with the vanity of an author and had insisted on seeing Polaroid tests of every shot first, fussing about his profile and the position of his hands and debating interminably whether his forehead didn't need a touch more powder to kill the shine. She heaved a sigh of relief as she hurried into the restaurant. It would be good to see Pauline again and catch up on what was happening in the outside world.

Barely had she sat down and ordered a spritzer, however, than she realized this wasn't going to be like old times. Pauline looked out of place in her smart Giorgio suit. Or maybe it was just that friendships owed everything to their context, and their own belonged among the social glitz of the capital rather than the casual, easygoing gentility of Charlottesville. Their conversation was full of false starts and mistaken turns, and when Hazel tried to enliven it by relating anecdotes of their honeymoon, she found herself sounding stilted and forced. Pauline seemingly sensed none of this: She held forth gaily with gossip of life in D.C., telling tales of low scandal in high places and high drama in low places. But for all she tried, Hazel found she couldn't muster any real involvement. That whole world seemed to have faded away into her past, subsumed within her new life and superseded by her new concerns, and listening to her friend she felt nothing greatly more than a detached interest, much as if she were reading the paper or watching the television. These were stories of other people's lives. They no longer touched her own.

This realization both shocked and saddened her. And when Pauline asked eagerly about the wedding escapade they'd planned together and whether the trick was still holding up, Hazel found herself reluctant to talk about it. That was a secret she'd buried for safety. If ever Matthew found out that the young woman who had come up to him at the reception had nothing to do with the real Isabel Hardiment but had in fact been an actress from Pauline's agency dressed and made up to look like her portrait, true in every detail down to the mole on her upper lip ... She shivered to think of the consequences.

"It worked like a dream," she said shortly. "The name Isabel hasn't cropped up once since. It's like we destroyed the negative."

"And you trust him?"

"'Trust' is a big word." She glanced at her hands and found her eye resting on her wedding ring. "You can never really know what goes on in someone else's mind."

"You can only judge a guy by what he does. How he performs." Pauline arched an eyebrow meaningfully. "How's that side of things?"

"He's no longer the manic obsessive he was."

"I mean things in the sack."

"Oh. Great. Really great."

"Here's to you, honey." Pauline raised her glass. "May all your troubles be little ones." She smiled. "Speaking of which ..."

"I'm not sure," responded Hazel, taking the point. "He wants kids, of course. Men always do."

"But you're not sure."

Hazel took a breath. Somewhere along the line she had to offer a confidence. That was what friendships were all about.

"I feel I'm only just becoming *me*," she confessed. "Ben's old enough to look after himself more and more. And I'm starting out on a whole new career. Having a baby would be like turning the clock back. When I think of the whole process, the nursing and feeding, the broken nights, the sheer exhaustion—it's like turning yourself back in to prison. You have to be saint to want to do it again. Or a superwoman."

"No you don't," her friend responded. "One in three of my girls have kids. They come back to work just as soon as they're in shape again. It's getting fashionable to have a young family *and* a career."

"I'm old-fashioned, then," laughed Hazel.

"Anyway, you don't need to work, honey. A full professor must make a bundle."

Hazel took the opportunity to steer the conversation away. The question still confused her. She felt torn in different directions.

"Matthew's not quite a professor yet," she said, "but we're working on that. The dean has promised to make him an associate at the end of the year if the book goes well." She warmed to her theme. "You'd be amazed at the internal politicking it takes. You think politics begins and ends in D.C.? I tell you, Pauline, you've seen nothing. The infighting and the backstabbing in the academic world is just unbelievable. I was taking some shots of the professor of English this morning. He's just won a big literary prize. He told me how he fixed it himself—buying off X with a grant, killing Y with a review."

But Pauline's eyes were glazing over: Petty politics in the corridors of academe were too small-time. For her, too, these were stories of other people's lives, and they didn't touch her own. Eventually, Hazel stopped, and an awkward silence fell.

Pauline turned her large blue eyes on her and smiled as widely as her face-lift would allow.

"It's good to see you, honey," she said with genuine warmth.

Hazel took her hand. "You too, Pauline. And you're looking so great."

"So do you," returned Pauline. "You missed your vocation. With your bone structure, you should be on the other side of the camera."

"You've got to be kidding," laughed Hazel.

For a moment, the old understanding seemed to flow between them again. Hazel said nothing more, afraid to break the entente. But then she realized she had nothing to say that wouldn't. They exchanged a smile, drank from their glasses, glanced around the room at the other diners, and when they finally broke the silence, they spoke at once.

"I have to be getting along." "I guess we should get the tab."

The meal was over, and the prospect of both the relief and the sadness at parting seemed to bring on a new talkativeness. They squabbled amicably over who should pay, then decided to split it down the middle and say that each was paying for the other. As they rose from the table and went out into the bright sunshine toward their cars, they chatted about their respective vacations and about the meal they'd just had and other similar generalities, more in the way of pleasant acquaintances than long-standing best friends. They kissed and, exchanging pledges to meet up again very soon for a proper chat, they parted.

Hazel watched Pauline drive away, hooting and waving, until her car had disappeared from sight, then she walked slowly over to her own. She felt a wave of wistfulness. It wasn't nostalgia for her life in Washington so much as a sense of regret that moving ahead necessarily meant moving away and leaving people behind, people who had been close when the time favored but grew distant when the time changed. Her time had changed. As she climbed into her car, her eye lit upon the small photograph of Matthew and Ben she kept tucked into the corner of the instrument panel. Yes, it had changed beyond recognition. Beyond anything she could ever have hoped for.

Through the open French windows came wild shrieks of laughter and the din of heavy splashing. Wrapped in a towel, her hair dripping onto the phone pad, Hazel jammed a finger in one ear and strained to hear the caller. It was the features editor of the *Post* asking if she would take a portrait of the new ABC News anchorman for a personality profile and offering a fee of three thousand dollars, plus expenses. She put her hand over the mouthpiece and waved to Matthew and Ben to keep down the noise, but the editor evidently misinterpreted the momentary silence as hesitation over the fee and quickly raised his offer to four. As she replaced the phone, she smiled to herself. Not bad for the work involved. More satisfying still, it showed she was gaining serious recognition as a portraitist. She'd have done this job for four *hundred* just for the prestige.

She switched on the coffee machine and, as she waited for the water to filter through, gazed out of the window at the naked figures of Matthew and Ben horsing around in the pool. They had such a good relationship, such an affinity. Ben had turned nine just the other week and he was beginning to shoot up. His hair was very fair, but in every other way he could easily be Matthew's son ...

Matthew's son. She thought back to her conversation with Pauline earlier that week and how the same issue had arisen over supper the previous night. She understood how Matthew would want children of his own. He'd make a wonderful father—he *was* making a wonderful father to Ben. For days now, he'd been taking time out from his work to build Ben a tree house, and he'd already begun to plan a detailed tour of the Civil War battlefields for Ben's summer vacation project. But it wasn't, and it never could be, the same. Ben was not his natural son, his own flesh and blood. Matthew loved him as a father, but deep down she sensed how he must really feel. She only had to ask herself how she would feel if she'd inherited a child of his by another woman. Wouldn't she secretly be forever looking for traits of its real mother, little ways and mannerisms, special looks and glances, an alien cast of face or some special feature of its physique expressing itself?

Yet if she knew that, why had she tried to draw him on it at supper last night? And persisted, too, under some self-punitive impulse to force the question beyond its comfortable limit?

"It's only natural," she'd begun, refilling their wine glasses. "You simply can't care for someone else's kids as much as you do your own. It's against your genes."

"Depends," he'd responded promptly.

"On what?"

"Depends if you see yourself as a member of a larger family, the greater pool of mankind." He'd eyed her seriously. "Your selfish gene theory comes straight from the materialism of the eighties. It's outmoded. There's a new global consciousness around. I bet we'll soon be hearing theories telling us our first genetic duty is to our species."

"Parents will sacrifice their lives for their child," she'd persisted. "I would die for Ben. But I wouldn't expect you to."

"According to your theory, you should only be prepared to die to save two of your children," he'd answered with that irritating, academic precision he assumed when he wanted to avoid the real question. "Ben carries only fifty percent of your genes."

"Say you're in a sinking ship and there's only one place in the lifeboat. Would you give it to Ben?"

"I hope I'd do so for any kid," he'd said carefully, then his face relaxed into a smile. "I guess you're right, Hazel. But then, I'd do anything for Ben because I love him."

Some devil had possessed her to go on further. "Suppose there are *two* kids on board this sinking ship. One is Ben and the other is your own natural son."

"Hazel, what are you trying to get me to say?" His longish face tightened into a pained frown. "It's hypothetical, and it's unfair to ask."

She'd felt suddenly abashed. She'd wanted to drive him into denying that he wished for children of his own, and thereby release her from the ever-present obligation she felt. Ever since she'd thought of marrying him, she'd lived with this silent worry in her mind. She'd tried to ignore it, to reason it away, but she knew it would surface in the end. On her own with Ben, she'd been complete: they'd been mother and son, a working unit of two, requiring nothing, lacking no one. But marrying Matthew had changed all that. She was no longer a single parent; she was now one of two parents, part of a larger family unit. And, by the standard of equilibrium, this family was one member short.

Matthew had never explicitly raised the issue, but the thought of it lying deep in his heart haunted her. If only she knew her own mind clearly. On the one hand, for all that Pauline said, she had her new life and career to consider. On the other, there was not only Matthew to think of but also Ben. There were times she'd look at Ben and wonder if he hadn't missed out on a part of childhood by living so much among adults; whether, for instance, his willfulness was just a stage or the direct result of being an only child. But then she'd ask herself whether having a brother or sister ten years his junior would make any difference. He would be fifteen when any child she conceived now was five. The damage, if any, was done.

The hiss of a drip of coffee sizzling on the hot plate brought her abruptly back to the present. Think of all the good things you *do* have, she told herself crossly. You have a beautiful son, a loving husband, a fine new home, a fulfilling career. That's the bottom line. Don't create crises where they don't exist.

Briskly she put the coffee jug on a tray, with a glass of juice for Ben, and carried it outdoors into the sunshine.

"Watch me, Mom!" came Ben's cry as she reached the poolside.

The boy stood poised on Matthew's shoulders, then with a whoop he dived into the water. The splash shot high in the air, showering her. She laughed. There was nothing else for it. She put down the tray and dropped her towel and, taking a deep breath, plunged into the water. She glided under her own momentum along the bottom to the far end. The cool, silent, aquamarine world seemed to soothe her thoughts, and she coasted to the rail, feeling all her anxieties flowing away. As she broke the surface, gasping for air, she saw Ben homing in on her underwater like a torpedo. She felt him grab at her ankles, and the next second she was head over heels in the water, spluttering and choking with laughter.

Later that day, when Matthew was at the library and Ben was at a friend's, she went into the bathroom. She stood in front of the medicine cabinet. For a moment she hesitated, weighing up her decision. Then, in a single quick motion, she took out her packet of birth-control pills and dropped it into the waste bin. She wouldn't tell Matthew. If he knew nothing, he couldn't be disappointed if nothing happened. But she'd try for a child. She had aired all the arguments for and against until her head ached. But one argument had tipped the balance. It was really very simple, only she'd chosen not to listen to her heart. The fact was she loved him, and as much as he wanted her child she also wanted his.

Otis glanced across at his daughter sitting rigid and silent in the seat beside him, staring at the road straight ahead. Why had she insisted on this crazy detour all the way east toward the ocean? He'd drawn the line at going down Northern Neck, where she'd begged him to take her. Fredericksburg was a direct drive up the highway north.

They had driven for miles now, in silence. Occasionally he'd address a remark to her, but she merely grunted. She really wasn't there. He tightened his grip on the steering wheel. Ever since he'd proposed driving her out to Fredericksburg to see if the old apothecary's shop where she'd worked the previous summer vacation might have a part-time vacancy, she'd been in a strange state, very intense and self-absorbed. What was going on in that head of hers?

They drove on, following minor roads through meadows and grasslands, where the fields were fenced by low walls and the trees formed a distant hem along the rolling hillsides. They drove past red barns with roofs shaped like Dutch hats, past fruit farms and wineries and the sites of old battlefields. From time to time she would speak a word, whispering it so softly to herself that he could barely catch what she was saying. It took him a while to realize these were names of places she was reading off roadsigns. "Christ Church," "White Stone," "Fair Port," "Tappahannock," "Culpeper." Old names, evoking echoes from the country's earliest colonial history. In those names he heard the resonance of the hardships and struggles, the triumphs and joys, of the first settlers. In his mind arose pictures of pitch-and-tar swamps, infested by mosquitos, of a hinterland of wilderness, rolling and thickly forested and infested with Indians, of meager plantations, exhausted earth, disaffected colonists, rebellious slaves ...

These names went way back to their own family's roots, too. Take Culpeper, for example. His own ancestor, Fergus McDowell, the first of the clan to settle in the Dominion, had married an Englishwoman who possessed a small fortune in land she'd purchased from Thomas, Lord Culpeper, one of King Charles II's cavaliers. That land comprised most of Northern Neck, as it happened. Curious that Josie should have been so keen to go there today. True, she'd shown quite an interest in family history of late. But he'd only learned of the connection himself quite recently, when a deed of land transfer came up at auction and he'd donated it to a local museum. Josie couldn't have learnt about it from the books at home.

Eventually the signs to Fredericksburg came up. In the town they stopped at Arbuckle's for an ice-cream soda then, leaving the car in the restaurant lot, they went off on foot through the quiet streets of the historic quarter. The late afternoon sun gilded the clapboard of the old, low-built houses, and their mellow brickwork glowed with its warmth. He slipped his arm into hers and gave it a squeeze. This was more like it, father and daughter, like the old times.

Half way down Caroline Street she stopped abruptly in her tracks. Her expression sharpened, then to his surprise she began slowly nodding her head as though satisfied about something. He followed her gaze across the road. There, shaking out a duster around the back of a small clapboard-and-tile building, stood a figure of a girl dressed in a starched pinafore, lace-up boots and white mobcap. Above, a signboard was swinging in the light breeze. It read, HUGH MERCER'S APOTHECARY SHOP.

Before he could check her, she slipped her arm out of his and stepped off the sidewalk into the road. She didn't look either way, just headed out across the road as though some invisible hand were beckoning her from the other side. A car swerved violently to avoid her, and a truck bearing down from the other direction blared its horn. He grabbed her and propelled her across the road just in time to avoid being run down.

"For God's sake, careful, Josie!" he exclaimed, shaken.

But she seemed quite unmoved. She'd hardly registered any danger. Letting out a breath of relief, he followed her along the short pathway and up the steps and to the front door of the shop. He'd certainly make sure she had the chauffeur deliver her and collect her if she did end up taking a job.

They went in. He looked around with a familiar eye. The place hadn't changed since he'd visited her there last year and she'd taken him around, showing him every exhibit in detail. Indeed, it had hardly changed in two hundred years.

The room was empty. Two vast and ornately decorated apothecary jars stood at either end of the mahogany and gilt counter. Between these spread an array of jars and pots, filled with powders and pieces of root and bark, together with a number of finely calibrated instruments for weighing and measuring. He recognized the grooved board for rolling pills and, beside it, the gum arabic and flour used to give the tablets their body. Behind the counter, shelves rose to the ceiling laden with more jars and vials, some in clear glass, others in blue or brown, each bearing a carefully handwritten label. Here was quinine, he remembered, for treating yellow fever. There were cantharides—little green-black blister-beetles known as "Spanish fly," taken by men even these days to enhance their potency. This jar contained ground crab's claw; a spoonful taken in warm milk with cinnamon and ginger root made the perfect cure for a hangover. Next to this stood a bottle of senna leaves, to send a person running to the "necessary," and beside it, in case that didn't work, a far more violent purgative, root of jalap.

He turned his attention to Josie. She was looking about the familiar room, drinking in every detail. It moved him to see her so keen and interested. An exclamation from behind made him turn.

"Josie!"

The dark-haired girl they'd seen outside was standing in the doorway, a broad smile of welcome on her face. Sweeping a loose ringlet back into her mobcap, she came forward and took Josie by the hands.

"My, it's good to see you," she said warmly, looking her up and down. A faint frown flickered over her face. She shot Otis a fleeting glance, then scrutinized Josie more closely. "Has something happened, Josie?"

Otis quickly answered for her. There wasn't a scratch or a bruise on Josie's face any more, and yet somehow the girl had been able to tell.

"She was in a small road accident," he said, "but she's over it now. Aren't you, Angel? Josie?"

But Josie appeared not to hear. She was gazing around the room, lost in her own thoughts, her features set in an expression of silent, deadly determination.

This is it, she thought. I know it is. This is the place. This is where it will happen. In this very room. Here it will all begin again. Here destiny has decreed our paths will cross. Now at last the moment is ripe, now at last the wait of three hundred long years is about to end.

FOURTEEN

R eady, Ben?"

"Ready, Matt."

Matthew nosed the gray Mercedes out of the driveway.

"'Then on to Richmond!'" he cried. "Wasn't that the great rallying cry of the Union troops?"

"I'm a Confederate," countered the boy. "They should have won. They deserved to."

Matthew glanced across at the tough, determined face, and smiled.

"Today you're a historian, and historians don't take sides."

"If it was happening today, *you* would. I don't see the difference. What makes the past so special?"

"To get at the truth, you have to be objective, Ben. Passions get in the way of your judgment."

He frowned briefly. This was a text for himself. His own obsessive passion had almost destroyed him; he now approached his work more coolly, more rationally. It was going well, too; steadily, competently, if not brilliantly. To be properly inspired, you had to care.

"Come on, Matt. It's all only stories. Our teacher says 'history' and 'story' are really the same word."

"You win," Matthew chuckled. "Now listen, I've got an idea for today. You know how stories always go forward: This happened first, then that, then the next thing. For a change, shall we explore the story backward?

Let's start with Appomattox and the surrender and work our way back to Petersburg and Richmond. Then we'll have some lunch, and this afternoon we'll do Spotsylvania and Fredericksburg. If we have time, we could take a quick look at Manassas, where it all started. What do you say?"

"Great," replied the boy.

From the McLean House in Appomattox where Lee surrendered his exhausted army to Grant and the nearby Surrender Triangle where the defeated Confederate soldiers finally laid down their arms and began the long walk home, they drove to Petersburg, south of Richmond, a crucial railhead laid seige by Union troops, whose fall brought about the final defeat of the South within days. Ben was fascinated by everything. He was awestruck by the great tunnel dug there by a unit of Pennsylvanian miners beneath the Confederate line, blowing a vast crater, and he could hardly be torn away from a young guide in period uniform demonstrating bivouacking, trench digging and other duties of a Civil War trooper. He was voracious for recording the information, too. He fired off reels of film with the camera he'd been given for his birthday, he made copious notes in his project book, he collected a mountain of pamphlets from the Visitor Centers and, of course, wrote his name in every visitors' book he could find.

The afternoon grew hotter as they worked their way north to the cluster of battlefields surrounding Fredericksburg where the fighting had been heaviest and bloodiest. They toured part by car, part on foot, inspecting trenches and gun pits, reliving the bitter to-and-fro of the war. At Chancellorsville, Ben cheered at the triumph of Lee's bold gamble, only to sorrow at Stonewall Jackson's mistaken and fatal wounding by his own troops. They drove through the dense scrubland of the Wilderness, where the two armies clashed in savage close-quarters fighting and on to Spotsylvania, another Confederate victory that elicited further whoops of joy from Ben. Thence they progressed into Fredericksburg itself where they visited the stone wall at Marye's Heights, the site of a lengthy bloodbath, with fifteen thousand Federal soldiers lying buried at its foot. Finally, weary and thirsty, they drove into the old center of town and made for a soda bar.

Ben was on a high. He chattered nonstop. Everything around him triggered off a question. Sitting on the bar stool in the window, he pointed to a small white clapboard building across the road.

"What's an apocary?" he asked, squinting to read the sign.

"Apothecary," corrected Matthew. "It's the old word for a druggist."

"Who was Hugh Mercer?"

"An apothecary."

"I'm not that dumb. I mean who was he really?"

"I believe he was a friend of Washington's and a doctor in the Revolutionary War. I read somewhere General Patton was a descendant of his." Matthew swallowed his soda with distaste, wishing it were beer. "You know what the British call the Revolutionary War? They call it the 'American War of Independence.' Shows an interesting different slant, huh?"

"Can we look inside?"

Matthew glanced at his watch. "Not if we're going to make Manassas. Or have you had enough for one day?"

"Mom took me to Manassas once when we had time to kill at the airport," replied the boy. "Come on, let's take a look."

"This guy Mercer lived a whole century earlier than everything we've been seeing. You'll only get confused."

"I thought we were doing history backward."

Matthew smiled and, leaving some money on the table, rose to his feet.

"Come along, then."

Ben led the way across the road and up the path to the front door of the old shop. It opened into a small room dominated by a veneer and gilt counter on which, between two vast apothecary jars, lay a selection of eighteenth-century medicines. Behind stretched shelves laden with gold-labeled bottles and specimen jars.

A dark-haired girl in period dress came forward with a broad smile of greeting.

"I'm afraid Dr. Mercer has been called away," she began.

Ben shot Matthew a look of disappointment, but Matthew squeezed his shoulder.

"She's pretending we're back in the eighteenth century—it's part of the act," he whispered, then turned to the girl. "I wonder, could you show us around then?"

"Certainly. Are you a doctor, too?"

"A doctor of science, actually," he replied, playing the game.

"Science?" she queried, feigning puzzlement. "Ah, you mean natural philosophy. That requires learning. It's different becoming a medical doctor, you know. You don't need qualifications to set up in business. Anyone can. Of course, it helps to stay in business if you cure more patients than you kill."

She paused as the door opened and in came a bronzed young couple wearing fluorescent T-shirts and dizzily patterned Bermuda shorts. She gave them the same introduction, then addressed the small group with a gesture toward the display on the counter.

"Let me show you some of the drugs and herbs we use to treat disorders," she continued. "In the next room, my colleague will show you Dr. Mercer's surgery, where he bleeds his patients, sets broken bones and performs amputations."

Ben shuddered and stood closer to Matthew. In a voice full of old-world courtesy, the girl went on to show them the porous stone used for purifying water and the copper still for distilling rose water. She showed them the preparation of beeswax and sperm-whale fat, mixed with sulfur, used to treat the "itch," a common complaint caused by infrequent washing, and the same, mixed with flour, for covering smallpox scars on the face.

"This is snake root," she went on, "an old Indian remedy for pleurisy, which we take steeped in madeira wine to make it palatable. Here's calendula, made from marigold flowers, which we make into a plaster for healing wounds. And this is calomel, which you know as mercurous chloride; mixed with pig's lard, it's also very effective in stopping wounds going bad."

Antimony to make the patient sweat, drool and vomit. Valerian, called "devil's dung" on account of its vile smell, used to treat epilepsy. Myrrh, as a mouthwash, used with licorice root as a toothbrush. Peruvian bark for curing "bad-air sickness," known today as malaria. Willow bark, taken for its salicylic acid and now, in these days, synthesized as aspirin. Matthew grew increasingly fascinated. Although Nathaniel Shawcrosse had lived a century earlier, many of these drugs would have had their place in his laboratory. This room, this girl, the whole atmosphere of the place seemed powerfully familiar to him. He'd been here a thousand times before in his mind.

The girl had finished with the shop and was leading them into the next room, the doctor's surgery. The young couple followed, horrified and yet intrigued, muttering loudly about the prehistoric conditions of life two hundred years ago. Ben hung back to scribble his name in the visitors' book, then hurried on through into the inner room.

Matthew lingered for a moment, examining a jar containing a dessicated toad, a common diuretic of the period. He only dimly heard the girl
introduce her colleague.

"This is Mistress Josephine, who will show you around the doctor's
surgery."

Finally he followed on into the inner room. There he glanced keenly
about him. Beside the quill pen and inkpot on the doctor's small desk he
noted the lancets and scalpels of all sizes and a large cleister syringe used
for enemas. Dressed similarly in mobcap, apron and a waisted, ankle-
length dress, stood the second girl. She had her back turned to the group
as she demonstrated a phlemotomy chart showing the various points on
the human body for letting blood. On the wall ahead hung a small mirror.
For a brief instant she looked up into the glass and he could see her face.

Their eyes met.

Those eyes! He felt the jolt like a physical blow. For a flash of an
instant he was back in his rooms in Oxford, that hot summer's night long
ago, in the company of that breathtakingly beautiful girl who had come to
visit him, the moment when he'd looked up to catch her reflection in the
mirror over the sideboard....

The rush caught him in the stomach, winding him. An exclamation
gagged in his throat.

She turned to face him. She let out a small gasp and the cupping glass
in her hand fell to the ground. She took a step backward and thrust out a
hand to steady herself. Her eyes widened, then very slowly they narrowed.

He caught his breath.

It was her.

Not in the face exactly, not in the mouth precisely, not in the blond
ringlets slipping from the cap nor in the particular tint and shape of the
gray-blue eyes, although at the same time in all of those things, but most
of all in the *look*. In the cast of the face, in the expression that lit the eyes,
in the character that shaped the mouth. And in the one indelible mark
that put the identity beyond doubt, there, above her upper lip, just where
the smile line broke, the small mole.

Choking, he forced out the word. It hardly sounded at all. "Isabel?"

She held his eye steadily. The world froze about him. He couldn't tear
himself away from her gaze. His mind reeled, his pulse drummed in his
temples, his throat swelled to rob him of speech. The room around him
darkened and faded away, leaving only this face in the center, this face he'd

so long yearned for, dreamed of, craved after, filling the whole of his vision and his being.

Gradually a smile stirred at her lips. It was a strange smile, a guarded smile, like the smile of a card player dealt a winning hand. It reflected some inner state of thought, an expression meant for herself rather than for him. And yet, most strange and chilling of all, it seemed like a smile of recognition.

It was impossible, crazy, absurd, but he had the overwhelming sense that she had been expecting him.

When eventually she spoke, she addressed him in the same half whisper. But hers was not a question. It was a statement.

"Nathaniel," she said softly. "Nathaniel."

And there he stood, numbed, mesmerized, unable to do anything except just nod his head slowly, in silence.

Suddenly he broke the spell. No! He was *not* Nathaniel! He hadn't heard the name! None of this was happening!

Giddy and sick, he grabbed Ben by the sleeve and dragged him, startled and protesting, out of the room. He stumbled into the outer room, choking, clutching at his chest.

Ben was tugging at his arm. "Matt!" he cried. "What's the matter? Are you OK?"

The first girl hurried forward. Her manner was abruptly modern, professional. "Sit down," she ordered, steering him toward a chair. "I'll call the doctor."

"Call Dr. Mercer, huh?" Matthew rasped.

He heard his own strangled, crazed laugh as if it came from outside himself. The world was mad, reason was reeling. Send for the apothecary and his leeches! What would he prescribe for hallucinations? A concoction of sassafras and marshmallow?

"Loosen his collar," the girl was saying.

Suddenly he was seized with panic. He had to get out! He had come face to face with the demon, he had seen the face of his own madness. He fought his way toward the door.

"I need air," he gasped. "Come on, Ben."

He tumbled out onto the steps and staggered down the small pathway. Ben hurried alongside.

"You sure you're okay, Matt?"

"It's nothing," he mumbled.

The boy steered him out onto the sidewalk. "I'm getting you back to the car. You're going to stay there while I call Mom."

"No!" he protested. "I'm fine. I just got dizzy. I'll be fine in a moment."

He stood still and took several long, deep breaths. Gradually his mind slowed its wild spiraling and he felt himself returning to earth. He closed his eyes for a moment. Then suddenly a violent, icy convulsion shuddered through him.

"Let's get the hell out of here," he growled, grasping Ben by the hand, and broke into a shambling run down the street.

Lifting the hem of her skirts, Josie hurried out of the room, down the narrow green corridor past the wig-powdering booth and out of the back door. She swept down the side path to the small white gate, where she stopped and stood looking out down the broad street.

There, heading into the distance, was the figure of the man, with the small boy scurrying alongside. Momentarily a school bus obscured them from her view, and when it had passed she just caught the tall figure as it turned a corner and disappeared from sight.

Slowly she made her way back indoors. The young couple were just leaving and the other girl was preparing to close up shop. Josie answered none of the anxious questions fired at her. In silence she went about her own duties, clearing the till, checking the takings, tidying the counter. When she came to the visitors' book, she paused, and a thoughtful frown crossed her brow. Slowly she opened it.

The penultimate entry had been written hastily in a child's hand. It read simply, "Ben Cavewood, Charlottesville, Va."

Gradually the frown dissolved, and in its place the small, interior smile returned.

The vacation came as a godsend: two weeks in the rented house on Virginia Beach, away from the labs and the library and the ubiquitous reminders at home.

Matthew threw himself into the holiday spirit with a will. He would rise at dawn and, to allow Hazel to sleep in, take Ben off fishing in Chesapeake Bay in the small sailboat he'd rented. Later in the morning, they'd all go into Norfolk to shop for food, then after a light lunch and perhaps an hour's siesta, they'd drive to Sandbridge Beach and walk along the narrow strand to Back Bay and the wildlife refuge, stopping for a dip in the ocean or to watch the teeming bird population through binoculars, then return home for a shower, a cocktail and a barbecue on the beach. At night, he would make love to Hazel with a desperation and a craving that frightened him, and he could only find sleep when holding her tightly in his arms. As the first steely light of dawn filtered in from over the ocean, he would wake and lie staring at her face, and such fearfulness would surge into his soul that he could hardly restrain himself from waking her and smothering his dread in her soft, reassuring embrace.

As August slid into September with no weakening of the intensity of the summer's heat, the vacation drew to its close. The final day arrived and, filled with anxiety at what might lie ahead, he loaded the baggage into the car and headed slowly back home.

There, a mood of restlessness consumed him. He couldn't work, or rather, he felt he didn't dare work. He prowled about the house, making things to do for himself. He devoted an unnecessary amount of time to Ben's school project and he spent at least two days putting up shelves in the small study off the living room so that Hazel could have her own proper office, and even when she gently pointed out she preferred to work from the chaos of the kitchen, he still went on and finished it. Outside, he busied himself repainting the pool border, erecting a cover over the carport, weatherproofing the lumber shed and doing a dozen other tasks he could just as well have left or had workmen in to do.

"Don't you think you ought to be working?" suggested Hazel one morning as he headed into the yard with a paint can and brush.

"I am working," he replied.

"I mean, *real* work. You haven't done a thing on your book for nearly a month."

He managed a disarming smile. "It's vacation."

"It soon won't be. Ben starts back on Monday. And the university goes back the week after, doesn't it?"

"I know, I know, but we've got to make the most of it."

She cast him a close, worried look.

"Is everything okay, Matthew? You're not getting a block or anything? You've got to make the most of this year. It's make or break."

"Yes, yes. Don't nag me, Hazel. It's all under control." He tapped his head. "I'm thinking while I'm painting."

But he knew he couldn't postpone facing up to the issue much longer.

Finally, one morning, he shut himself in his study and, with a dry throat, pulled out from the bottom of a cabinet full of papers the box-file marked ISABEL HARDIMENT.

Later the same day, he went to the labs. In the elevator he met Lyall, who greeted him with an ironic "Dr. Cavewood, I presume?" He didn't linger to talk but hurried on up to his lab and locked himself in. There he called up the files from the data-base in which he'd recorded the various sightings, along with his tentative hypotheses involving Nathaniel Shawcrosse's work on the "hidden truth of Christ" and modern quantum theories of the physics of consciousness.

Gradually he began to see a pattern emerging. And yet he couldn't believe it. If he was right—just suppose he was—then this was the most extraordinary, the most terrifying, thing that had ever happened in recorded history.

Driven to distraction by the struggle to rein in his feverish imaginings, he rose and kicked the chair away. He staggered around the room, groaning aloud, beating his head with his fists. Either he was mad or the world was. He went to the window. Below, he could see groups of undergraduates scurrying around, clutching course schedules and registration papers. The academic year was getting under way again. Time was moving relentlessly forward. He glanced at the wall chart showing his planned schedule for the book. By now he should be two-thirds through the writing, with all the basic research completed and documented. He'd slipped behind target again. Unless he stopped pursuing this side track and ruthlessly focused his concentration on the main job in hand, he wasn't going to make it. He was putting at risk his career, his future, his family.

And yet he couldn't put it aside just like that. He had to check. Just one short trip, just a few hours more, and he'd probably discover he'd got it all hopelessly wrong and there was a perfectly good explanation, and then he could lay the whole crazy, fantastical notion to rest and settle down to the task ahead with an easy mind.

The air was hot and still, and a sultry haze hung over the streets, softening the white clapboard facades and dissolving the further perspectives in a faint mauve glaze. It was shortly after noon, and the streets were curiously empty.

Parked round the corner out of sight, Matthew sat for a while in the car, summoning his nerve. He had no plan, he didn't know what to expect.

He had only hopes. He hoped she'd look different, behave differently, give off a different feel. He wanted her to cast blank eyes upon him and address him as a total stranger, a visitor like any other: "Good afternoon, sir. I'm afraid Dr. Mercer has been called away ..." And when challenged, to shake her head and say she'd never heard the name Nathaniel in her life. Then he'd know he had imagined it all. Madness was manageable. The other was not.

Eventually he mustered up the courage. He climbed out of the car and walked up the street. He turned the corner and, with his eyes firmly fixed ahead, walked over to the small apothecary's shop. Reaching the low gate, he continued without hesitation along the path and up the steps. He pushed open the door and went inside.

The shop was empty of visitors. From behind the counter the dark-haired girl greeted him with her standard smile of welcome, then her expression changed as she recognized him.

"I remember you," she began. "We were so worried."

He shot a glance toward the door to the inner room. It was closed. He cleared his throat.

"Is Josephine in?"

"Josephine?" repeated the girl. "I'm sorry. She doesn't work here any more. She left us two days ago."

His mind raced. What now?

"Did she say where she was going?" he faltered.

"Back to college, I guess."

"Do you know where?"

The girl shook her head. "She didn't say. She didn't talk a lot about herself."

"Excuse me," he persisted, "but could you tell me her other name?"

Here the girl's eyes narrowed with suspicion.

"Who are you?" she asked suspiciously. "What's this about?"

"I just need to know. It's important."

"I'm sorry, sir. I don't think I can give out that information."

"I'm a friend of the family's," he fumbled. "I thought I recognized her. I wasn't sure, that's all."

"Then you'd know her name. Her first name is really Josie, actually."

He felt himself blushing. He realized he was trapped. The girl held his eye defiantly. He couldn't think of a way of penetrating the blank wall.

"I guess it doesn't matter," he said, and turned to the door. "Thanks, anyway."

"Sorry I can't help you, sir."

Outside in the street, he paused for thought. Well, that was some reassurance at least. She wasn't just something he'd summoned out of nothing, a figment of the past sprung suddenly into the present. She was a normal person, born of normal parents, a person with her own history and context, with a childhood and a school record behind her and a home and family and friends around her. Good. Fine. So that was that. He'd imagined the rest.

With a cautious sense of relief, he returned to the car. He'd come away with what he'd gone for. The main issue was resolved. He might have to face up to his mind going off the rails, but at least he didn't have to confront the impossible.

At the same moment, back in Charlottesville, a cab was drawing up in the street outside Matthew's house. Inside, behind dark glasses, sat a blond-haired girl. She leaned forward to give the driver a curt instruction, and the cab turned round in the street and drew up again on the opposite side, at a discreet distance from the house.

For a full five minutes the taxi stayed there, its engine purring while the girl, silent and self-absorbed, scrutinized the house and the movements in and out. At one point, a red Pontiac driven by a slim woman with wavy dark-copper hair pulled out from the driveway and headed off toward town, passing just feet away from where she sat watching.

Eventually the cab drew away. It retraced the route it had come, down Rugby Avenue and onto University Avenue and then along McCormick Road, stopping at the point closest to the Ranges at the back of the West Lawn, where the girl got out and paid. Then it finally headed off the university grounds and away into the shimmering afternoon heat haze.

PART IV

FIFTEEN

It seemed the ferocity of the summer would never abate. Day after day, like a patient imbued with the unnatural strength of a fever, the sun burned pitilessly down through unclouded skies, scorching the lawns across the grounds, wilting the lime trees along the colonnades and turning to molten asphalt the narrow pathways that crisscrossed the campus. Such wind as stirred at all blew off the distant, baked hinterlands of Georgia and South Carolina, a feverish, suffocating wind that clung to the skin like a sticky film and made even the act of breathing a labor.

Even with the air-conditioning at full stretch the labs were uncomfortably close. Day after day, often frustrated and irritable, Matthew struggled to push forward his work but seemed unable to catch up on his schedule. Something was missing.

He had some breaks, however. His "Alchemy and the Scientific Method" was being prescribed as a set text, and on the back of this his publishers were reissuing an earlier book, *Science and Sorcery in the Seventeenth Century.* As for the Shawcrosse biography, too, he'd been lucky enough to lay his hands on all the documents he wanted, not always an easy task. From the John M. Olin Library at Cornell he'd obtained six notebooks of experiments on which Nathaniel Shawcrosse had collaborated with his friend Robert Boyle, the brilliant Oxford chemist whose major achievement had been to define the elements. The Smith Collection at Pennsylvania University had sent him several unpublished autograph letters of Shawcrosse's to Hooke and Newton and other leading scientists of the day. And, perhaps most exciting of all, right there in UVA, he'd discovered in the Cabell collection an important variant edition of Shawcrosse's *Prolegomena*. There was no shortage of material—he had it all there—but he couldn't quite fit it together.

And then, one morning, he had a breakthrough. It was the missing piece that made sense of the jigsaw. He came upon it quite by chance but instantly realized that this was to revolutionize his understanding of Shawcrosse's work and provide a clue to the central mystery of the man's life.

Among the Shawcrosse-Boyle papers that had arrived from Cornell was one notebook more dog-eared than the rest. Part of the final page had been carelessly folded back on itself. On the reverse, hidden in the fold and evidently missed by previous scholars, he had found a tiny, carefully drawn diagram. It looked so simple that at first he almost passed it over. It was the word *anima*—spirit or mind—written in Shawcrosse's familiar minuscule, that caused him to take a second, closer look.

Then its true significance hit him. This single, deceptively simple sketch encapsulated the whole substance of Shawcrosse's revolutionary insight into the relation of mind to matter:

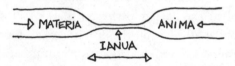

Dualists since Descartes, who saw the mind as separate from the body, had always foundered on a fundamental problem: How could the mind, which was immaterial, relate causally to the body, which was material? Shawcrosse, coming to the problem two decades after Descartes published his *Meditations,* leapfrogged the conundrum by proposing a theory that, in fact, prefigured much of the most advanced thinking in modern quantum physics. He proposed that mind *was* matter and matter *was* mind, and there was a free flow in either direction between the two forms of reality. Mind and matter met, and interchanged, at a point he called the *ianua,* the gate.

This brilliantly simple resolution of the link between physics and metaphysics was not destined to please the churchmen of course. If the distinction between the material and the immaterial was dissolved, what special place was left for an omnipotent, incorporeal God? Where was that essential gulf between the spirit and the flesh, between heaven and earth, between God and man, which necessitated a mediating priesthood to bridge? When challenged, Shawcrosse retorted with his famous heretical remark: *"Deus est Anima et Anima Materia"*—"God is Mind, and Mind is Matter." But abolish the difference between mind and matter, and you abolished the entire justification for the Church. Given the Church's virtual stranglehold on ideology, this was without doubt the underlying reason why Shawcrosse was damned and his work banned—and why, in consequence, for the three centuries to follow, the whole course of western thought was to lose itself down the Cartesian blind alley.

As he stared at this simple diagram, Matthew had the awesome sense that here, in his hands, lay more than merely the solution of a historical riddle; this was the key to a greater secret, the secret of the puzzle of substance and being that lay at the heart of the mystery of the universe.

"Free for lunch?"

Matthew looked up from the aged and discolored manuscript on his desk as Lyall's owlish face appeared around the lab door. He put down the magnifying glass and considered his friend carefully. Lyall never had time for lunch

"What's on your mind, Lyall?"

"Oh, just felt like a breath of fresh air."

Lyall gave an unconvincing smile and came over to the desk. He picked up the magnifying glass and leaned forward, his bushy eyebrows raised and his beaky nose twitching. He gave a visible start, then his smile returned and he let out a whistle of mock astonishment.

"What's this, an egg timer?" he remarked drily. "A right Leonardo, your chap Shawcrosse."

Matthew hesitated, not entirely sure about revealing his hand to Lyall. But who better to appreciate the significance of the find?

"Do you realize what this is?" he asked.

"I expect you're going to tell me."

"Shawcrosse's Gate. That's what I've dubbed it."

"Fascinating," replied Lyall distantly. He laid the magnifying glass down. His face was pale. He studied Matthew quickly, closely. "So, it's all going well?"

Matthew frowned. This discovery was to be the copingstone of the entire argument of his book. Had Lyall seen something that he'd missed?

"Come on, Lyall, this is beautiful."

"Yes, yes. It's splendid."

Then Matthew realized that Lyall was only concerned about schedules.

Hence the lunch. Up till now, he'd been concerned himself about his progress, too. Since his follow-up trip to Fredericksburg, he'd thrown himself into the book with renewed energy, almost with desperation—and not just to satisfy his obligations to the dean and the department, either. There was another reason: Lurking in the back of his mind was the constant anxiety that something was happening to his mind. Disturbing things had been going on ever since he'd started on the book. He recognized there were risks in identifying himself so closely and obsessively with his subject, but to understand the man he had, in part, to *become* him. The danger was in losing control of the distinction. He felt so close to Nathaniel Shawcrosse that at times it almost seemed to him they were merging. Until this book was finished, he would never be quite sure, never quite safe. He'd managed to keep control until now, but would he always be able to pull back from the brink? His brainstorm at Fredericksburg had really shaken him. What would happen next time if he really flipped?

Now at last this discovery held out the promise that he could break the block and bring the book to a completion, and that in turn would restore his mental equilibruim.

He met Lyall's eye innocently, to conceal the lie.

"I'm on target, if that's what's worrying you."

"So, no problems, then?"

"What the hell is this, Lyall? Worried about your investment?"

"Just wondering how things were going," responded Lyall easily. "We haven't had a chat for so long." He contrived a comradely chuckle. "You may have laid the ghost, old chum, but did you lay it to rest?"

"I don't get you."

"Just a joke." He tossed his car keys in the palm of his hand and cleared his throat. "Where shall we go? Remember when we'd slip round to the Kings Arms for a pint? What was the name of that girl behind the bar? Very obliging after closing time she was, if I remember."

Matthew smiled despite himself. It was typical of Lyall to defuse the atmosphere with a reference to their old Oxford days together. He locked the papers away in his desk drawer and rose to his feet. "Anywhere so long as it's cool," he said, and led the way to the door.

At lunch, Lyall was in great form. He'd chosen a small Thai restaurant downtown on Market Street—spicy food, he insisted, was the thing in hot weather—and he chatted over the meal with easy friendliness. Gradually

Matthew relaxed. Ever since he'd arrived in Charlottesville, he'd been too ready to mistrust his friend's motives. But Lyall had to be a politician, like anyone at his level. There was nothing sinister in his concern. If he was manipulative, it was perfectly transparent. For a while, he talked amusingly and without malice about Myra and her Farmington Club friends and how they managed to while away the time during the close season for hunting, then he switched the conversation to inquire about Hazel.

"She's wonderful," replied Matthew sincerely.

"And holy deadlock?"

"Can't think what I was waiting for."

"And how is her own work going? I saw a portrait she'd taken, in an in-flight magazine somewhere. Very perceptive. Very ... honest."

"Her client list reads like *Forbes,*" he smiled. "This weekend she's flying to Aspen. A publishing tycoon. Fifteen grand for two days' work. Hell, that's almost two months of what I earn."

"And you're grossly overpaid."

Matthew smiled. "You set it up."

"So, you won't be coming to the shindig on Saturday?"

"Oh?"

"The Restoration Ball. It's the event of the season. Really classy: dance cards and all. Some of the kids really go to town. Girls dress up in period ball gowns and guys go as cavalry officers. Strictly for graduates and above. Plenty of spare talent, though." Lyall leaned forward. "Myra is making up a table. Come on your own."

Matthew shook his head.

"I've got too much to catch up on."

Lyall raised an eyebrow. "I thought you were on target." He picked his teeth with a satay stick. "Colbert is with our party. It might be politic to be there."

Matthew tossed his napkin aside with sudden asperity.

"Colbert lives in a one-dimensional world. All he cares about is publication. He doesn't give a damn what's *in* the book or the paper so long as it gets published."

"He just happens to be handing out the jobs."

"Screw the job."

"Matthew," warned his friend, "you like it here. So does Hazel. You've set up home here. Ben's happy at his new school. You're not about to uproot. She won't love you for that."

"Leave Hazel out of this!" he flared suddenly, then he dropped his gaze and began etching the tablecloth with the prong of a fork.

"Easy, old chum."

"Look, I'm trying to hold it together," he said tightly. "I wouldn't risk things with Hazel for the world. But everything hangs on this goddamn book. Okay, I admit I *am* behind. I try and take weekends off from work. Weekends are sacred. It's kind of a deal with Hazel. When you've got a family, especially a new family, you want to spend time with them, not just come home exhausted and good for nothing and then get up in the morning and disappear again. I work at home to *be* there, though Ben doesn't understand and he keeps coming into my room, bless him. But in a way I like him to. It's what it's all about being a family. Wouldn't you rather spend ten minutes having fun with your kid than writing another paragraph? I mean, which is more important?" He paused, unsure how he'd let himself go so far. He shouldn't be offloading this onto Lyall of all people. "I try and help out with Ben, I collect him from school quite often, I take him places, put him to bed if Hazel isn't back, I make supper once or twice a week—the usual stuff, I know, nothing heroic, nothing like the model modern husband in the ads. And then there's the house itself; it's never-ending. You know how it is: The new clapboard is warping in the heat, the earth's so dry the pool is cracking, there's this to do and that to do and no time to do it." He met Lyall's eye. His frustration hardened to a small, steely, irreducible core. "I'm running like hell, I'm actually doing a pretty good balancing act, and I just don't need you or Colbert or anyone else giving me shit. Okay?"

Lyall's eyes had narrowed and his face was drained to an expressionless slab. Matthew had the feeling that this outburst was what he'd been after all along. Well, let him have his confession. He would talk to Colbert, but what the heck? Petty campus politics were of no significance in the greater issues at stake. To take Shawcrosse's insight and substantiate it in terms of the latest developments in physics was a challenge of a different order of importance. And if to achieve that he had to flirt with the demon, if he had to dance on the razor edge of madness, if he had to *be* Nathaniel Shawcrosse one moment and Matthew Cavewood the next, slipping like a thief through the gate from matter to mind, from reality to imagination, from being to becoming, then he'd darn well take the risk and do so.

He thrust out his jaw and glared defiance.

"Okay?" he repeated.

Lyall inclined his head slightly and his eyebrows peaked in an expression of pain.

"I understand," he said.

"Well, that's something, at least."

"I'll back you all the way, Matthew," Lyall added quietly.

"I don't care about the job."

"I'm not talking about the job. I know what you're taking on. Believe me, I do." He reached out a hand to his arm. It was meant as a gesture of comfort, but it failed. Men didn't make physical contact like this. He withdrew the hand. "Any time you want to talk ..."

"I've talked too much already."

"You may have things ..." He trailed off, then made an effort to brighten. "Well, if it comes to it, you'll know what I mean." He beckoned the waiter. "Shall we get back?"

Lyall brushed past his secretary and strode into his office, closing the door behind him. He went to his desk and, ignoring the pile of memo slips with messages received while he was out, took a small key from a cigar box in the top drawer. His private filing cabinet stood in the corner, a handsome piece of teak furniture matching the rest of the suite. He slid out the middle drawer to its fullest extent and from behind the furthest pocket took out a yellow envelope marked simply with the initials C.T. He returned to his desk and, sweeping aside the memos, emptied the contents of the envelope onto the blotter.

He worked quickly through the assortment of objects. There were sheets of yellow legal pad crammed with equations and random thoughts and self-addressed questions, such as "Bose-condensed states as the physical basis for consciousness?—check Frohlich." There was a university parking lot pass. A page of a notebook with yet more calculations and scribblings in the erratic, sloping hand of a seriously disturbed man. An appointments diary, the entries abruptly cut short, with the odd penciled hieroglyphic beside the date. Other odds and ends. A cheap pocket watch (why hadn't that been sent to the next of kin?). An invitation to the end-of-year departmental cocktail party (a very subdued affair, Lyall recalled, coming as it had just two days after the tragedy). A reminder from the library regarding overdue books, and another note with the information that the papers he'd requested from Cornell University had arrived.

And then finally the sheet of library scratch paper Lyall had been looking for. He'd been sure he'd seen that diagram before.

It was the identical drawing, an unmistakeable copy of what Matthew had just shown him. There were the words *Materia* and *Anima* enclosed within the same sideways egg-timer shape, with the neck similarly labeled *Ianua* and the arrows going back and forth in the exact same directions.

But what he hadn't noted before was that the paper bore a small mark in one corner. A date. He referred back to the invitation card to work it out.

Clark Tauber had made the same discovery just five days before he died.

Matthew took two iced coffees out onto the deck at the back of the house where Hazel was sitting deep in a wicker chair, reading the first section of his manuscript. He sat down opposite her and tried to detect her reaction. From time to time she adjusted her reading glasses or poised her pencil to make a mark, but otherwise she gave no hint of what she was thinking. She was as stringent and uncompromising in her judgment of his work as she was in everything else—very perceptive, too, and very honest, as Lyall had remarked about her own work. Her opinion mattered more to him than the vain and sophistical criticism of a dozen of his academic peers. A remark of Hemingway's came into his mind as he watched her: "The most essential gift for a good writer is a built-in, shock-proof shit detector." She was his detector.

He glanced at his watch. The limousine would be arriving any minute to take her to the airport. In the hallway her luggage stood ready: the camera bags, the film pouches, the tripod and lighting umbrella, the two aluminum briefcases, one containing her arsenal of camera bodies and backs, the other her battery of lenses, wide-angle, telephoto and zoom, and finally, as always, the small, battered leather case that held her favorite camera of all, the old Hasselblad her father had given her. This was a complete traveling studio. It was typical of her single-minded concentration on everything she did. As he studied her, sitting there so intently before him in the shade of the verandah, looking so fresh and composed in her light safari suit, he could hardly believe this was the same woman who, just an hour before, had lain naked beneath him, abandoned in the extremities of pleasure. He smiled to himself. One moment all body, the next all mind, but always, indivisibly, all woman. What do you say to that, René Descartes?

From the front of the house came the sound of tires on gravel. Hazel looked up and took off her glasses. She cast Matthew a long, considered look but said nothing.

"Well?" he coaxed.

"I can't say yet."

"Is it great or is it garbage? I can't tell. I'm too close to it."

"Yes, you are," she responded with a certain emphasis. She slipped the manuscript in her bag and stood up. "I'll let you know when I've finished."

"It's just a first draft," he hastened to remind her. "It'll need a lot of tidying up. You've only got the first section there, too."

The doorbell rang before she could respond with more than a smile.

"Well, here I go. Don't forget to drop off Ben's bag with his overnight things. And you will see you feed yourself, won't you? I've stocked up the fridge."

"Don't worry about me. Just take care of yourself."

He took her by the shoulders and drew her close. A shiver of desire ran through him. He tried to imagine how she would look to other men, in the airport lounge, on the airplane, at the conference, how she'd look, too, to the man staring directly into her eyes through the lens of the camera. Wouldn't they find her every bit as desirable, mysterious and alluring as he did? He felt jealous and curiously excited.

"Why don't you come too?" she murmured into his ear, pressing herself closer. "We can pick up where we left off."

"You'll be working day and night," he replied.

"So should you be!" she warned, pulling away. "I want to see the second section finished when I come back."

"In three days? Impossible!"

"Not if you have no distractions. I'll call every hour to check, and woe betide you if I find you out gallivanting."

"I might be in the lab."

"I'll always know, Matthew. Remember that." The doorbell rang again, more insistently. She clasped his face and kissed him fiercely. "And remember that, too," she added, then turned and headed briskly inside to answer the door.

* * *

The girl studied her reflection in the mirror. Her skin bore an ashen pallor, inflicted on herself slowly and painfully as the pile of blood-drenched tissues in the wastepaper basket testified. She peered closer and briefly touched up the edge of her bright scarlet lipstick, then stood back and examined the dress critically. Tight whalebone stays constricted her waist and the curving bodice thrust her breasts upward and almost over the square-cut rim. As she spun on her heel, the long flounced skirt flared in a sweep, revealing a flash of ankle in white silk stocking.

She closed her eyes and drew a deep, slow breath. In her hands she held a small fan, delicately engraved with mother-of-pearl. Tighter and tighter she clasped the fan, her fingers whitening with the pressure as it bent, until, with a sudden sharp *crack,* it snapped in half. She opened her eyes. Her gaze was focused on a point deep beyond the mirror. And slowly across her expression unfurled a small, careful smile.

Hazel replaced the phone slowly. No reply from home. Could he still be at the lab at this hour? She had no way of knowing: at eleven o'clock on a Saturday night the switchboard would long be closed. She took from her suitcase a small framed photo of Matthew and Ben and set it up on the bedside table. Gazing at it, she felt again a pang of loneliness. This was absurd! How could you be at dinner, or in a bar, or at a conference gathering, or in a palatial private office suite surrounded by aides and secretaries as she had been, and still feel lonely? Yet she did. She had felt like this all evening.

She stared from the photo back to the phone. It was more than that. She felt somehow uneasy. She had the vague, indefinable sense that something was wrong. But that, too, was absurd. She certainly didn't need to worry about Ben. Back in Washington in the days before Matthew, she'd often had to leave him with friends while she flew off on an assignment. She knew he was absolutely fine, anyway; she'd called him earlier at his friend's home and caught him on his way to bed. But she hadn't been able to reach Matthew all evening. If anything was wrong, surely he would have called. He had her number, and if she was out the hotel would take a message.

Wrapping her bathrobe around her, she lay down on the bed with the manuscript. If she couldn't speak with him, she could still be with him. Even if she couldn't tell him it was really quite brilliant.

* * *

The night was alive with dark excitement, and in the sultry air hung the smell of reckless midsummer dangers. Despite the stifling heat, Matthew shivered. He prowled about his laboratory, too uneasy to settle, too restless to concentrate on his work. He yearned for distraction, but he could not allow himself any respite. Yet danger sought him out. It came to him unbidden, now as before, and it was to alter forever the course of his life.

The hour was late. The electronic wall clock read exactly 11:00. He craved air, and regardless of the air-conditioning he had his windows completely open onto the night. The heat outside hung like a lead curtain, and scarcely a breath of wind stirred the sluggish air. The clouds lay in heavy slabs over the elegant Jeffersonian buildings, cast now and then into startling relief by a flash of sheet lightning. From the darkness below came sporadic bursts of laughter, while from the Rotunda way across the grounds filtered faint snatches of dance music—waltzes, foxtrots, polkas.

Matthew refilled his glass from the bourbon in the chemicals cabinet and forced himself back to his desk. He struggled to close his ears to the seductive call of the night. Half the university was out there, partying. His virtuous abstinence was pointless: For all the work he'd done, he might as well have gone along and played Lyall's little game of politics. A burst of flirtatious laughter rose from below; doors slammed, and a car roared away into the night, its engine dying away to silence through which floated the intermittent beat of a quickstep.

With a tormented groan, he pushed back his chair and went to the lab basin. He held his head under the tall spout until the cold water hurt. Mortify the flesh now to gratify it later. But would later ever come?

At first he barely heard the tap at the door.

When it came again, he decided to ignore it. He couldn't afford the interruption. As likely as not, it would be the janitor wanting a chat to help while away his night. Toweling his hair dry, he returned to his desk.

The tapping continued, light but insistent. Slowly, far away in his mind, deep in his memory, a faint bell struck. His heart pounding unaccountably, he stepped over to the door and opened it.

He caught his breath.

It was her. She stood before him. In all her astonishing beauty. Dazed, stupefied, he slowly drank in the vision. It was her, in every exact detail.

Her hair, the color of fine gilt, was piled high and fell in ringlets about her oval face. Her complexion was as pale as alabaster, its pallor heightened by the scarlet of her lips. Her eyes, a deep electric violet, wore an expression at once serious and whimsical. High on her upper lip, accentuating her mysterious half-smile, lay the small, dark beauty spot. Her whole skin seemed to glow with an inner luminosity, like a marble figurine lit from within.

Then his eye fell upon her dress. It was the very same period ball gown of cream silk, cut high and square so as to force up her breasts, with the same tight corsetted waist, ruched sleeves and long flounced skirt....

She was no hallucination. She was utterly real.

She fixed him with her deep violet eyes and slowly broadened her smile. It broke over him like a wave in slow motion, surging through him, sweeping him off his feet in its swell. He was powerless to resist.

Dimly, from the far distance, the words came back to him.

"Are you ... looking for someone?" He reached out a hand. It felt clumsy, made of rubber.

She nodded, and her smile grew arch.

"I was." Her eyes grew softer, the shape of almonds. She took a step forward. "Nathaniel."

She stepped into the lab. As she passed, he caught a trace of her perfume: sandalwood, saltpeter, and again that cool violet undertone that matched her eyes.

His throat was dry and swollen. He was suffocating. His stomach was melting. Everything seemed so slow, laden with such sweetness and inevitability. There were no questions, no puzzlement, no awkwardness, no surprise. Only a sense of complete knowingness. He had truly been here before.

He knew exactly how it would all unfold.

He would offer her a drink. Bending, he'd catch sight of her reflection in the window against the dark outside, standing with her pale neck thrown back, unbuttoning the fine lace ruff at her throat. She would pause as their eyes met, just long enough but not too long, before her fingers descended to her dress and began unlacing the tight curving bodice. He knew that when he turned from the cabinet he would find her standing barefoot before him, in a tightly whaleboned shift with her two pearly breasts struggling to escape from the top. When he offered her the drink, she would not take it but tilt her head back and purse her lips, and he would hold the glass against her lips as her tongue sought the rim and explored its shape, its rigidity. He would watch her hold the liquid in the pool of her lips, lapping her tongue and glistening her teeth, and his gaze would wander over her face like a climber cresting a hill onto a breathtaking landscape. And her mouth would lift into a smile that would eddy around the corners, making her small beauty spot dance.

And then she would reach for his hand and slowly draw it down onto her chest. The top of her shift would already be undone. Gently she would guide his hand inside and close it tight around one breast. A small sigh of pleasure would escape from her lips. The touch of her skin, the roundness of that young breast cupped in his hand, the nipple swelling between his fingers ... gradually a wild roar would rise in his blood and explode through his body. Tightening his grasp until she cried out in pain, he'd tear at the garments with his free hand, and with the sound of rending silk filling the air, nothing could ever stop him until she stood before him, trembling and breathless and completely naked.

SIXTEEN

Matthew woke slowly, reluctantly. If it had been a dream, he wanted never to leave it. Over and over again he replayed the scene in his mind, skipping one part and lingering over the next. She had slipped away into the night as suddenly as she'd come. He'd glanced at the clock: It read 11:21. Twenty-one minutes of silent, furious, ecstatic love. Twenty-one minutes of eternity.

Slow to recover his wits, he'd fumbled his way to the window. Far in the darkness below, he'd caught sight of her gowned figure skimming swiftly across the empty parking area and over the triangle of grass beyond. There she'd paused briefly and turned back. In a shudder of sheet lightning he could see her face upturned, the skin so pale, the eyes so bright, and that haunting smile, seductive yet strangely knowing.... He'd wanted to wave, to call out, but he hadn't been able to move. Across the distance between them, he'd felt her violet eyes boring into his own. Then abruptly she'd turned and vanished into the darkness.

He'd let out a howl of rage at his stupidity. He'd flown to the door and, without stopping to lock up, raced down the corridor. He'd taken the emergency stairs three at a time and, careering past the surprised janitor, burst out into the sultry night and set off after her at a stumbling run. Taking a short cut, he'd curved round the back of the School of Education, crossed Emmet Street in a diagonal and slipped round the far side of Monroe Hall. As the flat white dome of the Rotunda came into sight over the pavilion roofs, he'd glimpsed her fleeing figure twenty yards ahead and fallen back into the shadows. Her step was light and skipping, and she held up her flowing skirts as she ran. He'd tracked her along the serpentine brick wall, through a narrow passageway and out onto the broad cloistered lawns. At the end stood the Rotunda, its doors and windows open onto the night. Groups in evening dress, some in old period gowns, lounged on the columned portico, drinking and talking, while on the lawns, by the light of lanterns and flares, couples danced barefoot on the grass. From the cover of a doorway he'd watched her pause briefly to adjust her hair, then calmly and with dignity sweep across the lawn and up the broad flight of steps, to be swallowed up quickly into the swell of light and music.

The bedside phone rang.

He started. Hazel! Guilt flushed through him. For a moment he stared at the receiver, letting it ring on. Whatever happened, she must never know.

Shaking, he picked it up. Hazel's voice broke in at once. She sounded anxious. And very close. For a frantic moment he thought she'd flown back early.

"Matthew? Are you okay? You didn't call. I've been so worried. What took you so long answering?"

"I was in the bathroom." He forced some strength into his voice. "I stayed late at the lab. Lost track of time. How's it going, angel? I was just thinking of you."

"Liar," she laughed. The relief in her tone was palpable. "All you think of is your work, I know you."

"How are you making out? Mr. Big giving you trouble?"

"He's being sweet as pie. He's actually a very shy man." Her voice fell to an excited whisper. "Matthew, you wouldn't believe this place! It's gold-plated from top to bottom. Everything's here: heli-skiing on the glaciers, an Olympic bobsled-run, a whole mountainside of artificial snow. You should see my room! Guess what it's called. The Delilah suite! I could have a bath in asses' milk if I wanted." She gave a girlish giggle.

He let her talk on, listening more to the timbre of her voice than to the words. As the conversation drew to its close, she reminded him he'd promised to collect Ben and take him out for Sunday brunch and said she'd be home tomorrow as planned, fifteen thousand dollars the richer.

"Let's blow all of it," she proposed.

"On gold faucets and milk baths?"

"On something grand. A safari in the Serengeti. A cruise to the Galápagos. We'll go in January. It'll be your reward for finishing the book."

"You're on," he replied, feeling a sharp stab of panic. The book *finished?* Since last night everything had changed.

"Till tomorrow, my darling. 'Bye."

"'Bye." He held the receiver tighter. He had so much he wished he could unburden. "Hazel?" he began.

"Yes?"

"I love you."

"I love you too, Matthew."

He replaced the phone slowly. His mouth was dry and sour with the taste of treachery, and his stomach felt leaden and sick. Something had happened—he didn't know quite what—but he sensed he'd passed through a door and nothing would ever be quite the same again.

The alarm clock caught his eye. Eight-thirty. Four hours until he had to collect Ben. He leaped briskly out of bed. Before all else, he had to know for sure. A dream was hardly a sin.

In the west the sky lowered angry and purple, threatening to crack the grip of the heatwave. A silent wind had risen, and across the sleeping campus the dust-parched trees stirred cautiously, as if mistrusting the promise of rain carried on the breeze. Matthew rubbed his eyes as he drove toward the lab. Everything seemed surreal. He felt filled with dread, as much for what he would find as for what he might *not* find.

The door of his laboratory was unlocked, as he'd left it. A glance inside told him all he needed to know. The room was in total disarray. The floor was littered with papers and printouts, retort stands and assay dishes were spread in confusion on the bench top, swept aside in the heat of passion, and beneath the window lay his shattered bourbon glass. On the floor beside the desk something caught his eye. He bent down and picked up a small, silk-covered button. Hard evidence.

Who was she?

He locked the door and slowly retraced his steps of the night before, around the back of the School of Education, across Emmet Street and along the far side of Monroe Hall until he reached the serpentine wall that led into the lawns. He slowed as he came in sight of the Rotunda. Why did he think he'd find a lead there? Why even assume she was at the university? His mind flashed back to the apothecary at Fredericksburg. He had not the faintest doubt that this was one and the same girl. Her friend had said she'd gone back to college; that could be anywhere. If she was at UVA, surely he would have seen her before. Perhaps she had a boyfriend at the university and had just come in for the ball. Anything was possible. He had no idea where to start. He didn't even have a proper name. Mistress Josephine at the apothecary could be anyone in real life. Should he look for her in the phone book under "Hardiment, I."? he asked himself with a crazed chuckle.

Outside the Rotunda, a small army of students was at work cleaning and tidying up, collecting spent flares, retrieving stray glasses and raking the heavily trampled grass for cigarette butts and other debris. Dodging past one student hosing down the steps, he went inside the large circular hall where others were dismantling the music system and taking down the lights. Collapsible tables lay stacked against the walls, crates of empty bottles stood in piles by the door and in the air hung the smell of stale smoke and drink. He looked around with growing despair that he could ever hope to reconstruct anything of the night from this.

He sauntered down the sweeping staircase to the basement. A dark-haired young man sat at the Guides Service desk, waiting to take a group of visitors on a tour around the university. Judging by his washed-out complexion and the empty pots of coffee surrounding him, Matthew guessed he'd been at the ball the previous night, too. The Guides had organized the event; perhaps they'd kept a guest list? As he was approaching the desk, Matthew caught sight of another student with a Guides Service badge standing in an alcove behind, pinning numbered photographs onto a large beige-covered board. His pulse quickened. These were photographs taken at the ball.

He began to scan the prints—couples dancing and talking, groups at table drinking and laughing, some taken by surprise, others striking poses, but none with the girl he sought. Just as he was about to give up, the student reached for the last print in his box and held it in place on the board while he fumbled for some thumb tacks. Matthew peered closer.

It showed a couple, a dark-haired girl in a long dress with a plunging neckline and a tall, athletic young man with clean, chiseled features. In the background, almost beyond the reach of the flash, caught in half-profile and walking out of the frame was her, his girl of the night.

He turned to the student with as much nonchalance as he could muster.

"Looks like one helluva party," he remarked.

"Sure was, sir," replied the boy.

Matthew pointed to the girl. He couldn't think of a subtle approach.

"Do you know who she is?" he asked.

The Guide met his eye without surprise.

"That's Josie McDowell," he replied with a dry smile. "You won't get anywhere with her, sir. I mean, she doesn't talk to anyone. Keeps herself to herself."

Josie! His pulse jolted. What had the girl in the shop said? "Her first name is really Josie, actually."

"You don't happen to know where she lives?" he asked hoarsely.

"She's on grounds. West Ranges." The student smiled weakly. "I was down for that pad myself. I guess the luck goes with the looks."

Matthew gave a start. At this very moment he was standing within a few hundred yards of her!

Mumbling his thanks, he turned away and headed out into the lower cloisters. His heart was pounding. He wasn't ready for this. He hung back in a hidden corner and tried to prepare his thoughts. He was poised on the brink of a monumental and irreversible step. Right or wrong, he couldn't tell. He only knew he had to do it.

Taking a deep breath, he stepped out into the imminent storm.

He tapped on the heavy, old wooden door. No sound came from inside. He tapped again, lightly but insistently. Still silence. He looked about him. The cloister was empty, the world aslumber. Was she still in bed, sleeping off the party? Perhaps she had company. He tapped once again, this time more tentatively. Nothing stirred, not even a footfall or the creak of a bed.

He stared stupidly at the door. He hadn't reckoned on finding her out. With a quick glance over his shoulder, he reached for the handle. The door wasn't locked. Slowly, tentatively, he opened it and put his head round.

"Hello?" he whispered.

Silence. An empty bed, an empty room. Quickly he slipped inside and closed the door behind him. He leaned against the back of the door and waited for his eyes to grow accustomed to the penumbra.

Apart from a pencil of light filtering through the curtains ahead, the room was in darkness. In the far corner stood a large, low bed. The sheets were rumpled and a white lace coverlet lay half tossed off onto the floor. Beside the bed stood a small dressing table and a wicker chair over which was draped an embroidered Chinese robe. To the right, between a writing table and a bookcase, an archway led to a small inner room, perhaps a bathroom. Along one wall stretched a built-in wardrobe covered by a brocaded curtain, beneath which he could just make out the flounce of the cream ball dress with its lace and blue silk trimming. On the floor, amid a profusion of books and papers, stood a leather ottoman and a curious object resembling a small samovar. Far from the usual student posters, the walls bore a strange assortment of drapes and artefacts—one was a threadbare tapestry depicting Primavera sowing flowers, another an early celestial chart showing the movements of the heavens—while over an armchair sprawled a large, frayed piece of velvet-patterned silk that bore the unmistakable stamp of the house of Fortuny.

Filled with conflicting impulses, he crept over to the window and drew back a corner of the curtain to let in more light. His eye fell on the dressing table. Lying on a wad of tissues in a circle of dried blood, glinted a naked razor blade. Above, slipped into the frame of the mirror, he noticed an assortment of party invitations, lecture schedules and the personal cards of sorority colleagues, while the glass itself was papered with yellow self-adhesive notelets carrying reminders of classes and textbook references. Finally, propped up among bottles of rose water and cleansing lotion he found a student identity card. He examined it in the light.

The name was Josie McDowell. The picture was hers. The evidence conclusive.

As he replaced the card, he noticed a small vial of perfume. He raised it to his nose. Spicy as sandalwood, smoky as saltpeter ... the smell evoked her to his senses with a rush.

Suddenly he was filled with alarm: she might come back at any moment and catch him snooping. At the door, however, he hesitated. He would leave a note first.

He went to the desk and rummaged through the drawer for pen and paper. At the bottom, lying face down, he came across a handful of snapshots. He glanced through them quickly. One showed her as a little girl at Disneyworld, hand in hand with Mickey Mouse. Another at seven or eight, standing outside the porch of a grand house beside a gaunt woman with staring eyes—her mother? In a third one, she was on horseback, and clearly now an adolescent. In a fourth, on a yacht, deep-sea fishing, with a man whose face was very familiar.... Of course, this was Otis McDowell, the senator, her *father!*

He put the photos hurriedly back. The whole thing was crazy. He was projecting again. Or else this Josie McDowell was living a fantasy. Maybe she'd read somewhere about this tragic young seventeenth-century beauty, Isabel Hardiment, and she'd latched onto her. She'd done some research into her story and grown obsessed with her to the point—a point he knew too well—where she'd started identifying herself with the historical character. Of course she wasn't *actually* Isabel. How could she be?

And yet she was. He knew she was.

He beat his head with his hand. Which of the two was real—the phantasm of the night embodying the long-dead Isabel, or the modern-day senator's daughter taking a graduate degree at this university?

Then an idea occurred to him. He'd settle the question by a test. Finding a pen and a sheet of paper, he began to write in the sloping minuscule hand he knew so well.

If thou shoulds't ever doubt the power of my love,
Sweet Lapidus, . . .

There he stopped, leaving the stanza uncompleted. Only the real Isabel, to whom these lines had been addressed, could possibly know them and recall the rest.

He rose. From his pocket he took out the small silk-covered button and placed it on the note. Then he closed the curtain and, with a final glance about him, slipped out of the room.

It was only when he reached his car parked at the rear of Monroe Hall and felt the tension in his nerves beginning to ease that a chilling thought struck him. From the date of birth on the ID card he worked out that she had just turned twenty-two. His mind went back to the night in Oxford fifteen years before. He'd been twenty-two himself then. But Josie McDowell would have been just seven. That small girl he'd just seen, photographed with her mother on the steps of her home.

Who the hell was the girl who'd visited him back then?

Josie hastened her step as the menacing growl of thunder grew closer. An unnatural chill had entered the air, like the ominous chill of a man sickening with a fever.

She had risen early and gone for a walk in the deserted Sunday dawn. She'd roamed the grounds in circles, breaking into a run one moment and halting abruptly in her tracks the next, never settling in any one place for more than a moment.

The sky was growing darker, as though presaging an eclipse, and distant thunder tumbled angrily around the vast bowl of the heavens. The first rain began to fall, thick clotted drops that fell with a smack onto the metalized paths and sank instantly into the thirsty, cracked earth. A steamy, sweaty scent rose from the ground. Suddenly, with no further warning, the clouds burst open. The rain fell in sheets, obliterating all but the closest trees and buildings. Cars slowed to a crawl, their drivers unable to see ahead, and everywhere sharp cries filled the air as people scattered for cover.

Josie remained standing in the open, her arms upraised and her face upturned to the lash of the rain. A wild, long-drawn-out laugh burst from her throat. From the trees where they were sheltering, a group of students looked on with pity. A passing jogger steered off course, giving her a wide berth.

Drenched to the skin, she slowly turned and wove her way back to her rooms. She walked without hurry, holding her body erect and her head high. She let the rain stream down her face and neck as though she barely noticed it. Figures huddled in doorways shrank back as she passed. She looked neither to right nor to left. Her gaze was fixed on a point in the distance. And as she went, from time to time, she broke into a chuckle, a small private chuckle of pure glee.

She reached her rooms and went inside. There she stood for a moment looking about her, with the rain dripping off her in pools on the carpet. From across the room she saw the note.

As she read it, her expression hardened.

Nearly, she thought, very nearly. Just one more step, and the trap is sprung.

"Matt, what makes thunder?" asked Ben pensively.

"Come on, Ben, we've got no time for that." Matthew adjusted the flowers in the vase and stood back to check the effect. "Is your room neat? Did you clean out the rabbits as I asked? Dammit! I left the washing on the line."

"It's the thought that counts. That's what Mom always says. Anyway, the new maid starts tomorrow."

"Ben, the idea is to make the place nice *now*. Nice for Mom to come home to." He eyed the boy critically. "You've got dirt all over your shirt. Go upstairs and put a clean one on. Hurry, or we'll miss her. And then we'll look like losers."

Eventually they were ready. Matthew locked the house, and they hurried through the rain to the car. The drive had become a river in spate, running a rich red. He sighed; the silt would have to be shoveled back and the troughs in the gravel laboriously filled in. More work when time was already too short.

The storm had raged all morning and only now, in mid-afternoon, was it beginning to abate. The sky was clearing from the west as they drove onto the open highway, rolling the thunder clouds toward Richmond and the flatlands of Tidewater and Chesapeake beyond. Gradually his tension began to ease. He glanced across at the boy, who sat staring out of his window at the sporadic forks of lightning receding into the distance.

"If you want to know," he smiled, "thunder is actually caused by lightning. The discharge creates thermal changes which cause wave disturbances in the air. That's what makes the bang."

"Thanks, prof," replied Ben with a cheeky grin. "I guessed it wasn't God with a rumbling tummy."

"You know, it wasn't until the eighteenth century that they knew that lightning was actually electricity," he mused, half to himself.

His thoughts wandered along their well-worn path. He wondered what Nathaniel Shawcrosse, earlier still, had believed lightning to be. He gave an inward chuckle. *He* should know, if anyone; he only had to think himself into Nathaniel's mind. Or ... did he only have to ask? He thought back to the previous night and a shiver of excitement ran up his spine. He glanced across to find Ben scrutinizing him oddly. The shiver turned to a flush of guilt. Did his face betray his thoughts? Hazel would see through him at once. He must cast the events of the night out of his mind. It had just been a moment of midsummer madness, nothing more.

"Benjamin Franklin discovered that," the boy was saying. "He got a shock from holding a kite in a storm."

"Good for you, Ben," he replied, clapping him on the knee. "Now, do you know who discovered electricity in the first place?"

It seemed no time before the signs for the airport came up and they were heading through the low concrete sprawl of cargo warehouses and freight depots. They parked in the short-term area and, with only minutes in hand, hurried through the humid, fume-laden air into the cool of the terminal building.

Hazel's plane had just landed, and they took up position by the main arrivals area. They watched impatient businessmen pushing their way through, nuns in summer habits coasting serenely past, harassed mothers trying to marshal uncooperative kids, roughnecks in check shirts and wide-buckled jeans drinking from cans as they walked, families of blacks with kids impeccably dressed in Sunday best, Hasids shuffling along in black homburgs and ankle-length overcoats ... a whole cross-section of America seemed to be processing past them.

Then came Ben's excited cry. "There she is!"

She hadn't seen them. Matthew put a restraining hand on the boy's shoulder. He wanted to enjoy the moment, watching her from a distance as she came forward, walking with that easy, fluid movement of her hips, her copper-beech hair bouncing in gentle waves with each step and her strong, open face lost in thoughts of its own. He felt he was discovering her all over again. He knew with a rush of absolute clarity why, for all that there might be the occasional midsummer mistake along the way, she was the only woman he could ever wholly, fully and eternally love.

She had almost passed them when he released Ben. The boy sprang forward like a retriever.

Her face lit up with surprise and delight.

"What's this?" she exclaimed. "A welcoming committee?"

Ben threw his arms around her, then delved into a bag she was carrying.

"Did you bring anything back for me, Mom?"

"Something for later, darling," she laughed, kissing him. She turned to Matthew. "You're crazy. You should be working."

"I've been working like a maniac. Give me a break."

"But now we've got two cars here."

"So? You take Ben. He's dying to tell you all about thunder and lightning. Eh, Ben?" He picked up her bags, then hesitated. "There's something I have to tell you, Hazel," he began gravely.

Alarm flashed across her face.

"What's that?"

He leaned forward and whispered in her ear.

"I love you and I'm crazy for you."

Turning before she could reply, he led the way to the exit. His conscience was easy, for this was the absolute truth.

Three days later, Matthew was at work in the lab, wrestling with the opening of the third and final section of the book. Evening was drawing on, and he wanted to get back home before Ben's bedtime. Hazel had hired a baby-sitter, and they were going out to supper at a new restaurant out of town that Lyall had recommended. She needed a break, too. She'd been working flat out since she'd got back from Aspen. It might be different kind of work from his own—manual, not mental, as she often reminded him, meaning that it was better paid. Different in its output, too: He could spend a day without writing a single word, but she never left the darkroom without something to show for her time. She was productive without being obsessive. He'd dearly like to know her secret.

With a weary sigh, he pushed his papers into the desk drawer and switched off the word-processor. As he reached for his jacket hanging on the back of the door, he noticed a small envelope in the bottom of the letter basket. This hadn't come by internal mail: he'd cleared the basket earlier in the afternoon. It had been delivered by hand.

The letter was addressed to Dr. Matthew Cavewood and marked PERSONAL. Even before he opened it, he knew who had sent it. That slender, sloping handwriting was unmistakable.

He went over to the window and, filled with conflicting hope and dread, he opened the envelope.

Inside was a single sheet of paper. It was the note he himself had left. Except that the missing lines had been added to complete the stanza.

> ... or seek that I its strength should'st prove
> And fiery trial of its potency prepare,
> By Egypt's ancient art I hereby to thee swear:
> Eternity's elixir swift shall I achieve
> Lest e'er my love the loss of life's sweet breath should'st grieve.

It was unsigned.

He read and reread the familiar lines, numb and confounded. This love poem had never been published, anywhere. He'd only found it himself after a good deal of painstaking detective work. Josie McDowell was a straightforward graduate whose subject, he'd discovered, was chemistry. She was hardly a scholar learned in the arcane byways of science history. Just possibly, he granted, she might have come across some reference to this young Englishwoman who lived three hundred years ago and have taken a closer interest in this figure, even perhaps looked up the odd reference in the scanty material available in the libraries. But it was simply not conceivable that such a girl could have known about this.

The conclusion was as chilling as it was inescapable.

He had called into the void and she had returned the echo. However it could be, and whatever it meant, these two were one and the same person. Josie McDowell *was* Isabel Hardiment.

SEVENTEEN

For the next few days, Matthew kept to his study at home and immersed himself in work. He didn't trust himself to go out without ending up at Josie's door, and he knew that even if he could contain himself inside his lab, he'd only spend his time at the window with his eye on the entrance steps of the chemistry building across the way in the hope of catching a glimpse of her. By immuring himself at home he hoped to put temptation beyond reach while he resolved the dilemma he faced. Deep down, however, he knew he was only pretending to give the issue a fair hearing. From the moment she reappeared in the doorway of his laboratory, the seal had been set.

For a start, he couldn't deny the inestimable value this extraordinary situation could have for his work. If Josie McDowell really could recite to the very letter a love poem that had lain buried in archives virtually since it was written, what secrets and insights must she be able to offer into Shawcrosse's scientific work, especially into those missing parts which had been deliberately suppressed? As Isabel Hardiment, she'd been Nathaniel's lover, his collaborator; as Josie McDowell, she was a contemporary living witness of his life and times! The implications for the biography were mind-boggling. She was, literally, a voice from the past. Never had a historian had such an opportunity to realize his wildest dreams.

The risks were fearsome, though. He was embarking upon a love affair. He might pretend he could limit it to an affair of the mind, but he couldn't trust himself to keep to that. Hadn't he already crossed the threshold? He felt sick with guilt over Hazel. What if she found out? Even if he could somehow keep it concealed—supposing that were possible with someone of Hazel's intelligence and intuition—could he really live at ease with himself while he was deliberately and systematically cheating on her? Was the prize worth the price?

And there were other, unknown dangers of meddling too closely in Shawcrosse's work. Dangers to his mind, his sanity, perhaps worse. He was launching out into the perilous waters of the human psyche, tapping the deep, dark, unseen powers of matter and being. Did he have any idea what he was getting himself into?

Yet he'd already made up his mind. All this agonizing was simply to justify to himself the act he knew he was about to commit. Ultimately, he felt one overriding compulsion. He craved her.

Fifteen years ago, his life had been turned upside down by a dream of ultimate sexual ecstasy. Since then he'd sought to relive this moment with various women, some of whom he'd loved and some he hadn't. Finally he'd met Hazel, and he'd fallen in love. This was a true love, in which he'd discovered a different, deeper kind of ecstasy. With Hazel, sex was many things and many modes; it was always wonderful, but it was not transcendental, it never risked the limits of oblivion. True love could never be true sex. When he and Hazel made love, they brought to their bed everything that they shared outside it: all the laughter, the surprise, the hopes and joys, even the quarrels and frustrations. They were making love as the people they were. But with that angel of the night, no people as themselves were involved. Quite the reverse: she'd offered him an escape from himself, from the gravity that kept his soul earth-bound. With her, he'd stood outside himself, he had known oblivion.

He'd grown to expect never to relive that ecstasy; he'd been granted one glimpse through the doors of delirium, and the doors had remained closed ever since. Until just the other night, when his angel returned. But by now his life had moved on. He was no longer the young, unattached postgraduate of his Oxford days. He had a life, a context, a family. He felt like a figure in a children's fable, cursed by his wish coming true.

And yet one thing outweighed all the rest. He wanted her, desperately. He only had to picture her framed in the doorway of the laboratory, her violet eyes shimmering, or standing before him with her dress half undone and her lips raised for a kiss, to feel an overwhelming swell of desire for her. His mind was in a turmoil and his body in a fever, and he couldn't contain for much longer the volcano bursting within him.

The fall that year fell suddenly. The unusually late heat had prolonged the summer beyond its time, and the onset of cooler, damper weather precipitated the season's turning. Josie woke that Sunday morning to find the slender maple tree outside her window had turned yellow over night. It was a signal to prepare.

She had buried herself in her room, cutting classes and skipping meals. She had only ventured out once in the past two days, to go to the library to collect the books she'd ordered: *Wild Plants and Herbs of America, A Neurochemistry of Toxins and Poisons* and a facsimile edition of Gerard's *Herball* of 1597. She had studied, planned, prepared. One by one, everything was coming together and slipping into place, and now all was ready. Except for the one final and crucial preparation.

She spent the morning carefully arranging the room, then in the afternoon she put on a jacket and, taking a willow basket and a sharp knife, she let herself out into the sunshine of the cloisters. From her neighbor Mandy's room as she passed came the muffled sound of copulating. With a frown, she quickened her step. She stopped by Newcomb Hall to call a cab, then slipped around the rear of the building and along the side of the library to meet the cab on University Avenue. Within ten minutes she was sitting silent and composed in the back of the car, heading out westward toward the hills.

Ten miles out, on impulse, she told the driver to fork off left. The road wound through the village of Wintergreen and took them into the foothills of the George Washington National Forest. In the far distance rose the smoke-blue peaks of the Allegheny mountains, while in between snaked the majestic ridge of forest etched by tracks and rivers. Whenever the road branched, she told the driver to take the smaller track, until they found themselves bumping along a rocky trail that eventually grew so narrow that the driver had to pull off into a small clearing and come to a halt. She instructed him to wait there for her, warning him she might be gone quite a while. Then, clasping her basket and knife, she set off on foot.

Here, the country rose in a gentle sweep through fields and wild meadows that bore little sign of the hand of man. At times she waded waist-deep in golden grasses, at others she fought her way through thorny thickets and dense clumps of bushes. All around her the leaves were turning, some already falling, and the hills and glades were cloaked in the febrile reds and yellows of autumn. From time to time she stopped and bent to examine a plant, occasionally snipping off a cutting and adding it to her basket.

In a hedgerow she came upon a sprawl of wild bramble and picked a handful of the leaves and berries. Next she collected some verbena growing beneath a laurel bush, a soft, hairy plant that yielded a lemon smell when the leaves were crushed. From a marshy stretch she culled several long stems of the fragrant meadow-sweet, while not far off, on thinner, rockier soil in a hollow that formed a natural sun trap, she discovered a small, straggly clump of marjoram. Valerian, the heal-all plant, she also found, and beneath a mountain ash a mat of sow-bread, a species of cyclamen and, in Gerard's prescription, "a good amorous medicine." She even chipped away some of the white, decaying part of the ash tree itself for the aphrodisiac properties it, too, possessed. She smiled to herself as she slipped the fragments of rotten bark into her basket. "Remember, Nathaniel, how at dinner in London once your friend John Evelyn gave you some of this—what did he call it?—'sweet powder for gallants,' and you brought it back and we tried it one night?" She moved on. Her hands were trembling.

Her basket was full, but she carried on. She hadn't yet found the one rare, special plant she sought.

Though the sun was now sinking, she was hot, weary and thirsty. After a while she came upon a small stream and slaked her thirst from the pure, ice-cold water. As she rose, she let out an exclamation.

There it was.

The plant lay like a large, straggly rosette, almost flat on the ground. The lower leaves were long and narrow, the stem leaves fatter and wavy, in all somewhat resembling a large radish, while nestling in the heart was a cluster of orange-yellow fruits each about the size of a cherry tomato.

Atropa mandragora. The American Mayapple. Otherwise known as the mandrake.

She glanced up to check the sun. There was still some time to go before sunset. She sat down on a sandy mound and took out a small well-thumbed book.

"Mandrake," she read. "Contains the alkaloid atropine, the active principle of another member of the solanaceous family, *Atropa belladonna,* the deadly nightshade.... Exerts a narcotic effect on the central nervous system, blocking the activity of the vagus nerve to cause an anaesthetic effect....

"Much false superstition surrounds the mandrake. The Greeks considered it an erotic plant, on the basis of the Doctrine of Signs, for the root strongly resembles a man's genitals. Apuleius in the second century noted it as a cure for demonic possession. In the Middle Ages it was believed to grow under the executioner's gallows, receiving its seed from the blood of those hanged there, and anyone daring to touch it was inviting death.... Its root, which goes very deep, is hard to extract, and when pulled up the demon inhabiting it is supposed to let out such piercing shrieks that the perpetrator is killed on the spot."

She closed the book and put it back in her pocket. "We know all about the mandrake, don't we, Nathaniel?" she muttered half-aloud with a tight smile. "We have taken it to its limit. We discovered how to harness its transcendent powers, to suppress the lower, material functions and release the spirit to fly uninhibited and free. This is our secret. But there is no turning back. Once you have tasted the mandrake and known again the ecstasy, Nathaniel, you will be mine. Forever."

First, she drew a circle around the plant and carefully cleared away all the grass and weeds within it. Then, starting at the circumference, she began digging.

With nothing more than an angled stake to clear the earth, the work was difficult and before long her hands were raw and blistered. From time to time she glanced up at the sun: the root had to be drawn, wholly and undamaged, at sunset. Gradually the hole grew deeper and the mound of dirt higher. Inch by inch she picked away at the soil around the plant until she had isolated the whole root system. By now, the sun was declining fast. She was trembling with exhaustion, but the prize was in sight. She stood back and waited for the right moment. Just as the last rays of the sun were filtering through the tips of the trees above, she moved forward and, taking hold of the root in both hands, gradually eased the plant in its entirety out of the ground.

Later that evening, back in her rooms on the grounds, she cleared a space on the floor. Taking the grate and tray from the fire, she laid out the bramble leaves and berries on a metal tray in the center of the floor, struck a match and set fire to the pile. A bitter-smelling green smoke filled the small room, fumigating the bedchamber of demons and evil spirits. Next, she made up a potpourri of the verbena, marjoram, meadow-sweet and valerian in a glass punch bowl and crushed it until the scents rose to drown the odor of the smoldering brambles. Finally she prepared the bed, slipping a sprig of verbena inside the pillowcase, and with a silken cord she carefully looped the mandrake root on the bedhead where it would hang to dry before being ground to powder and made ready, all in good time, for its purpose.

She sat down in the floor, cross-legged, her head swimming in the melange of fumes and scents, and focused her mind on thoughts of love. She had laid the trap and it only remained for her lover to step into it.

She lost track of time. The small fire burnt itself out. She lit a single candle. All was calm and quiet in the room. In the distance odd sounds could be heard—voices, laughter, a blown exhaust—but all so far away. She sat staring through the shadows at the door, waiting, knowing.

When the tap came, she did not rise at once. She waited for the door to open. Nathaniel stood there, in the doorway, the light from the cloisters behind him, his face in shadow but his eyes burning out of the darkness.

Slowly she rose to her feet at last and reached out her hand to draw him inside.

For the first few days, with that false brilliance of a light bulb before it burns out, the atmosphere at home appeared to grow brighter.

Matthew told himself that so long as Hazel never suspected, he wasn't causing her hurt. What the eye didn't see, the heart could not grieve over. But gradually the strains began to show, and he grew to feel increasingly under siege. The threat, however, lay not from Hazel but from himself. She could live happily in innocent ignorance, but he could not live happily with the lie. His conscience was to prove the traitor.

That night, he'd stayed only a short while with Josie. With a prodigious strength of will, he'd refused the lure of her bed. That, at least, relieved him of some of the burden of guilt. He returned home to find Hazel already in bed and asleep. He took a long shower, careful to wash away any possible traces of scent or lipstick or other marks that might betray him, then climbed into bed and folded himself around her warm, soft body. She stirred sleepily and, reaching for his hand, drew it tight to her breast, then fell back to sleep. He lay staring at the pattern of the moonlight on the ceiling, too excited to sleep, filled with irrepressible elation. Partly this was a wicked satisfaction with himself for having resisted the temptation. Was he cheating on the woman he loved? Not really, he told himself, although in his heart he knew that not repeating the act didn't absolve him of blame for committing it in the first place.

But beyond anything else his elation was for the sheer dizzy thrill of the experience of *her*—of being with her, of talking with her, of seeing with privileged access through her eyes into the past. She gave him a direct line into his subject. She made it live, because she had lived it. It was incredible, it defied reason, it was unimaginable, yet it was undeniably true. She knew things no one else possibly could; she had been there.

She talked at one point about the wild genius Robert Hooke, speaking of him as though he were just a colleague in the faculty at UVA. She reminded him of an anecdote (she *reminded* him?) about the time when, during a dinner at Christ Church, the fiery Robbie had had a furious row with Isaac (meaning Newton), accusing him of stealing his work, and challenged him to a duel. And how it turned into an unseemly brawl of fisticuffs in the middle of Tom Quad, with the great and arrogant Newton ending up half drowned in Mercury fountain. And then how he himself (*he himself?*) had fished Isaac out and taken him back to his house in Merton Street. And didn't he remember how at dawn the following day, Newton had gone back to Christ Church and spent hours tossing pebbles into the fountain, puzzling over what, in a world governed by gravity, allowed the water to splash upward? Didn't he remember?

He looked across at Hazel, lying contentedly asleep beside him. She would never understand. How could she? If he told her anything at all, he'd have to tell her everything. She'd never be able to separate the sexual from the intellectual. Both were infidelity. No, he simply couldn't tell her. Not yet, at least. Not until he'd reconciled it himself.

For three days, he held himself in check. He spent the evenings cooking the family supper and helping Ben with his homework and the night lovemaking. Things Hazel said would constantly surprise him—wise and witty things that made him see her with fresh eyes—and laughter filled the house. At times he would find his mind drifting off, and once or twice he didn't hear a remark she addressed to him and she'd tease him with her usual "Yoo hoo, Matthew, come back to this century," and the moment would pass and everything continue as before, smooth and harmonious.

On the fourth day, his resolve faltered and he visited Josie again. Finding her out, he slipped a note under her door to say he would come by in the afternoon and hoping she'd be in. When he arrived she was waiting for him in her Chinese silk robe, quite naked underneath, and this time he succumbed to the temptation and, behind her closed doors and beneath her spell, discovered once again the ecstasy of oblivion.

That evening, he began the tree house which he'd promised to build Ben. And that night, he made love to Hazel with a desperate, savage passion that left her bruised and breathless.

By Sunday, the pressure was building to a head again. It was evening, Ben was upstairs in bed and Hazel was sitting at the kitchen table, pasting photographs from her latest assignments into her portfolio.

Matthew paced the room, unable to settle. He felt caged in. The nights were fast drawing in now, and against the darkness outside the windows reflected back the scene in the kitchen, making him feel hemmed in by mirrors. He fixed himself a whisky, but poured it down the sink after one sip; a drink wasn't what he needed. He glanced through the *Post,* but found nothing to hold his attention. He flicked through the television channels, then switched off with a sigh of frustration.

Hazel looked up from her photos.

"Matthew, sit down. Or go upstairs and work."

He stared at the window. The panes were streaked with rain.

"I think I'll go out."

"Oh?"

He turned. "What do you mean, 'oh?'"

"It's late. And it's pouring. It's no time to go jogging."

"Who said I wanted to go jogging?"

"You used to go jogging every day. What happened? Saving your energy for other things?"

"What other things?" he snapped.

"Hey, ease up! You *are* in a bad way, Matthew. Do whatever you want, but stop prowling around. It's driving me crazy."

"Sorry. Mustn't disturb the bread-winner at work."

She laid down her scissors and regarded him carefully.

"What exactly is eating you, Matthew?"

"Nothing."

With a shrug he picked up her portfolio and began idly leafing through it. Suddenly a face leapt out at him. Josie McDowell, with her father Otis! A flush of guilt and excitement ran through him. He looked closer, unable to tear his eyes off her. She was so different! Shorter hair, rounder face, shallower eyes—a wholly different look. And no trace of that small mole on her upper lip. Had she covered it with makeup, or had Hazel for some reason retouched it out?

Behind him, Hazel's chair scraped on the floor, and a moment later he felt her arms folding round him. He turned the page quickly, keeping his face averted for fear it might betray him.

"It's still the damned book, isn't it?" she said with sympathy.

He latched onto the escape route. He answered quickly, too quickly to check the asperity that came out in his tone.

"Does it matter? In a single day you can make what I make in a month. I don't know why we pretend."

She drew him round to face her.

"Now listen, Matthew," she said seriously. "Don't make an issue where there isn't one. Whatever I earn is ours, for the family. If I happen to make good money at the moment, that's our good fortune. If it's more than you make, that's because my work is more commercial. Your work is creative and intellectual. Yours is fundamentally more important than mine. Never forget that."

He found himself careering off on a false tangent. Anything to deflect attention from the thoughts he'd been thinking.

"Don't be patronizing, Hazel!" he responded. "I'm sick of hearing how valuable my work is, what a vital contribution it's making to the sum of human knowledge, how it's helping bridge the gulf between the arts and sciences. That's all crap! This book will sell five thousand copies world-wide, maximum, and ninety-nine percent of those to libraries. Only a handful of people will actually *read* the damn thing, and most of those will be other academics wanting to knock it to protect their own butts. Its real message just won't get through. Not to the people that matter. The wider audience."

"Why not?" she challenged. "Look what happened to *A Brief History of Time*. It's on the bestseller list."

"That's different."

"I know what you're going to say. Then write a popularized version."

"You mean, a commercial version."

"If that's what you want. Matthew, we don't need the money."

"I don't want the money, for God's sake! I just want to reach people."

Her manner softened.

"Well, *I* think you're brilliant," she said with quiet sincerity. "You don't have to stay an academic all your life if you don't want to. You can turn your hand to any number of things."

"Like what?" he snapped. "Like renovating derelict houses? Building tree houses for a profession? Become one of those pool designers we pay thousands of dollars to? Life has got to be more worthwhile." He checked himself. "I'm sorry, angel. I don't know what's gotten into me."

She stroked his cheek tenderly. "You've been going at it too hard these last weeks." She slipped her hand into his arm. "Come on, come upstairs. I'll take your mind off things."

She led him to the door and switched off the lights. In the hallway he stopped and drew her tightly toward him. She was being so painfully sweet and understanding. Why did he feel this drive to hurt her, to provoke her? He was the one deserving blame, not her, and yet all evening he'd been looking for things to blame her for. He didn't understand.

"I'm sorry," he murmured, burying his face in her neck. "Forgive your fond and foolish man."

As the internal conflict mounted, Matthew began to realize he had to find a way of reconciling his compulsion with his conscience.

He was seeing Josie every other day now, sometimes just for fifteen minutes, other times for the whole afternoon. Sometimes, too, for all his resolve and to his greater guilt, he would end up making love with her, but for most of the time they met to talk, to act out their roles as Nathaniel and Isabel, to return, for those minutes or hours, back to that earlier century. Entering her room was literally to step back in time. At times they would laugh until they ached, at others they'd quarrel and dispute, but mostly they just talked together, quietly in the half-light, reclining on the bed or on the rugs, with the aroma of herbs dousing their senses. Afterward he would hurry back to the lab and write up his notes. Already he'd accumulated a mass of astonishing information: details of experiments, formulae, recipes, herbs and medicaments, social tidbits, gossip of the day, motives, insights into Nathaniel's struggle with the Church, clever ruses of Isabel's to escape her father's eye, their laboratory and its equipment, their love and its flowering, anecdotes, too, in profusion. One day she told him of the student with a fever whom the college physician had bled to death with fifty leeches and a dozen cupping glasses. The next, she reminded him laughingly of the time that Robbie Boyle brought some bizarre contraption to their lab to demonstrate the relationship of mass to pressure in a gas and the infernal thing exploded. She told him things that no one who hadn't lived in those times could possibly know. He had stumbled on a gold mine beyond the wildest imagining.

He couldn't conceive of giving her up; he simply couldn't live without her. And yet he couldn't live with himself while he kept it going with her. Something had to give.

It was a brief encounter with Lyall at the laboratory that finally pushed him toward a working solution, unsatisfactory though it proved to be.

It was approaching four o'clock and he was just heading through the main door for his rendezvous with Josie in her rooms when he heard Lyall's throaty voice behind, hailing him across the lobby.

"Matthew, old man, I've been looking for you!" The professor bustled through the door after him. Pausing on the broad step outside, he glanced furtively about him. "Got a minute?"

"Sure."

Lyall shot him a penetrating glance, then looked down at his feet where fallen leaves swirled in small eddies, caught in the gentle autumnal breeze. He cleared his throat.

"I think you ought to know something, Matthew," he began, meeting his eye at last. "I don't have time for gossip as a rule, but a little rumor has come to my ears. It concerns you and a certain chemistry graduate. Now, this is not strictly any of my business—"

"Correct," retorted Matthew, turning away. "It is not."

Lyall's hand restrained him. "I think you should listen to what I have to say."

"Listen to gossip?"

"Matthew, I'm not talking to you as head of the department. This is strictly off the record. I'm talking to you as a friend. A friend of Hazel's and the family."

"Leave Hazel out of this."

Lyall pulled a comradely smile.

"Look, we're men of the world. I have my little flings, God knows. But I never mess on my own doorstep. That's cardinal rule number one. It's unprofessional and it creates all kinds of nasty problems. In a close community like a campus, it's impossible to keep anything quiet for long. Tongues wag."

"I'm sorry, Lyall, but I don't have time—"

"I'd hate those tongues to wag in Colbert's ears."

"If Colbert is dumb enough to make his appointment decisions on the basis of rumor—"

"Suppose this 'rumor' gets to Hazel's ears? I'm thinking of how she'll feel."

"Come off it, Lyall! Don't pretend. Anyway," he glared, conscious that he was trapping himself, "what a person doesn't know can't hurt them."

Lyall shook his head. "I'm not making moral judgments. I'm only saying that you should think of what you're doing before you get in too deep. Look, old lad, she's only a student. They're all the same—pretty young things, but immature. If you really need to stretch your wings, I could suggest—"

"Thank you, Lyall, but I don't need any tips from you." He glanced at his watch. "I must be going."

Lyall stood back to let him pass.

"Think about it."

"I already have. Now, if you don't mind ..."

Muffling an impatient oath, Matthew turned and hurried down the steps into the golden autumn sunlight. He cut diagonally across the lawns and took the shortcut around the back of Monroe Hall. As he went he felt acutely conscious of people's glances. Was it just a "little rumor" or common knowledge? Perhaps Josie herself had heard those mutterings in corridors and faced those knowing looks. He hastened his step, anxious to forestall anything she might do.

"Suppose this 'rumor' gets to Hazel's ears? I'm thinking of how she'll feel." How she *will* feel: He'd used the future tense, not the conditional. Matthew bit his lip. Whatever precautions he took, however carefully he kept the affair clandestine, somehow, some day, from some source, Hazel was bound to get to know.

His conscience knew what he was doing was wrong. He recognized that this was at the root of his behavior toward Hazel. It was the old, familiar loop: feeling guilty at cheating on her, he wanted to provoke her to react angrily so that he could then accuse her of being intolerable and thus feel justified in going on cheating. It didn't work with Hazel because she reacted with sympathy and understanding—which in turn enraged him further. The only way to escape from this vicious circle was to find a means of persuading himself that he was not, in fact, doing anything wrong.

He would recognize what he had in effect become: two people.

The man who was married to Hazel, who lived with her and loved her, the man who had been talking with Lyall on the steps of the laboratory just a moment ago—this was Matthew Cavewood. But the man now walking along the serpentine wall toward the Ranges, the man who any moment would be entering a young woman's rooms and there revisiting his past life, this was Nathaniel Shawcrosse. Could the second man be charged with the crimes of the first?

For a moment he paused in his tracks. It seemed at first to resolve everything. There need be no more conflict of loyalties, no more internal angst, no more torment of guilt. Until he realized the implications: he was admitting to a split personality.

The peace of mind came at a price, and the price was madness.

EIGHTEEN

To Matthew's surprise, the madness felt most natural. In fact, hardly mad at all. As a *modus vivendi* it felt positively comfortable. Since the night of the ball, he had not doubted for a moment that Josie was Isabel; he knew. The only puzzle for him had been how. How could a modern-day girl actually be someone who had died three hundred years ago? He was now spared from having to confront that brain-numbing conundrum. Madmen had their own logic; they weren't bound by objective reasoning.

Within a week or two, a steady routine had begun to develop. Every other afternoon shortly after three o'clock, Nathaniel Shawcrosse would make his way across the grounds to Isabel Hardiment's room, and there they would talk and perhaps make love and work on his *Tractatus Novae Naturalis Philosophiae,* his definitive statement on the New Science, and discuss the preoccupations of the day. And every evening around seven, Matthew Cavewood would leave the department of physics laboratories and climb into his gray Mercedes and head home to his wife, Hazel, and there they, too, would talk and perhaps make love and discuss his work and the preoccupations of their own day—incidents of local crime and global violence, gossip from the campus and scandal from the capital, along with the whole spectrum of domestic concerns from her latest photographic assignment to Ben's nightly homework.

A mind might inhabit two places at the same time, however, but a body could not. It was inevitable that before long there would be a slipup.

The evenings were drawing in noticeably, and the first hints of dusk had now begun to fall across the grounds as he left Josie's rooms. One particular day, as the hour to leave approached, she became strangely quiet. The room was half in darkness; she liked to draw the last light from the day before lighting the oil lamps. The air was still heady with smoldering incense, and in the background the clock on the mantelpiece continued its relentless measured tick. He was reclining on the bed, talking in a rambling fashion about a feral boy discovered in the wild who was the current talk of the town. She was sitting in the armchair, naked but for a silk slip, hugging her knees and staring at him with large, sad eyes.

Suddenly she clamped her fists over her ears. For a while she sat with her teeth clenched and face screwed up in pain, then without warning she rose and swooped across the room to the mantelpiece where, with a violent thrust, she swept the clock off onto the floor. It fell with a shattering crash, and was silent.

He understood. He, too, hated the sound of the minutes passing. Each tick of the clock brought their time together one beat closer to its end. He seemed hardly to arrive before he had to leave. Always snatched afternoons, too, never proper evenings or whole nights and days.

She glared down at the broken clock with a ferocity that took him aback, then looked up at him, focusing her bitterness on him. He felt suddenly aware of how much he was taking and how little he was giving. That was the sorry rule in affairs between married men and single women. Theirs was far different to that, of course—an infinitely more extraordinary and special—and yet he'd been treating her just like any bit of stuff that Lyall might be knocking off. But what could he offer? There simply was no more time he could give, no more commitment he could make.

"I could maybe manage to make an evening sometimes," he offered, conscious of how lame it sounded. "Come around eight or nine and stay till midnight or so."

She came up and stood in front of him, fixing him with a steely stare. Her response was a single, taut word.

"When?"

"I don't know," he fumbled. "Tomorrow maybe?"

"I shall have the cup prepared."

He didn't follow her meaning—but then, so much of what she said was unfathomable. Her eyes glowed out of the dark at him, penetrating his soul. The intensity of the gaze began to unnerve him. He took refuge in physical contact. He reached forward. Working his hands beneath her slip until they clasped the smooth mounds of her buttocks, he gradually drew her up onto the bed until she was stretched on top of him. She yielded without demur, raising herself on straightened arms so that her breasts, hanging full within her slip, brushed across his face. She tossed back her head as the pleasure began to bite, and from her throat came a low gargling cry that swelled with the roaring in his temples, until he felt his whole being lifting off the ground and spiraling higher and higher into a daze of stars.

But Nathaniel had not thought to check with Matthew. If he had, he'd have found in Matthew's diary the following night was booked. Lyall and Myra were coming to dinner.

Josie spent the following day making careful preparations. She cleaned the small room from top to bottom, and above the door she intertwined sprigs of dog rose and wild honeysuckle that she'd collected in the escarpment along Jefferson Park Avenue. She added perfume to the potpourri and slipped fresh verbena inside the pillows, then settled down to prepare the mandrake.

The mandrake root was fat and flaccid, with the bloated whitness of a drowned man's flesh. It hadn't properly dried out yet. But events were moving too fast. There was no time to wait. The hour for the cup had come.

Wrapping the plant in a newspaper, she hurried to the chemistry labs where, on a bench well out of sight, she cut it into slivers. These she dried carefully over a retort. Dessicated, the flakes now crumbled easily, and before long she had reduced the root to a pile of whitish gray powder. Evening was drawing on when she finally returned to her room. There she made ready the small samovar, laid out wine and sweetmeats and the special lacquer bowl, and finally took a shower and annointed her body with essential oils and sweet-smelling unguents. Then, wrapped in her Chinese embroidered robe, she sat down cross-legged on the bed to wait.

Eight o'clock became nine, and nine became ten, and there was no sign of him. She sat as still as a statue, her face frozen in a hard and bitter grimace. Around and around in her mind went the same thoughts: It's all happening again, just as it happened before. The betrayal, the deceit, the false promises, the broken trust ... but not so soon! It is not time yet. Everything must proceed in its ordained pattern. The sequence cannot be broken. The betrayal and the revenge—that comes later, all in good time. First comes the cup. He must drink the cup. Once he tastes of the cup, there can be no turning back. He will be caught in the inescapable web. And the next stages, proceeding one after another with unrelenting necessity, can then begin.... Yet should a broken promise go quite unpunished?

As the first strokes of a distant clock chimed eleven and the last of the candles was sputtering out, she finally rose from the bed. She went over to the wardrobe and, from under a pile of clothes, she took out an old, long, slender, bone-handled butcher's knife.

Matthew barely slept that night. It had been a terrible evening. Lyall and his wife hadn't left until well after one in the morning. And he'd drunk too much. He'd only remembered they had people coming to dinner when he found Hazel laying the table, and by then it was too late to get a message through to Josie. As the evening wore on, his frustration built up into anger. First he took it out on Myra, whose snobbish gossip always infuriated him, but although Hazel glared at him, Myra herself seemed too thick-skinned to notice, while Lyall patently enjoyed the spectacle of his wife being baited. Then he had a go at Lyall himself, who kept making little remarks full of double entendres and sly insinuations. The meal dragged on interminably, as cocktails became wine and wine became liqueurs and one course followed another in agonizingly slow succession, and no amount of impatience on Matthew's part could hasten its conclusion. In the end he took his rage out on himself for his own stupidity and decided there was nothing to do but get drunk.

With the dawn came the panic. What if breaking Josie's trust had broken the spell? Suppose she refused to see him again? The convenient partitioning was breaking down and emotions were spilling over from one side to the other. As he shaved that morning, he was so distracted that he cut himself, and the bleeding could only be staunched with a clownishly large sticking plaster. He bolted his breakfast and left the house before Hazel and Ben had even stirred, and with a pounding head he clambered into his car and drove a painful path to the university.

The morning was bright, and a fresh autumnal wind carrying the scent of burning leaves swept through the low brick cloisters. As he reached Josie's door, he paused to collect his thoughts. From the other rooms people were beginning to emerge, some perhaps off to breakfast, others even at that hour bound for the libraries. Maybe she had already left, too, and he would find the door locked and a note in his pigeonhole at the department. He tapped tentatively. There was no reply. He tried the door. It was open. He stepped hesitantly inside.

The room was in semidarkness. The bed, it seemed, was empty. The air was fusty with the odor of stale incense. He took another step, into a pool of cooler air ... unnaturally cool....

She was there!

He whispered her name. He looked to one side and the other. Then he turned. He stifled a gasp.

She was standing behind the door, motionless. In her upraised hand she held a long, slender object. It was almost invisible in the low, gray light. She moved, and he instantly caught the razor-sharp line of the blade. Before he could check her, she stepped forward and brought the knife down in a swift stabbing thrust. Twisting, he sidestepped the stroke. The blade flashed past him, slashing the sleeve of his jacket as it passed. He stumbled backward. The samovar toppled over with a loud clatter. She was coming for him again, moving in jerks like a mechanical toy, her eyes boring through him and her face twisted in a demonic mask.

He tripped over the ottoman and fell backward onto the bed. In a flash she was upon him, the knife poised directly above his face. As she brought it down, he caught her wrist in mid stroke, with the point of the blade just inches from his cheek. For a moment he held her locked in his grip, then suddenly she relaxed her pressure on the knife and let it drop. He jerked his head to the side, but not quite fast enough. The blade caught his cheek a glancing blow as it fell, cutting a shallow gash on the point of his jawbone.

He flung her off him and rolled aside.

"Jesus Christ!" he swore. "What the hell are you up to?"

She crawled to her knees and glared at him from the floor.

"Never do that again," she hissed slowly.

Confused, he blustered.

"Never do what? You'd better never do *that* again! You could have killed me."

"Remember that."

"For God's sake!" He was recovering but still trembling from the shock. Appease her, he told himself. Get her talking. Say anything to quiet her. "I know, I know, I didn't make it last night. I couldn't. I'd forgotten we had people to dinner. There was no way I could reach you. For what it's worth, my evening was shit. I hated every minute. I could only think of you." He heaved a breath. "That's why I came now. And this is what I walk into!"

She had risen to her feet and was looking at him, through him, with cold, dead eyes. He had the feeling he was suddenly a stranger, that she didn't recognize him. It was as though she'd drawn the blinds down between them.

Sick, angry, he felt a sudden impulse to kick sense into this madness. Just what *was* he dealing with here?

"Now look, Josie," he began brutally, climbing to his feet, "I think we'd better get certain parameters straight——"

The look of horror on her face checked him. Josie, he'd called her Josie! Well, she *was* Josie, goddammit! Or she *had* been. Wasn't that so? Wasn't this the pretty little girl in the photo, standing with Mom outside the big house? The university graduate with Dad in the *People* magazine portrait? When had it happened? When had she changed?

No, no! This was the forbidden question. He pressed his fingers against his temples. The division was collapsing. Here he was, being Matthew Cavewood in Nathaniel Shawcrosse's house. He had broken the rules.

He sank back onto the bed. To admit questions was to doubt, and doubt would destroy this precious, fragile miracle. He closed his eyes and began to think thoughts of Nathaniel, to evoke his spirit, to resonate with his being. Gradually he felt the change coming over him.

After what seemed an eternity, he felt a light touch on his cheek. He looked up to find the girl standing over him, her face filled with a tender, sorrowful beauty. He took her hand and pressed it against the wound. It hurt, but he wanted it to.

"Forgive me, Isabel," he muttered.

He left having laid a hostage to fortune. The implications only hit him as he was completing his notes on the computer at the lab. The following week he was due to be giving a paper at a conference at the University of Illinois. It would be a two-night stay. And he had invited her along.

At first he decided not to think anymore about it. He hadn't even written the paper yet, and that alone made the prospect seem beyond concern. He didn't want to think about the deadly rage she could flare into, either. He believed she'd never intended to do him serious harm—she'd let go of the knife, after all, not actually tried to use it—but it gave him a chilling glimpse of her potential if he wrongly provoked her. As if in compensation, however, she provided him that morning with an astonishing insight into Shawcrosse's concept of "flux" as the medium operating at the mind-matter interface. From the safe distance of the laboratory, the whole scene looked just the jealous outburst of an aggrieved mistress, and he was content to leave it at that.

As the day of the trip approached, however, he grew increasingly nervous. At home, he tried to behave as though it was just another routine conference, part of the academic round, but he was filled with a growing anxiety that something would go wrong. First it looked as though Lyall would be passing through Champaign-Urbana at the very same time. Then, with the overcompensation of the guilty, Matthew suggested to Hazel that she joined him on the trip, and to his utter alarm she accepted at once. They could make a holiday of it, she proposed, and drive to Chicago or somewhere interesting for a few days' break. Up until the last moment it seemed that she was coming, and only an unexpected tooth infection of Ben's kept her back.

Even then, she was bent on driving him to the airport. He had arranged with Josie that he'd pick her up on a corner, a short walk from her rooms but discreetly off campus, and drive her to the airport himself.

"You've got better things to do, angel," he told Hazel as he buckled his overnight case. They were within minutes of having to leave.

"Wrong. I'm free as air." She reached for her car keys.

"There's Ben. I'm thinking about his tooth."

"An outing will do him good. You know how he loves spotting planes."

Matthew glanced at his watch. This was getting critical. Any minute now, Josie would be setting off for the rendezvous.

"I'm driving myself, thanks all the same, and that's that," he said firmly, then mollified his tone. "I need to think about the paper. God knows what I'm going to say."

She cast him an intense, puzzled glance but said nothing. He busied himself with his case, afraid she might read his mind. He just had to keep talking and moving. He reached to kiss her. Her body was stiff, unbending.

"You won't be missing anything," he said. "No gold taps and milk baths for me. This is strictly work."

"I should hope so," she said doubtfully.

"Don't be silly, darling," he laughed. "You think anyone would chose Champaign for a vacation?"

At that moment Ben ran up and, glad of the diversion, Matthew bent down and gave him a big hug. Then he straightened, reached for his suitcase and headed briskly out to the car, chatting to Ben as he went, telling him to take care of his tooth and promising they'd really get down to work on the tree house when he came back. At last he threw the case in the back of the Mercedes and was ready to go.

He turned to Hazel, standing pale and watchful, and took her in his arms. This time, her body softened into his embrace and she returned his kiss with a curious fervor. And as he finally drove away, he could see her figure in the rearview mirror, waving him off almost as though he were going to war.

Several streets away, he drew up and wiped the traces of her lipstick off his mouth, then set off again quickly, before he could feel the sting of shame. Back at home, Matthew's wife would be tidying up or calling her agent or fixing a coffee or playing video games with her son in the den. Ahead of him, Nathaniel's mistress would be coming down the hill toward the corner of Main and 14th Street. And he had just moments in which to make the transition.

Josie had brought a large suitcase that clanked as it moved, and it wasn't until they'd reached the hotel in Champaign that he understood: she'd brought along a pair of candlesticks and the small samovar. And it wasn't until he'd returned upstairs from the lobby, where he'd gone to call Hazel, that he realized her purpose.

The room was transformed. The only light now came from candles, which lent the place a mysterious, conspiratorial air. She was sitting cross-legged on the floor with her Chinese robe wrapped loosely about her, stirring the bowl of the samovar as it came slowly to the boil under the flame of the spirit lamp beneath. Beside her lay a small lacquer bowl containing some roughly ground grayish white powder. As she reached out to add another pinch to the brew, the movement of her sleeve fluttered the candles, making the shadows dance on the walls. This was an alchemist's coven.

He felt momentarily disorientated. Barely a minute ago, he'd been in a modern hotel lobby, talking down a line to another person hundreds of miles away. Passing through this door, he'd stepped over the threshold into an earlier century. This room was a time bubble caught within the present. He blinked hard. Was he in the now or the then? Perhaps both. Time is parallel and interchangeable—one of Shawcrosse's precepts.

A steamy, rootlike smell rose in the air. His head began to swim, and he became aware of a strange melting sensation creeping through his body.

He met her eye as she looked up. He knew without needing to ask what she was preparing. It stirred echoes deep in his memory. He spoke the word slowly, in a whisper. It had the ring of a magic spell.

"Mandragora?"

Her eyes glowed deep violet in the half-light, their gaze profound and intense.

"Of course."

In silence, following the bidding of some familiar yet forgotten ritual, he began his own preparations. First he made his ablutions, then the libations. Finally, clad only in a black bathrobe, he sat down before her and accepted the bowl she proffered.

The draft was bitter and sharp, and his throat tightened involuntarily against the dilute poison. Slowly they passed the bowl between them, sipping in turns until it was almost empty. At first, he felt only a knotty constriction in his stomach, but gradually this dissolved into a glow of warmth, which spread quite suddenly and fiercely through his body, from his bowels to his chest and outward to his hands and feet. As it rose up his back and neck to the root of his brain, he felt a sharp, explosive jolt as though the lid of his skull were being blown off, and then abruptly, with a roaring like fire tearing through a forest, he felt himself being sucked upward and out of his body. As he rose to the ceiling, he glanced down and saw his own body, now naked, moving on top of hers and a moment later her head jerking back in a gasp of pleasure, then he was bursting through the ceiling, through the very roof above, and blazing like a shooting star into the brilliant darkness of the firmament.

Hazel stared at the small glass vial in her hand. A hazy morning sun filtered softly in through the bathroom window, and she tilted the tube to the light. It looked as though ... She shook it gently; she'd give it another thirty seconds, just to be absolutely sure. Finally she released the small rubber stopper and drew out the plastic tester stick. A deep purple spot stood out clearly on the impregnated wadding.

There could be no doubt at all. She was pregnant.

Yet she wouldn't quite believe it. She read the instructions over again in case she'd made a slip. She didn't feel different. She pressed her breasts and they weren't especially tender. She tried to remember how she had felt with Ben, but it was too long ago. Some women claimed they knew the very moment they conceived, others seemed to have no idea right up until the labor. Here she had the medical evidence in her hand, so why did she doubt it? This was something she'd wanted, something she'd planned. What was she afraid of?

She understood. Doubt was a precaution against disappointment, an antidote to the joy in case something should go wrong. She counted off the months on her fingers: October, November ... it would be born in June. A child of summer. They'd do up the room next to Ben's; that would make a lovely nursery. What would they call it? If it was a girl, she'd like to give it her mother's name.... Steady on, she told herself. Don't count your chicken; the hatching day is a long way off yet.

As she stood at the window, stretching her gaze out across the dewy expanse of lawn to the tall plane tree ankle-deep in fallen leaves, she felt an irrepressible joy surge through her. She must tell Matthew at once! With a glance at her watch on the sink, she hurried through to the bedroom, flung herself onto the bed and snatched up the phone. He would be over the moon.

As the hotel switchboard answered, however, she hesitated, then replaced the receiver. The news was far too wonderful to break over the phone. Besides, he was probably on his way home by now. She had a better idea. She thought back to how he'd surprised her at the airport the other day. Oh boy, would she surprise *him!*

She drove fast, afraid she'd miss him. Ben had been kept in after school for some minor misdemeanor, and when finally she'd collected him she ran into roadwork delivering him to Elaine and Harry's. She'd arranged for him to stay the night with them: she was carrying Matthew off to a quiet country hotel. She'd break the news over dinner.

Further roadwork delayed her on the approach to the airport, and by the time she'd parked and hurried into arrivals, Matthew's plane had been on the ground fifteen minutes. Knowing he had only carry-on luggage, she decided she'd best intercept him at the parking-lot exit. She was turning to retrace her steps when she caught a glimpse of his head standing out above a crowd of other passengers coming down the long arrivals corridor. With a sigh of relief, she stepped up to the barrier to wait.

The press momentarily cleared, and she saw he was carrying two bags, one his small overnight case and the other a large suitcase. Beside him, strolling at the same easy pace, was a slender girl with blond hair. Hazel smiled to herself: the rogue would chose the prettiest girl on the plane to help with her luggage! For a moment she thought she'd lost him, but when the press cleared she saw he had moved to the side of the gangway and was bent over an open suitcase. As she watched, he took out a shaving bag—she thought it was a shaving bag—and slipped it into his own case, then stood up. The girl slid her arm into his, and together they moved slowly forward toward the barrier.

A few numb seconds passed before the truth hit Hazel. It caught her like a whiplash. Grasping at the rail, she watched in shock as Matthew and the girl walked right past her, then crossed the concourse and headed toward the exit.

She wanted to scream but all that came out was a tight, choking moan. She wanted to rush after them and tear them apart, but her limbs wouldn't move. Somewhere in the back of her mind, she recognized the face of the girl, but she couldn't quite recall from where. It wasn't important. The fact was all that counted.

She bit hard on her knuckles. She blinked hard, as if this was a dream from which she could wake herself, but it was all too real. She was dying. The walls of the world were collapsing in on her, crushing her, suffocating her.

Standing there, unable to move, she pressed her fists into her pockets and screwed her eyes tight against the pain. Matthew, Matthew, she wept inside, how could you do this to us? Now of all times, how could you?

NINETEEN

Through a mist of tears, Hazel drove in pursuit, and within a few miles she had the gray Mercedes in her sight. She slowed down and followed at a discreet distance. Through the rear window she could see Matthew and the girl laughing. Who was she? She caught her briefly in profile, and suddenly she recognized her. Josie McDowell, Senator McDowell's daughter! What was Matthew doing with her? He couldn't be giving her a ride home; this wasn't the route to Richmond. Wasn't she supposed to be away at Northeastern, anyway? Hazel was stricken with sudden uncertainty. Maybe it was perfectly innocent after all. Maybe he had genuinely met the girl on the plane and she happened to need a ride to Charlottesville. Perhaps he was even going to bring her to their home for a drink on the way.

From the way they looked at one another, she knew she was clutching at straws. The proof was not long in coming. Instead of taking the exit to Rugby Avenue and home, Matthew drove to Main Street and parked up a small side road. For a full fifteen minutes the two stayed in the car. When Josie emerged, she looked flushed. She stood straightening her clothes and hair while Matthew retrieved her case from the trunk. Finally, she kissed him good-bye and, pausing at the corner of the street to give him a small wave, headed off toward the university grounds. A moment later, the Mercedes pulled out and drove slowly away in the homeward direction.

Hazel sat in her own car, paralyzed. None of this was really happening. It simply wasn't possible to be so deliriously happy and so utterly cast down in the space of the same day. She shut her eyes tight and waited for the terrible spell to break. But it didn't. This *was* happening. And worse, it had happened before to her, just like this.

She pounded the steering wheel with her fists. She hated men. They were two-faced shits, the lot of them. She should have known. Hadn't she learned her lesson with Clay? When Matthew came along, she'd foreseen the danger, and for a long time she'd kept her distance. Time and again she'd warned herself to keep some inner corner safe and separate, some unbreachable refuge to which she could always retreat. But in the end she'd weakened. She'd committed herself to him, heart and soul, and now she was paying the price.

Suddenly she felt trapped, frantic to get away from there. Starting up the car, she set off at a furious pace without any idea where she was going. She found her route taking her into the dying sun. Filled with a desperate urge to cheat the encroaching darkness, she drove faster and farther. Finally, on the crest of a ridge deep in the hills of West Virginia, she pulled up and climbed out of the car. She couldn't outrun the problem. She had to stop and *think*.

The wind was cold, but its chill bite upon her flesh made her feel curiously alive. As she stood watching the sun setting behind the far mountain ranges, an unexpected calm gradually settled over her. She had faced worse before, and she'd pulled through. She didn't need a man or a man's love. She had lived alone for close on ten years, and in that time she'd raised a happy child and pursued a successful career. Ben was hers, and no one could take that away. The life growing inside her, too, was inalienably her own. She was not the helpless victim of a cheating husband: she was her own self, strong and capable and responsible for all that happened in her own life.

She would be pragmatic. She wanted this child, and she wished for it to grow up knowing its father and thriving in a harmonious atmosphere. For its sake as much as her own, she had a duty to try and save her marriage. She had won Matthew back once before, and then she'd been up against the most potent of all possible rivals—a woman created by his own imagination. But what was she dealing with now? Just some flighty young college kid, quite a pretty one, admittedly, but nevertheless made of flesh and blood and altogether a perfectly regular adversary such as a million wives were facing at that very moment across the breadth of the country.

She would keep her pregnancy secret, *her* secret, the haven to which she could always retreat. If she told him, it would only force his decision and create a resentment that some time later would explode under stress. She didn't want him back under any kind of duress. And if she didn't get him back at all, then she needed her options open.

Resolute and composed, she headed back to the car. But the moment she closed the door, she was assailed by a wave of despair and burst into tears. This tough talk was just words. How could you react reasonably when your deepest feelings were at stake? The heart never listened to the head. You could tell yourself a thousand times that your man was a worthless shit and you owed it to yourself to quit, but that counted for nothing in the face of a single thought whispering in your mind that you loved him.

She had to find a way. Whatever she'd done, whatever he didn't get from her and had to look for in this girl, whatever the problem was, she'd fix it. She would wind down her work, if that was it: she knew he resented it, however much he said he didn't. They'd make the marriage work together. They'd build the home they'd always planned. They were almost there. Don't shoot us down, Matthew, she wanted to cry. Not before we've had a chance to fly. Not now that we have what we've always wanted, our own child.

Eventually, she storm in her heart blew itself out, and feeling drained and numb she returned to Charlottesville. She had no more rage and no more resolve. She just felt empty.

She heard Matthew hurrying across the hall as she slipped the key into the front door. The anxiety on his face dissolved to relief.

"Angel! Thank God! I've been so worried. It's almost nine! I was beginning to think something had happened. Why didn't you call?" He looked past her. "Where's Ben?"

"Ben's staying over at Elaine and Harry's," she replied coldly, brushing past him.

He caught her by the arm and pulled her toward him. She let him kiss her. His touch felt merely dead.

"I bought him a wildlife video," he went on, following her into the kitchen. "It was all I could find at the airport. And something for you, sweetheart. Sorry about the gift wrap."

He handed her an airport store bag in which was a box of Godiva chocolates. Expensive confections, the gift of a guilty conscience.

"I see you didn't get out much." She laid the chocolates aside; she'd give them away.

"I was on the go the whole time," he replied easily.

"I bet you were, Matthew."

"The seminar took up the first day. Then I spent the whole of yesterday at the physics department. I ended up having dinner with Max Feldman. You remember M-M-Max, with the stammer? He sends you his l-l-love. We had a good laugh. You should have been there."

"I think not."

She reached for the vodka, but he took the bottle from her.

"Sit down, angel. You look dead beat. Instant Death, on the rocks? C'mon, I'll fix supper. Fancy pasta and salad? Pesto, or carbonara?"

"I'm not hungry."

"Just you wait." He put a pan of water on to boil and began chopping a lettuce. "Aren't you going to ask me how the paper went?"

"I can see from that smug grin all over your face."

"It knocked their socks off, angel."

She sat back with her drink and watched him. She could hardly believe that this man had spent the last days and nights with another woman. Nothing in his manner betrayed the least guilt or remorse or any hint that anything had happened at all. He prepared the supper, lit the candles, poured the wine, told anecdotes about Max Feldman and other characters at Champaign, inquired keenly about what she'd been doing, showed genuine concern about a problem she was having with a client who wouldn't pay, and afterward he reached for her hand and settled his large, dark eyes upon hers with such transparent good humor and pleasure that she felt filled with doubt and confusion and began to wonder if she'd got it all wrong.

Yet she had seen. His performance tonight astonished her. Either he was simply a superlative actor or else he genuinely saw nothing wrong in what he had done. It didn't seem to mean he'd stopped loving her; if anything, he behaved more warmly toward her than when he'd left on the trip. Perhaps this was just another example of how men "compartmentalized." They divided their lives into sections, like a submarine where if one section blew the boat would still go on. He probably saw no contradiction in being with a girl one night and his wife the next. If there was no contradiction, there could be no deceit. Life, for him, could go on exactly as before. Nothing substantive had changed.

This realization left her feeling angrier than ever, for she saw how impotent it made her. You couldn't win back a man's love when he hadn't withdrawn it in the first place.

Angry, too, that he should get away with it. There might be no contradiction for him, but there was for her. For her, life could not go on exactly as before. Not in an atmosphere of deceit. Would he dare deny it?

He was switching the lights off in preparation for going to bed. She remained in her chair, not moving. She met his puzzled glance with an open challenge.

"Matthew, is there something you want to tell me?"

"What?" he responded quickly.

"You should know."

He came over to her and put his hands on her shoulders.

"Like how much I missed you?" he smiled easily.

Her glare made him step back.

"Matthew," she began coolly, "what were you doing with the McDowell girl in your car?"

He started violently.

"What? When?" he snapped, a flush rising to his cheeks.

"This afternoon, at the airport."

"You were at the airport?" he asked with incredulity.

"Don't keep answering me with questions, Matthew. I saw you. I followed you."

"You were snooping on me? That's shocking! I'm ... flabbergasted."

"Just tell me."

"She was on the plane. I offered her a ride. That's all."

"To Charlottesville?"

"She's at the university."

"I thought she was at Northeastern."

"She transferred. We got talking on the flight. She's doing a masters in chemistry, under Magnus Fairburn. Quite a bright kid."

"And you were talking about chemistry all that time you were parked round the corner off Main Street?"

"What is this, Hazel? A police interrogation?" He struggled to bluff his way out. "I demand to see a lawyer!"

"She didn't happen to go up to Champaign with you, too?"

"Of course not! Why should I take her? I wanted you to come, remember?"

"Is that the truth, Matthew?"

"For God's sake, stop this, Hazel. Whatever's in your mind, forget it. I met her on the flight back, okay? That's the end of it." He went to the door. "I'm going to bed. You coming or not?"

She let him go ahead. She needed time alone to cope with the shock of his blatant lie. No one you'd just met on a plane would have your shaving bag in their case. After a good while she followed upstairs but stayed in the bathroom until she was sure he would be asleep. She didn't want to have to face the issue of bed. She couldn't kiss the lips that had uttered such a barefaced untruth.

Too troubled to sleep, she wrapped her bathrobe around her and went upstairs to her large attic studio. She paused for a moment in the pale moonlight that streamed in through the skylights, then abruptly snapped on the light. Thought was a traitor to the heart. She leafed through a drawer of files in which she kept the master copies of her photographs until she came upon the originals for the *People* magazine profile. She spread them out on the desk and, bringing the lamp closer, examined the face of the girl smiling sweetly back at her.

She had certainly changed. Her hair was different, for a start. In the photos she wore it tied back in a bow, whereas the girl this afternoon had worn it piled high, with ringlets falling either side of her face in a strangely old-world, courtly style, strangely like that old portrait of Isabel.... Her face seemed thinner now, too, and the bone structure more pronounced. She looked somehow more mature than in the photographs, more interesting, more calculating.

The smile on the face now mocked her. She bit her lip. This was the girl her husband was screwing.

She reached for a small brown bottle from the cabinet over the sink. The label read, HYDROCHLORIC ACID: HANDLE WITH CARE. Laying the print on a ceramic dish, she carefully unscrewed the bottle and dribbled a few drops of the virulent liquid onto the surface. With a soft hiss, the emulsion sputtered and scorched, dissolving the whole of the girl's face, and within a moment nothing was left but a vicious, brown-rimmed hole burned in the paper. The eyes, the hair, the sweet and mocking smile, all were gone.

Over the next days, Hazel grew progressively more unnerved by the atmosphere of calm normality that reigned at home. Matthew gave never the least hint of the lie he'd told or the double life he was living. He wasn't simply papering over the cracks; for him, it seemed, there were no cracks. Everything was harmonious, in balance. She was living with a schizoid, and it was driving her crazy. She felt her grip slipping. Her resolve to hold back was constantly on the point of cracking. Worse, she found her anger rebounding off the blank wall upon herself. She almost began to blame herself. Little hidden insecurities started coming to the surface. What did she lack, what was she failing to provide, that he was driven to look for elsewhere? What had the little bitch to offer?

Well, for one thing, the girl was younger. She was graced with a younger body.

Alone, standing naked before the mirror, Hazel examined her own body critically. She pinched the skin on her thighs—not much superfluous there. Her stomach was flat, her breasts were full and still firm enough not to need support, and only the faintest stretch marks betrayed that she had borne a child. True, a few crow's feet radiated out from the corner of her eyes when she smiled, and two small vertical lines puckered her forehead when she frowned, leaving white ghost traces where she'd squinted in the sun, but it was still the face of a woman younger than her years. Even so, from then on, every morning after taking Ben to school she did her aerobic exercises, and in the afternoons she worked out for an hour at the health club. It did her morale good, if nothing else.

Then, too, the girl was a student. No doubt she flattered Matthew's ego and made him feel the big professor. Her work didn't threaten him.

One morning, Hazel cleared the kitchen table and removed all signs of her own work. From now on, she'd play down her career. She'd never mention it to Matthew, and if he asked she'd merely brush it aside. She'd conduct her business strictly during the hours he was out of the house and never let it intrude upon evenings and weekends. She would encourage him to talk about his own work, however, and, above all, she'd listen.

Finally and most cruelly of all, the girl was free. Romance flourished on the unknown and the impulsive; domesticity was its death.

Hazel decided that she would think bigger. She would no longer let her life be dominated by household concerns. She'd go out more often, she'd get tickets to concerts or the theater, she'd get back in touch with Pauline and her friends from D.C., she'd invite people to dinner more often and accept more invitations out. For the next three or four weeks, she stuck to her resolve. She did it for herself but, unexpectedly, Matthew seemed to reap benefit from it, too. Gradually, she came to the realization that this whole strategy was counterproductive. Everything she was doing was merely making it easier for him! The harmony she was fostering at home was exactly what he wanted. In effect, she was simply reinforcing the status quo.

The issue finally came to a head one windswept afternoon in early November. She was at home, catching up on her accounts. The sun was dazzlingly bright and the air chill, and the leaves swirled in wild flurries with each gust of wind. She felt seized with quiet desperation, as though she were witnessing the last gasp of the dying season before the dark winter rains and snows set in. On impulse, she picked up the phone and dialed the department, and within a moment she was through to Matthew's lab.

"Hi, angel," came his cheery voice. "What's new?"

"Drop whatever you're doing, Matthew," she commanded. "I'm coming over to take you out."

There was a moment's silence.

"Ah," he said cautiously. "Where to?"

"Anywhere. Let's go into the country. Have you noticed what a beautiful day it is?"

"I, uh, I can't be that long," he fumbled. "I'm seeing Lyall at four."

He's lying, she thought. I can hear it in his voice.

"I thought you said Lyall was out of town," she said sweetly.

"Did I?"

"Why don't you check? I'll hold."

"Well, it's a committee meeting," he responded. "I guess he doesn't have to be there."

"Then you don't either. Oh, forget it, Matthew."

"Hazel," he offered, "it's two-thirty. I could meet you in town for an hour."

"Forget it, I said."

"Wait." He searched further for something to mollify her. "Tomorrow's the weekend. Let's all have an outing then."

"I meant just the two of us. Tomorrow's too late."

"What do you mean, too late?" he said quickly.

"It's supposed to rain," she replied innocently.

He let out a sigh. "I'm sorry, but you know how it is. Meetings, and all that."

"I know how it is, Matthew," she said quietly.

"We could go to a movie tonight."

"We'll see. Good-bye, Matthew."

As she replaced the receiver, all her pent-up rage exploded. This was absurd and debasing! What the hell had she been doing these interminable past days, bending over backward to be everything to him? Why should she have to be the superwoman—his wife, his mother, his partner, the career woman, the housekeeper, and on top of all that, his fucking mistress? Was he some kind of superman? He was just a cheating slob. Screw him!

She'd get to him. She'd penetrate that smug self-satisfaction. She'd confuse him, unnerve him, destabilize him, turn him on the rack of his guilt. And she knew how. His conscience was his Achilles heel.

I'm seeing Lyall at four. The lying hound. She knew exactly where he would be at four o'clock. And she would be there, too.

To the casual eye, the woman was just a visitor wandering around the university. She wore a trench coat with the collar turned up against the wind and a scarf that concealed her dark copper hair and much of her face. The camera hanging from her neck looked somewhat professional for a tourist's, however, with its fat, 400 mm telephoto lens and its heavy machine-shutter pistol grip. For a normal visitor, too, she seemed to take a curious interest in the department of physics, not an especially outstanding building architecturally, outside which she waited for quite some minutes with her lens trained on the large revolving door before suddenly firing off a series of shots, then slipping quietly away across the lawns.

Only a careful eye would have noticed that she was following the tall figure of a man striding purposefully some thirty yards ahead of her, looking neither to right nor left as he skirted the dorms and, heading around the back of Monroe Hall, made a direct line for the West Ranges. No one there paid any special attention as the woman slipped behind a pier in the old brick cloisters just as her target reached a low wooden door and, raising her camera in time to catch the door opening, fired off another rapid volley of shots.

The first envelope arrived at the department in the morning mail. It was a stiff envelope in ivory parchment but with the address typed on a self-adhesive label like a circular. Matthew tore it open carelessly, ready to consign it to the bin.

Inside were three postcard-size black-and-white photographs. He took a moment to recognize the figure hurrying out of the revolving door of a large brick-faced building. He made nothing of the man in the second photograph striding across an open space, though in the background he recognized the dome of Cabell Hall. But there was no mistaking, in the third, the man who was snapped stepping through a small doorway, and the girl whose liquid eyes shone out from the shadows of the room beyond.

He whipped the photo over. On the reverse, typed again on an adhesive label, was simply a time and a date: 4:03 p.m., Friday, November 7. The other two bore a similar mark, varying only in the time. He snatched up the envelope and peered inside. No accompanying note. The postmark showed it had been mailed from Charlottesville around noon on the Saturday.

He broke out in a sweat. Was this some campus crank with a grudge? A jealous admirer of Josie's, hoping to warn him off? But why no message? Perhaps that would follow, an ugly threat or some demand for blackmail. Never give in to blackmail, he told himself boldly, and with sudden decisiveness he tore the photographs into small pieces and tossed them into the wastepaper basket.

But all day the images haunted him. Who was behind it, and what was the motive? On reflection, he reckoned it was unlikely to be blackmail: After all, it was no secret he was seeing Josie—Lyall had hinted it was all over the campus ... Lyall! Of course! The creep was trying psychology where persuasion had failed. But would the professor of physics really resort to such a childish and time-consuming device? And why should he really take the trouble? The threat of a phone call to Hazel would be enough; he didn't need photographs.

Oh my God, he suddenly realized, it's Hazel! She knows! The photos were clearly taken with a powerful telephoto lens. Hazel has the means and the motive. Lyall has told her, the sneaking bastard.

That afternoon, he left for the library around three o'clock and spent the next hour trying without much success to concentrate on a series of puzzling marginal glosses in a notebook of Newton's. At five to four, he left the building by an exit at the side and made a detour around the back. Taking service passages and rear alleys, he finally reached the Rotunda, where he slipped along the West Lawn, hugging the side as closely as possible, and through the narrow passageway that led into the Ranges. Every few steps he glanced nervously over his shoulder. The buildings seemed to have eyes, and from every window and doorway he sensed he was being watched. A prowling car, a figure stopping to light a cigarette, a fleeting face at a window—everything seemed suspicious. Even when he reached the Ranges, he hung back in a corner until he was sure the cloisters were quite empty, and then he hurried across to Josie's door and slipped inside without knocking.

Once in the sanctuary of her room he felt more at ease; but still not easy; Hazel was on his mind.

The room was low lit, and Josie was in her silk robe, kneeling over the samovar, preparing a concoction of some kind—the mandrake once more, he guessed from the bitter scent. He felt uncomfortable, unready for a trip. He refused the bowl she proffered and lay back on the bed cushions. She rose and slid her body alongside his. Her robe fell open and her breast brushed his hand. She stroked his head in slow, soothing movements. Closing his eyes, he waited for Matthew to ebb away and for Nathaniel to take his place. But Matthew refused to go; he stayed there, thinking, watching.

Her hands reached inside his shirt and inched their way down his stomach, but her touch failed to arouse him. He stood outside himself, looking at his body lying on the bed, being caressed by this exquisitely lovely girl, and yet he felt numb, the caresses fruitless, even mildly irritating. He shouldn't have come there at all, certainly not in that frame of mind. He tried to shut his thoughts out and focus his senses entirely on what was happening to his body, but each time he felt the stirrings of a response the observer standing beside him would intervene, dissipating the desire. All the time the same thing was going around and around his mind: "Hazel knows, Hazel has found out, Hazel knows I'm here this very moment."

He was about to say something in explanation, but Josie put a finger on his lips. Her eyes smiled knowingly.

"Mary knows," she said quietly.

Mary … Hazel … his world was in a spin. He swallowed hard and just nodded.

"That is how it must be," she said conclusively.

He sighed and closed his eyes again. This was all getting beyond him. He abandoned himself to the slow, sensual touch of her hands, and gradually, at last, he found his thoughts at last fading into the distance and his body yielding to the swell of desire.

* * *

Matthew returned home, steeled to own up to the truth. He found Hazel ready with a drink in one hand for him and in the other an old copy of a seventeenth-century English parson's diary she'd picked up at Heartwood's bookshop and thought might interest him. All evening she was easy and engaging, and never for a moment gave any hint she knew anything. He bit his tongue. He didn't know where he stood. It was like fighting shadows.

He knew he wouldn't rest easy until he'd made completely sure, however, and over a fireside drink after supper he tried to draw her as obliquely as he could.

"About the other day," he began. "I wanted to say sorry. You know, when you called and said let's go to the country."

"I didn't really expect that you'd give up your work," she responded without looking up.

"I was in the middle of something tricky," he admitted.

"Of course you were, Matthew."

He hesitated, unsure if he could detect sarcasm or not.

"I felt really bad," he went on, "especially since it rained all weekend."

"Don't even think about it. It was just a passing fancy."

A passing fancy. Could she be playing with words?

"So what did you do in the end?" he inquired nonchalantly.

"I can't really remember. Ah, yes. I took my car in to have that rattle in the muffler fixed. An 'intermittent fault,' they said. That's what they call a thing when they can't fix it. All very boring." She sipped her brandy. "Mom called today. She asked what we were doing for Thanksgiving."

"What did you say?"

"You know, she's getting old, and I really think ..." She regarded him frankly. "She's not expecting you to come too. You have so much on your plate."

"Of course I'll come!" he exclaimed. "Screw the book for once."

Her face lit up with unfeigned delight. "That's wonderful. She'll be really pleased."

He bit his tongue. He'd been too quick. Thanksgiving was a time he dreaded. Like Christmas, it brought simmering issues to the boil and drove dormant conflicts into the open. The holiday created a natural four-day break. Four days he could have spent working on his subject ... at least, around his subject. Josie wasn't going to like this one bit. And he'd just thrown away an opportunity offered on a plate. He'd better lay the ground for a way out. He cleared his throat.

"We'll have to drive," he began. "That's a good day on either side. There's no point in going all that way for less than a week."

"You can fly back early, if you're worried about work."

"Even so."

"You don't have to come, Matthew. I said you didn't."

"I was just thinking of the logistics."

"Then I'm sure you'll work it out."

His escape route had been cut off. Best not to push it anymore now, he thought. The vacation was ten days off, plenty of time to think something up. But then, he wanted to spend it with Hazel and Ben just as much. He rubbed a hand over his forehead. He couldn't sustain the balancing act much longer. But what did he himself want? To be with Hazel or with Josie?

The answer was, with both.

Two days later, another letter arrived. This time it came to his home address. Luckily, he got to the mailbox first. He recognized the envelope at once.

Inside were three more photos. The first showed him slipping round the back of the library, the second lurking in the corner of the cloisters and the third letting himself into Josie's room. Once again the date and times were exact. And again, there was no message nor any clue as to the sender. What in Christ's name was this?

It began unnerving him. He couldn't go onto campus without feeling he was being watched. With Hazel being so sweet at home, his unease visited itself on Josie. Things were reaching their critical mass. The entente between Matthew and Nathaniel that kept his conscience at bay was slowly and irrevocably crumbling. He could no longer be both men, just as he could no longer have both women.

Soon, very soon, a choice would have to be made.

TWENTY

Here, let me." Matthew intercepted Hazel at the front door and carried the two large suitcases over to her car. The trunk was already packed with boxes and cartons and photographic equipment and there was hardly room for the cases.

"And these," she said, handing him two tote bags. "There's only Ben's things to come now."

"And the kitchen sink," he smiled. "Angel, you're out of your mind. You're only going for a week."

She said nothing. In the early morning light her face was pale and drawn. Her eyes were red-rimmed, as when she'd been spending too much time in the darkroom. She hadn't been working for days, though.

"You look tired," he went on. "I don't like you driving all that way alone."

"I've got Ben for company. We'll be fine." She turned away.

"It's not right," he persisted. "I ought to be taking you. I could drive you there and get a plane back."

"No, Matthew. The point is for you to stay here and work. As soon as we get there we'll be able to relax."

Suddenly he understood why her eyes were red.

"Hey, come on," he soothed, stroking her head. "A week is no time at all. I know—I'll fly out and drive you all back! What d'you say?"

A look of profound sadness passed across her face.

"You're all talk, Matthew," she sighed.

"I mean it."

"It doesn't matter." A sardonic smile was appearing. It showed in the lines that slipstreamed her eyes, but the eyes themselves were still soft, vulnerable. "Thanksgiving is about kids, anyway. It's a chance for Ben to see his Gran and his uncles and aunts. It's not about us."

Matthew felt confused. He sensed a subtext in all she said, but he couldn't be sure of what without pushing his luck to the limit.

"It's a time for families to be together. This is crazy!"

"Don't go on. We've been through it all. You'll get far more done on your own."

He paused. Hazel was going off for a week. It was wonderful and it was terrible. Yet he felt strangely unreal.

"I'm missing you already," he said truthfully.

"You're so sentimental," she said with a brusque sigh and met his eye pointedly. "You had the choice. You made the decision. End of story." Ben had appeared on the porch, laden with bags and toys. "Climb aboard, darling," she called out to him. "Say 'bye to Matthew."

Suddenly, the caravan was on the move. Before Matthew knew it, Hazel was in the car and Ben safely belted in his seat. She wound down the window and handed him a bunch of letters, asking if he'd mail them for her, then gave him a short, abrupt kiss and started up. Matthew followed the departing car to the end of the drive and stood in the road until they were out of sight.

He retraced his steps slowly. He tossed the letters into his own car and went indoors and made himself a cup of strong coffee. Echoes of Hazel's remarks kept coming back to him. "You had the choice. You made the decision. End of story." Was there a parallel text here?

The coffee tasted foully bitter, and he threw it away. He spread a cold English muffin with grape jelly, but he couldn't stomach it. He took a glass of juice to his study and stood staring out the window at the great tree at the foot of the lawn on which a scattering of yellow leaves still clung tenaciously. Everything was happening slightly out of phase. Hazel had left too quickly. He was due to see Josie in the afternoon, and that was too soon. He wished more than anything he could have sent Hazel off happy and cheerful, not with that hard, sorrowful look on her face. Fleetingly he toyed with the idea of jumping into his car and setting off after her, flagging her down on the open highway.... But then there was Josie waiting for him, with a week of dangers and delights in store. Damn it, he thought with sudden asperity. He'd have felt a lot better if Hazel hadn't always been so sweet and reasonable, if she could have provoked a fight and screamed and stormed off! She was too damn smart. She knew, of course she knew. She was getting out of his way to give him the time and space to make up his mind. Or the rope to hang himself.

He pressed his head in his hands. Hazel ... Josie ... Hazel ... Josie ... Each was so wonderful, so extraordinary, so necessary. How the hell could he make up his mind?

And when he said "Josie," who did he really mean? The daughter of Senator Otis McDowell or the daughter of Dean Hardiment?

That afternoon, he stayed with Josie later than he'd intended, laying plans for the week together. In the morning he'd promised to take her on a trip across the state to Northern Neck, a long, rugged peninsula carved out by the Potomac and Rappahannock where the two rivers fed into Chesapeake Bay. It was a thinly populated region, much of it still primitive, undrained marshland, offering little of interest besides a handful of semiderelict plantation houses and other echoes of early colonial settlement. He couldn't imagine why she was so insistent on going. She'd spoken of the place several times before—always, now he came to think of it, when under the influence of the mandrake. What on earth did she want to do there?

The evening was dark and blustery. He glanced at his watch as he hurried through the cloisters toward his car. Hazel would be arriving at her mother's about now and he wanted to be at home for her call. As he climbed into his car, he remembered the letters she'd asked him to mail. Waiting at the traffic lights, he riffled idly through the envelopes. An airmail letter to a magazine in Tokyo. A postage-paid reply card. A letter to her agent in Washington, with the address typed on a self-adhesive label....

He froze. He knew that typeface, that label, that ivory parchment envelope.

He posted the letters at the first mailbox he found and drove home fast. A terrible truth was dawning. He grazed the fender on the gate post as he swung into the drive, but he didn't stop. In his haste, he dropped the door keys on the porch and fumbled around in the dark, cursing himself for forgetting to fix the broken light. Inside, he could hear the phone ringing. It was intercepted by the answering machine, but when he'd finally let himself in and reached the phone, it had cut off. It was Hazel. She'd arrived safely. He played the message back several times, trying to read her tone of voice. She sounded tired and subdued. She was checking in as a formality, he felt, not really expecting him to be there.

He hurried upstairs to her studio. He glanced around the room: blackout curtains on the windows, backdrop drapes in various colors, a central stool surrounded by tripods and reflective lighting umbrellas, a wardrobe for props, a bureau, a large workbench, filing cabinets, equipment racks, a drawing board for pasting up....

Where should he look? The wastepaper basket?

He upended the basket on the floor and rummaged through the cuttings and trimmings. Crumpled up at the bottom he found a print from which the center had been carefully cut out. The background that remained showed buildings, cloisters, doorways receding out of focus. Slowly, with a dreadful certainty, he reached into his jacket pocket and took out the envelope that had arrived in the previous day's mail. He found the photo of himself outside Josie's door and laid it over the hole in the background.

It fit exactly.

In his mind he saw her red-eyed with weeping, and now he understood. He heard her voice again: "You had the choice ... end of story." He heard himself exclaim at the amount of luggage she was taking, "You're only going for a week," and he remembered how she'd said nothing in reply.

She has left me, he thought. Walked out of my life. Oh *Christ*.

His first reaction was angry self-justification. It was her fault for snooping on him! She should have confronted him and had it out in the open, not played this cheap, demeaning trick. But in the next instant he checked himself. She *had* confronted him, and he had denied it openly. He had no right to play hurt when she was the one hurt. What must she have suffered, seeing him running off to his girlfriend in the afternoon and that same evening facing his lying smiles and his treacherous excuses? She deserved admiration for behaving with such dignity and self-restraint. But she'd touched him where it really hurt. His shame and confusion told him he had treated her abominably.

This was the moment of choice.

But how could he chose? How could like be compared with unlike? The two women were so completely different. Complementary, not alternative. It was impossible to weigh one in the balance against the other. He went to the kitchen and, with a tumbler of straight bourbon in his hand, paced up and down the room, struggling with the dilemma.

Hazel was like a continent waiting to be explored, full of promise and surprise. Life with her was always fresh and exciting, yet she could be easy and comfortable when the mood was right. She was glamorous, she dressed well, she looked good. In bed she was both shy and bold in a blend that drove him crazy. Emotionally she was strong, intellectually she was rigorous. She was incapable of compromise. She was the toughest critic of his work. She pushed him, she inspired him, she made him strive. He admired her. He respected her. He envied her a little for her forthrightness and certitude about everything. God help him, he loved her.

He swallowed a large gulp, and turned to pace the room in the other direction.

Josie—Isabel—was altogether different. She was his eyes and ears into a lost world, a channel down which he could travel into the heart of history. She was a living being from a past century. No gift could be greater that the gift she brought him. He was consorting with a living seventeenth-century beauty! It was a thrill beyond imagining. She was a demon. She represented madness, unreason. Magic and intuition were her familiars. Her continent was a wonderland of the impossible. Her touch was mysterious, compulsive, erotic. She made sex, not love. Transcendent sex. He lost himself in her. He needed her, he feared her. With her, he flirted with mortal dangers and danced on the razor edge of madness, but, God help him, she made him feel alive.

He passed his hand across his nose and inhaled the intimate scent of her body. A pang of desire swirled through his body.

He checked himself. This was decision time. He poured another drink and looked around him, searching for signs to help. He saw Hazel's face before him, alternately sad and brave, her eyes red with concealed tears. He gazed at the bulletin board by the sink with the photos she'd taken of Ben and himself. He looked at Ben's homework lying unfinished on the table. He saw about him a dozen signs of the home and the family life he was helping build for them all and he was now about to destroy, and he thought to himself, I can't do this.

The moment he came to the decision, he felt it could never have been otherwise. Quickly, before a counterargument could upset the scales, he went to the bookshelves and took out a road map. He spread it on the table and studied it carefully. Five hundred miles—a good nine hours' drive. The clock read a quarter after eight. He'd throw a few clothes into a bag and get on the road right away.

But what about Josie? He was due to collect her for the trip to Northern Neck early in the morning.

If it must be done, he told himself, then do it swiftly. A clean cut is the kindest. Don't go and see her; there'll only be a hysterical scene and your resolve won't hold firm. Do it at a distance—send a message.

He poured another drink, reckless of the long drive ahead, and taking pen and paper from the sideboard, settled down to compose the most difficult letter of his life.

Ben was asleep, having worn himself out running around the small yard with her sisters' children that had come over to greet them, and Hazel herself was well ready for bed. As she waited for her mother to vacate the bathroom, she wondered why Matthew hadn't called back. Sitting at the kitchen table, she listened to the wind rattling the screens and the sounds of a neighbor's party filtering through the shutters. The dark, the music, the air itself carried the smell of the deep South. A thought half-formed in her mind, a confused thought relating geography to rhythm, a typical idea that would excite Matthew, and she looked up, half expecting to find him there. Her eye lit only upon the phone. She bit her lip.

The toilet flushed, vibrating the partition wall, and her mother emerged. Her face glistened with night cream under the fluorescent light and her hair, without support, seemed surprisingly thin and insubstantial. But her eyes were tender and understanding, and as she kissed her goodnight she held her long and close, as if she instinctively understood why she had come home.

Alone, Hazel glanced round the meager kitchen. She looked at the noisy old-fashioned fridge, the small single sink, the table covered in scorch-marked plastic and the chairs that didn't match, and she felt ashamed of their own kitchen back home with its double sink and its state-of-the-art refrigerator and their hickory-wood refectory table and all their little knick-knacks collected from antique shops and garage sales....

Theirs? She drew herself up sharp. The house in Charlottesville might become his or it might become hers, but it would never again be theirs. From now on, the real "they" was just the two of them, herself and Ben.

It was midnight. She'd give him one last try. She hauled herself up from the table and reached for the phone. She let the phone ring and ring in case he was taking a shower or playing music with the volume right up, then slowly replaced the receiver.

No reply. Not even the answering machine. So, there it was.

In the bathroom cabinet she found a small bottle of sleeping pills. She'd take anything not to have to think. Thinking hurt. Her thoughts were all of how it might have been and how it should have been and how, dear God, it wasn't.

The drive was interminable. The highways were empty, and for long stretches in the large open spaces between towns, the only light came from a sickly, swollen moon. This was darkness as they'd have known it in the seventeenth century. Matthew put his foot down a little harder. He was leaving that behind.

On and on he bored into the night. At times his mind wandered and the car veered across the lanes. A dull ache drummed constantly in his temples and his eyes felt scorched and raw. In the early hours, in that no-man's-land where time holds a truce, he was beset with specters of his own guilt and anxiety. He saw himself rejected by Hazel, shunned by Ben, cursed by Josie, mocked by Lyall, dismissed by the dean. All he could do was drive a little faster.

As the night wore on, the moon veered around to cast the distant foothills of the Appalachians in surreal relief. Finally, as he crossed the state boundary from North Carolina to South Carolina, the first steely yellow streaks of dawn began to appear on his left. By imperceptible degrees the sky grew brighter until, quite abruptly, heralded by a peachy blush, the rim of the sun slipped above the horizon. He pulled off the road and climbed out onto the dirt shoulder to watch the day break. The sight filled him with a powerful, pagan awe. He felt naked, humble, an insignificant speck standing before mighty celestial forces. At the first glimmerings of warmth on his skin, he shivered.

He thought of Josie but, strangely, he could only summon a faint image of her. She seemed so far away, left back in the darkness, her power dimmed like a radio signal with the lapse of distance. His thoughts turned to Hazel. He seemed to see her image in everything. The sky unfurling above him, the plains stretching beyond, the highway forging ahead, all seemed to bear the gentle, grave look of her eyes. He rubbed his eyes. This was just an unslept mind playing tricks. But as he returned to the car and set off again, he felt strangely at ease with himself. He knew he'd been right. It had always been Hazel.

He lost his way in the suburbs of Atlanta, and the streets were coming alive by the time he eventually drew up outside the house where her mother lived. For a moment he stood on the sidewalk, stretching his aching limbs as he took in the unfamiliar surroundings. This was a part of Hazel's background he didn't know and, to his shame, had never really made the effort to. After her father had died, her mother had handed the diner on to Hazel's two sisters and bought this modest one-story prefabricated home. It stood in a row of others of the same type, each bearing the stamp of pride and parsimony.

He felt embarassed to arrive so empty-handed, but he couldn't go for anything now, for he had been spotted: in the front room window a net curtain was stirring. Steeling his nerve, he stepped up to the door. It opened before he could ring. Hazel's mother stood in the doorway, weighing him up and down. Then a knowing smile gradually cracked her wrinkled face.

"So, you came." She ushered him indoors. "Hazel's still asleep. You look beat. And half starved. Grits and bacon all right? If that monkey Ben has left any."

The wind woke Josie. A sudden gust billowed the curtain and sent a bowl crashing to the floor. She switched on the bedside light. Potpourri lay scattered over the floor. She climbed out of bed and shut the window. As she went for a dustpan and brush she stopped. An envelope lay on the rug. It had been slipped under the door.

She smiled, seeing the handwriting, and put it on her bedside table while she cleared up the scented petals and pieces of aromatic bark spread over the floor. Finally she climbed back into bed and, settling herself comfortably among the pillows, opened the letter.

She read it twice. She snatched up the envelope and checked for anything else inside, then let it drop. With a long, strangled moan, she sank back and beat her head on the pillows, panting and howling with every blow. She suddenly sat up and grabbed the letter and tore it into a hundred pieces, then she slid gasping to the floor, where she lay doubled up in a crouch, hammering her fists and beating her forehead on the floor until they were bruised and raw.

Slowly and gradually, a deadly calm came over her, like the calm at the very eye of the storm. With tear-stained face and bedraggled hair, she rose unsteadily to her feet. She stood for a long while in the center of the room, breathing deeply and slowly. An expression of lethal tranquility glazed her face. Only her white-clenched fists held rigid down her sides betrayed the tension in her being. Slowly she unclenched her fists and, opening out her fingers to their fullest stretch, she raised her hands and held them up in front of her breasts. She held them there, like five-bladed weapons, as a hard, thin smile slowly cracked open across her mouth.

It has begun, she thought. Events must now follow their ordained course. First, it must be the wife. Then the boy. And last of all, it shall be the man himself.

PART V

TWENTY-ONE

They left the car beside an old Dutch barn and, following a hard-core track raised above the level of the ploughed land, struck out across the wide, wind-scoured plain. Above, gunmetal gray clouds laden with rain rolled swift and low across the vast expanse of sky. Hazel walked slightly ahead, her figure bent into the wind and her long, scarlet coat standing out shrill against the silver-gray backdrop. She held her arms wrapped tightly around her, as if she were trying to contain something within her.

Matthew followed a step behind. He felt light-headed, partly from exhaustion and partly from the relief at unburdening his heart.

That morning he'd woken her with breakfast on a tray and, sitting at the foot of her bed, he'd confessed everything. He knew she knew, of course, but he'd pretended she didn't. He'd tried to make it sound like a commonplace student-tutor affair, thinking she would find that easier to understand and hence to forgive. He'd played down the reality and referred to Isabel and the whole thrilling and terrifying aspects of their relationship in a brief aside. He had underestimated her intelligence, though. She had listened to him coolly, quietly.

"Of course I *forgive* you, Matthew," she'd responded in a tone suggesting that the real issue had little to do with forgiveness.

But by then he hadn't been listening; he could only hear the exhilaration swelling in his heart. He'd felt inspired with all the strength and love in the world. Everything would be all right—he'd *make* it all right. His conviction would carry them through. His faith alone was enough for both of them. She'd sat upright in bed like a statue, wearing a sad and weary half-smile, and gradually he found her cool reserve eating away at his confidence. Finally the conversation—his monologue, rather—had ended abruptly and unsatisfactorily when Ben came bursting into the room saying her sister and her family had arrived and they were starting the preparations for the festive dinner. It wasn't until well into the afternoon that Matthew had managed to find a way of being alone with her again.

They were alone now, but what could he do with the moment? He watched her figure picking her way ahead of him, battling against the wind. From the way she held herself, he could tell she seethed with anger and hurt. He must take it slowly and softly. Hurt needed time to heal.

He lengthened his stride until he was alongside her. Her windswept face was sealed in on itself. He let the silence continue a while longer before speaking.

"This reminds me of our walks along the Mall," he ventured at last. "The wind, the leaves, the smell of the chill in the air. A good brisk walk, then home to your apartment." He paused, leaving the rest unsaid. "Life was so simple and straightforward then."

"Simple and naive," she corrected.

"What happened?" He shrugged. "I guess we grew up."

"We grew apart."

"That's not true, Hazel," he said with a stab of pain. "I feel we're closer than ever before. These things are bound to happen. It's a stage all marriages go through. It can actually bring people together."

"It can separate them, too."

"It won't separate us. Not if we decide it won't."

"You really think it's that easy, Matthew?

"I know it is."

She stopped and faced him. The wind swept her hair across her face, but she kept her arms firmly clasped about her middle.

"This isn't a scene in some biography you're writing, Matthew. This is real life. If you really understood what was going on, you wouldn't keep saying 'the past is past' and 'let's turn over a new leaf' and all those easy platitudes. It's you all over, Matthew, just playing with words and feelings."

"But I mean it all," he protested. "I've given you my solemn word. It's over with her. Ended. Finito."

Her eyes filled with sorrow and pity.

"I'm sorry, Matthew."

"What more can I do? I can't rewrite history."

"You can stop writing history."

"What does that mean?"

"It's not about promising this or promising that. It's about facing up to reality."

"I've told you the truth."

"You're not telling yourself the truth, Matthew. You can't expect me to feel differently while you refuse to be honest with yourself." She held up a hand to check his protest. "So long as you persist in this childish delusion of yours, you'll never see things as they are."

He fought to keep his frustration in check. Of course this had to be the sticking point. It always had been, and no doubt it always would be. But right now he'd hoped to brush that side of things under the carpet.

"The facts may be weird, bizarre, whatever you will," he said obstinately between gritted teeth, "but they are still the facts and I can't change them. This person is *not* Josie McDowell. She is not the girl you photographed. She may look like her, but she isn't. She is someone entirely different. She changed."

"She changed?" echoed Hazel drily. "Is this some kind of metamorphosis we're seeing here? She wakes up one morning and finds she's turned into a romantic seventeenth-century murderess. How convenient for you. Your wildest fantasy realized."

"I don't know how or when it happened. I only know it did."

"And you and she, alone in all the world, know this?"

"Maybe there's a doctor or a shrink somewhere who's looked at her."

"But not locked her up. She's presumably safe enough to be let loose on campus. I wonder if her father knows. Or is she Isabel Hardiment just with you?"

He sighed in frustration. "I can't explain it myself—"

"That's not good enough, not from you, Matthew. If you can't explain it to yourself, how do you expect to convince me?"

"I agree it sounds crazy—"

"Stop!" she cried suddenly, pressing her fists to her temples. "Why can't you just admit you've just been screwing around, without trying to cover it up with all that garbage? Why don't you recognize that this is just the old story of the professor sleeping with the pretty student? You're inventing that crazy business to salve your conscience. What makes screwing some seventeenth-century witch any better? A reincarnated fuck somehow doesn't *count?*"

"I didn't say it made it any better ..."

"Then drop it! You don't need it. Having an affair with a student may be tacky and banal, but at least it's normal. It happens all the time. This Isabel creation of yours is nothing but a psychological excuse. It was weird enough when she existed just in your mind. Now you say she's become flesh and blood. Don't you think that's just a bit too handy? Come on, Matthew: morally, emotionally, intellectually, it *stinks.*" Her voice was cracking. "You make all these fine speeches about how the thing's over, you pledge undying faithfulness, you give your word of honor, but what's it all worth? If you can't be honest with yourself, how can you be honest with me? How can I *trust* you?"

He bit his tongue. He would never convince her. The gulf was unbridgeable. Trying only made it wider.

They walked on in silence. From time to time he glanced across at her. Her lower lip was trembling and her eyes were tearful. He couldn't renounce what he knew to be the truth. Yet he had no proof to offer her. She was bound to think he was just screwing a pretty student and no more. The reality was too way out to get across.

"Nothing matters," he said quietly, "so long as we love each other."

She turned with a deep sigh.

"Of course I love you, Matthew. You know I do."

"Well, then."

"That's not the point."

"It's the only point."

She smiled faintly. "You really believe that, don't you? You honestly think a kiss and a cuddle is all it takes, and everything will be back to normal."

He took hold of her by the elbows and drew her closer. The kiss muffled her words. He felt her body melting into his. But then, abruptly, she pulled away. Her face was flushed.

"I hate you, Matthew! I could kill you."

"Yes, yes, I'm sure you could."

"I mean it! I could shake you and throttle you. I could kick this stupid shit out of you."

Their eyes met. In her gaze he saw a look of harsh, angry sexuality.

Deeper still, he found himself looking into a cauldron of rage, a rage that went beyond this particular moment and his specific transgression: It was the eternal, silent anger of all women abused and deceived throughout the ages. And yet it was coupled with a desire so potent that it left him almost physically winded—the greedy, rapacious desire of a woman who has scented the smell of raw power.

When she spoke, her voice was rough, guttural.

"Come on," she rasped.

Together, each forcing the pace on the other, they headed back toward the car. The wind at their backs quickened their steps. As they reached the car, she caught him by the sleeve and steered him toward the derelict barn. He pushed open a wooden door hanging on one hinge and drew her inside. The air was fusty with the smell of old hay. A flurry of birds rose and escaped through holes in the roof.

They fell upon each other, starving for reunion. She tripped on a pole and fell back on the hay. He was on top of her in an instant, tearing open her clothes and devouring the flesh of her neck and breasts. She closed her fingers around his throat, tightening her grip until he was almost choking. He would strangle sooner than release her. He thrust into her savagely, mercilessly, dragging the cries from her throat until they reverberated in one continuous howl around the rafters. His mind was blowing. It had never happened like this with her before! He was exploding out of his body, rising up to the stars, shooting into the furthest reaches of space.

For a small eternity he coasted out in the timeless vastness. When finally he began on a gentle glide path back down to earth, he found tears were streaming helplessly down his cheeks.

Josie turned the bay hunter's head toward the distant woods and, digging her heels into its side, broke into a canter through the tousled sea of yellow grass. As she crested the meadow ridge, with the Pamunkey river glinting in the steely morning sunlight, she let out a cry and spurred the horse on to a gallop. The wind snatched the cry from her lips and flung it far behind, where it vanished unheard.

As the lake came into sight through a ragged fringe of birch trees, she reined in the horse to a trot. Here, the ground grew softer and the first marshland plants began to appear. After a while she dismounted and proceeded slowly on foot, with a canvas bag in her hand, searching about her as she went.

Briefly she paused over a clump of ferns, but then passed on. The powdered root of the male fern could cause paralysis, but there was barely enough to kill a child here.

She walked slowly around the lake's edge, stopping every few paces to examine a plant. At a crop of wild foxglove, she hesitated.

Dead men's pillies? she wondered, then shook her head. Taste too foul. You'd have to mix it in a grand sallett or an olla podrida. Or put it in a grand battalia pie. Among the cocks' combs, the oysters, capers, ox palates, truffles, morels and spices, the berberis, the ash keys, the nasturtium buds and all the rest, you wouldn't even taste the vilest henbane! She gave a short laugh. But a pie is impossible. No; I need something that's tasteless and lethal in small doses.

She found a thorn apple on the far side. The whole plant was a cocktail of toxic chemicals, but in the wrong dose it worked as a narcotic, even an aphrodisiac, sending the victim into an erotic delirium. She looked about her. In the woods beyond, she might find an amanite—death cap, say, or even the scarlet spotted fly agaric—though it was rather late in the season for mushrooms.

I know, she thought. I have it. The very thing.

She moved on, with more purpose in her step. She had gone twothirds of the way around the perimeter of the lake when she began searching a small marshy area of dense vegetation. Suddenly she stopped and parted a thick clump of bull rushes. She let out a sigh of satisfaction.

Cowbane.

From the canvas bag she took out a small book entited, *Poisonous Plants of America.*

"Cowbane, *cicuta virosa,* also known as water hemlock," she read quickly, "is extremely poisonous to man. It is found in wet places at the edges of lakes, ponds and ditches throughout the United States. The distribution is very local and it is never abundant. It has been eaten in mistake for parsnips, with fatal results.

"The active principle is a resinous substance, cicutoxin, found in the yellow juice of the roots and in small quantities in the stems. It is present in its greatest amount between late fall and early spring.

"Cowbane acts as a convulsant. Small quantities of the fresh root are sufficient to cause death, a piece the size of a walnut being fatal. Symptons of cowbane poisoning are nausea, widely dilated pupils, vomiting, delirium, violent convulsions and death from asphyxia. Autopsy examination reveals nothing diagnostic, except parts of the plant in the stomach contents."

She closed the book with a slow smile. She returned it to the bag and took out a small trowel. She cleared the surrounding ground and began carefully digging away the earth from around the root. The juice from a walnut-size piece of root would be just right: convenient, undetectable and absolutely lethal.

Lyall sprang out of his car and was half way up the front steps of the department building before the engine finally coughed itself out. Thank God the vacation was over and people would be back in their labs and offices again! There was so much to do. He'd been asked to chair an interuniversity science research committee, he'd just pulled off a major governmental grant for a research project into high-temperature supercon-ductivity and, on top of that, he was standing in for Colbert for the semester while the dean was away on sabbatical leave. But he liked to be under pressure; it produced results.

Fleetingly he noticed the slim blond girl through the glass of the revolving door, leaving the building as he was going in. It was a good few seconds later that a bell rang in the back of his mind. He stopped and turned. She was half way down the steps before he'd placed her.

Josie McDowell.

What was she doing here? Visiting Matthew? He frowned. He hadn't seen Matthew near the lab for days. It was time he checked. What he'd seen the other evening at dinner wasn't good.

He took the elevator to his own floor; he'd call Matthew from his office and suggest a drink. But as the door opened he thought better of it, and pressed the button for the top floor instead. There, he tapped on Matthew's laboratory door.

"Matthew?" he called cheerily.

There was no reply. The door was locked. He frowned momentarily, wondering what else Josie McDowell could be doing in this building. Then he noticed the note lying on the floor, slipped half under the door.

He bent to pick it up. He opened it. The handwriting looked most unusual, almost old-fashioned.

You have betrayed me, Nathaniel. You had it in your power to break the cycle and forge a new history. But you chose otherwise. Now events must take their course. Do not hope to escape necessity.

Good-bye, Nathaniel. God forgive you. God help Mary. Had you but chosen, it need not have been so.

The note was signed simply, "I."

For a moment Lyall stood staring dumbly at the note. A terrible cold dread stalked through his veins. "I" was Isabel, of course. Nathaniel ... Isabel.... What was this crazy game they were playing? Were they insane? Did they have any idea of the danger? Jesus Christ!

He looked again at the note. Something about the signature stirred a deep memory. He had seen that particular letter "I" with its loops and ser-ifs somewhere before, quite recently. Suddenly, with a flush of alarm, he realized where. In the small appointments diary that had belonged to the unfortunate Clark Tauber. He recalled exactly the pencil mark next to the actual date of the tragedy—a circle and, inside, exact in every loop and serif, a tiny initial "I."

For a moment, he stood absolutely still as he struggled to come to grips with the implications. He reread Josie's note. "You have betrayed me.... You had it in your power to break the cycle.... God help Mary."

Mary?

Mary Shawcrosse. Nathaniel's wife.

Holy Christ, he swore softly. Hazel! Hazel was in danger.

He hurried downstairs to his office and grabbed a phone. This was a matter for the police. Then he checked himself. No: Better take it to Matthew and let him deal with it. He alone knew what was really going on. But where was Matthew? He sat down behind his desk and tried to work it through more carefully. Maybe he was taking this too quickly.

There was the experiment to think of.

He might just give Matthew a little more rope. But not Hazel. Hazel had no part in it. Her life was directly at risk. He must get to her and tell her. He'd borrow the note for a while and slip it back under the door later, where Matthew would find it in his own time.

He reached for the phone again and dialed their house. Hazel answered. Good—she was at home. He put the receiver back down with-out speaking and, checking his pocket for his car keys, headed briskly for the door.

Hazel had to be warned, and that should be done face to face.

* * *

"Are you telling me what this is all about?" smiled Hazel from the passenger seat. "Or is it a magical mystery tour?"

Lyall returned the smile grimly as he swung his car left into University Avenue. He was relieved he'd found her alone at home. Persuading her to drop what she was doing and come with him was the easy part, though. He cleared his throat. Now came the crunch.

"You know how fond I am of you both," he began. "The last thing in the world I'd want to see is anything happen."

"Nothing's going to 'happen,' Lyall," she laughed.

He swallowed. "You're not going to like this, Hazel. I'd rather hoped not to be the one to tell you."

She sighed sympathetically.

"You're going to tell me about Josie McDowell."

He spun round. The car swerved into the center of the road before he steered it straight again.

"So you know?"

"Matthew has told me everything."

"Well, that's something at least," he breathed. "It'll make what I have to say a lot easier."

"Please, Lyall. I don't want to hear the sordid details. As far as I'm concerned, the chapter's closed."

"Not quite, Hazel."

"Wrong."

"We'll see."

He glanced across at her. Her expression was hurt, impatient. He drove on in silence. He turned off under the railroad bridge. A hundred yards down a side street, he pulled up. Ahead ran a broken chain-link fence beyond which lay a marshaling yard filled with railroad carriages and trucks. The railroad track ran over the bridge to a small elevated station that stood sandwiched between a complex of gravel silos and the School of Medicine buildings, then swung away from the university campus toward downtown Charlottesville.

He switched off the engine and met her eye.

"Does the name Clark Tauber mean anything to you?"

"Should it?"

"Come with me. I want to show you something."

"Lyall, is this really necessary? I know all I need to."

"You don't, Hazel. Come on."

He climbed out of the car and, turning up his coat collar against the wind, headed toward the marshaling yard. He led the way through a small gate in the fence and stepped across the tracks to a broad open area of rubble. He stopped a short distance from the main railroad line.

"Clark Tauber was Matthew's predecessor in the fellowship, in my department," he began. "Like Matthew, he was a brilliant mind. He didn't have Matthew's flair and insight, but as a theoretical physicist he was next thing to a genius."

"Lyall—"

"Now, Tauber was working on the physics of antimatter, and in his research he came across the work of a man whose name you *will* know: Nathaniel Shawcrosse. Shawcrosse *was* a genius. He was the first man to propose a theory of matter in which there was a two-way flow between the material and the immaterial, a kind of transubstantiation in which, under certain conditions, matter actually became mind, and mind matter ..."

"I've heard all this before."

"What you haven't heard before, Hazel, is that Clark Tauber committed suicide. Nor why he did."

The shrill whistle of a locomotive cut through her exasperated sigh. A moment later a goods train lumbered into sight. It clanked past them, lurched through the station, then rattled away out of sight.

A hint of alarm sharpened her expression.

"I hope you're not suggesting that Matthew is suicidal, Lyall."

He continued as though he hadn't heard her. He pointed to a spot on the tracks a few yards away.

"That's where the train ran into him. Or rather," he corrected himself, "where *he* ran into the train."

"Lyall, please—"

"At the inquest, the driver of the train said something very interesting. He said Tauber never saw the engine, even at the last second, though the day was perfectly fine. He said Tauber seemed to be looking *through* the engine at something beyond it, something he was running *toward*." He paused as a frisson ran over his skin. "There was one other witness, a footplate man," he continued. "The whistle of the train made him look up. He saw Tauber running along the track shouting some gibberish about a bell. A bell? Everyone naturally assumed he'd gone over the edge. He'd been close to cracking for some while."

"Well?" Hazel's face expressed unfeigned impatience now.

"Clark Tauber was as sane as you or me. He had come here to meet someone. A woman."

"Really, Lyall, I can't see the point of all this."

"Wait till you hear who that woman was." He held her eye. "What that footplate man heard Tauber shout had nothing to do with bells or any such nonsense. Clark Tauber was calling a name. *Her* name."

"Belle?"

"Nearly. I believe he was calling out, 'Isabel.'"

A sudden spurt of color shot to Hazel's cheeks.

"For God's sake, Lyall," she flared, "what kind of joke is this? Are you completely crazy?"

"I'm deadly serious."

"You astonish me!" she fumed. "I'd always credited you with more sense and brains. Don't talk to me about Isabel! This whole thing is absurd, pathetic. It's a farce."

"Think for a moment." He felt his own heat rising. "I know it sounds strange—"

"Strange? It's crazy, disturbed, *delusional.*"

"That's how it seems to you, Hazel, and I do sympathize. These things are difficult to get to grips with. But try not to let your feelings get in the way. No one fully understands the physics of the mind, but we do know that certain things are possible that run counter to common sense."

"I don't want to hear."

"Listen to me, woman!" he spat. She fell silent, taken aback by his ferocity. He continued more quietly. "Until now the whole of science has been based on Aristotelian logic. Everything sprang from three basic axioms. But the logical fourth axiom was always ruled out: "a" *and* "not a." That says a thing and its opposite can exist at the same time. The moment you admit that principle, as we're now beginning to do, all kinds of bizarre and crazy-sounding things become logically possible. Like travel through time. Like thought power. Like the transmission of matter without loss of energy—maybe even without energy itself. And, of course, the old mind-body dualism goes right out of the window." He paused as he reached his point. "It is by no means inconceivable that a person—a spirit, a mind, a soul, whatever you like to call it—can survive the death of the body and, at some later date, rematerialize in another one."

But Hazel was backing away, her face filled with anger and distress.

"For pity's sake," she said. "Why don't all you theoreticians just go back to your playpens and leave those of us who have to cope with the real world alone?"

"Because this *is* the real world. Isabel exists among us. In the living flesh."

"Oh my God! Has Matthew sold you that line? Where's your objectivity?" She broke off. "I'm sorry. I don't want to talk like this anymore."

"But, Hazel—"

"Would you please drive me back? Or I can call a cab."

Lyall bit his lip. This had gone badly wrong. He'd alienated her before he'd even reached the real purpose of the meeting. He thrust his hands in his pockets and, angry with his mishandling, led the way slowly back toward the car.

"Let's remain skeptical, then," he said finally. "Let's just say that Matthew and this girl are engaged in a weird and sinister piece of playacting. Let's also say that, crazy as it may be, Josie *believes* she is Isabel Hardiment and that Matthew is Nathaniel Shawcrosse. Will you go that far?"

"I don't see the point," responded Hazel tautly.

He reached into his inside pocket and handed her the note.

"Read this."

He watched her closely as she quickly skimmed it. She frowned briefly, then handed it back with a brief shrug.

"The girl's crazy."

"She's dangerous, Hazel. You know who she means by Mary?"

Hazel blanched but quickly recovered.

"I'm not fazed. I've dealt with this before, if you remember. Even you agreed then that this Isabel was a figment of Matthew's imagination." She met him full in the eye. "Look, it's all in the mind. And I can handle Matthew's mind."

Lyall shook his head.

"Things have changed. The situation is quite different. We now have a girl who believes she is this Isabel in the flesh. She feels she'd been betrayed. She is angry and hurt. Someone is going to pay. And she's going to see it happens just like it did before." His gaze carried the full intensity of his anxiety. "Hazel, can you handle *her* mind?"

They had reached the car and climbed in before she replied. She was visibly shaken, but he could tell she strove to sound relaxed, even slightly provocative.

"What should I do, then? Adjust my space-time frame? Zap her with thought power?"

He rested his hand on the ignition key.

"It's not for me to say. I just wanted to tell you, to *warn* you. Just recognize you are in real danger, Hazel, and take care. That's my advice. Never underestimate the power of delusion." He slipped the envelope back into his pocket. "I'll put this back in Matthew's lab where he'll get it when he comes in. It's up to you to decide how you're going to handle it. But for God's sake, understand the danger."

She let out a sigh. She clearly hadn't bought any of it.

"Message received. Can we please go now?"

Hazel, can you handle HER mind?

Hazel stood under the hot shower, but inside she was shivering. She had no doubt of her own grip on reality. What alarmed her was the shaky grip of others around her. She could explain Matthew's delusional imaginings as the result of the strain of his book and the obsessional way in which he worked. They had started when he'd begun it, and it was a sure bet they'd evaporate as soon as it was finished. Pray God that day came soon.

But Josie? She found it impossible to imagine her as anything but the normal, smart, sweet girl she'd met by the lake at Hanover Park. Had she really flipped over the edge? Or was it Matthew himself and his obsession that had infected her and dressed her up in the role of his own fantasy?

She recalled with a light shiver the documents she'd once found on Matthew's desk—transcripts of the seventeenth-century chaplain's chilling account of the proceedings against Isabel Hardiment and of her execution for murdering her lover's wife.

God help Mary.

Reaching forward, she turned the shower to cold. She stood there as long as she could bear it, until she could no longer tell if the water was freezing or burning on her skin. Then she dried herself quickly, roughly, and with her flesh tingling from the mortification, slipped into her robe and went downstairs to pour herself a large neat vodka.

As the alcohol scorched its path through her, she felt fired with a towering, rebellious anger. She wasn't going to submit to this mental blackmail. No one was going to threaten her. How dare Lyall "warn" her! He was as lunatic as the others in this intellectual madhouse. There was reality, and there was fantasy. There was fact and conjecture, reason and supposition, evidence and theory. The world was divided into those who lived with their feet on the ground and those who floated with their heads in the clouds. At the end of the day, reason and truth had to triumph. One had just to cling on to that, and all would be well.

She'd darn well go and see for herself. She'd pay a visit to this changeling creature, this Josie McDowell turned seventeenth-century murderess.

TWENTY-TWO

Atlanta was one thing, but back home at Charlottesville quite another. Brave promises traveled badly. The objectivity Matthew had gained with distance he lost with his return. Josie remained constantly on his mind. He couldn't shut off the flow of thoughts, images and memories that filled his waking hours. No manuscript, no textual notation, no historical detail however trivial seemed to have any dimension without her to give it life. She was nowhere and yet everywhere. In his study. In his bed. In his mind. He felt like a person who had cut off his own limb to free himself from a man trap. And the pain was all the greater because he'd severed the limb deliberately. He missed her, and by God it hurt.

He worried constantly about her, too. He wondered anxiously about how she was feeling and what state of mind she was in. He was, after all, responsible for her. He'd rejected her at the moment when she most needed love and understanding—and, goodness only knew, psychiatric care, too. He'd heard nothing from her: there hadn't been a single word or any hint of a communication. It was all he could do to keep himself from sending her a note or going to see her. For ten days now, ten days of painful silence, he had forced himself to keep clear of the university and busied himself at home, revising the early parts of his book, a self-imposed and frankly unnecessary task.

Finally, one morning, he rose early and ventured onto campus. Not to see Josie, just to see about her. He contrived to cross paths with her neighbor on the West Ranges, a girl called Mandy, as he knew from the visiting card in its slot on her door. But Mandy had seen nothing of Josie, either. Josie hadn't put in an appearance at the dining hall or the library for weeks, and her chemistry friends said she'd been cutting her lectures. At night, Mandy heard her pacing about her room, but in the daytime all was quiet.

He went over to the department. It was time he looked in at his lab, and besides there might be some message left for him since he'd last asked Lyall's secretary to check his internal mail.

There was. A note had been slipped under the door of his laboratory.

Instantly he recognized the handwriting.

"You have betrayed me, Nathaniel ..." it began.

He read it carefully, several times. His stomach tightened, and his flesh went very cold. He took the note over to the window and read it once again. Gazing sightlessly out over the parking lot and the parkland beyond, he debated what he should do. He understood this note. He understood every word of it. He recognized the threat. He had suspected Josie might attempt some act of revenge. And now it had come.

This changed everything. All those days of nostalgic regret and sentimental self-searching had evaporated in the instant. Everything was very clear, very certain. Josie was not to be pitied; she was to be feared. She was not to be desired but shunned. And, above all, she was to be stopped. For her threat was aimed not at him, who deserved it and could handle it, but at one who was innocent of any part of it all—Hazel.

His immediate thought was to call Hazel and tell her not to move until he got back, to stay inside and not to open the door to any strangers ... but then he remembered she was out on a job that day. He'd make sure he was home first and bring it up at supper. He could hear her sarcastic retort, though. For her, Josie was just a rejected girlfriend, psychiatrically disturbed perhaps but nothing more, certainly no real danger to anyone. In her mind, this was a perfectly commonplace case of a jilted college kid fired with predictable jealous rage. She was wrong, dangerously wrong. Somehow he'd have to convince her that what she was really up against was quite different. This was a crazed, vengeful seventeenth-century witch.

A crazed, vengeful seventeenth-century witch. Jesus Christ. What would Hazel say to *that?* Her earlier taunt echoed in his ears: "Some kind of metamorphosis? ... That's not good enough.... If you can't explain it to yourself, how do you expect to convince me?"

He pounded the window sill with his fist. Right, he said aloud. Once and for all, and before anything else, I am going to get to the bottom of this. I am going to find out what is happening and how it happened and just who the hell we are dealing with.

There was the before and the after. One, the girl who was born and grew up Josie McDowell; the other, the woman who had lived and died Isabel Hardiment. There must have been a moment of transition. A point of change when the switch took place. Focus on this, he told himself.

The obvious person to ask was her father, Otis McDowell. Matthew played through the likely conversation in his imagination. It wasn't promising.

"Senator," he begins, "I have to tell you your daughter is suffering from a serious delusional condition. Crazy as it sounds, she actually believes she is the mistress of an English alchemist living in the seventeenth-century."

The Senator frowns.

"Tell me, Dr. Cavewood, is Josie a student of yours?"

"No, sir, but I know her well and I'm concerned about the state of her mind ..."

"How well do you know my daughter, Dr. Cavewood? Are you in some way involved with her?"

Matthew gulps.

"The fact is, sir, Josie has projected this fantasy onto me. She sees me as this alchemist, her lover ..."

It wouldn't get him anywhere, except hauled up before the board of governors to answer a charge of ethical misconduct.

Then a better idea occurred to him. He thought back to when Hazel had done her piece for *People* magazine. Josie had then been at Northeastern Illinois university—he remembered that, because before coming here he'd been in Chicago himself, the local rival. Now she, too, was at UVA. Presumably she had transferred at the time of the ... transformation. In which case, perhaps her old tutor or professor at Northeastern might provide a clue.

Sensing the trail warming, Matthew settled down at his desk and began making a series of calls. First he spoke to the registrar at Northeastern, who gave him the name of the chemistry department chair. By good chance, the professor was in his office.

He recalled Josie perfectly.

"Remarkably smart girl," he reported. "A great sadness to see her leave us. We held her place open, of course, but her father wished her to be closer to home. One can understand that, after what happened with the accident."

"The accident?"

"You didn't know about that?"

"Not in detail," Matthew bluffed.

"A road accident. Late at night. She lost control of her car and ended up in a ditch. She got out, but a car ran her down as she went for help." The professor paused, as if uncertain how much of this was useful. "They said it was a miracle she survived. I believe they thought they'd lost her at the hospital."

"When was this?"

"Let me see. April, I guess. Yes, early April. The summer semester had just started."

Matthew swallowed. The visitations had stopped in early April. His mind flashed back to the wedding reception. He could hear Isabel's words even now: "Farewell, Nathaniel, farewell, and adieu."

"You don't recall which hospital?" he asked in a tight voice.

"Why, yes, right there, in Charlottesville. I remember one of the faculty was visiting UVA and spent some time with her. But I forget the name."

"Martha Jefferson Hospital?" Matthew suggested.

"That's the one."

"Thank you, Professor. Thank you very much."

Matthew made his next call in person. And once again his luck was in.

At Martha Jefferson Hospital, he tracked down the surgeon who had operated on Josie. He managed to catch him just as he was leaving the emergency room and returning to his office. He spoke to Matthew as he led the way briskly along a labyrinth of corridors. He was a tall, precise man, with honed features and delicate hands more appropriate to an aesthete than a surgeon-physician. He seemed quite happy to talk about the case, which he remembered well.

"She was D.O.A.," he was saying. "We don't get too many of those walking out of here."

"I'm sorry?" Matthew didn't understand the jargon.

"Dead on arrival," the surgeon explained. "Of course, it depends what you mean by death."

"There are ... degrees of death?"

"Sure. She was clinically dead. All the external signs of life were absent—consciousness, reflexes, respiration, cardiac activity and so on—but she wasn't dead in an absolute sense. While the metabolic processes of the tissues are still working, resuscitation is still possible. That is, up to the point when the brain cortex becomes irreparably damaged."

"How soon is that?"

"About six minutes, give or take. We can get individual organs like the heart and lungs to function again after that, but we can't bring the whole organism back to independent life."

"Tell me, doctor," inquired Matthew carefully. "How long was Josie McDowell clinically dead?"

"Two, possibly three minutes."

"Enough to cause any brain damage?"

"We ran every check in the book. We could find no effects on cortical functioning."

"And no associated ... psychological effects?"

The surgeon misunderstood him.

"You mean her, uh, *experience?*"

"Yes," responded Matthew, sensing a new lead. "I was wondering about that."

The surgeon led the way into the elevator and hit a button. A grimace of distaste soured his thin face.

"These so-called near-death experiences," he said deprecatingly. "So much garbage gets written about them. They tell us far more about the dying brain than what lies beyond the grave."

Matthew felt his pulse quicken. Did Josie have a near-death experience?

He'd read numerous first-hand accounts of people brought back from death. One thing was most striking: their experiences were all virtually identical, starting with an out-of-the-body experience, generally viewed from above, followed by the sensation of traveling through a dark tunnel toward a dazzlingly bright light. The whole experience was invariably shattering and often life-changing. For many people, it was clear proof that the spirit survived bodily death. In Josie's case, had something happened during those critical moments between death and revival to change her personality? Or maybe to awaken some deep, dormant pool of memories? So many of the minute details she knew of daily life in seventeenth century Oxford could be ascribed to cryptomnesia. Many, however, he had to admit, couldn't. The love poem, for one.

"Of course," the surgeon was saying, "there's a simple physiological explanation. The tunnel sensation has to do with how the visual cortex is structured, how the information is mapped. As you shut down the system, you get a kind of "coning" in the retina. You find the same thing in epilepsy and migraine and with drugs like LSD and mescaline."

"And the bird's-eye viewpoint?"

"That fits the way memory models are structured in the brain."

By now they had reached his office. He paused outside with his hand on the doorhandle. Matthew had one more question he just had to put.

"This may sound crazy, but could you imagine this experience altering a person's consciousness? Could a person wake up afterward with, literally, an altered self?"

"Altered personality, maybe," he granted with a puzzled look, then shrugged, "I can't speak in Josie McDowell's case. She was transferred to a clinic in Richmond as soon as she was able to be moved. Nearer to home, I guess." He frowned. "I do recall that she said some pretty weird things when she came around, though."

"Weird things, like what?"

He paused, groping through his memory.

"I remember she kept saying she wanted to be taken to some place called Fairmont. She was very insistent that that was where she lived. We all knew where she really lived, of course. Patients can be very confused in the first days. I only remember that because there's a Fairmont on Northern Neck where my wife's family comes from." He looked at his watch. "I'm sorry, but I really must ..."

Matthew took a moment to come back to reality. He mustered a smile as he met the proffered handshake.

"Of course, doctor," he said. "Thank you, you've really been most helpful."

He walked slowly down the corridor, so slowly that people in a hurry kept bumping into him. Gradually, he felt, the pieces were beginning to fit. She had gone into that hospital as Josie McDowell and come out as

Isabel Hardiment. She'd died and been revived, and the change, the switch, the transformation or whatever it was, had happened in the process.

Was Isabel just one face of Josie? He thought of Sybil and Eve and the other cases of multiple personality. But then, where was the Josie personality? It seemed totally eclipsed by Isabel.

Or had she come back not as a different personality but as a different person? It wasn't at all the same thing. Hazel's brutal phrase flashed into his mind: a reincarnated fuck. Was he to imagine that Isabel might somehow be reincarnated in Josie? Perhaps he should consult Professor Stevenson, a medically trained doctor working right there in Charlottesville who had made a lifetime's study of cases of reincarnation....

He rubbed his aching forehead. Wait, he told himself. Guessing wasn't the way. He had to start with what he knew. And start at the beginning. What was the first thing the surgeon had said the new Josie had kept talking about? "She wanted to be taken to some place called Fairmont. She was very insistent that that was where she lived.... I only remember because there's a Fairmont on Northern Neck....

A way-out hunch began to form in his mind, and he quickened his pace. Soon he broke into a run, down the corridors, through the main reception hall and out down the front steps to where his car was parked. Within a minute he was heading fast back to the university, and not much afterward he was drawing up in the parking lot at the rear of the Alderman Library. Here he was on solid ground. This was his field, his expertise. He knew, if anyone, how to squeeze the secrets out of historical archives.

Hazel hung back in an archway, her heart pounding. Ahead of her stood the door. Her legs were paralyzed, her brain numb. She'd wrapped up her day's photo assignment early to come here, and now that she was here she couldn't think what on earth she was doing. What was she hoping to achieve? What should she say? A couple of students in tracksuits jogged briefly past, nodded a greeting and disappeared, leaving the cloisters empty once again. She felt embarassed, as though caught loitering. She had to go ahead, or go away.

She stepped forward. Perhaps Josie was out anyway. In the afternoon, most students would surely be in the labs or the lecture halls or maybe on the games fields. That would be a relief.

She tapped. Sounds of movement came from within. Her heart leapt into her mouth. There was no going back now.

The door opened quickly a quarter of the way, then stopped abruptly. Josie's face peered out from the shadows inside. Surprise, shock, then suspicion flashed in quick succession across her pale, washed-out face. The door closed an inch. Her eyes narrowed warily.

"Yes?"

"I'm Hazel Cavewood."

"What do you want?"

"I'd like to talk with you."

This was as far as she'd prepared her script. Josie's expression tightened.

"I have nothing to say to you."

The door began closing.

"Wait." Hazel reached forward. "I'm not here to argue or recriminate. I'm not about to say let's bury the hatchet and be friends, either. I just ..." She groped for a workable line. "Matthew has told me everything. I just wanted you to know there are no hard feelings on my side."

"Should I care what you feel?"

"And I'm sorry. I know what it's like to be hurt."

"Save your pity! You'll need it."

Hazel bit her lip. The moment was slipping away. All those vital questions would remain unanswered. In despair, she made a last, blunt attempt.

"Josie—" she began, then deliberately checked herself. "Or should I call you Isabel?"

At this, a curious transformation seemed to come over the girl. Her face brightened briefly, as though an idea had suddenly occurred to her, and she shot a glance behind her into the room. A careful half-smile twisted across her face, but her eyes remained hard and wary. She sized Hazel quickly up and down.

"It's Josie," she said slowly.

"Of course it is." Hazel swept a strand of hair away from her face and feigned an absentminded look. "We've met before."

"Oh?"

"When I came to photograph your father."

"Ah," said Josie distantly, keeping her eyes on Hazel's face all the time and watching her closely. "You came to photograph my father."

"It seems like a long time ago."

"Yes, a long time ago."

A brief pause fell. Suddenly Hazel felt idiotic, standing there in the open, trying to read clues into the empty small talk. It was perfectly obvious this was one and the same girl that she'd ever been. A little confused, perhaps, and understandably defensive, and somehow changed in her appearance and her clothes and in the way she did her hair. But it was Josie McDowell all right.

She took a step back.

"Well, I said what I came to say. I'll go now."

For a second time the curious look came over Josie's face, the flash of an idea, then the careful smile and the narrowing of the eyes. She opened the door fully.

"No, no. You must stay. You must come in."

"Don't let me disturb you."

"You *must*."

"I won't stay long, then," said Hazel as she went inside. "You've probably got essays to write. Or are you working on a thesis? I guess you're a graduate. Matthew didn't say."

She bit her tongue. Why was she chattering on like this? For God's sake, leave Matthew out of this, too. No need to rub the girl's nose in it; she was behaving in a very civil manner. It took her a moment to register the light frown that passed briefly across Josie's face at the mention of Matthew's name. Hazel remembered that part of their little love game was playacting as Nathaniel and Isabel. She shuddered. Nothing could be more nauseating than the intimate pet names of your husband and his whore.

She cleared her throat; she had to find an excuse to get out of there. But Josie had already opened the curtains and turned on a table lamp and was sweeping a pile of clothes off an armchair onto the floor.

"You will take coffee?" It sounded like more of an order than a question.

"I really think—" began Hazel.

"Sit down. Please."

Josie went to a small kitchenette in an alcove, leaving Hazel with no option but to stay. Hazel turned her back to the bed and tried not to think of what had gone on there. She looked around the room with disquiet. It was unlike anything she'd known in her own student days. Her eye settled briefly upon a silver frame on the desk, and she noticed it was empty. As she glanced around her, half curious and half afraid of what she might see, she was gradually overwhelmed by a sense of unreality. The room and its rich and ragged furnishings, the baskets of herbs, the faint smell of incense, the samovar beside the ottoman, everything seemed so extraordinary, so otherworldly. This was indeed the stage for theatrical games. She could feel the power of the spell, and grudgingly she could see how Matthew had been seduced by it.

But most unreal of all was the conversation that ensued between them when Josie finally brought in a tray of coffee and cookies. They studiously avoided any further mention of Matthew, but since he was all they had in common, they were left exchanging insignificant small talk in an atmosphere of stilted politesse. Josie had a curious manner of speaking in short, cropped, eliptical sentences that made Hazel wonder if she'd had some accident, possibly a minor stroke. That might explain, too, why she'd transferred to this university in mid-year. As if to compensate, Hazel found herself doing all the talking, chatting away as though for the life of her this was a ladies' coffee morning at the Farmington Country Club.

"These cookies are delicious," she murmured appreciatively. "They look homemade. An old recipe?" she added, trying for some levity. A seventeenth-century recipe was what she wanted to say, but she couldn't be sure how it would go down.

"My mother's."

"I'm sorry. You lost her when you were quite young, didn't you?"

"She died long ago." She offered her the plate. "Have another."

"I couldn't, thank you."

"You must take some home, then."

"No, I couldn't take them."

"But you must. I'll find a bag."

As Josie rummaged around in a sideboard, Hazel studied her thoughtfully. So many questions flooded her mind, but she felt too numbed by the bizarre quality of it all to make sense of very much. Josie was strange in so many ways—the intensity of her eyes, the way she spoke, the things she said. Astonishingly composed, too, for a jilted mistress meeting her lover's wife. One thing was for sure, though: Whatever fantasy role she played behind these closed doors with Matthew, it *was* a fantasy. And the pitiful thing was, she could see it and Matthew himself couldn't. He was locked in a world of his own creation, a world where present and past, reality and fiction, were indistinguishable.

This proves it, she thought to herself as she finally bade Josie good-bye and hurried off through the cloisters, clutching the bag of cookies she'd pressed on her. Matthew was seriously disturbed; she now knew it for a certainty. It was time she had it out with him, once and for all. He just had to get psychiatric help.

She quickened her step and broke into a gentle jog. On reaching the car, she collapsed into the seat. She felt dizzy, and her stomach burned with a painful stitch. God, was she so unfit? She sat still for a moment while she recovered. Her eye fell upon the shopping bags on the floor beside her: smoked oysters, Chesapeake Bay prawns, a bottle of Moët.... What the hell did she have to celebrate?

Her freedom. Whatever else, she had nothing to worry about from this girl—at least, nothing she couldn't handle. That ridiculous note Lyall had shown her was just another piece of theater, part of the same absurd little game. Meeting Josie just now had proved what she'd believed all along. The whole thing was in Matthew's head.

She could relax. Josie might remain a difficulty, but not a danger.

Josie closed the door and stood with her back pressed against it while the steps disappeared away down the cloisters. Then with a wild whoop she threw her arms in the air and danced around the room, crying out in delight.

Oh, the sweet, sweet justice!

She swept away the crumbs from the plate on which she'd served the cookies, taking care not to let any fall into her own food, then she closed the curtains, lit the candles and switched off the lights. Carefully she prepared a fumigating incense of aromatic herbs and dried hawthorn bark, then went round the room sprinking rose water on the chair and carpet and anything else the woman might have touched. She rinsed her hands three times and, undressing, put on her Chinese robe and lit the spirit lamp beneath the samovar. From the lacquer box she took two small pinches of the whitish gray powder and sprinkled it into the water in the bowl, then settled down to seek the purification of her spirit in the sweet, slumbrous embrace of the mandrake.

* * *

Back in the 1920s, the University of Virginia had been bequeathed a major archive of historical documents relating to the period of the early British settlements, and this included the nation's finest collection of early land title deeds. During the past few years, these had been transferred to microfilm and an elaborate cross-index set up. The whole was housed in the basement of the Alderman Library, in a large windowless room known on account of its constant temperature and humidity control as "the humidor."

The archivist was a bespectacled, bulb-headed man whose somber dark suit and white gloves, worn to protect the manuscripts he handled, gave him the appearance of an aging butler. He explained the system in onerous detail to Matthew before guiding him finally to a microfilm reader. There were gaps, he warned, but the data bank contained over eighty percent of all land and real estate transactions recorded in the first hundred years from the first permanent settlement at Jamestown in 1607.

Matthew waited until he was alone before calling up the menu.

KEYWORD? the screen asked.

He typed: ISABEL HARDIMENT

A second menu came up, asking for further information on dates, place names, type of transaction. He selected the option, "Information Not Available."

SEARCHING, flashed back the screen. PLEASE WAIT.

A few seconds later, a list of names unscrolled down the screen.

01: HAMMICK, Joshua K
02: HARAKIN, Joseph Ezekiel
03: HARDIMENT, I
04: HARDY, Samuel Jeremiah
05: HARINGTON, William Ebenezer

With a drumming pulse, he typed in the code 03. Back came his reply.

HARDIMENT, I. Deed of purchase of estate at Fairmont, Northumberland County, Va., dated 17 March 1682. First recorded title: Thomas Lord Culpeper. Land registry ref. 03867/22b. Archive ref. NN/256c.

He felt the perspiration prickle his skin. A reference to Fairmont again. And Northumberland County lay on the northern tip of the peninsula of Northern Neck.

He mustn't get carried away. The initial "I" could stand for Isaac or just as likely, in the Latin, for James. All the other names had been men. Was it likely in those days that land transactions would be effected with women?

He noted down the archive reference and asked the librarian if he could see the actual original deed of purchase. After a lengthy wait, the man brought a heavy parchment scroll and a pair of white gloves for him to wear. With trembling hands, Matthew untied the ribbon and unfurled the scroll.

WHEREAS by this deed made and entered into this 17th day of March in The Year of Our Lord MDCLXXXII between Sir George Barrington Swithin, Bart., and I. Hardiment, gentlewoman ...

He swallowed. His mouth was desperately dry.

A woman!

Could she be Irene, or maybe something exotic like Iphigenia or Innocenta?

No, this was no coincidence. This was Isabel—his Isabel.

Hazel opened the fridge and took out the champagne and prawns. Her eye caught the bag of cookies she'd hidden at the back where Ben was less likely to see them: The boy could eat his way through a package at a sitting and leave no room for a proper meal. Behind her, she could hear Matthew prowling restlessly around the room. She smiled wearily. She knew what he wanted to talk about. She wondered briefly whether she should tell him about her visit that afternoon, but decided it would only open up the wounds again. As far as she was concerned, the matter of Josie McDowell was closed. The only matter for discussion was Matthew himself. Not for Matthew, though, it seemed. Ever since he'd got back, he'd been hovering around, waiting for his moment to broach the subject. Now that Ben was upstairs in a bath, they were alone at last.

She straightened too fast, sending the blood rushing to her head, and felt suddenly faint. She steadied herself against the fridge until the wave passed. Her legs and feet felt icy cold, and she went over to the thermostat on the wall to turn up the heat. He was too preoccupied in opening the bottle and pouring out the champagne to notice. He handed her a glass and raised his own in a brief toast. His face was hard and unsmiling.

"Hazel, this is very important," he began. "It concerns you and Ben—all of us. It's about Josie."

"Please, Matthew. That's all over."

"For her it isn't. She's got it into her head that ..." He broke off and pulled out a letter from his pocket. "Here. Read this. You know everything. You'll see what we're up against."

It was the note Lyall had shown her. She glanced at it, then handed it back dismissively.

"So?"

"You know who 'Mary' refers to?"

With a sigh, she helped herself to a prawn and washed it down with a small sip of the champagne. She'd spin the glass out all evening. God, how she craved a proper drink. And how tired she was of all this Josie and Isabel nonsense!

"Wake up, Matthew," she said wearily. "The play's over. The curtain's down. They're turning the lights out. Broadway's packing up."

"Believe me, angel, this is for real," he retorted. He took a step closer. "We're dealing with a deranged mind. Deranged and dangerous, Hazel. Are you hearing me?"

His deep-set eyes burned with vehemence. How often she'd seen that look. She shivered. It seemed so cold everywhere. Maybe she was coming down with flu. She ate another prawn and offered him the plate. He refused.

"They're delicious," she said. "You can taste the ocean."

"I believe you could be in serious personal danger, Hazel ..."

"I'm in serious personal danger of screaming, Matthew."

She felt herself perilously close to the edge. She took another prawn. She wasn't hungry; in fact she felt rather sick. It was just displacement activity.

"There's something you should know," he was continuing. "I did some research in the library today. Isabel Hardiment did not die how and where we've always thought she did."

"Matthew ..." she warned.

"I believe she died right here, in the United States."

"For God's sake, drop it!" she cried. "I don't give a damn if the poor woman died on the moon! I've had enough of this whole absurd farce! I don't want to hear that damned name ever again, do you understand? Never, never, never."

"But this letter ... it's a threat ... a direct personal threat ..."

"Do you think I'm scared of that girl? She's a perfectly regular, normal kid. She may be weird enough to play those dumb games of charades with you, but she's not deranged. *You're* the one with the problem, Matthew. Face up to it."

"Angel—"

"Cut it out!" she shrieked.

She went over to the sink, to put distance between them. Her stomach was burning in the way it did whenever she was angry. Maybe she'd eaten too many prawns; she'd been devouring them furiously, angrily, one immediately after another. She poured herself a glass of mineral water and drank it back in one gulp. God, how could she ever break free of this vicious iron cage clamped round her soul?

"Hey, are you okay?" she heard him ask.

How cold it was. It was like standing in freezing water. She couldn't feel her feet at all. Nor her fingers, either. But her stomach felt hot, very hot. It was as though her whole body's warmth was drawing in from her extremities and concentrating in her center.

"Hazel?" His voice was tinged with alarm.

She'd read about Arctic explorers who lost their toes from frostbite. It didn't hurt at the time. It can't hurt if you can't feel. A sudden flood of nausea swept over her. Was it the taste of champagne? Too acidic, corked, just bad? Or the prawns? Oh my God, the prawns!

"I feel ..." she began.

But she got no further. Her stomach suddenly burst into flames. Molten lava flowed in her intestines. Invisible hands closed around her throat choking her, smothering her of breath. Her feet, her ankles, her legs, her fingers, her hands ... icicles, dropping off one by one. Her whole being was imploding on her stomach. A furnace of pain roared within her belly. The flames turned to knives. The knives sliced and jabbed, turned and twisted, all blade and barb, all slash and stab. She choked on her scream. She clutched at the sink, doubled up, crumpled in on herself. Her cry rent the air. The pain, oh God, the pain, the pain.

TWENTY-THREE

Matthew stood at the foot of the hospital bed while the doctor bent over the comatose figure. Could this be his vibrant, energetic, life-loving Hazel? Her face was deathly pale and her breathing so shallow as to be almost imperceptible. Tubes led from her nose and mouth, a drip fed into her arm, and a skein of thin wires linked her chest and wrists with monitors that blipped and bleeped with disturbing sluggishness. A nurse stood checking the dials and screens; her expression betrayed no hint of what she read in them.

Matthew rubbed his eyes. He felt desperately tired. Through the window filtered the cold, reluctant light of early morning. He'd been back and forth to the house several times already that night, collecting Hazel's overnight things and arranging for Ben to be taken care of. While he was away the last time, she had been moved out of intensive care and into a large private room. A new doctor had come on duty, too, an affluent figure with his starched white coat, graying temples and early winter-sports tan, who was at this moment in the process of making his own diagnosis. At length he straightened and, handing the clipboard to the nurse, turned to Matthew.

"She's going to be fine," he announced.

"How long will you keep her here?"

"A few days, perhaps a week." The doctor paused and frowned. "You're a lucky man, Dr. Cavewood. If we hadn't taken her in right away and had her stomach pumped ..."

"My God," breathed Matthew, "I'd no idea it was so close."

"Food poisoning can be very serious when there's a child involved."

"Oh, Ben's all right. He didn't eat any of those things. He was already in bed, thank God."

"I was referring to the baby."

Matthew looked up sharply.

"The baby?"

"The fetus, I should say."

"I'm sorry, doctor. I'm not with you."

The man's face deepened into a puzzled frown.

"You do know your wife is pregnant?"

"Hazel's *pregnant?*"

"Ah, I see." He recovered from his surprise and reassumed his professional distance. "I would guess she's still in the first trimester, though we'll check with an ultrasound." He cleared his throat. "Food poisoning can cause problems at the early stages of pregnancy, but I don't think we need worry unduly in your wife's case. We'll continue to monitor the fetus over the next forty-eight hours, of course, and I'll check the results of the tests, but I don't anticipate any complications."

But Matthew was hardly listening. His mind was in a tumult of joy and disbelief. He stepped closer to the bed. A child! *Their* child. Did she know? Of course she knew; nothing ever caught Hazel by surprise. Then why hadn't she said? And it was going to be all right. "I don't anticipate any complications." Christ, that was a close call.

Finally the doctor left, and Matthew drew up a chair beside the bed and gently stroked her pale, needle-bruised hand. Her eyelids briefly flickered and for a moment the monitor's blip quickened, then gradually she sank back into her deep, drugged sleep.

I'm sorry, my sweet darling, he mumbled to himself. I've been so blind and self-absorbed. But all that's behind us now. We'll make a fresh start, I promise. Right now your job is just to get better. Nothing else in the world matters than that you should be well—you, and the little life inside you.

Matthew insisted that Hazel take a period of convalescence and, taking Ben out early from school that weekend, drove the family off to Virginia Beach to the old clapboard house on the ocean which they had rented during the summer. There he set about nursing Hazel to health, allowing

her to do nothing but rest and take it easy and leave the caring and cater-
ing to himself. He took Ben back to school on the Monday morning and
returned to spend the week alone with her. Every day they went on a walk
along the ocean path, each time progressing a little further until by the
end of the week, when he collected Ben back once again, she was strong
enough to walk for the whole afternoon.

The weather, up to this time crisp and bright, abruptly deteriorated,
and by the Friday night great storm clouds were rolling in over the ocean
like sheets of black tarpaulin. The wind rose to gale force, and all next day
a violent storm raged, forcing them to stay behind closed doors. Ben sat
with his face pressed to the window, watching the waves exploding against
the rocks and flinging great sprays of spume high into the air, to be caught
by the wind and sent lashing against the panes a second later. He prayed
fervently that they would be marooned there for the rest of the school
semester and have to be rescued by helicopter—in time, though, for
Christmas.

That evening, as usual, Matthew made a fire from driftwood and they
all gathered round to talk about the day. With Ben helping, he cooked
supper while Hazel sat in the rocking chair by the fire, reading and dozing
by turns. Later, after Ben was upstairs and asleep, the two of them sat
together, cocooned in the warmth of the fire, exchanging the occasional
smile of contentment, while outside, safely beyond the shutters, the squall
continued to rage unabated. At these times it seemed to Matthew that
nothing could exist outside this small paradise. He found whole hours
going by without his having had the slightest thought of Josie and the
turmoil he'd left behind. All that seemed to belong to another place,
another time. It had just been an illusion, a nightmare that dissolved with
the coming of the day.

On the final Sunday afternoon, however, just like the last time they'd
been here, as they packed up the rented house, loaded the car and headed
westward back to Charlottesville, he felt the tension beginning to mount
again. The storm had blown itself out, leaving the woodland slopes
stripped of leaves and spreading a slippery mulch over the surface of the
highway. As they drove they sang along to the radio and cracked idiotic
jokes in that end-of-vacation mood of slightly unnatural hilarity, but that
did little to subdue his underlying unease. The past week of paradise had
been the dream. Ahead lay the reality.

When finally they reached home, it was already dark. Instinctively,

Matthew made sure he was first to the door and, once inside, quickly glanced around, then checked the mail the maid had piled on the hall table. Bills, circulars, bank statements, an airmail letter from Bonn University, a package for Hazel from a magazine ... nothing worrying. What had he been expecting? He wasn't sure. That was the trouble: He sensed danger poised to strike, but he couldn't tell what or from which quarter it might come.

Cautiously relieved, he unloaded the car. Then, bolting the front door, he went into the kitchen where Hazel was busy unpacking the food and checked the answering machine for messages. Lyall had called, hoping Hazel was better. (How did he know? Mathew wondered: He certainly hadn't told him.) There were several calls for Hazel from her agent and from friends, but most were for himself—the university grants office, the pool maintenance service, a double-glazing sales company, the faculty administrator, a visiting historian from Berkeley, in addition to the usual invitations to meetings and talks and social events. In between these calls, he noticed, the machine had recorded a series of *bleeps* where people had rung but left no message. People ... or a certain person? He turned away briskly; he wasn't even going to speculate. He'd fix himself a whisky and go through his mail.

As he was pouring the drink, the phone rang. Hazel, being nearest, picked it up.

"Hello?" she called into the receiver. "Hello? Who is it?"

After a moment the line evidently went dead, and she replaced the phone with a puzzled shrug.

"I hate it when people do that," she frowned.

"A wrong number," he offered.

"It always makes me suspicious."

"It happens all the time." He forced a cheery tone into his voice. "Can I fix you a drink? A small glass of wine can't do any harm."

"You're sure?"

"A little every now and then is perfectly okay. You're past the danger period."

"I mean, you're sure about that call?"

"Well, it can't be burglars," he smiled. "Unless they're particularly dumb. They've had all week to break in." He wasn't thinking it could be burglars. He didn't know what he was thinking. He'd rather not think at all. He delved into the drawer for a corkscrew. "Red or white?"

"I'm sticking to juice." Her frown lingered for a moment longer, then with a shake of her head, she reached for a knife and began chopping an onion. He stood behind her and put his arms round her waist. The perfume of her hair and neck filled his senses. "Move out of my way," she said, brushing him off. "If you want to be useful, get Ben into his bath. Tell him it's lights out promptly tonight. He's got school tomorrow. And you'd better get down to some work yourself, too, Matthew. You can't keep taking time off for any excuse."

"I'll remember that next time you're at death's door." He hung back at the door. "It's good to be home, huh?"

"Hurry up, and take that drink with you. I can smell it from here."

With a smile, he left the room. As he crossed the hallway, he caught his reflection in the windows against the darkness outside. Anyone could be looking in.... He quickly swept the curtains shut, and stifling a gnawing sense of unease he continued on his way upstairs. *Was* it so good to be home?

Hello? Hello? Who's there?

Josie cupped her hand over the mouthpiece and carefully hung the phone up on its cradle in the roadside booth. For a moment she stood motionless, a look of frozen disbelief on her face.

Impossible! she choked. She must be dead, she has to be! Oh God, she's cheated me. Stolen me of my revenge. No, no! I can't allow this. The cycle must work itself through. She cannot escape what is coming!

Slowly, as if in a trance, she turned away from the phone booth and, blind to the traffic, cut diagonally across Main Street and headed into the campus grounds. Gradually she quickened her step. She headed up the sloping lawns of the grounds, guided by the floodlit dome of the Rotunda, floating like a majestic crown above the university. Skirting the lawns, she made her way along poorly lit pathways until she reached the Ranges, where she slipped unseen along the cloisters and into her room. There she threw off her cloak and made straight for her desk.

This time she shall not escape me.

Through the bedroom window, Hazel watched Matthew in the driveway below, swathed in the car exhaust billowing on the cold morning air, as he scraped away at the frost on the Mercedes' windows. She hung back behind the curtain, in case he glanced up and saw her.

He'd risen early, explaining he had a mountain of work to catch up on at the lab, but when it came to going he'd seemed strangely reluctant to leave, and he'd only finally headed off after making her promise most insistently to take care. She'd assured him over and over that she was absolutely fine now, but that didn't seem to relieve his anxiety. It was only when she heard the front door closing that she realized what lay behind it all. He still had that wretched girl's threatening note on his mind! Oh God, wouldn't they ever be free of all that? Suddenly all the joy of the past week seemed to evaporate. They'd come home to find nothing had changed. She should have known better than to hope it had. She sighed in exasperation; there was a limit to human patience.

She watched him climb into the car and head off down the drive. At the end, however, instead of turning right into the road to go to the university, she noticed he went left. This would take him straight onto Route 29, the main highway that ran north to Washington and connected in the south with the interstate to Richmond. As she turned away, her eye fell upon the bedside clock and she focused her thoughts on more immediate concerns. She'd better get moving. Ben would be late for school if she didn't hurry.

She delivered Ben to school as the last pupils were arriving and returned straight home, planning out her day as she drove. She'd spend the morning catching up on calls and correspondence. Elaine was picking Ben up from school with her boys and taking him home to play with them; she herself had nothing booked until four o'clock, when she was due at the doctor's for a checkup, and an appointment at the hairdresser's afterward. She collected the mail from the box at the end of the drive and, while waiting for the coffee to filter, riffled through the small sheaf of envelopes.

One, on heavy bond, stood out from the rest. It was addressed in fine, sloping handwriting to MRS. HAZEL CAVEWOOD and marked PERSONAL, and on the back it bore the sender's address: HANOVER PARK, HANOVER, VA. 15812.

She tore it open. It was from Otis McDowell, written in his own hand.

Dear Mrs Cavewood,

I'm writing to you on a matter of some delicacy. You may understand when I say it concerns your husband and my daughter, Josie.

Josie came to see me recently in great distress. It seems that she has become the focus of certain unwelcome, I would even say bizarre, notions in your husband's mind. I do not wish to write more. I assume you are aware of what I refer to.

I would like to meet and talk this through with you confidentially. I feel sure we can find a way of straightening it out between ourselves, without having to involve outside parties.

I have business in Charlottesville this coming Monday, November 29. Could we meet for a drink or an early supper, say, at Duner's Restaurant on Rte. 250 West, at 6:00 p.m.? Don't trouble to confirm: I shall be there in any event.

Meantime, I rely on you to keep this strictly between ourselves.

Sincerely,
Otis McDowell

Hazel reread the letter. Monday, November 29: My God, that was today! She glanced at the date at the top of the letter. It had been written a full week ago. She checked the envelope, but the stamp appeared to have escaped the franking machine. Evidently it had got delayed in the mail.

She read it a third time. *"The focus of certain unwelcome, I would even say bizarre, notions in your husband's mind."* This was real trouble. It meant Matthew's problem was no longer a private matter they could keep within the walls at home. It was now public. True, Otis spoke of meeting her "confidentially" and of "straightening it out between ourselves." He might not tell other people, perhaps, but what if Josie did? Things like this always leaked out. What would it do to Matthew's career? His year was almost up, and he hadn't yet produced. Dean Colbert would be back from his sabbatical at the beginning of the new year, now just a few weeks away, and Matthew's whole future was coming up for review. He had to get back on track and see to this accursed book, and the last thing he needed was to risk a damaging scandal. At a university like this, where the undergraduates still subscribed to that old Jeffersonian code of conduct, the Honor System, she could only guess at the stringent standards of ethical behavior expected of the teaching faculty. If it became campus gossip, he could kiss good-bye any hope of an associate professorship. He would never recognize that, of course. He never understood that what counted was not the actual but the perceived rights and wrongs of a case. You couldn't spend the time she had in Washington, D.C., without learning that at least.

She folded the letter and slipped it into her purse, then reached for the phone. She'd schedule her hair appointment earlier in the afternoon. She might as well go in fighting looking good.

*   *   *

FAIRMONT, VA., WELCOMES CAREFUL DRIVERS, read the teetering sign, its enamel surface peppered with buckshot. Matthew braked sharply as a tractor ahead swung left across the road without signaling and lumbered down a track toward a rust-streaked barn.

The town consisted of a single road running from one end to the other like a flattened spine, lined by houses and stores, garages and shops, lying just one block deep. Here, the pearly mist that hung over the countryside had lifted, and through it percolated a pale, shy sun that washed the ramshackled clapboard buildings in a diffuse, shadowless light.

The church alone stood apart. It was positioned on a small hillock some way back from the road and the flow of commerce, like a port abandoned over time by the receding ocean. Matthew's pulse quickened as he pulled up beside the small wicket gate. The crouching doors and windows and sharply pointed steeple of the church bespoke its early colonial origins. The date was certainly right, but the chances were slim that they'd have records going back that far.

The church was surrounded by a graveyard bordered by a threadbare yew hedge. In the far corner, a gardener with close-set eyes and a slack jaw was raking dead leaves onto a smoldering bonfire. The smoke filled the damp air with a rich, dank perfume. Matthew huddled into his overcoat and, torn between hope and dread, stepped over to examine the first headstone. He progressed systematically, reading each in turn until he'd come full circle. He hadn't found what he was looking for. The graves themselves had clearly been recycled: None of the headstones was more than a hundred years old.

As he let himself into the church, his heart finally sank. The interior had been modernized: Slatted wooden benches in varnished pine formed the pews, while above a plain table laid with an altar cloth rose a stained glass window in an abstract design. But then, to his surprise, he noticed that the original flagstone floor had survived. Looking further, he saw, set into the floor at intervals down the aisles, a number of larger slabs of darker, slatelike stone. Tombstones.

The surfaces had been worn smooth by the feet of generations so that the inscriptions were only partly legible.

With mounting excitement, Matthew knelt to examine the first. All that was left was a cartouche at the head showing a dove bearing an olive branch, and at the foot the words "O Death ... thy sting?", with a date beneath it: MDCLXXIX.

A seventeenth-century tombstone!

He hurried on to the second, then the third, better preserved than the others.

A violent shiver ran through him. Falling to a crouch, he began painstakingly to piece together the inscription. It read:

INMEMORIAM
IsabelJaneHardimentMcDowell
Beloved Wife of Fergus Jeremiah McDowell
Released from the Tribulations of this World
23rd November 1689
Aged 29
After an Illness first contracted upon the Sea Voyage from England
and Suffered with Exemplary Fortitude

*

*The First Man is of the earth, earthy: the Second Man is
the Lord from Heaven
—MATTHEW*

*

"I shall return, Nathaniel"

He broke out in a flush of dizziness.

Isabel Jane Hardiment McDowell, Beloved Wife of Fergus Jeremiah McDowell ...

Jesus Christ!

There, incredibly, engraved on the slate tablet before him, was the evidence of a link he could never have guessed at. On that one stone he could read the whole extraordinary, tragic story.

Isabel Hardiment had somehow, God knew how, escaped the gallows in England and fled to the colonies of America. There, a year later, she had bought an estate in Fairmont, Northumberland County. Subsequently she'd married a certain Fergus McDowell, probably a first-generation Scottish settler, and died seven years later. It was a fair guess that she left issue—male issue of necessity, to carry on the name of McDowell. And now the fruit of that issue, some twelve generations later in a direct line of descent, was a girl with the same oval cast of face, the same blond hair and intense blue eyes, the same characteristic mole on her upper lip ...

But was it the whole story? It left the question at the core still more tantalizingly out of reach.

Who exactly was lying beneath that slate slab, reduced to dust by the worms and maggots of centuries? If that was Isabel Hardiment, then who was the girl living today, full of youth and vitality, probably sitting at this very moment in a small room off a cloistered yard at the back of the main lawns at the heart of the campus of a university not a hundred miles away?

How did it happen?

If memories actually did lie in brain cells and were transmitted through the genes, he could imagine that Josie had inherited Isabel's memories and, at the critical moment of near-death, when her brain was given a kick-start it somehow called up an atavistic bank of memory files in error.... But that was scientific rubbish. Memories were not physically located in the brain, in fact, and genes did not code for them either.

He simply did not know. He didn't have the apparatus to tackle the question. Frankly, he was defeated. It was time he paid Professor Stevenson a visit.

As he slowly retraced his steps to the car, he found his thoughts turning to Nathaniel. What had become of *him*? Had he engineered Isabel's survival from the gallows? It was not unknown for relatives to bribe the executioner to cut down a condemned prisoner while he was still just about alive. Had he helped her slip the country, perhaps even joined her later over here? Or died on the way, and she went on to marry someone else?

But one thing he couldn't rid from his mind was the ambiguous phrase incised in the hard stone and strangely unaffected by the attrition of time: "I shall return, Nathaniel." The more he pondered the words, the more he detected a sinister undertone. Was this simply a promise, a vow of love between two hearts torn by tragedy and separated by insurmountable barriers, a cry from the heart for a lost love? Or was it a threat, a cry of vengeance from the grave upon a lover for some unforgivable act of betrayal?

Many great religions believed in reincarnation, of course. Hindus and Buddhists held it as an article of their faith. So had the ancient Celts and the Greeks, and even some early fathers of the Church, such as Origen and Saint Jerome, were sympathetic to the doctrine. But the second Council of Constantinople convened by Justinian condemned it outright, and thereafter reincarnation became a Christian heresy—a ruling of which Nathaniel Shawcrosse was later to fall afoul. Even in the modern day it was rejected by the churches of Rome and of other Protestant nations. In their view, we had one life on this earth only, and for it we would be held to account on the Day of Judgment.

For himself, however, Matthew had no difficulty in theory with the concept of a discarnate spirit becoming reincarnate. Shawcrosse had embodied the principle in his Gate, after all, and it was gaining surprising endorsement with advances in modern physics. But it was a far different matter to accept that here was a real and actual living case.

He reached Charlottesville shortly after noon. It took him a while to locate the place he was looking for, and it was well into the afternoon by the time he found himself outside the organization's headquarters, a brick and clapboard house on a side road off Main Street. Outside, a noticeboard read, DEPARTMENT OF PERSONALITY STUDIES, A DIVISION OF THE UNIVERSITY OF VIRGINIA HEALTH SCIENCES CENTER.

Arriving without an appointment, Matthew found that the professor had just left on a trip to Sri Lanka. His assistant offered to help, however. She led him down a corridor festooned with spears and masks and other mementos of exotic lands and showed him into the library, where she got for him a pile of books and articles.

The first book was entitled *Twenty Cases Suggestive of Reincarnation.* All the cases appeared to be of children, and all from the Indian subcontinent. He cast her a doubtful glance.

"You'd expect to find cases there, where reincarnation is taken for granted," he remarked. "What about right here, in America?"

"Oh, yes," the assistant replied at once. "There are American children who claim to remember previous lives. Many come from families who hold an actively negative attitude to it. It can be very alarming. We get a lot of correspondence from worried parents."

He skimmed a number of abstracts. Nothing quite matched his case.

"Tell me," he tried, "do these kids who remember previous lives actually believe they have always been that person, from the time they were born? I mean, you don't ever get cases where a person has an accident, let's say, and *becomes* another person afterward?"

"A walk-in, you mean."

"A walk-in?"

"Well, we prefer to call them 'cases of the possession type.' They're rare, but not unknown." She dug a small pamphlet out of a box file. "Maybe this case would interest you."

A chill passed through Matthew's veins as he read the pamphlet.

The case concerned a young married woman called Sumitra in a village in northern India. She apparently died and was revived. After a period of confusion, she stated that she was, in fact, someone called Shiva who had been murdered in another village. The details she gave corresponded exactly with the facts in the life of an actual woman called Shiva, also young and married, who'd lived some sixty miles away and had met with a violent death about two months before Sumitra's own brush with death. The evidence for the switch was overwhelming. Sumitra knew her way round Shiva's village, for instance; she recognized her friends and relatives, she exhibited instinctively the habits of a Brahmin, Shiva's caste and a higher one than her own....

"And then, of course," the assistant went on, handing him an open book, "you have the case of Jasbir."

Jasbir, a three-and-a-half-year-old boy, appeared to have died of smallpox. His father asked the other men of the village for help in burying him, but as it was late they decided to leave it until morning. A few hours later, the father noticed the body stirring, and gradually the boy revived completely. When after some weeks he recovered the ability to speak, he showed a remarkable transformation of behavior. He said he was the son of a man called Shankar of a different village and that he wanted to go back there. He would eat no food at home, claiming he belonged to a higher caste, and indeed his obstinate refusal would have led to his second, and permanent, death had not a kindly Brahmin neighbor agreed to feed him. This she did for a year and a half.

More details of his previous life in the other village began to emerge. He particularly described how, during a wedding procession, he had been given poisoned candies by a man who owed him money; made giddy, he'd fallen off the wagon on which he was riding, suffered a head injury and died.

News leaked out, and gradually the story was corroborated. A young man of twenty-two called Sobha Ram had indeed died in an accident exactly as Jasbir described, just before Jasbir's own close call with death....

Matthew puzzled over these two cases for a while. The similarities with Josie's case were chilling. But equally glaring was the one major difference: the lapse of time. In Stevenson's cases, the gap between the death of the first person and the possession of the second was short, a matter of months if not merely days. Indeed, it seemed the lapse was shorter when the earlier lives had ended violently. Death, even near-death, by hanging could hardly be a more violent end. And yet the interval was three hundred years!

For three centuries, Isabel had bided her time, waiting for the moment and the opportunity—a suitable host body to present itself within the area of her reach. In Josie she found a young girl, rushed to hospital after a car crash, who for a few vital minutes died in the operating room, a brief but sufficient window through which an invading spirit could enter. But Josie was not *any* host: She was her own blood, her own stock—herself in the flesh today. This was no case of random possession; this was deliberate. Isabel had carefully and knowingly chosen her vehicle.

Because she had a purpose.

The conclusion hit him with the force of a physical blow, for it meant that she had been waiting not only for Josie but also for him. He was the other, necessary part of her purpose.

He thought back to the various times she had appeared to him: the hallucinatory dream in Oxford, the ghostly presence at the bedroom window, the apparition in the backyard, the fleeting images of the boy in black. She had been tracking him all this time! He was as necessary to her purpose as the real Josie.

Why him?

Because she saw him as her Nathaniel. And that, in turn, was because he had made it so. His obsession with the character and life of Nathaniel Shawcrosse had been so total, his self-identification as a biographer with his subject had been so powerful, that to a real degree he had become him. Not by reincarnation but by resonance. By the sheer power of his obsession, he had become another man.

The realization froze him to the spot. He had stirred up terrible, potent, unpredictable forces. Unwittingly he had sent out a call and Isabel, waiting in the wings of time, harboring her purpose, had answered the call and found the means to return.

Was her purpose to relive the grand passion of her life, to complete a love cut short by death? Yes, but it was also more sinister. Something unspeakable had happened to her, some ultimate act of betrayal. Her driving need was to resolve this. She wanted to recreate the passion but also to change its fate. To redirect its destiny and set it right, and so to lay to rest the pain and rage that time had been unable to assuage. That was the threat behind the curse, "You have betrayed me, Nathaniel." In rejecting her, he had unwittingly stumbled over a trip wire and unleashed her terrible, implacable will to vengeance. *"Now events must take their course,"* she'd written. *"Do not hope to escape necessity.... Good-bye, Nathaniel. God forgive you. God help Mary ..."*

Mary!

Suddenly he let out a howl of horror. In a flash he grasped the full and awful meaning of the threat. He turned and set off in a desperate, stumbling run toward his car.

Hazel! he cried aloud. Stay where you are! Don't move! I'm coming!

Waiting at traffic lights, Hazel checked her face in the rearview mirror. The hairdresser had done well—just the right fullness and wave. With her little finger she touched up the edge of her lipstick and softened the line of her eye shadow. Glancing down, she flicked a speck off the lapel of her pale gray silk suit and eased up the jacket so as not to crush the hem. She looked good and she felt good. A head start with the senator.

She drove slowly, with time to kill. After a short while she had left the town behind and was driving through open countryside. Twilight was falling fast, and a piercingly bright crescent moon etched the distant mountain ranges in sharp profile. On either side of the road, ploughed meadows and pastures stretched up to a treeline of fir and spruce, all gradually merging into a single dark monotone. For a while she was caught behind a lumber truck, but she made no attempt to pass it. She wanted to time her arrival right, and to arrive fresh and relaxed.

Shortly the sign came up, DUNER'S RESTAURANT: 1 MILE. With the dashboard clock turning ten past six, she swung her car off the highway onto the broad, metalized drive that ran in front of the low restaurant building. She coasted into the floodlit parking area and pulled up.

As she climbed out, she looked about her in puzzlement. The restaurant itself was floodlit, too, but it looked strangely dark inside. Where was everybody? A pickup with a flat tire stood parked by the far fence. Across from it stood a silver Olds; the grime on its windshield suggested it hadn't been driven for a while. A van bearing the restaurant's name stood over by the service entrance, alongside two steel garbage dumpsters. Otherwise the parking lot was empty. No sign of Otis or his limousine. For all she'd contrived to be late, she'd ended up being early.

As she approached the restaurant, she slowed. The lighting inside was low, perhaps to create an intimate atmosphere, but she couldn't see much of anyone. She reached into her purse to check the letter. No, she hadn't mistaken the day or the time.

Then she understood. Of course! The restaurant was closed on Mondays, and the senator had arranged to have it opened specially. My God, she thought, he must be worried, to go to such lengths. If discretion was so vital, why couldn't they have driven around in his car for a talk? She smiled to herself: He was a real old-fashioned gentleman, the kind that wrote his personal letters himself and took a lady to cocktails or supper if he had something delicate to discuss.

The sign on the door said OPEN. She went in. Inside, she hung back and cast around her. The tables were laid, the linen fresh and the glasses polished. The table lights were on, and in the background light music softly played. But there seemed to be no staff in evidence, let alone other customers. She glanced at her watch. Quarter past. This was the right place, wasn't it?

Just then the swing door to the kitchen opened and a girl with short dark hair and tinted glasses came out. As soon as she saw Hazel she came forward with an apologetic smile.

"I'm so sorry," she said in a slow, soft drawl. "I didn't hear the door. You must be Mrs. Cavewood. You're due to meet Senator McDowell."

"That's right," said Hazel with some relief.

"He's just called. He's been held up but he's on his way. He says please have a drink and he'll be with you very shortly." The girl ushered her to a table. "What can I get you, ma'am? We have a selection of cocktails ..."

"Just a glass of water, thank you," replied Hazel.

"Perrier?"

"That will do fine."

Hazel idly studied the waitress as she went to the bar and set about pouring the drink. She looked like a student paying her way through college. She herself had earned money waiting tables in her time. She gave the girl a friendly smile when she returned and took a long, refreshing mouthful from the glass. She'd forgotten how strangely bitter mineral water sometimes tasted.

"Thanks, I needed that," she said. "Where are you from?"

"Fairmont, Virginia. You won't know of it."

"And you're studying at UVA?"

"Right."

Hazel took another long pull of the water and glanced at her watch. The dial seemed a bit blurry. She blinked, and the hands came back into focus. Twenty-five after.

"When did he say?"

"Any time now," replied the girl.

"This all seems ... rather strange," said Hazel. Her voice seemed to come from just outside herself.

"It's how it should be."

"I hate being late for a date."

She didn't recognize what she was saying as her own words. The girl paused before replying. When she spoke, her voice was slower and silkier than ever.

"You're not late for your date, Mrs. Cavewood."

Hazel looked up sharply. Something about that face seemed curiously familiar. Maybe all girls today had a look in common. And yet ... She laughed aloud, a short staccato burst that took herself by surprise. What was she thinking? This was crazy.

"Hardly a date," she slurred. "More of a business meeting. We have things to discuss. This and that. Matters of mutual concern."

What was she saying? The girl's face wore a strange, hard smile. Hazel found her gaze rooted on a small mark on the girl's upper lip. Beneath a layer of foundation, she could see the ghost image of a small dark mole.

Gradually the girl removed her glasses and fixed her with intense violet eyes. Hazel gave a start. Those eyes! But the hair? The hair was dark and short....

"Matters of mutual concern?" echoed the girl, her smile withering into a twisted curl.

Then she saw the single wisp of blond hair that coiled out from under the thick dark locks, and she understood. She understood everything.

"Oh my God," she gasped.

She struggled to her feet. The room swirled about her. She raised her hand; it was as heavy as lead. She tried to cry out; a great stone slab had settled upon her lungs. She looked at the glass of water, then at the girl. The girl was clutching a heavy wooden mallet, the kind used for tenderizing meat. Her eyes were piercing, mesmerizing. The room began to revolve faster and faster, like a giddy catherine wheel. Suddenly Hazel broke her gaze free and cast frantically around her. The place was empty. There was no one to help. No one to hear. The world was pitching like a ship in a storm. She clutched the table to steady herself. Her feet were set in concrete, her joints locked, her eyelids leaden.

"Why?" she choked. "*Why?*"

But Josie made no reply. She merely tightened her grip on the mallet and took a step forward.

TWENTY-FOUR

The mallet caught Hazel a glancing blow on the shoulder. The pain scorched through her like a flame, jerking her brain out of its fog. With a cry, she flung the empty glass full in Josie's face and stumbled for the door. It wouldn't open. Frantically she tugged and twisted the handle, but it seemed to be stuck.

The girl was coming forward, her eyes blazing, her arm raised to strike again. Hazel rushed her. Coming in under the blow, she threw her off balance and sent her flying into a table. It crashed to the floor, shattering the crockery and glass. The mallet flew out of her hand. Hazel fell upon her, and for a moment held her pinned to the floor.

"Stop this madness!" she cried. "Listen to me! Whatever's the matter, let's talk. We can settle it without fighting."

Josie glared up at her, her expression contorted with hatred, then suddenly she spat at her full in the face. In the second that Hazel relaxed her grip, the girl squirmed free. Hazel grabbed at her hair. The wig came away in her hand. Her long blond hair flying, Josie scrambled away toward the fallen weapon.

Hazel was breathing heavily. She felt dizzy and sick. She could feel the adrenaline burning in her stomach, alternating with great waves of drowsiness that kept trying to swamp her. Josie had reached the mallet and was climbing to her feet. For the first time a jolt of real terror shot through Hazel. She was drugged and trapped in a room with a crazy psychopath.

She backed deeper into the restaurant, stumbling her way through the tables. A small conservatory annex led off the main dining room. Surely there was an escape here? In the far corner stood a glass door marked EXIT. She hurled herself at it, but it, too, was locked. Summoning her remaining strength, she seized a chair and smashed it against the door, shattering the glass into a large jagged hole. She was climbing through the gap when the girl grabbed her from behind. She fell back into the room, ripping her skirt on a spike of glass and gouging a deep cut in her leg. She thrust the girl off her and blundered half-crazed around the tables into a corridor. To the right lay the rest rooms: no, not there, she'd only get trapped in there. Ahead was the kitchen. There would be a phone in the kitchen—and knives.

In the kitchen, the venetian blinds were closed. Overhead strip lights illuminated the large room with a cold glare that glinted dully off the stainless steel and aluminum of the pots hanging on overhead racks, the sinks stretching along one wall and the array of slicers and peelers standing on the work surfaces. Air freshener overlaid the stale smell of cooking. In the center stood a large work island with an open base, and above it was suspended a row of sharp knives, arranged in size order like pipes of an organ, from the heaviest cleaver to the lightest filleter. Just as she was taking a long, thin carving knife, there was a distant *click* and the lights abruptly went out. In the sudden darkness, she let the knife slip out of her hand. It glanced off the work top and clattered away across the hard tiled floor.

At that moment the door opened.

Falling to a crouch, she wormed herself in under the work island. There she waited, barely breathing, as the footsteps came closer and closer. Slowly her eyes grew accustomed to the dim light filtering through cracks in the blinds. A pair of legs came into view. They stopped just inches away from her, then turned and slowly walked away. She felt a great wash of drowsiness and fought with all her strength to keep her eyes open. She heard the steps recede, then abruptly go quiet. The girl was back in the dining area where it was carpeted.

Cautiously she crawled out of hiding and, retrieving the knife, tiptoed back to the door. In the corridor she turned and headed deeper into the building. Surely it must lead to a service entrance. She felt her way along the wall in the dark. The corridor turned a corner. At the end where it turned again she could see a glow of light. But footsteps were approaching again. She clasped the knife tighter, but her grip was already weak.

She fumbled her way along the wall until she found a door. As she opened it, a rancid smell met her—the food larder. Quickly she hid inside. The door had a line of ventilation holes at eye-level. Carefully she peeped out. The girl was prowling down the corridor. A moment later, she came back and paused briefly. They were now standing no more than a foot apart. Hazel smothered a cough. With all her willpower she forced her legs to support her. The moment stretched interminably. Then, as carefully as a panther, the girl moved away.

Finally, cautiously, Hazel opened the door an inch. The corridor was clear; all was quiet. Shaking uncontrollably, she traced her way toward the light. As she rounded the final corner, she saw hope at last: a wire-glass door marked, FIRE EXIT—PUSH BAR TO OPEN.

She dragged herself forward. Through the door, in the light of the floodlights, she could see the outside service area—pallets, beer crates, garbage dumpsters. Suddenly her foot struck a fire extinguisher canister, and a sharp metallic clang echoed around the corridor. She froze. Honing her ears, she listened for steps behind her, but all remained silent. Carefully she reached for the bar and tried to push it. It was too stiff; she'd have to thrust it open, risking the noise. She grasped the bar in both hands. Nervously she shot a final glance behind her, but the corridor was empty. Then, summoning the final resources of her strength, she turned and ...

Christ alive!

Josie was there, at the glass, sprung up at her like a jack-in-the-box, her face pressed against the pane, wild-eyed and crazed and murderous.

Hazel screamed. She staggered backward. She tripped, and fell. She flung out a hand to break her fall, but in vain. Her head caught the side of the metal fire extinguisher, she crumpled to the ground, and abruptly her whole world went black.

Twenty minutes later Josie was at the wheel of the red Pontiac, heading back to town. She drove erratically, swerving all over the road and veering off the curb like a pinball. She sat forward in the seat with one hand clenched around the steering wheel and the other held upright to check the flow of blood seeping through the napkin tied around it.

She glanced at the dashboard clock. She'd be back in town just after seven. A thin smile twisted itself across her tightened lips. A lot had happened in the three hours since school let out. But at the new apartment, her young guest would be sleeping soundly.

It was late in the afternoon when Matthew stumbled down the steps of the department of personality studies headquarters and raced to his car.

His mind was in a daze. Here he was, a man of the late twentieth century, driving a car on a modern highway, with gas stations here and shopping malls there and scientific materialism triumphant everywhere, and yet it was all just a gigantic stage set tricked up to look convincing from the front but which proved hollow behind. The truths behind this comforting facade were profoundly disturbing. Truths that turned the common idea of time and causality on its head, truths that destroyed the belief in the distinction between mind and matter, truths that allowed a woman buried in a church three hundred years ago to be living and walking the streets today.

The closer he drew to home, the faster he drove. He should have known! It was folly to have left Hazel alone like that. A pattern was repeating itself, a pattern in which the past was gradually closing in on the present. The moment he pulled into the drive, he saw her car was not there. Even so, he rushed indoors and called her name. There was no reply. Then he remembered that she had a hair appointment. He breathed a sigh of relief. He could intercept her there. She wouldn't be out for a good while yet.

He took a can of beer from the fridge and replayed the messages on the answering machine. The last was from the hospital doctor, saying the results of the tests had come through and asking him to call. Matthew waited interminably while the hospital switchboard beeped the doctor. When finally they were connected, the man sounded puzzled, his professional aura of confidence shaken. It wasn't seafood poisoning, he reported, but some kind of vegetable toxin. They hadn't yet identified it, but it looked like some poisonous berry or seed. Could Ben have concocted something which his mother had accidentally eaten?

Matthew slowly replaced the phone. A gong was drumming softly in the back of his mind. Vegetable toxin ... poison berries, poison seeds. Isabel had been a noted herbalist....

No, this was absurd. It wasn't possible. There was no way Josie could have given Hazel anything to eat.

Troubled, he made himself a pastrami sandwich, but couldn't stomach it. He glanced at the clock. Ben would be all right at Harry and Elaine's for a while yet, and he wouldn't need to leave for the hairdresser's for a good forty minutes. Maybe he'd go and meet her there before she left. Meantime, he'd try not to think about anything.

He sat down and turned his attention to the morning's mail lying on the table. Hazel had been through her own already, as he could see. As he reached forward, his eye lit upon an opened envelope that stood out from the rest. It was on heavy personalized stationery, and addressed to Hazel by hand. Out of curiosity he picked it up and turned it over. The address engraved on the reverse gave him a start. Otis McDowell was writing to Hazel? Oh God, he thought instantly. Josie has gone to him and said something ... he'd lodge a complaint ... the dean would arraign him before the board and all hell would break loose. Josie's campaign to destroy him had begun.

Then he frowned. Something didn't quite figure. Would Josie really go to Otis when she didn't actually recognize him as her father? And how would he react to the revelation that his daughter was not the Josie he had reared but some other creature from a different century—assuming, of course, he didn't know already?

And another thing. Would Otis McDowell really write his own letters? Perhaps, if what he had to say was exceptionally confidential or delicate. But then, why write at all and risk committing himself to paper, when a phone call would have done?

And then, come to think of it, didn't Otis have difficulty writing with ease? Matthew remembered the first time Hazel had shown him her portrait of the senator, signing papers at his desk, he'd thought she had got the negative round the wrong way, for he was holding the pen in his left hand, and she'd explained how he'd lost his right arm in a shooting accident....

His frown deepened. He took out his pen and, holding it in his left hand, traced out the address on the envelope with the point of the cap. The slant of the characters was impossible to follow. Then he transferred the pen to his right hand, and now the flow of the characters followed naturally. There could be no mistake. Otis was left-handed, but this letter had been written by a right-handed person.

Suddenly he recognized the color of the ink! And, looking closer, he recognized the sloping "l" in "Hazel" and the unusual "w" in "Cavewood."

His world lurched violently.

He grabbed the phone and dialed the hairdresser's. He would tell Hazel to wait there and not move at any cost until he was there. From now on, until he'd sorted this all out, he literally wouldn't let her out of his sight.

He called. The conversation was brief. When he put the phone down, his shirt was damp with perspiration.

Hazel was not at the hairdresser's. She had rescheduled her appointment. She had an early supper date with someone important—some political big shot, she'd hinted, though she hadn't said who or where.

Releasing a pent-up breath, he turned back to the envelope. He was overreacting. It had obviously been addressed by Otis's secretary. He'd call and find out where they were meeting, and escort her home.

He obtained the number of Hanover Park from Information and called up. As the phone rang, he wondered idly where they had gone: All the decent restaurants in the area were closed on Mondays.

"Senator McDowell's residence," came the secretary's silken voice. "I'm sorry to keep you."

"This is Dr. Matthew Cavewood," he began. "I need to get in touch with my wife urgently and I believe she is meeting with the senator this evening …"

"You must be mistaken, sir. The senator is out of town. We don't expect him back until the end of the week. Dr. Cavewood? Hello? Are you there?"

But he had already replaced the receiver. It was all becoming clear. Sickeningly clear.

Snatching his car keys, he hurried to the door. Christ alone knew where she was and how he'd find her.

Josie was not in her room. Of course she wouldn't be. He tapped on her neighbor Mandy's door. There was some shuffling inside, then Mandy's voice called out, "Who is it?"

"Matthew Cavewood."

"Just a sec." More shuffling and whispering, and the door finally opened. Mandy stood clutching a robe around her naked body, her hair awry and her face flushed. "What's wrong?"

"I need to find Josie."

"She came by earlier," she said, stifling a yawn. "She wanted to take my car, but I needed it. I guess she took a cab."

"Where did she go?"

"Search me."

"Which cab company? I'm sorry. It really is important."

"Try ABC Cars. Or Luxicabs. Luxicabs gives student discounts."

"Thanks, Mandy. Sorry to disturb you. If you see her, you might ..." He gave a faint smile. "Forget it. You've got better things to do."

He strode briskly to the Rotunda. There was a pay phone in the basement. When he arrived he found it bore a sticker OUT OF ORDER. With an oath, he broke into a jog and headed across the grounds to Newcomb Hall where there was a bank of phones.

He called Luxicabs. They had no record of picking up a Josie McDowell. With mounting despair, he called ABC Cars. The man took a while to shuffle through his papers.

"Nothing today by that name, sir," came the response.

"There must be!"

"I guess you're out of luck."

His mind whirled frantically. A wild idea suddenly occurred to him.

"Try under another name."

"What's that, sir?"

"Hardiment."

"Hold, please." The man put down the receiver while he dealt with another call. In the background, Matthew could hear a babble of voices coming in over the radio. Eventually, after an agonizing delay, the man returned to the phone. "Yeah, I have a Hardiment. Collect at corner of McCormick and University Avenue and take to Duner's Restaurant on 250 West."

Matthew slammed down the phone. In a flash he was out of the building, down the steps, across the lawns and round the back of Minor Hall where he'd illegally parked his car, and within another minute he was roaring up Ivy Road and heading west out of town.

DUNER'S RESTAURANT: 1 MILE, read the signboard. Matthew accelerated. As the low, floodlit building loomed up through the dark, he eased up and swung off the road. He skidded to a halt and sprang out of the car. He looked around him with disbelief. The lot was empty, the restaurant closed. No sign of Hazel's car.

He slammed his fist on the roof. The trail ended here. Josie had lured Hazel to this place, knowing it was going to be deserted, then they'd gone off somewhere in the Pontiac. He looked about him. A pickup with a flat tire, an abandoned Olds, a delivery van without a driver, an unmanned incinerator, a whole restaurant in total darkness. Who could tell him where they'd gone?

He went up to the front entrance. The sign on the door read SORRY, WE'RE CLOSED. He tried the knob; it was locked. He peered inside. He could see the tables laid for the morrow's meals, but the building was in darkness. With a sinking heart, he went around the side in case ... in case what? In case there was a caretaker or a security man who had something to say? Absurd! He passed the service entrance and tried the door there, but it, too, was locked. He picked his way past stacks of plastic beer crates and continued around the back. He came to an annex, evidently a recent addition....

He stepped forward quickly. It had a door to the exterior marked, FIRE EXIT—DO NOT OBSTRUCT. The glass in the door had been smashed. He examined it more closely. Onto one jagged piece of glass clung a small fragment of material. Gray silk. He knew who had a suit in that gray silk.

"Hazel?" he howled. "Hazel!"

A frenzy of desperation seized him. Kicking out the pane with his heel, he clambered in through the frame and blundered through the room into the dark interior. He crossed a corridor and burst into the kitchen. He fumbled for the light switch, but the power was off. For a moment, defeated, he stood quite still. Absolute silence. Odd, he thought; surely there'd be some sound, a buzz of fridges and freezers, maybe even low-level heat. He shivered. Maybe Josie was still there, lying in wait behind a door. Carefully he retraced his steps into the corridor and felt his way along the wall. Suddenly he tripped, and his legs buckled beneath him. Something solid was lying on the floor, solid like a body! He fell to his knees and fumbled in the darkness to define the shape, then stood up with a sick flush of relief. It was only a bundle of laundry.

He began feeling around the walls. There had to be a box with a breaker switch somewhere. He groped around for a while with failing hope until suddenly his hand touched cold metal and he knew he'd found it. Lights sprang on everywhere.

She was not in the dining room. Not in the kitchen. Not in the rest rooms. Not in the food larder nor in the linen store. Not in the office, not in the storeroom, not in the broom closet.

"Hazel?" he called.

Still silence, but for the buzzing now of fridges and freezers.

A terrible thought occured to him. He returned to the kitchen and went over to the large chest freezer in the corner. With trembling hand, he gradually opened the lid. A fog of frosty smoke coiled out, blurring the shape of what lay inside. As it cleared, he peered in. Slabs of meat, packs of burgers, bags of french fries. Nothing else.

As he lowered the lid, his eye rested upon a large, walk-in fridge standing against the wall behind the door.

He gritted his teeth. This had to be the last shot. He reached for the handle and, closing his eyes, swung the door open.

He was thrown backward by the body as it fell out. Before he could react, it collapsed in a limp sprawl across the floor before him.

She's dead. My Hazel is dead. Our baby is dead. There is nothing left. Life is ended.

He knelt beside her, filled with an icy calm. His mind was absolutely clear. No more issues, no more questions, no shades of hope and possibility. He'd take Hazel to hospital, then go after Josie and exterminate her.

A trace of blood oozed from a gash in her forehead, and he reached forward to wipe it away. The blood was still flowing? A surge of hope shot through him. He grasped her wrist and felt for a pulse. It was faint, but unmistakeably there! Her flesh was cold as marble, yet living. He pressed his lips against hers. He could feel her breath, slow and shallow. She seemed drugged into unconsciousness. How had she survived? Had the cold slowed her metabolism right down? But then, the fridge wasn't that cold—the power had been switched off.

He tore off his overcoat and jacket and wrapped them round her, then drew her up and held her tight to him to warm her body, rocking her back and forth as he whispered desperate words of encouragement. Gradually her breathing strengthened, and her body began to twitch and jerk violently as though she were fighting off an attacker in a nightmare. Then suddenly her eyes flickered half open. She winced in the glare of the light.

"Matthew?" she mumbled.

"It's me. I'm here. You're safe now, my darling. Everything's all right."

"The baby?"

He turned his head away. He didn't know, he didn't dare think. For he had felt the seat of her skirt, all cold and sodden and sticky and damp, and raising his hand found it smeared with rich, black-red blood.

"Fine. Just fine."

Matthew glanced across at Hazel as she lay in the hospital bed. Her face was pale and sunken, her eyes were half closed and her head lolled slack on the pillows. Into one arm fed a blood line, into the other a saline drip. She herself had been lucky. She hadn't suffered any hypothermia, and the drug, a plant-based sedative, was by now beginning to wear off. But the miracle was that she hadn't lost the baby. The bleed had been serious, and she was going to have to stay in hospital for a while and spend as much time as possible lying down, but somehow, against all the odds, the tiny life within her had survived.

Briefly she stirred and rolled her head toward him. Her eyes wandered, unfocused.

"Please, Matthew," she mumbled. "I'm so worried about Ben."

He leaned forward and squeezed her shoulder.

"Don't worry. He'll be fine. He's probably on his way to bed by now. You know how relaxed they are."

"Just call, huh?"

"Sure, angel."

He left the room and asked the nurse if he could use the phone on the reception desk. He dialed Harry and Elaine's number. The phone was answered almost at once. In the background he could hear shrieks of laughter. The kids were up to their bedtime pranks. Ben wouldn't want to be dragged away from the fun.

"Hi, Elaine, it's Matthew," he began. "Sorry for dumping Ben on you all this time. Look, I need to ask a real favor ..."

"Ben?" Elaine interrupted in a puzzled voice. Muffling the mouthpiece, she yelled at the kids to make less noise. "I'm sorry," she returned. "Ben isn't here."

"Not there?"

"But Hazel picked him up."

"*What?*"

"I saw her driving off. The red car, right?" Her tone grew alarmed. "Is something wrong?"

"You're sure?"

"I got there late. The whole class had left. Even the teachers were packed up and ready. You know how they quit on the dot. Matthew? Are you there?"

His let the receiver sink slowly onto its cradle. For a moment he was too paralyzed even to think. This nightmare was never ending. Ben ... *Ben ...*

Oh my God.

Numb, like a man on his way to his execution, he went back into the corridor. There he stopped. He couldn't do this to Hazel. She simply wouldn't be able to take it.

As he came into the doorway, she looked up eagerly. He bent to straighten the bedclothes as he spoke, unable to face her as he told the lie.

"He's fine," he said briefly. "He sends you his love. I didn't tell him what happened, of course. We'll break the news tomorrow." He managed to meet her eye and muster a comforting smile. "Now, you try and rest. I'm going home to pick up some things for you. Don't worry if I'm gone for a little while. I have to get some gas on the way."

"Matthew?" she called drowsily through the mist of the drugs.

"Yes, angel?"

"It will be all right, won't it?"

"You'll be on your feet in no time."

"The baby, I mean."

"Of course it will. If it can pull through all of that, it's got to be a helluva tenacious little thing."

"Like its father." She pulled a face. "Oh no, spare me that," she groaned.

"Now, you just rest," he smiled, bending to kiss her.

A sudden look of anxiety flashed across her face. She craned her neck forward and returned the kiss fervently, desperately.

"Promise me you'll take care, my darling," she said.

"Of course I will."

"Promise me."

"I promise, angel."

He turned away and, with a heart like Judas, he left the room and slipped quickly down the corridor and out of the hospital.

Josie looked from the sleeping boy to the empty beaker of 7-Up. She nodded with satisfaction. He would be out for a good twenty-four hours. And then he'd have to pray someone found him. The rest of the building was empty for the Christmas vacation and there'd be nobody to hear his screams.

She lingered for a moment. Briefly she ran her finger over the soft, youthful face, tracing the salty tracks on his cheeks left by his tears.

Pity the child, she thought. So plucky, so cheerful, so easily deceived. It's always the innocents that feed the sacrificial altars. He has to die. That is the pattern. That's how it was before and how it must be again.

She closed the bedroom door quietly. She stood for a moment looking around the living room of the small, top-floor apartment she'd rented for the vacation. Her eye rested on the phone. Taking a knife from the kitchen drawer, she cut the line. With a final glance around, she let herself out into the dark and empty corridor, double-locking the door behind her, and within a minute she was heading back across Jefferson Park Avenue to her own room on the grounds.

TWENTY-FIVE

Matthew drove the short distance to the university at breakneck speed. Ben.... His mind whirled. If Hazel was meant to meet Mary's fate, then what was in store for Ben? What had happened to Nathaniel's own son, Barnabas? History didn't tell; it was lost in the infuriating silence that followed Isabel's hanging.

He cursed himself a thousand times. How could he have been so blind? Obsession, infatuation, conceit: All these things parading as legitimate scientific curiosity. And this was where it had landed them. Should he go to the police? He could imagine trying to explain to some stalwart, corn-fed cop behind the desk at the local precinct station that there was a seventeenth-century psychotic at large in the town, bent on a homicidal mission of vengeance. No: He'd have to handle it himself.

He ran the car onto the curb and tore across the road toward the West Ranges. The night was dark and overcast, and the grounds wore its bare winter vacation mask. In the libraries and halls occasional lights still burned, and here and there windows sparkled with Christmas decorations, but the lamps tracing the lattice of pathways were dimmed and on the Ranges themselves the windows were dark. He passed two figures huddled deep in anoraks, but otherwise the lawns and cloisters were deserted.

He reached Josie's room within a moment. He prayed God she was in. He burst in without knocking.

The sight that met him pulled him up sharp. He blinked, disorientated. Briefly he had the same sense of stepping back in time that he'd experienced the first time on entering this room.

The place was lit solely by candles. Deep in the looming shadows he could see Josie sitting cross-legged on the ottoman in her Chinese robe. Her hair was piled high and fell in ringlets around her oval face, and the telltale mole on her upper lip stood out strikingly against the pallor of her skin. Her feet were bare. In front of her lay a large, ornate silver dish in which glinted a curved ceremonial knife.

He blundered forward.

"Where is he?" he demanded. "What have you done with him?"

She raised an eyebrow and cast him a withering look.

"You're late," she said coolly.

"Where is he? Where is Ben?"

"I would mend your tone."

"Where is the kid?"

"The child sleepeth."

His temper swelled, and he clenched his fist. God help him, he'd strike her. He cast about him. Where was she hiding him? A rough shape lay on the bed. He tore off the coverlet—it was only a bolster. He stormed over to the kitchenette, then into the bathroom, calling the boy's name as he went. Silence met him. He returned and stood before Josie, glaring.

"Well?"

"You're a fool, Nathaniel," she said quietly. "A tragic fool."

"Cut that out!" he shouted.

"I warned you!" she hissed. "You had your chance! You knew what you should have done. Now it's too late, and there's nothing you can do about it. Things must take their course. It's the pattern of necessity. First it had to be Mary—"

"You blew that," snapped Matthew. "Hazel's fine. She's safe."

A sudden agitation broke her composure.

"You're lying! She is dead. I know she is."

"Wrong. I found her myself. At Duner's restaurant. Okay?" He pressed forward. Even as he spoke, he knew this was fatally the wrong tack. "So much for your goddam 'pattern of necessity.' Come on, the charade is over. Now, just tell me what you've done with Ben ..."

She snatched up the knife and jabbed the point toward him.

"Forget him," she spat. "You won't see him again. Don't blame me. You brought it on yourself."

Suddenly an uncontrollable fury seized him. Knocking the knife out of her hand with a sharp sideways chop, he reached forward and grasped her round the throat in a vicious stranglehold. Her robe fell open to reveal her naked breasts, their beauty now an insult. He tightened his grip.

"Where is he?" he snarled. "Tell me, you little bitch."

Frantically she clawed at his fingers, but his grasp was inexorable.

"Tell me!" he roared, shaking her violently. Any moment he felt her neck would snap, but he didn't care.

Suddenly, as she was choking, her eyes widened in a different kind of horror. A look of raw terror beyond anything he'd ever seen came over her face. She let out a long, bloodcurdling shriek. He struggled to hold her firm, but she was possessed with insane strength. As he fought to restrain her, he realized that her eyes were strangely focused on something beyond him, something in the distance, or in the distant past, as though she were reliving some unimaginably terrifying memory. A memory of her own strangulation by hanging?

Awed, he let his grip relax. With a sudden jerk she twisted free and flung herself across the room, where she remained crouching in the corner, choking and coughing and sobbing in extreme distress. She was trying to speak. Her words came out disjointed and inarticulate. He held back, shivering with horrified anticipation.

"Go on," he whispered hoarsely.

Her eyes rolled wildly and her face twitched with small convulsive tics as she struggled to get the words out. They stumbled out all broken at first, but gradually as she relived the nightmare, they began to develop a flow. She spoke in a voice he seemed to recognize. A voice he had heard once before, that sultry midsummer night in Oxford all those years ago.

It was Isabel herself speaking.

"The Ordinary has been to visit, the hateful and insidious serpent. His priest's robes smell of capon's grease, his breath is sour with greed. He tells me it is to be done tomorrow. Tomorrow at noon. I am to hang in the company of two common criminals. 'As our Lord Christ,' I mocked him. He shook with the devil's own rage. 'I would fain have you whipped for blasphemy,' he cried. Then he began again at me: *'Repent, confess, repent, confess. God is merciful: He will forgive your sins.'* But wherefore have I sinned against God? How is natural justice a crime?

"The gaoler arrives. He unlocks the cell door. He says I have a visitor.

My heart leaps with joy. It is you, my Nathaniel! You hand him a coin, and he leaves us for a minute together. The other women in this stinking pit gawp and mutter. I try and imagine we are alone. You reach toward me, but I pull back. I do not wish to be touched. My hair, my clothes, my skin, all about me is foul. We will not touch until we meet again. Then I will be clean, cleansed by death.

"You see how I am troubled by the priest and you comfort me. 'Sweet my soul,' you say, 'do not upset yourself with that foolish prelate. Content you with the joy that lies ahead and embrace your release. We leave nothing behind that is dear to ourselves, each to the other being most dear. As one, we shall travel that journey together and there, in the world beyond, find the peace and harmony that has eluded us in this.'

"These and many other sweet words you speak. But haste, the gaoler returns! 'The plan,' I cry, 'tell me the plan!' You whisper quickly, imparting the particulars of time and place and that wherein I must do my own part. The man is rattling his keys. You grasp my hand.

'Tomorrow we shall meet in Paradise,' you vow. 'My eternal soul upon it.'

"In a sudden you are gone. I weep. No love has ever been so sundered. The gentler women seek to console me, but I do not weep for my fate: I weep for yours. I weep out of love."

Here she broke down, sobbing.

Distressed in his turn, Matthew made a move to reach forward, but thought better of it. He felt dizzy, spellbound. He was listening to Isabel speaking to Nathaniel! A year before, he'd have given his soul to spend a day inside the skin of Nathaniel Shawcrosse. And now he was there—with his soul in forfeit?

"The night lasted an eternity," she continued, a little recovered. "At dawn, the Ordinary comes once again and offers me God's pardon if I will confess and repent. 'For the King's pardon I will confess,' I say, 'but wherefore for God's? I fear not God's judgment. We are all His children: from Him we come and to Him we return. There can be no sin in us, for we are made in His image and likeness. We are mind made matter, and to the immaterial we all shall return—even you, Mr. Ordinary.' He curses me for an obstinate apostate and tells me to look to my dress and appearance, for the crowd are expected in force, the execution of a woman of such egregious youth and beauty being a most choice rarity.

"I am numb. My limbs are paralyzed. The seconds pass, each one a lifetime. At last, at the appointed hour, they come for me. The other women bid me good-bye, many in tears. Outside, I swoon, my condition being so wasted. The light of day is so dazzling after the gloom of the dungeon that I fancy I am already in heaven, but as they herd me into the cart and I see the other two felons due to hang, I know the ordeal is only beginning. The sheriff calls his men to order, the horses are given the whip, and the terrible procession sets off.

"My heart is in my mouth lest our plan should be discovered. As we approach the inn at Holborn, the place where by tradition the condemned are given refreshment on their last journey, I almost faint with dread. When the innkeeper comes forward with three similar jugs of ale, I all but pass away. But then he turns to the sheriff and calls out, 'Surely a lady so sweet of looks deserves something sweeter than ale.' Upon which he hands me a stirrup cup of mead.

"The moment I taste it, I know you have triumphed! Oh my brave and beautiful Nathaniel, I think, see me drink, and drink you, too! I hold up the cup in a salute to you, and drain it in a gulp. I am filled with indescribable joy. Before the day is out we will be reunited for eternity! Even at this very minute you will be on your way to your lodgings and preparing the mandrake so as to do for yourself what the hangman is about to do for me. Hurry, hurry, I cry. Oh how I long for Death's embrace.

"The draft is working fast, and I am afraid I might collapse before the final moment. The crowd is now growing thicker. Faces press forward, leering and jeering. Hands reach over the edge of the cart and claw at my skirts. The Ordinary is leaning close over me; I can smell his stale breath and his fusty vestments. *'Repent, confess, repent, confess.'* The world is lurching about me. I fear I might not hold my bowels and I will disgrace myself ...

"At last we reach Tyburn. The crowd is ranged on stands before the gibbets. A hideous howling arises as the cart draws up to the platform. Rough hands help me out. I am fainting. Suddenly out of the press, close by, peers my father's face: severe, judgmental, stricken. I want to acknowledge him, but from his plain, hooded black habit I know that shame has driven him to conceal his identity. Father, father, I cry silently, why hast thou forsaken me?

"Then the executioner begins his work. They stand me upright on the platform. I shut my eyes, but I can't shut out the terrible baying of the mob. My legs are already numb, and the cold is fast spreading upward. I pray it might engulf me in time.

"I feel them put the rope over my head. I feel the rope against my neck. Rough against my skin, rough and tight and heavy ..."

Suddenly her hands flew to her neck and with a throttled gasp she shrank backward.

"No! No!" she choked.

Matthew fell on his knees in front of her.

"Go on!" he hissed.

With a drawn-out cry she collapsed on the floor, knocking a candlestick off a table, and lay there, writhing in convulsions and clawing at her neck to free herself from the noose. Her breathing came short and broken, and for a moment he was afraid she might suffocate. But then, quite suddenly, her body straightened, gave several violent, convulsive jerks, then abruptly went still.

"Isabel?" he whispered.

He brought another candlestick up and bent over her supine form. Her eyes were open but unseeing. Her breathing was shallow and fast. He saw a vein in her neck pulsing and made a rough count of her pulse rate. She was in a state of shock. He'd better get help. Medical help. And the police.

Slowly he rose to his feet and, with his back turned, bent down to pick up the fallen candlestick. He didn't immediately register what happened. It was a full two seconds later that the wild shriek penetrated his consciousness. He turned and saw it happen, but he was taken too much by surprise to react at once.

Like a whiplash the girl had leapt to her feet, sprung across the room and snatched up the knife from the floor. Her eyes blazing with hatred, she went for him, slashing the blade through the air in wild, vicious swipes.

"You devil!" she screamed. "You cheating monster! Miserable coward! *You didn't do it!* You betrayed our pact! You wouldn't go through with it. You thought you'd let me die and go on living yourself."

"Hold it—" he protested, backing away.

"I know it! I saw you."

"You *saw?*"

Her lips peeled back in a cruel sneer.

"You never expected this, Nathaniel. I was not quite dead when they cut me down. That was the mandrake. It slowed everything down. My father had given the hangman money and he allowed them to cut me down as soon as I had stopped twitching. They took me to a carriage where the physician was waiting. The physician revived me. I was alive but, God knows, I wanted to be dead. I wanted to be with you, in the life beyond, and I was still trapped here in the mortal world, all alone, with you gone on before ...

"But damn your soul, you were not! You were back in Oxford, back at home with your brat of a son, laughing at your clever trick, feasting in college and enjoying all the things of fleshly life. I know," she hissed. "I came back secretly."

Matthew stifled a gasp. He sensed he knew what was coming next.

"I couldn't stay in England. You remember Thomas Lord Culpeper, with his estates in the colonies? My father knew him well. He booked me on the next passage to America. I thought constantly of ending my life. I only wanted to be dead, imagining you dead. For my father's sake, though, I had to seem to be going into exile. It was only a pretense: I planned to take my life during the voyage, but first I had to return to Oxford to collect my few possessions and mementos. I couldn't bear to leave without paying one last visit to your laboratory, which had been the scene of so much joy. So, at the dead of night I stole out of the deanery and crept through the college to the laboratory. A light was on inside! I was filled with outrage. Who would dare to trespass, when you were hardly even in your grave?

"So, very quietly, I opened the door."

"And?" he stuttered.

"I saw *you,* Nathaniel."

"My God," he breathed.

She paused, whitefaced and shaking.

"It was then that I vowed I would kill you," she said in a low, acid whisper.

Matthew couldn't move. He was transfixed with horror.

"I sent you poisoned sweetmeats, as a gift from a student," she went on with a twisted laugh. "Your poor little Barnabas ate them. You didn't know that was how he died? Of course you could hardly have suspected me, but you could at least have diagnosed the form of poison. Yew berries, it was. Anyway, you escaped me, and I had to leave before I could try again. So, you got away. I swore on my eternal soul that I would find you and finish the business and so lay this troubled history to rest. And unlike you, Nathaniel, I keep my vows."

* * *

She was standing between him and the door. The blade glinted in the candlelight. He swallowed hard. The girl was crazed, possessed. But he was a strong, grown man. He studied the way she held the knife. If she lunged at him, he might just catch her by the wrist and twist it out of her grip.

The physical odds were in his favor, but the psychological odds were against him. She had waited all these years, consumed with hatred and driven by the thirst for revenge. She represented the triumph of phenomenal force of will over the constraints of time and space. How could he hope to match the sheer strength of that will? He felt a sharp stab of fear. He was up against an unimaginably powerful mental force.

And worse: Even if he did somehow manage to disarm her, what then? He'd go for help. But what help? Only she knew where Ben was hidden. Would the police succeed in extorting a confession out of her where he had failed? They'd send out a missing person's call, put up posters, make house-to-house calls ... and hand Josie over to the shrinks. How would they diagnose her? He knew the incredible truth, but would anyone listen to him, let alone believe him? No, he had to stay right there and front it out. The only weapon against a mind was another mind.

Finally he spoke. He contrived to make his tone gentle, almost indifferent.

"Put that down," he said. "You don't need it."

"Keep back!" she warned. "Think of the boy."

"That has nothing to do with us."

"It's why you're here."

"Very well. Let's deal with him first and then we can talk, you and I."

She gripped the knife in both hands, keeping it pointed at him.

"It's too late for that, Nathaniel," she snapped.

He gave a small shrug and, steeling his nerve, slowly turned his back on her and took a careful step away.

"I'm going to the bathroom while you think about it," he said.

As he passed he caught her expression in the dressing-table mirror. His prosaic nonchalance seemed to have thrown her momentarily off balance. Steadily, without glancing over his shoulder, he made his way into the bathroom and turned on the light. Squinting against the sudden brightness, he looked quickly around him. A curling iron. A hairdryer. Pots of makeup. Nothing to use as a weapon.

No, that wasn't the way. The worst thing was to threaten a madman. You had to work within the madness, not confront it head-on. You had to play along. And that meant that here, if he was to have any hope of rescuing Ben, he must play the part of Nathaniel Shawcrosse. A humble, penitent Nathaniel Shawcrosse.

Gritting his teeth, he switched off the light and opened the door. Sudden blackness surrounded him. But not so sudden as the violent blow that struck him on the back of the head, nor so black as the pitch-black world that then abruptly engulfed him.

Pinpricks of light. Brilliant stars. Strange pagan figures, white-robed Druid priests and soothsayers, dancing in white robes before him ...

As he struggled to focus through the blur of pain, he gradually realized he was staring into the flames of candles. He screwed up his eyes and peered beyond into the moving shadows. On the wall beside him hung the faded tapestry. He must be lying on the bed. He stirred, but he couldn't move his arms or legs. Then he felt the ropes, and he understood. He was bound, hand and foot.

The girl emerged out of the shadows. She held the silver dish in both hands like a salver, and on it lay the knife. The candles lit her face from beneath. Her skin bore a pale, silky sheen that seemed to radiate coolness. The air in the room was heavy with the smell of incense he knew so well, but the ritual she was preparing to perform was cruelly different.

She knelt down beside the bed and laid a cloth on the floor. There was a curious abstraction in her manner, as though she was governed by a force from outside. He had the chilling sense that she had rehearsed and elaborated this final moment of vengeance over and over in her fantasy, until every detail of the act was immutable and had to be performed in its exact and correct sequence. As he struggled in vain to find any play in the ropes, his mind was struggling with equal desperation to find a way of breaking into this seemingly invincible replay of history. Wild ideas swam through his head. Could he not, for instance, reenter the flow of events somehow at an earlier point, before the critical act of betrayal, and pick up a thread from there from which to weave a new history?

He studied her face. She appeared locked in some kind of trance. Her movements were slow but deliberate. She showed no hint of any feelings. Then, slowly, she raised the bowl and pressed it against the bare flesh of his neck. With her other hand she brought the knife up and laid the blade gently against the side of the neck just below his ear. He was transfixed with terror. If he moved the slightest muscle, he knew she would strike. She had only to draw her hand down and she'd slice deep into his jugular. For a moment she paused, as if fascinated, almost hypnotized. Time held its breath. He felt perspiration trickling down his cheek.

Barely moving his lips, he whispered her name.

"Isabel?"

Her eyes flickered, but she didn't break her gaze.

"Isabel, look at me. Look at Nathaniel."

Slowly she turned and met his eye. Her gaze was distant, dead. He could feel the sweat running down his collar now. He spoke again, very carefully, very sweetly.

"If thou should'st ever doubt the power of my love, Sweet Lapidus," he began.

She gave a small start. Her eyes peaked in puzzlement.

"Do you remember, my sweet love?" he went on in a caressing tone, knowing he was talking for his life now. "Do you remember how it was? Those mornings at work in the laboratory, those afternoons walking in the fields by the river? That day we rode out to Shotover Park and made love among the bluebells and the bracken?" He sighed, "Those days were always sunny. You remember how, in the evenings, we'd go back to the lab and take the cup? We'd lock the door and snuff out the lamps all but one, and you would prepare the mandrake, you always knew just how much to use, and we'd drink it together out of that chalice you'd purloined from the deanery. That chalice! How we laughed at the blasphemy!"

He broke off, feeling strangely disorientated. How had he known about that? Was he inventing or ... remembering? He went on, not knowing where the words came from.

"We'd spread furs and cushions on the couch and we'd lie down together and wait for the potion gradually to take us out of our bodies, do you remember that, Isabel, do you?"

The knife slipped from her hands. It glanced off the bowl and fell to the floor with a clatter.

"Do you, Isabel?" he repeated in an insistent whisper.

She let out a small whimper. Her eyes had grown round and moist, even tender, and they gleamed with tentative hope. He knew that look so well. He'd seen it a thousand times, from that very first moment in the chapel at Sanctus Spiritus when their eyes had met across the aisle, until the final moment in the gaol as the door clanged shut behind him and their eyes had met through the iron bars, and in hers there had been such a look of simple trust....

A serpent's voice sneaked into his mind. How do you know all this? it whispered. Only Nathaniel Shawcrosse himself could know the half of it!

Her whole face had softened. He could sense the balance tipping. He had touched her deepest weakness: a divided heart. She was driven to hate, but more even than that, she wanted to love. She yearned for everything to be as it should have been. A noble, tragic love, sealed by a death pact.

"Isabel," he whispered, "let us do it now. Do what we left undone. And be free for ever."

She faltered, her heart and mind at war.

"Fond, foolish Nathaniel," she sighed. "If I could only trust you."

"Prepare the mandrake."

"And let you cheat me again?"

"I shall not. That I promise you."

"What is your promise worth, Nathaniel?"

"Do it, Isabel! Cut me free. I shall not leave. I will stay right here, and together we'll right the wrongs and settle our account once for all. From now on we shall be at peace with one another. Come now, do as I say."

She hesitated. A sudden draft made the candle flames flicker. The shadows loomed alarmingly.

"Isabel," he whispered softly.

She fixed him with a long, intense gaze. In it he could see hope battling with mistrust, love struggling with hate, reconciliation wrestling with revenge. He waited, barely daring to breathe. After all this time and this grief, could love prove the stronger?

Finally she stood up.

"I will prepare the cup."

He sat on the bed, rubbing his wrists where the rope had chafed the skin. She was kneeling over the samovar, her back to him. Five paces away stood the door. He could easily make a break for it.

No, he thought. Think of Ben. Cheated a second time, she would be implacable for eternity. He might manage to have her committed to an asylum, but he'd never feel safe for himself or his family. Bars and locks couldn't keep in an unquiet soul. No; he must go through with it and just pray that a way would reveal itself whereby he could lay her spirit, once for all, to rest.

And yet, as she turned and came toward him with her slow, knowing smile, bearing the cup before her just as she had done so many times before in that very room, he knew he would not leave even if the door were open. An involuntary shiver of excitement uncoiled in his stomach and rippled through his body. He was caught under the spell.

At the first taste he knew the dose was lethal. He held it in his mouth without swallowing it and spat it out discreetly into his sleeve as she raised the cup to her own lips. But already he could feel the acrid, bitter liquid burning the sides of his mouth, and within a few seconds the first swirling waves of giddiness were rising deep at the root of his skull. A sudden urgent craving seized him. Let me go just a little of the way, he prayed: grant me just one last, short glimpse of heaven.

Already his feet and hands were growing cold, his body was opening up and he could feel the first tugging as his spirit struggled to detach itself. Hold on, another voice cautioned. Keep within yourself, don't separate, don't go out there! But he knew it was too late.

She handed him the cup. It was almost empty.

"Finish it," she slurred.

"I'm already gone."

"We'll share it."

She drained the cup, then bent over him and dribbled the potion into his mouth. He swallowed a little: God help him, he couldn't prevent himself from swallowing a little. Almost at once he felt himself separating. From one remove he observed her. He could see tears flowing down her cheeks. A lump rose in his throat.

"Don't be sad," he said.

"I'm not sad, I'm happy. Happier than I've ever been. I never knew it would be like this." Her voice dropped to a whisper. "Can you see it? The light, the colors ... so bright, so wonderful. Can you hear the music? Oh Nathaniel, hold me, hold me tight ... tighter ... I can't feel you ..."

"I'm here, Isabel." He clasped her half-naked body to him. "I'm with you."

He was rising slowly, unsticking like a balloon. For a while he hovered above the bed, looking down upon their two figures entwined in a tender embrace, and he found himself wondering with a mixture of pity and astonishment at all the struggle and tribulation of this earthly life, all this groping around in darkness and ignorance. Everything was really so simple, so clear, so obvious. He laughed aloud with joy, and the peal echoed around the universe. He felt himself to be as minute as the smallest speck of matter yet as vast as creation itself. He was like the skin on the ocean, everywhere and nowhere. Everything was in his power, but there was no need to use it. All was perfect, in harmony. At last he understood.

He was floating upward through a vast tunnel toward a bright light. It was brighter than a thousand suns, yet not in the least dazzling. Its rays seemed to pour inward, not outward, drawing him forward into its welcoming glow. Ahead of him he could see Isabel, a look of beatific joy on her face. She smiled and reached out a hand.

Wait! hissed the inner voice. Wait, Matthew!

Matthew? No, no. Matthew is left behind. Matthew is back among the struggle and tribulation, the darkness and ignorance, among cars and houses and places and people, back with Hazel and with Ben....

Ben! Oh my Christ.

Isabel was floating away from him, sucked into the node of light.

Nathaniel, she called, come on!

I can't. I must go back.

She had reached the light. It was diffused as though by a vast silk membrane of unimaginable fineness. She hovered for a moment on this side, she turned, she reached out her arm, she tried to arrest herself, she called out to him. Suddenly he knew that it was in his power to recall her or to send her through. This was the Gate! The frontier between matter and mind, the very boundary between the body and the spirit.

He focused the full strength of his will upon her.

"Go, Isabel!"

She hesitated. Perplexity flashed across her face.

"Go, I say! Go where you belong. Now, Isabel, now!"

Slowly, before his astonished gaze, like a substance dissolving in a bath of acid, her body bled through the membrane and vanished, leaving only the ghost of her face, sorrowful and forlorn, lingering briefly on the surface until that, too, finally evaporated into pure spirit.

Frantically he bent his mind against the force drawing him with an inexorable gravitational pull toward the core. Straining every nerve, he gradually found himself reversing the upward rush, and haltingly, in fits and starts, he began clambering back down the tunnel away from the light and toward the darkness below. From time to time great cosmic gusts tore at him, threatening to sweep him back into the well of light, but he clung on with every ounce of his willpower, affirming his mortal reality by shouting his own name aloud, "I am Matthew! Matthew Cavewood! Let me back!"

Suddenly, abruptly, he was hovering again above the bed. There the girl's body lay still and quiet. His own, however, was thrashing about wildly. It looked so ugly, so mean, so corrupted. He shuddered. Must he go back?

He must, and fast.

Get in! he yelled to himself. Get in there!

With a terrible howl of pain, he felt himself being sucked back in to his old, tired, rotten mortal carapace.

Then, with a sudden convulsion, he jerked upright. He looked around him. He was seeing through his own eyes again.

He glanced at Josie. Her eyes were open, her eyeballs rolled back up to the whites. He felt her neck. The veins were still. She was dead ... or just near death?

A sudden panic gripped him. Quick! Close the Gate! She mustn't get back in!

But how? Nathaniel Shawcrosse's precept came into his mind: "All is resonance." Somehow he had to break the resonance between the body down here and the spirit out there.

Staggering to his feet, he grabbed two candlesticks and placed them on either side of the body. His head was bursting with the force of his thought.

"Keep out, keep out," he chanted aloud.

A sudden chill swept through the room. He fancied he could feel something brushing his cheek, like bat's wings. She was there! She was everywhere—around, above, beneath—trying to break back in.

"Isabel Hardiment," he yelled at the top of his voice, "I conjure you to stay away! Keep out of this girl's body! Go, and never return. Go and find your own peace. Out, out, I say!"

He shouted until he was hoarse. He raged around the room, flailing his arms and filling the room with hideous oaths and ugly imprecations so as to prevent the spirit from settling. He felt as if he were beating off a flock of greedy vultures. But the drug was still swirling through his veins and his strength was progressively failing. Any minute the spirit would dart in under the barrage and retake possession of the girl.

Suddenly he realized her eyes were wide open and staring. The windows of her soul were open! In a flash he swept the coverlet over her face. In that instant he fancied he heard a long, thin, high-pitched shriek reverberate through the room. Slowly, it seemed to die away until it lost itself in the far distant ether. No sooner had it died quite away than he became aware of a distinct change in the atmosphere. The tension began to lift. The threat seemed to recede upward and away, and slowly, gradually, a great calm settled over the room.

The dizziness washed over him in thick waves. He sank onto the bed. For some time—whether minutes or hours he couldn't tell—he seemed to lose consciousness, but the voice kept breaking in with relentless insistency: "Fight, keep fighting, don't give in just yet!"

Painfully he struggled back to his feet. He fumbled for Josie's pulse. She was alive, thank God, but she needed help.

But Ben? Where in God's name was he? He could be somewhere in that building, on the campus, in the town, in the woods, anywhere. Josie must have left some clue in the room. Surely she had.

Frantically he searched the room. He upended her purse onto the floor. Nothing there. He groped his way to her desk and ransacked the drawers. Finally, rummaging in the wastepaper basket, he struck lucky. Deep at the bottom of the pile he found a notification from the telephone company advising of a transfer of service into the name of I. Hardiment. The address given was 1515 Jefferson Park Avenue, Apartment 5A.

As he lurched toward the door, he froze. He could hear a distant howling, like terrible mocking laughter. It was coming from inside his head. He was going mad. He clamped his hands over his ears, and the sound stopped. Then he realized it was police sirens. Hazel! Thank God. In the hours that had elapsed, she must have come around, called the house, then Elaine's, and found neither he nor Ben were there, then knowing Josie was at large, made a terrible guess and called the police.

He was standing in the center of the room as the police burst in. The officer at the head took two steps inside and froze. He let out a low whistle of disbelief.

Matthew barely had the strength to hand him the letter.

"The kid's at this address," he croaked. He gestured toward the unconscious girl. "Call for an ambulance."

He took a step forward, but his legs buckled under him. He swayed like a tree about to be felled, and as the world about him faded into gray, unable to keep up the fight any longer, he let himself gradually crumple to the floor.

TWENTY-SIX

Matthew stood at his study window, looking out at the great ash tree, its bare boughs rimmed with snow and etched stark white against the darkening February sky. From downstairs filtered the sounds of a party in full swing. Friends, neighbors, colleagues—all were there to celebrate his appointment. He had landed the associate professorship.

He sighed. He couldn't deny feeling some satisfaction with life. Things at home couldn't be better. Hazel was now five months pregnant and, though she still had to take things carefully, she was enjoying the pregnancy; by being selective in the assignments she chose, too, she was managing to advance her career while devoting more time to her family. As for his own work, the biography was now finished and in the hands of the publishers. He'd been fortunate enough to avoid a damaging scandal over his involvement with Josie McDowell and her sudden, tragic illness, and especially fortunate in that the general consensus of opinion (which he later discovered had been fostered by Lyall) regarded her bizarre behavior as no more than the result of severe amnesia brought on by the accident. He was more than just exonerated, too: in offering tenure and a salary above the scale with his promotion, the dean and faculty were pointing out a starry future for him. Yet, if he were honest, the triumph felt somehow incomplete. He'd won the job for his work on Nathaniel Shawcrosse—a revolutionary piece of work by the standards of any other biography—but he was dogged by a sense that the story was not quite complete. One thing still wasn't there, and only that thing could lay the bitter cycle of history finally to rest.

A board creaked behind him. He turned to find Lyall standing in the doorway, nursing a tumbler of whisky and watching him from behind his thick glasses.

"Sitting out your own party?" he queried.

Matthew smiled faintly.

"Just thinking."

"Drink, not think: That's what parties are about." Lyall came forward and scrutinized him. "What's up?"

"Nothing." Matthew struggled to break out of the sudden wave of depression he felt. "Everything's fine. Terrific. Never felt better."

"With all due respect—bollocks." Lyall took off his glasses and breathed on the lenses and cleaned them. "Come on, what's eating you?"

"Well, just the usual, I guess." Matthew let out a frustrated sigh. "I go around and around in circles. I know what I experienced and I know what is objectively possible, and the two just don't mesh."

"If they ever did, we'd be out of a job." Lyall was smiling, but his eyes were hard.

"The key factor is energy, I can see that," he went on obstinately. "That's okay while the mind is attached to a living brain. But when it gets detached, as at death? It's got to establish a relationship with some other source of energy." He managed a smile. "Hardly party small talk, huh?"

But Lyall was frowning, his levity vanished.

"This just happens to be the big question of all time," he said drily. "Crack the mind-body problem, and next stop Stockholm."

"What is the self: That's the question." Matthew couldn't break out of the familiar loop of thought. "I know you believe the brain creates the self. For you, the personality is a product of billions of neuronal selections and gradually engraves itself on our nervous system. But the mind is surely more than the brain that creates it."

"Yes," admitted Lyall carefully. "That's precisely the conundrum."

"So there's no logical reason why it shouldn't survive the death of the brain."

"None at all."

"But it would need a new source of energy. Either there's some ocean of immaterial wave fields out there that we all plug in to when we die, or," and he paused to weigh his words, "it could take over the brain of another living person. As happened with Josie McDowell."

Matthew watched his friend closely for his reaction. The other day he'd stayed up half the night with him, recounting the entire story, and he'd had the strange feeling throughout that Lyall knew something he wasn't divulging, as though he somehow wasn't showing his hand.

Lyall considered his glass, now empty.

"Feelings are energy, too," he offered. "Love, hatred, anger, revenge. These could fuel a spirit independently."

Matthew shivered involuntarily. Lyall had touched a nerve.

"She's still there," he said quietly. "I can feel her anger and hate still burning. She'll never give us peace."

"Not *her* anger, Matthew. Yours."

"I'm not angry."

"You're consumed with anger. You're angry with her for making you feel guilty."

"Spare me the psychoanalysis, Lyall. I don't feel guilty."

"It stands out a mile off! You blame yourself for what happened to Hazel, for what Ben went through—for what's happened to Josie, too, for God's sake." Lyall grasped him by the arm. "Listen, Matthew, it's not your fault! The girl brought it on herself. You couldn't have done anything else."

Matthew turned away. His voice was choking. He couldn't bear to think of Josie. He had, quite literally, robbed her of her self. He'd cast out the invader but failed to restore her own in its place. Who *was* the pale, vacant-eyed girl he'd visited at the clinic? No one, a nonperson. A pang of anguish shot through him as he thought back to the afternoons spent together in her room and the moments of ecstasy shared. He had destroyed what he had most loved.

"You haven't seen her," he said tightly. "It's terrible. She's just not there. It's like looking at a living corpse. A vacant shell. The empty husk of a person."

"I'm sorry."

For a moment the two men stood in silence. From the party downstairs came a roar of laughter. Lyall gestured with his glass toward the door.

"You're getting maudlin, old man," he said. "Come and join the party."

"You go on. I'll join you in a moment."

Lyall hesitated, began to say something but checked himself. At the door, however, he turned, as if he felt he couldn't leave on a downbeat note. His voice was forcedly cheery.

"Well, you can thank your lucky stars you didn't end up like Clark Tauber," he said.

Matthew gave a start. He turned to face his old friend. Hazel had told him how he'd taken her to the railroad yard and shown her the spot where this man, his predecessor in this very appointment they were celebrating, had been killed. An appalling thought was boring through his brain.

"What did you say?" he asked quietly.

Lyall seemed to sense he'd made a mistake. His grin broadened, and two red patches flushed his cheeks.

"There's always some guy worse off than you, that's all I mean."

"No. You were saying about Tauber ..."

"Ach, Tauber. That's history. I guess, working on the same things, you have the same obsessions. Maybe even the same delusions."

Matthew felt his fist clenching. The thought was hammering away more insistently.

"You don't mean delusions, Lyall," he said with deadly quiet. "You mean that this guy Tauber actually experienced what I experienced. He was working on Shawcrosse before me. He had the same ..." he groped for the word "... the same visitations. *And you knew it!*"

"Come now, old chap—"

"You knew he was having hallucinations, and you knew they were of Isabel. You were tracking his work all along. That's why you had his library copy of the *Proceedings* on your desk that time I came to your office. And—"

He broke off. Suddenly he understood with absolute clarity the double game Lyall had been playing all this time. The more he thought back to their ambiguous relationship over the past months, the more he realized how his so-called friend had been manipulating him.

He took a step closer.

"So, when Tauber died," he continued in a growl, "the goose that laid the golden egg had died. You haven't got the brains to do the work yourself, but you knew you were onto what was, what could be, the greatest advance in science in modern history. You were going to be there when it broke, and you were going to ride on anyone's coattails who'd get you there. So you set out to find another goose. You didn't have to look far. I was the perfect choice: an old friend, building an academic reputation, working smack in the center of the field—Christ, I even did my thesis on the subject! So you lured me here. You put together a package of grants and benefits and promises of 'associate professorships' and all that, just so you could have someone carry on the work."

"Matthew, please—"

"And I delivered. But I delivered too well. Things began to happen. *Real* things, not just things in the mind. Suddenly we weren't dealing with hallucinations and visions, we were dealing with an actual flesh-and-blood materialization. Your precious experiment was getting out of hand. But what did you do then?" He spat the words out. "Tell me, my old friend and buddy, *what?*"

Lyall had turned white. He stared out from behind his heavy glasses, beads of cold sweat starting out on his fleshy forehead, but he said nothing. Matthew gathered his breath and continued, his jaw clenched with cold ferocity.

"Nothing! You stood on the sidelines and watched. You wanted to see how far it would go. What would happen. I was your private experiment, and you had to see how it played out! You knew everything—you'd been into my files, hacked into my database, read my notes—and you knew I'd set off a time bomb. And, you two-faced shit, you knew what the dangers were."

"Well, I did try to warn you," Lyall fumbled at last. "I warned Hazel, at least."

"Bullshit! You could have stopped it. You could have prevented all of it. You could have saved Hazel from what she went through. She nearly lost our child, for God's sake. And think of Ben. And Josie. Josie might not be a goddam cabbage now if it wasn't for you. Just one word, one small word at the right time, that's all it would have taken." He stepped back. It was a reflex of disgust. "Don't you talk to me about guilt," he said bitterly. "Don't tell me not to blame myself. Just tell me how you can go on day to day, going to meetings, running your department, without feeling the burden of guilt yourself. Because, Christ, I tell you, I may have trouble with my conscience, but I would hate to live with yours for the rest of my life."

For a long while, neither spoke. Lyall stared into his glass, turning it around in his hand like a man examining a diamond. Finally he looked back up at Matthew and broke the silence.

"Quite a speech," he murmured. "From the heart, too. I hear what you say. Of course," he added, still toying with the glass, "none of this need go further than this room. People have such a distressing habit of ..." He trailed off. He shrugged. "Pity, really. We nearly got there, you know. Ah, well. Science has lost a Shawcrosse. Close the shutters, bring on the dark ages."

Matthew turned away. He had to rest his eyes on something other than Lyall's treacherous face. The great tree stood pale and stark in its nakedness against the dark night. He had a sudden wish that he could be that tree, standing solemn and contained within itself, braving the seasons and the vagaries of time, knowing nothing, feeling nothing, just being. Behind him, he could hear Lyall shuffling his feet and clearing his throat.

Matthew didn't turn.

"Just get out of here," he said quietly and with finality.

Otis looked up from his book and sighed. He felt sorrowful and yet somehow grateful at the same time. Josie had been home two weeks now. Getting her out of that clinic had been the best thing he'd ever done. If they couldn't cure her, why should they keep her?

He sat back in his chair. He liked this time of night best, when the household had gone to bed and he had his girl all to himself. A log on the fire momentarily flared, casting a warm glow over her pale and frozen features. He put the book down and reached across for her hand. It was limp, lifeless.

He smiled comfortingly. He knew she couldn't register it. Perhaps he did it for his own comfort.

"You know how long since I last read a novel?" He shook his head. "I don't know myself. Ten, maybe twenty years. Maybe not since you were born. Mountains of reports and papers, and not a single good story."

He rose to his feet a little unsteadily. He was feeling old. There seemed no point now in struggling against the inevitable. The light in his life had gone out. He refilled his tumbler from a decanter and raised the glass.

"Your health."

He moved the wheelchair a little further back, in case the fire was too hot on her face. Briefly he traced a finger over her silky blond hair, then turned aside, stifling the pang. Dear God, why had he been robbed of all of her? Even when she came back after the accident, for all that she behaved strangely, she'd still been able to talk, to laugh, to run, to play. Now she could do nothing; she *was* nothing. The doctors came and went, diagnosing her condition according to their own speciality. They spoke of catatonia, of hysterical withdrawal, of encephalitis lethargica, sleeping sickness, the condition that matched the symptoms closest. They put her on a course of L-dopa injections after a spinal tap revealed a deficiency of the neurotransmitter dopamine in the brain, but that had no effect: the cause, whatever it was, lay elsewhere. Electroencephalographs showed sluggish brain activity in the cortical areas associated with the higher functions, and the various scans they ran identified low metabolic rates in the main consciousness areas. The symptoms showed up clearly in one diagnostic test after another, but the actual cause eluded all the specialists. None of them had come across a case quite like this. She was awake yet asleep. Alive yet dead. Active yet passive. A person yet....

With a tremulous sigh, he looked away. His eye came to rest on the photograph on his desk. She had been so utterly beautiful. She was still beautiful, but her beauty was inanimate, in the way of a statue or a still life. She could move her eyes to see and her mouth to eat. She would turn her head at a loud noise. But her face never registered anything, neither thought nor feeling. It was not a mask concealing something behind; there *was* nothing behind. She was an empty room.

"Tell you what," he said, forcing the cheerfulness into his voice, "let's have some music."

He went to the bookshelf and pressed a button. A false-fronted cabinet opened to reveal a music center. He reached for a compact disc, then a tape caught his eye: the tape they'd retrieved, still playing, from the wreck of her car in the accident that had started it all.

He inserted the tape and took his drink back to the fire. In a moment, the cheerful beat of the Beach Boys filled the room, bringing with it all the fresh, open-air optimism of the sixties. How naive and dated that sounded now. Life was more complex, more confused, more bitter. He went back to the stereo. This tape was altogether too brash for his mood.

As he turned, he caught a glance of Josie's face. He stopped in his tracks. A tear was trickling slowly down her cheek. And her mouth, her lips ... was that a wince of pain ... or could it even be ....

She was smiling!

It was a faint half-smile, and it faded almost at once, leaving her face as vacant as before. But it had unmistakably been a reaction! A wild surge of hope rose in him. His mind flashed back to the doctor who'd treated her after her accident. "A person is the sum of their memories," he'd said. If you could restore the memories, couldn't you then restore the person?

Hurriedly he rewound the tape and played it again. Kneeling close by her side as the music began again, he scrutinized her face.

Nothing.

He turned the volume up. He switched tracks. He tried the other side. He ransacked his collection for music he remembered she'd liked. He tried everything he could think of. But nothing he did could coax from her even the smallest flicker of expression, let alone a repeat of that enigmatic smile, and eventually, filled with sorrow and disappointment, he laid the rug gently over her legs and slowly wheeled her out of the study and up in the newly installed elevator to her bedroom.

Ben hovered outside the sitting-room door. Inside, Mom and Matt were talking in soft voices. They always talked in soft voices these days. He tiptoed past into the kitchen and opened the fridge. Celery sticks, cucumber, salad—these days, too, the fridge only ever contained things that were good for you. He rummaged around. Wasn't there anything worth having? He was starving. He reached deeper in. Behind a jar of low-fat mayonnaise he came upon a small paper bag. He recognized the contents by their feel. Cookies!

Quickly he snatched the bag and retraced his steps upstairs into his bedroom. There he dived into bed and, huddling under the duvet, opened his contraband. Just as he was reaching into the bag, he heard footsteps approaching up the stairs. It was Matt, coming to tuck him in.

As he opened the door, Matthew must have caught the sudden flurry of movement and heard the crumpling of a paper bag.

"Come on, Ben," he said. "Show me what you've got there."

"Nothing. Honestly." Ben raised his hands innocently above the covers.

"You know you mustn't eat candy after you've brushed your teeth."

"It's not candy. It's cookies." He delved under the duvet and produced a paper bag. "Mom hid them at the back of the fridge. Keep a secret?"

"Come on, hand them over. I'll put them on the shelf. You can have them in the morning and not before. Promise me?"

"Okay," replied Ben, feigning a sullen expression.

Matthew tucked him in, kissed him and turned out the light.

"Goodnight, my boy," he said. "Sleep tight."

"Night, Matt."

Matthew went downstairs, smiling to himself. He knew that the moment his back was turned, the boy would be at the bag. As he came into the sitting room, Hazel looked up inquiringly. She was sitting on the sofa, with a cushion propped in the small of her back, flicking critically through a mail-order catalogue for maternity wear.

Matthew smiled.

"The little wretch," he said. "I caught him eating cookies."

"Where did he get those?"

"From the back of the fridge. He thinks you hid them there."

"Oh not those!" exclaimed Hazel. "They must be stale by now. Anyway, I'd have thrown them out of the house long ago if I'd remembered."

"Remembered?"

"That girl made them, with her own fair hands. She made me take a bag that time I went to see her." She shuddered.

Dimly he thought back to the time. It was only a couple of months, but it seemed so long ago. That was the day Hazel fell terribly ill with food poisoning. Or what they'd taken at the time to be food poisoning....

It was a full second before the realization hit him.

"Oh my God!" he cried and rushed to the door.

He was up the stairs in an instant. As he burst into Ben's room, he saw the boy quickly hide something under the covers again. He ran forward and snatched it out of his hand. It was a half-eaten Hershey bar. He spun round. On the shelf stood the bag of cookies, untouched.

"I said I promised," said Ben innocently.

Matthew laughed aloud with sheer relief and hugged the bewildered child. He looked up to see Hazel hurrying heavily into the room, her face pale and taut.

"What's wrong?" she cried.

"It's all okay," he breathed. "Everything's completely okay."

And yet he could never be quite sure. He couldn't quite feel at ease.

If feeling were energy, was it his obsession that had evoked the spirit of Isabel? Thank God he'd finished the book at last and he was free of that. Whatever her motive might now be—wherever she was—and whatever

grudge she might still harbor or revenge she might seek, Isabel was impotent. She was a shade, a spirit, a flame deprived of oxygen.

Or so he told himself. As he went about the university, though, he
found himself looking out for her in this guise or that. One evening he
thought he saw the boy in black hovering at the corner of a building, but
it turned out just to be an undergraduate waiting for a ride. He strictly
avoided the Ranges; that would be courting trouble. But driving home at
night, he would still look up at the bedroom window just in case there
might be some hint, a fleeting shadow perhaps or the briefest ghostly
luminance. He was almost disappointed to see nothing.

Yet he sensed her presence about him, although he couldn't be sure it
wasn't a projection of his own nostalgia. It was not a malevolence he
sensed, though, more a vast and unquenchable sadness: all her vengeful-
ness had turned to sorrow. And this touched him profoundly. For a brief
moment in his life he had shared a love, a passion, an excitement, such as
he had never believed could exist. Yet like Nathaniel before him, he had
rejected her, he had betrayed and abandoned her. Could he not find some
way of setting her sorry, unquiet spirit at peace?

The days drifted into weeks and the weeks into months. The snows
came and went, the buds returned to the trees, and with the greening of
the land came a resurgence of hope and life. Hazel was doing fine and the
baby inside her thriving. In the happiness that filled those days, all
thought of the anxieties of the year before were forgotten. Ben was settled
at home and doing well at school, and he hadn't had a recurrence of his
nightmares for months. And by now Matthew himself was working on his
next project, a biography of James Watson, the joint discoverer of the
structure of DNA. The Shawcrosse book, now just published, brought him
numerous offers to write other definitive biographies—he'd already had
propositions to do Galileo, Newton and Einstein—but he'd declined them
all. From now on, he was sticking strictly to living subjects.

Finally, one gentle day in May, he received a bulky airmail letter
which contained within it the seeds of a resolution.

The package came from a scholar at the Sorbonne in Paris who had
chanced upon a review copy of the Shawcrosse book. The scholar was making a study of French seventeenth-century deathbed confessions, and he
had amassed a major collection of manuscripts. Some were recorded on
parchment and written in formal court French, while others had simply
been taken down on scraps of paper by village priests in semiliterate

provincial dialect. One such confession, recorded at an address in a poor *quartier* of Paris and dated November 23rd, 1689, purported to be the confession of a certain "Natanyel Chaucrosse," also called "L'Anglais." Was this perhaps—the scholar politely inquired—Nathaniel Shawcrosse, the natural philosopher from Oxford?

The text rambled on over several pages. His French being poor, Matthew asked a professor of modern languages for help in translation. He collected the transcript late the following evening from the professor's house and took it home. Hazel was asleep and the house quiet. Filled with mixed anticipation and unease, he crept upstairs to the study and settled down at his desk to examine the text.

Gradually the final piece of the mystery at the heart of Shawcrosse's life fell into place. A pitiful story of bereavement, deprivation, degradation and finally death emerged from the pages of the confession.

Within months of the death of his wife, Mary, Nathaniel Shawcrosse lost his last remaining child, his son Barnabas. He was inconsolable. The boy's death shook him out of his lifelong apostasy. He saw the tragedy as God's judgment upon him. Faced with this potent sign of divine retribution, he underwent a conversion.

But he converted not to the Anglican faith, now triumphant in England, but to the Church of Rome. He was drawn by its mysteries, its rituals, its certitude and, above all, its promise of absolution. His enemies came out from hiding. They had tried constantly to silence him, to ban him from teaching, even to deprive him of his stipend, but so far he had always eluded them. Now, by turning Papist, he had put into their hands the weapon of his destruction. Led by the implacable Dean Hardiment, they turned upon him. His laboratory was ransacked and his equipment destroyed, and a great fire was lit in the main college quad upon which, amid scenes evoking the Grand Inquisition, all his books and papers and experimental notes were unceremoniously burned. And he himself was hounded out of Oxford.

He left England a broken, disgraced man and settled in Paris where he believed his newfound faith would find a ready welcome. He was penniless and destitute, and his own health was failing. He was taken in by a priest in Montmartre, and for a while he earned his *croute* by teaching English to the artist colony. But he could not give up his scientific work, and in secret he continued his experiments, using makeshift equipment cobbled together out of bits and pieces scavenged from wherever he could. One day, performing an alchemical transmutation, he started a fire in the house and was promptly turned out into the streets.

He ended up in a garret above a brothel in the Marais district, a marshy, unsalubrious quarter choking on the damp vapors from the Seine. His health deteriorated sharply. Winter was approaching and he had sold his only coat. He fell ill, and began to cough blood. The madame, a sympathetic woman who felt for this eccentric exile, paid for a doctor herself; besides, his nighttime coughing was turning away trade. The doctor prescribed bleedings, but the leeches could not fatten enough to drop off by themselves and had to be prized off. Infection set in. His fever rose, and he fell into delirium. The madame called a priest. Between bouts of feverish raving, he had moments of total clarity, and it was during these, and at his fervent behest, that the priest began to take down his verbatim confession.

It was an appeal for forgiveness, addressed not to the Almighty but to a woman. A woman called, simply, Isabel. In one passage after another, the disjointed narrative was interrupted by a terrible cry wrung from the heart: "Forgive me, Isabel, I beg you!" But the full burden of Nathaniel's torment only became apparent in the penultimate paragraph, where he struggled to explain himself before this silent and unanswering judge.

"I wronged you, Isabel," he pleaded. "I failed you. I could not bring myself to leave my beloved boy Barnabas alone in the world. I could not let him, at his tender age, having already lost his mother, grow up bereft of the love and guidance of a father. I cared nothing for my own life, only for his. Isabel, Isabel, believe me, I could not do this to him. I told myself my natural time would come in its own course, and then you and I would be united. What are a few years on this mortal plane in the eye of eternity?

"And then my beloved boy died. His innocent soul was taken in retribution for my sin.... I sought absolution in the Church...." Here the text was corrupted.

"Now it is my time. I go forward, trusting in the great and manifold mercies of the Lord. I shall seek you in the beyond, Isabel. And I trust that when we meet, you will show mercy and forgiveness. We have both suffered grievously, and it is meet we should heal our wounds and embrace one another in the spirit of forgiveness. Hear me, Isabel. I am going fast. I can see the light. I can hear the singing. Are you there, my beloved?"

Matthew pushed back his chair and stared out of the window into the darkness. He felt deeply moved by the pitiful story. There were a host of questions, old and new, but he was prepared to accept that the answers would never be known. History could never be quite complete.

As he sat there, he had the powerful sensation that, in those last minutes, a profound change had taken place in the relationship between himself and Nathaniel Shawcrosse. All along, he'd been obsessed by the mystery of Shawcrosse's death. Knowing at last how he had died seemed to dissolve the confusion of identities at a stroke. Now perhaps, for the first time, their relationship could be as it always should have been—that of biographer and subject, the recorder and the recorded, each separately and distinctly himself.

And, by extension, his relationship with Isabel had profoundly altered, too. Freed of the burden of Nathaniel's identity, he found himself looking at Isabel and feeling for her with a new objectivity. Seen from this remove, the tragedy of her situation filled him with pity and sympathy. Poor Isabel, she couldn't have known the circumstances of Nathaniel's death; she'd had no notion of why he'd reneged on his vow and how that had tortured him, nor how he had begged her forgiveness with his dying breath. By then she was living on the other side of the known world, eking out a tenuous existence on some malaria-infested tobacco plantation, far from any contact with her past life. Her last and abiding memory of Nathaniel was of a lover who had betrayed his faith, a man who had reneged on his pledge, not the heartbroken father torn between his vows to her and his duty to his son, the penitent racked on his deathbed by an unassuageable guilt.

She could not have known this. That was the root of the whole tragedy.

Matthew pressed his fingers against his temples. Could he marshal all his powers of mind and somehow get one final message through to her? Couldn't he tell her the truth and let her hear Nathaniel's dying confession? He peered into the shadows of the room and willed her to present herself.

"Isabel," he whispered aloud. "Come to me."

Silence. Nothing stirred, no hint of her presence could be felt. It was as if shedding the persona of Nathaniel had robbed him of his power over Isabel.

He was shivering; the room had grown cold. He glanced at his watch: the heat had gone off. He stretched wearily; he really ought to get to bed.

For a few minutes longer he strained to call up the spirit, but to no avail. Finally, with a defeated sigh, he rose to his feet.

As he stepped into the center of the room, it hit him, that unnatural chill like an unexpected cold current in the ocean. His pulse raced.

He looked up and addressed the empty shadows.

"I know you are here, Isabel," he whispered urgently. "Listen to me! Hear me. You must know the truth."

For a full twenty minutes he spoke to her, talking to her as though she stood before him once again in the flesh. He read aloud passages from Nathaniel's confession and begged her to make her peace with him. Nathaniel was out there, he said, waiting for her, yearning for her. The peace she sought lay with him and those of her own kind, not here among the mortal and material. Go there, he urged her. Search for him. Find him. Forgive him.

He said all he could say, then stood silent and motionless, waiting for a sign that she had heard. The minutes passed, and nothing showed itself. Then, quite gradually, he realized he was no longer feeling cold. He took a few steps in each direction. The chill had vanished. The air throughout the room was even and warm.

She had gone.

He returned slowly to his desk. He felt both released and strangely bereft. He was safe and yet sad. The danger had gone out of his life and, with it, some touch of transcendence. He looked at his hands, at the desk, at the objects in the room: all was base, material, earthly substance. He was where he belonged, but it was all leaden and made of clay.

As he slowly gathered the papers together he glanced over the prologue to the transcript. He paused. "Paris, 23rd November 1689": something about that date seemed familiar. Suddenly he realized what it was. Rummaging quickly through his files, he pulled out the text he'd copied down from the tombstone at Fairmont, Virginia.

Though separated by three thousand miles of land and ocean and in total ignorance of each other's condition and whereabouts, Nathaniel Shawcrosse and Isabel Hardiment had departed this life on the very same day.

"It's coming. One more push. Breathe it out. That's it! You're there. Here we come. Great! That's just wonderful!"

Carefully the obstetrician slithered the wrinkled, purplish infant up onto Hazel's stomach. He looked up.

"Hazel, Matthew," he beamed. "You have a fine little girl."

A girl. Matthew pressed closer. There was something he had to see. He knew it was crazy, even superstitious, but he needed to be sure. All along, he'd had this tiny nagging doubt.

He examined the small newborn creature. The capping of fine dark hair was a promising sign, but that could always be shed and blond hair grow in its place later. He peered closer, at the tiny face. Through the whitish vernix he scrutinized the mouth, the lips, the cheek. Finally he stood back and let out a slow breath. Perfectly clear. No hint whatever of any mark.

He looked at the baby, then at Hazel, and felt a great surge of supreme joy. This is our child, he thought. Our own beautiful, perfect child. He reached for Hazel's hand and squeezed it tight. She looked radiant. Her whole face was flushed with triumph and bright with wonder. Through eyes misted with tears, she smiled at him. They had come through.